Beyond the Rim of Light

by

Alex Stone

Published by
Melange Books, LLC
White Bear Lake, MN 55110
www.melange-books.com

Beyond the Rim of Light, Copyright © 2012 by Alex Stone

ISBN: 978-1-61235-396-8 Print

Published in the United States of America.

Cover Art by: Mae Powers

Acknowledgement

Special thanks are due to Randall Murray and Penny Mattern for their insights, suggestions, and corrections and to Mae Ann Powers and Jane Carver for their fine editing. Thank you also to my publisher, Nancy Schumacher. This novel could not have been completed without their help.

Beyond the Rim of Light
Alex Stone

Captivated by the beauty of the planet Arden , xenobiologist and survey team leader Marissa Latham wants to preserve it and its dominant species, the rheodactyls (rheos). However, a treaty between the Usian Confederation and the Delphian Empire requires the clearing of Arden despite Marissa's insistence the rheos are sentient. Unsupported by others, she is determined to reverse that decision when a rheo attack on the survey team closes the planet to all. Angered by events, Marissa takes action that has unexpected results. Exiled beyond the edge of the universe, she is transformed.

From the unsuspected warp and weft of the universe to the pleasure world of Satina IV, Marissa fights to save Arden, the Rheos, and the friends who were condemned along with her.

About the Author

Alex Stone is the pen name of the writing team of Nell DuVall and Steven Riddle. Both have several published short stories and Nell has two published novels with another one scheduled for an August release. Steven is a poet and essayists. Both have degrees in science.

Prologue - The Lamp

"Our lamp is spent, it's out!"
-*Antony and Cleopatra, IV 15*

Clambering out of the shallow depression in the cave under Orm's Monolith, Marissa Latham crept toward the flickering light. Pausing, she stared, unable to hope, to believe. On a rock ledge, a lamp wavered and popped. Carved, with layer upon layer of filigree, the lamp had two chambers, one encasing the other. At the heart of this intricate sculpture, a small flame danced on a wick that floated in a pool of shiny liquid.

She couldn't identify the material of the lamp. It resembled stone, largely green with veins of gray. As she reached out to touch it, the light sputtered and died in a sudden cold breeze.

Lunging forward in the darkness, she grabbed for the ledge. Her fingers inched along it until her right hand touched the smooth, still warm lamp. A lamp, more than a mural, an artifact to take back with her, offered proof positive of rheo intelligence.

Something grabbed her wrist. She gasped and struggled.

Someone or something tore the lamp from her hand.

Jerking backward, she came free and fell to the cold stone floor. From the blackness, a loud shriek rent the air and echoed from the walls. Shrill trumpeting almost deafened her.

Her heart pounding, Marissa scrambled backward. Away, away from whatever inhabited the cave. Then she stopped. The lamp. She needed the lamp.

"Wait," she cried to the faceless, nameless presence.

Echoes and then something like a whispered hiss answered her. The thing in the darkness threatened. Her muscles refused to move. Time stopped.

Another stealthy sound.

Fear foremost, she turned and ran. Her pulse raced and drove her toward the safety of the glowing lumina in the previous chamber.

With one quick grab, she scooped up the light along with her pack. Marissa sprinted toward the daylight certain a creature writhed through the cave after her. At the last moment, she remembered to stoop to avoid the low ceiling of the corridor entrance.

On her knees, she crawled as fast as she could toward the growing sunlight. Outside, she raced along the streambed. A hasty glance back revealed nothing followed her. She slowed, but off to her right, across the plain, a dark herd of rheos massed. At least a dozen of them galloped toward the Monolith at breakneck speed.

The team!

Desperate and breathing hard, Marissa raced back to where she had left her crew. She scrambled up the talus pile between the stream and the armored vehicle, dislodging scree and stones. As she crested the other side, she saw more rheos in the south, approaching even faster than the first group. Tesde, N'Bert, and Tad worked on the Monolith face, unaware of the threat.

Sliding down the talus, Marissa ran toward the three. "RHEOS!" She pointed across the fields.

About fifteen hundred meters from the scouter, the galloping rheos bore down on them. Tesde and Tad stared at her a moment before they too saw the approaching herd. When they did, they just stared. Marissa raced toward them. She tried to shout, but she had too little breath for it.

At last, she reached them. She shoved them toward the armored transport. "Inside! Now!"

The dust cloud raised by the rheos stretched out toward the limits of the now much shorter shadow of the Monolith. They would overrun the team in minutes. N'Bert had already climbed into the transport. Tad hauled a huge sample bag, and Tesde dragged the gravscooter toward the armored bulk of the vehicle.

"This isn't a drill," Marissa shouted. "Move your asses!"

She pushed Tad and Tesde toward the scouter. Tesde shoved the scooter out of the way and scrambled inside to help Tad pull in the samples.

Marissa dove after them and slammed the doors. She counted her heartbeats, every second expecting the attack. Nothing happened.

What were the rheos doing?

A good thirty seconds later the ringing and pounding of rocks sounded against the surface of the transport.

She lay against the door panting. Raising her hand, she looked at her chron. Her trip into the cave had taken the better part of four hours. She hadn't even noticed.

Tears trickled down her cheek. "I had proof. I swear I had proof."

Three sweating, silent people stared at her. Sylvic, chewing a huge wad of stim, didn't even glance at her, but cringed with each rocky impact.

One by one, the vidscreens went dark.

* * * *

Aboard the expedition ship, Marissa lay on the narrow bunk in her tiny cabin. That left Captain Quincy and the ship's med jammed against the opposite wall. If Quincy gained a few more kilos, he would have to stand half in the hatchway.

The med packed away his equipment. "You show signs of stress from a traumatic experience." He offered her several ampoules, but she glared back.

Behind him, Quincy grimaced. "Take it! That's an order." He nodded to the med and then faced Marissa. "I'm recommending a brief rest—in quarters."

Head woozy, she blinked and glowered at him with narrowed eyes. "I'm under arrest?"

"No." He flicked an imaginary piece of lint from his uniform. "For now, you're best off in your quarters. Consider it a request."

The ship's med handed her the ampoule. "Works for me every time."

After a second look at the captain, she clutched the capsule with grudging reluctance. She'd really bungled this time. Quincy and the med left her no choice. They watched and waited for her to take the medicine. Seeing no way out and wanting them gone, she swallowed it. Her glance focused on the red marks on her wrist where the thing in the cave had grabbed her arm. The med hadn't even mentioned it.

She lay back and soon images of Arden filled her thoughts. Then, darkness encased her.

Chapter One - Crossroads

"Beauty itself doth of itself persuade the eyes of men without an orator."
-Rape of Lucrece

"The grass stoops not, she treads on it so light."
-Venus and Adonis

A flurry of golden dust motes greeted Marissa Latham, the Crossroads Survey team leader, when she stepped from the landing pod's hatch onto the surface of the planet Arden. Invigorating air, heavy with the tantalizing scent of hot grass and some herb—sage?—met her, a welcome change from the expedition ship's months-old recycled air. She both looked forward to and dreaded this survey.

The image of the orbiting expedition ship with its belt of drones girding its circumference rose in her mind. Those drones, overgrown egg sacs, would swarm toward the planet with the agents of Arden's destruction. Science now modified a planet to any use. The survey team she led would analyze, record, and document the natural state of this planet prior to reforming. As a xenobiologist, such waste and wanton destruction of life appalled her, but changed nothing in the world of politics. Shrugging off disgust and frustration, she focused on the beauty before her.

"Breathtaking," Tesde, the dark-haired survey geologist, marveled as she joined Marissa. Her voice reflected admiration and a little awe.

A filmy lime scarf fluttered in the breeze and added color and flair to Tesde's regulation beige field suit. Her neat cap of black hair made Marissa conscious of her own untamed mass of red curls. The cool elegance and neatness of her friend only emphasized her own haphazard, slap-it-on style. Marissa had never garnered any awards or accolades for her appearance.

"Yeah, just like Mikla Arden's holos," Marissa agreed, "only so much better."

The factual descriptions of previous surveys and even the pictures hadn't fully prepared her for the rich golden tint of the sky or the lavender colored savannas that stretched endless kilometer upon kilometer, except where broken

8

by huge rock formations or scattered clusters of spiny wickabrush. Nor did they convey the rich aromas that delighted and refreshed spirits.

With the binocs on high, Marissa watched the large, oddly fluid animals—probably the dominant native species—rheodactyls. Like the dorsal fins of Xhank's Dolphin cleaving the water of Drisna, the rheos gracefully broke the surface of the grasses for a moment to emerge from the brush only to recede once more. They ran with long, undulating strides, up and down in herd unison, to form the crests and troughs of one unified animal ocean. Their massive bodies flowed over the ground at nearly twenty kilometers an hour. The six-legged, lizard-like creatures moved with incredible grace for such large animals. How their hydrostatic structure worked comprised one puzzle Marissa hoped to answer.

Arden's beauty and peace surrounded and soothed her. She inhaled the air to again savor all the tantalizing scents of this paradise.

"Hey, Marissa," Tad, the pod pilot, med-tech, and mechanic, spoke on the communit, demanding her attention. "Where do you want to set up camp?" At least with him, her long-time companion along, she had someone who understood her.

With the assistance of the grav cushions, the pod would hover just off the ground and damage nothing. Held in place by grav units, the camp too would float centimeters above the ground and wouldn't kill the native grasses, although the lack of sunlight during their three-week stay probably would.

"Give me a minute." She pulled out the survey chart.

The previous team had recommended this position twelve kilometers southeast of Orm's Monolith to avoid the grav anomaly it caused. In the distance, the tall stone finger loomed on the horizon. The Monolith, two and a half kilometers in height, dwarfed all nearby topography. Distant cliffs outlined the plain as a broad valley. Despite rising more than a hundred meters tall, they formed mere lines on the horizon by contrast with the Monolith's enormous bulk. Tesde would study it to verify the grav anomaly wouldn't affect the proposed buildings or activities of a mall world. The large groups of rheodactyls recorded periodically by Mikla's survey in its vicinity only added to Marissa's interest in the Monolith.

With these concerns in mind, she touched the map and searched for rocky patches nearby. Fine-tuning the scan, she located a shelf about seven tenths of a kilometer farther from the Monolith. Nodding, she sent Tad the coordinates and then damped the map.

"Really, Marissa," the survey's know-it-all physicist N'Bert Fashvoralian's voice sputtered over the communit, exasperation evident. "What's wrong with here?"

"I want to keep the flora and fauna intact until we leave."

"You need a sharp dose of reality," N'Bert grunted. "Our mission is get in, get out, and reform the planet."

"So? I don't want to muck up our survey results."

The communit transmitted his sharp intake of breath. "You're the designated leader for now, but I'm the Regulations Monitor. Doing things your way caused a few problems in the past."

Filling her lungs, Marissa then expelled air in one slow breath and focused on slowing her pulse. "I know the regulations, N'Bert, but no impact for *now*. Take the pod to those coordinates, Tad."

"Got it. Will you and Tesde join us on board?"

The other members of the five-person team, Sylvic Prentiss, the archivist, and N'Bert Fashvoralian, Regulations Monitor and nominal physicist, had stayed on board with Tad. While Sylvic spent her spare time immersed in her favorite vids, she had the qualifications for her job. She had worked off world before. As for N'Bert, the less Marissa thought about him the better. Too bad, he also considered himself the rightful team leader.

Thoughts of him made her shudder. "No, we'll walk and absorb a little local color. After so long on the ship, my legs need stretching."

"Right," Tad acknowledged and eased the pod forward.

She could almost see his grin. He knew her views on N'Bert. She and Tesde followed the pod on foot as it moved forward.

"Marissa…" Tesde paused, twisting the ends of her scarf together and peering sideways at her. "As a xenobiologist, this survey of Crossroads is different for you."

"Crossroads! I hate that name." Marissa dug her nails into her palms. "For this survey, it's still Arden. I'm glad Mikla named it that. The name invokes the ideal, the epitome of grace. Renaming makes no sense and doesn't change the fact it's a real world with its own creatures. I hate reforming. Why change something so…so perfect?"

Tesde, dark eyes open wide, gave her an odd look and turned to gaze at the landscape. "No one will ever see it quite like this again." Opening her mouth to speak further, Tesde instead stopped and knotted her scarf. A sigh followed. "Reforming doesn't change the basic geology, so the things I study won't change."

She faced Marissa with empathy and compassion filling her dark eyes. "Studying the life forms here, you must view things differently. Hard as you may find it, you have to distance yourself from Crossroads—sorry, Arden. A place can become too important—"

The abrupt pause reminded Marissa of Tesde's ambiguous status as a Guest, tolerated and used, but not quite accepted by Confederation citizens. Science and animal behavior Marissa understood, but people, especially their emotions and politics, left her uneasy and uncertain how to respond.

A large sigh escaped her. "It's all right, Tesde, really. The survey only lasts a few weeks. Based on the ones I've done before, I'll have time only for the survey itself."

The heat of the sun baked the fragrant herbage, so every step they took toward the campsite released aromatic incense. Confusing emotions engulfed Marissa as she surveyed the vast plain—pleasure in its beauty, a tinge of anger at the future, and a sense of helplessness. A gentle breeze rippled the covering of coarse purple grass.

At their next step, a rush of wings, all colors of the spectrum, rose from the grass. Her heart skipped a beat. Arden's Avian Arvos. They whirred up, clucked, shrieked, and settled down a few meters away. The previous survey had found no birds on Arden, but recorded bird analogues. For such a dry planet, the diversity of life forms astounded Marissa.

The refreshing breeze sent the grasses into long rolling waves. By the time she walked halfway to the campsite, Arden's beauty enthralled her. "Zero impact," she muttered.

This place, this planet Arden—even the original name breathed some of its rich glory—Inspired her. Reforming affronted her sense of the sacredness of life and represented waste at its most extreme. Bad science and morally wrong, it would be doubly wrong for Arden.

Her opinion would not change the Will. Barring something in the Monolith's grav fields or something about the rheos, Arden would become one more mall world. For a brief moment, an endless procession of gray buildings with garish signs filled her vision. Appalled, she shook her head, and the lavender savanna replaced the horror of Arden's future desolation.

* * * *

With camp established and leaving Tesde, Sylvic, and N'Bert to unpack, Marissa tapped Tad on the shoulder. "Let's have a quick look. The previous survey shows a rheo habitat not far from here. We'll start there."

After pushing the little floater out of the pod, Tad slid into the driver's seat, and Marissa jumped in beside him. He set the vehicle in motion to skim over the ground, leaving a light trail of golden dust behind. With the breeze in her face, she sat back and enjoyed the ride.

Mikla Arden had designated the site they approached as Home-4. A stand of wickabrush and a huge cinnamonberry tree marked the place. They framed the narrow space leading into an open area he described as a resting place. Two large rheos grazed before the only way through the wickabrush. Tad eased the floater forward, and the largest rheo raised its head to consider them.

"We'll look inside later," Marissa said. "Just drive past for now so we can relate its location to the work plan."

He skirted close to the area defined by a line of scrub. A few grazing rheos ignored them. Several munched on the nearby wickabrush while others with long slender digits on their highest forelimb delicately snatched flitterwings. Pulling out her notecomp, Marissa recorded a few entries. One rheo, more bloated than the others, gazed in their direction.

"Tad, is that a female?"

"What?" He pulled himself up from under the windscreen for a better look. "Female? You're the biologist, not me."

"Arden's survey recorded the dominant species as the rheodactyl, yellowish green in color with hydrostatic skeletons. Sexual characteristics?" Marissa scanned the survey index. "Yeah, here it is. The females are smaller and darker in color than the males. That fits."

"Nothing else?"

"Umm, not much. Maybe this one is gravid. We know so little. The earlier survey recorded nothing on mating practices, gestation periods, or any known predators. They didn't stay long enough to get that data."

"Hey, that's why we're here, we'll compile that data."

"As much as we can in three weeks. We need more time. No one knows the life span of these animals or any of Arden's species."

"What's the DNA tell you?"

"Humph, not a lot. Their leathery hides resemble reptiles, but other features reflect mammalian characteristics—warm blooded, but no hair, and no data about mammary glands or bearing young alive."

Tad turned the floater to avoid a clump of wickabrush. "Maybe this one will tell you."

"Not in three weeks."

"You could dissect her." He grinned at her.

"Don't say it even as joke." Marissa glared at him. "You know how I feel about that." She pulled at her wind-tangled hair and smoothed it back. "We do as little damage as possible."

"With reforming coming?" The doubt in his tone added to her defensiveness.

"I hate that word."

The wind ruffled Tad's hair, almost the same gold color as the wickabrush. "You think I don't know that? Hey, don't take this too much to heart. We're here to record what we can before reforming. Nothing will remain as we see it now."

"So why remake it?" Marissa gazed at the landscape, longing to keep all of it safe.

"I'm with you, but the Will says otherwise, so we do our duty and complete the survey."

"Unless we find something. Something about the rheos themselves." She tapped the pen against the notecomp. "If only we can do that."

"Well, you've got three weeks, but..." He stopped the floater and focused on her. "Marissa, don't get too attached. Sometimes you care too much."

"Yeah, it's hard not to do that. Anyway, get some samples for me."

"Might as well. All I have to do is locate, record, and dump them in the collector cells, right?"

"Yeah, lucky you." Marissa grinned. "No hand labeling, no grubbing in the mud. Nice and sanitary. Oh, wear your gloves. You never know what irritation plants and insects might cause."

"I'm a med tech and a big boy, remember?"

Leaning over, she kissed him on the cheek. "You bet I remember. Just wait until tonight. Now, get on with it." She gave him a playful push.

For a moment, she watched him as he snapped holos of the area and then focused on some bones and nearby fecal material. The stuff of science. With automated data recording and reduction, as long as Tad kept the equipment going, the survey work would be routine. The automated analyst even identified areas for further study and suggested several possible hypotheses for interpreting the results. However, the final choice remained with the scientist. Intuition, experience, and luck still had roles to play.

With a sigh, Marissa turned back to observe the scattered group of rheos.

* * * *

To N'Bert's disgust, by the third day into the survey work, Marissa started giving all the rheos names. So far, she had identified Savage, the largest male of the group, who cowed all the others when he rose to his full height, Daddy-Long-Legs, another long-limbed male, and Europa, the gravid female. Another male she called Thom after an old school pal. She couldn't quite bring herself to call one N'Bert. In her view, the individual rheos deserved better than to be saddled with anything associated with him.

That evening in the dining dome, Marissa relaxed and stretched out her legs. Tired after a long day in the floater, she didn't even protest when Tad, Sylvic, and Tesde left her alone with N'Bert.

"This place amazes me. We should keep it just as is," she said and then wished she hadn't. Why leave N'Bert a chance to protest?

He pinned her with a disgusted glare. Not as tall as Tad and dark instead of blond, he had a short, muscular build. Black hair sprouted in a thick beard and flowed up into a dark tangle of hair. She could almost like him, if he'd just drop his complaining.

"The Confederation signed a treaty over Crossroads. You of all people know that. No life forms of significance exist here. Other than grazing and keeping the local fauna in check, the rheos serve no purpose."

13

Sighing, she looked toward the sunset. "We don't know that."

If only Tad had taken pity on her and stayed. She resigned herself to N'Bert's rant. If he ran on too much, she'd leave. How had he ever taken the Triple Crown in his field—Dirac Honors, the Planek Seat, and the Shoedmier Prize—yet parroted regulations verbatim rather than focusing on science? A self-styled expert in all matters, he offered her plenty of unwanted advice.

N'Bert snorted. "So? It doesn't matter once the Will has been spoken. No one, even you with your connections, can change that. Politics and treaties determine this planet's future. The previous team collected enough data, and I, for one, have other things to do."

His reference to her family and their political influence along with that knowing look of his made her squirm. The thought of reforming this paradise made her stomach churn. "We have a survey to complete and more samples to collect. Politics should never drive science."

He laughed at that. "At times your naiveté stuns me. No one cares about useless animals."

"I care." She emphasized each word. The image of Europa rose unbidden. "The rheos are the natives; we're the invaders."

His eyes glistened, small obsidian chips. "Don't confuse life and intelligence. The rheos only want their next meal."

Overwhelmed by frustration, she dug her nails into her palms. She struggled to accept they—she—had no alternative. The Will had been spoken, and all obeyed the Will. Surely, it could be reversed. She believed it, knew it, yet she recalled no instance of it ever happening.

Determined not to lose her temper or let him provoke her more, Marissa pushed herself up out of the grav cushion. "Good night." She headed toward her quarters, hoping to find Tad there to help her forget N'Bert and reforming.

* * * *

A rattle at the pod flap woke Marissa. She fumbled for the chrono—just after six in the morning. Another, louder tap sounded

"Marissa?"

Recognizing Tesde's voice, the excitement in it alarmed Marissa. She wormed out of the sleeping pouch, but woke Tad in the process. He squinted one blue eye and gazed at her. "What's the noise?"

"I don't know," she said. "It's Tesde."

She groped at the bottom of the pouch for her clothing. "Hang on, I'm coming," she called. As soon as she had covered the essentials, she raised the flap.

Outside, Tesde shifted from foot to foot. "The rheos are doing something weird. I thought you'd want to see."

"Okay, give me a minute." Marissa closed the flap and pulled on her beige

14

field suit. "Tad, I'm going with Tesde to check what's up with the rheos." She yawned. "I'll be back by eight for commlink."

He blinked, rubbed both eyes open, and glanced at the chrono. "Commlink? So you won't be back until lunchtime?" He grinned and ducked.

"No, I'm making my report on time today." She ruffled his blond hair. "I want to talk to Quincy." She kissed him and dashed from the pod.

In the floater hovering outside, Tesde, punched coordinates into the auto navigation interface. As soon as Marissa jumped in beside her, Tesde pushed the throttle. The floater moved off slowly, but soon crossed the lavender grass and golden dust of the Arden savanna at a swift pace.

"I went out early to collect some samples between Home-4 and the Monolith."

Intoxicated by the sage-and-cinnamon scent of the sun-warmed flora, Marissa barely heard Tesde.

"The young ones," she continued, "are gathered just outside the camp. They're doing a sort of dance."

Arriving at the site in minutes, Tesde eased the floater closer to the group. Even from a distance, Marissa could see their unusual behavior.

"Stop here," she said. "I don't want to spook them."

Jumping from the floater, Marissa raised a set of holo-binoculars to her eyes. Fumbling with the focus, she finally closed in on the group. Juveniles, as Tesde had said, gathered in a loose circle. When she first saw the six-legged lizard-like creatures twenty days ago, Marissa found the rheos' movements oddly fluid. Now she considered them the epitome of grace. As she watched, she realized they wrestled with one another.

"I'll be," she muttered.

"What is it?"

"They're playing a game to establish dominance."

"Oh, is that something odd? Don't all species do that?"

"No, not all. However, you're right. It's common behavior among social animals. Even sheep do it."

Delighted, she watched the young rheos push one another back and forth, switching opponents. The grappling went on for nearly half an hour. Finally, the biggest one huffed himself up like Savage, the large adult she had designated as the alpha male. This youngster loosed a loud bellow, and the others retracted their front legs and bent before him, rumps raised, in a gesture of submission.

Marissa lowered the binocs and glanced at the chrono on her wrist. Five minutes to eight. She looked around to find Tesde crouched near a rocky outcropping, combing through scree and selecting chips for her sample bag. The jumble of stones looked ordinary to Marissa, but then mineralogy and

15

geology weren't her areas of expertise.

"Come on, Tesde, let's get back to camp. I've got commlink."

Tesde looked disappointed. "I hoped to get a few more samples, maybe even get over to the Monolith today."

Orm's Monolith loomed on the horizon. The previous survey team had noted the gravitational anomaly and speculated it might interfere with the grav cushions needed to hold the eight domes of the survey camp in place.

"We'll go there later, I promise. Let's get back to camp. I have to report to Quincy."

Tesde closed her survey kit and got in the floater with Marissa. As they sped toward the camp, they disturbed a swarm of flitterwings that morphed into an iridescent rainbow as they rose and settled again in the tall grass.

"I've never been anywhere so beautiful," Marissa marveled aloud. "The more time I spend on Arden, the more I'm convinced it's paradise."

"Oh, Marissa, please, please don't get too attached to this." Tesde glanced sideways at her.

As Tesde steered the floater into camp, Marissa looked at her chrono. It read ten after eight. When the floater halted, Marissa jumped out and raced toward the communication dome.

"Thanks, Tesde," she yelled over her shoulder.

Inside the dome, cool silence enveloped her. Marissa sat in the shadows across from the black set and looked at the instructions again. So many dials and switches—why couldn't they make it with just one on-off button? Most people would find it easy to use, but the commlink would elude her forever.

After a minute of twiddling, she sent the commlinkup code. Thirty seconds later—at eight thirteen—the screen cleared, and the display glowed with the stocky image of Captain Heironymous Quincy, feet apart and arms at his side. Just behind his shoulder hovered her personal monitor Walt Fenster, his cheek bulging with his usual wad of wasso gum.

"You're late, Commander Latham." Captain Quincy's voice wavered between avuncular concern and exasperation. "You are scheduled to report on time every day."

"I'm sorry, sir. I was making observations of rheo behavior in the field." Having missed yesterday's commlink, Marissa struggled with guilt. Why should Quincy of all people have this effect on her? Yeah, he was her commanding officer, but not her father.

Walt Fenster, on the other hand, always annoyed her. His assignment as her personal monitor after her recommendations about Benaria had not met 'Confederation Standards' rankled. She preferred to ignore him.

"Latham, don't give us lame excuses. You look like you just rolled out of bed."

Walt's piercing gaze made her all too conscious she hadn't washed her face or combed her hair. She pushed a stray curl out of her eyes and sat a little straighter.

"Well, let's hear your *observations*." He popped his gum for emphasis.

She could almost smell the smoky-sweet stench of it, and her empty stomach turned. Marissa gave them a quick sketch of the activities of the previous two days, and the results of the tests the team had run. She even recounted events of the morning. Overall, her report went well.

Quincy stared at her. "That's all?"

Marissa blinked, but couldn't think of anything more to say. She glanced from Quincy to Fenster, who still scribbled in his notecomp.

Quincy's face grew red. "Your main mission is to complete the geosurvey. We need precise data on the area around Orm's Monolith. We can't afford mistakes. You've had almost three weeks on the surface, and you haven't relayed one bit of information we can use."

Marissa sensed he struggled not to yell at her.

"Captain Quincy," Fenster chimed in, "all of Latham's reports center on the rheodactyls. Perhaps, as a xenobiologist, her focus is too narrow for the leadership position she occupies."

Fenster's words ruffled her. The Confederation had never encountered a life form like the rheos.

Quincy waved off her monitor's comment. "Marissa, if the Confederation doesn't see results soon, they'll reassign you and give the job to someone else."

"What? No, we're doing vital work here." Her fists clenched and unclenched.

"Since when is counting useless animals considered vital, Latham?" Fenster smirked.

"Since when is monitoring a woman from space considered a real job, Fenster?" His smug expression vanished, and they glared at each other.

"Humph!" The captain broke the silence. "You two can fume all you want as long as I get those survey results." He awaited her reply.

"Captain Quincy, I have something to ask you."

Quincy raised his eyebrows. "What?"

Inhaling, Marissa breathed out, determined to push as far as she could. "I need three more weeks. The data you want will take more time."

Rolling his eyes, Fenster scribbled more notes. Quincy looked thoughtful, but didn't answer. Hope dribbled away as each second passed.

Then Quincy smiled at her. "Well, Commander, you're in luck." Fenster stopped writing, and turned to stare at the captain, his mouth agape. "The Delphians delayed the supply ship. I received the news an hour ago. Don't get too excited. It's a few days late. I can give you one more week, that's all."

Another week. Marissa crossed her fingers. She'd make it enough. "I'll take it."

"Remember, when the week ends I expect complete survey results on the Monolith. Once the supply ship arrives, they'll start the terraforming without further delay. You'll have to have your whole team packed and ready to leave the planet. Are you clear on that?"

"Yes, sir." Marissa's head swam with urgency and hope. "Thank you for the extension." Before Fenster could make any more snide comments, she switched off the commlink.

No sooner had she stepped outside the communication dome than spiky-haired Sylvic Prentiss confronted her. "Tesde said you went to Home-4 this morning. Did you collect any data?" Her cropped pink hair reminded Marissa of the savanna grass. It even waved a little in the wind.

An amused giggle escaped Marissa. "Sorry, Sylvic, I didn't think to take my notecomp."

"My job, Marissa, is to archive all the data we acquire. I can't document what you don't give me." Her pale gray eyes skewered Marissa.

"Don't worry, Sylvic. I saw nothing of interest to you. Why don't you ask Tesde about the rock samples she collected?"

"She's already given me a fully configured report of her morning's work, including elemental analyses." Sylvic turned in a huff and stomped off toward the transport pod.

Off to see her cohort, no doubt, Marissa thought. N'Bert spent most of his time aboard the transport pod. What he did, he neglected to tell her. She preferred not to know. As long as he kept the team well fed, she could tolerate his unwanted advice.

"Sorry about that." Tesde's voice interrupted Marissa's thoughts.

"Huh?"

"I didn't mean to make you look bad to Sylvic," Tesde explained. "The geology here is so stimulating, I enjoy doing the reports."

"Everything here is stimulating." Marissa took a dramatic, deep breath of spicy, warm air and exhaled loudly. "Besides, I do enough to make me look bad." She grinned at Tesde.

"How did your report go?"

"Great. I got the extension we needed."

"Extension?"

"Yes, we have another week to gather more data. Quincy insists we get the info on the Monolith. We'll scout out a site this afternoon, and then the whole team can spend all day there tomorrow."

Her words had the desired effect—a girlish sparkle appeared in Tesde's dark eyes. "Orm's Monolith, the opportunity of a lifetime. I'll do my most

18

important work there, I just know it." She stopped, a thoughtful look on her face. "I'd better go get my analysis kits together. I'll be in the lab dome if you need me. See you later." She walked away, twirling the ends of her scarf.

* * * *

The team had completed most of the ecological surveys using Mikla Arden's report to guide their work. Today, Marissa and Sylvic Prentiss, the archivist, had just finished mapping and recording the wickabrush density and community structure at a site north of the camp and the Monolith. No surprises, no journal-shattering articles, just standard results for a savanna/low brush community. They found a few odd organisms, but odd organisms no longer rated a note in a netjournal, much less a full article. The sheer numbers of reports and galactic diversity militated against anyone noticing.

After Marissa submitted the names and descriptions via the net to the Commission on Phyletic Nomenclature, some archivist, when she pulled herself away from the vids long enough, would check the records and register them with Marissa's name as author. The thought of each organism with her name attached still thrilled her.

"Going by the Monolith," she shouted to ensure Sylvic heard her over the sound of the wind blowing past them in the open floater.

Laughing aloud, she delighted in the brisk breeze and warm sun. The familiar scents, the spacious landscape, and even Sylvic added to her pleasure. The effect of the wind on Sylvic's pink spiky hair amused her. Except for the color, Sylvic's head didn't differ much from the savanna when the breeze blew over it. When Marissa banked the floater sharply, Sylvic braced herself and cursed at the disturbance. Her eyes stayed fixed on the holocube she held clenched between her knees.

"Sylvic, turn that thing off. Aren't you recording all this?" Marissa made a sweeping gesture to encompass the plain in front of them. She laughed again at Sylvic's answering scowl.

"Is it official survey material, and is it archivable? I don't think so. And so, no." She turned back to the holocube.

Banking to the right, Marissa released the stick to auto. She pushed herself up to let the rush of wind lift her hair and cool her face. Grumbling, Sylvic turned the minicube to watch the dancing figures from another angle.

Marissa shook her head in disgust and gazed out at the gathering herds of rheos. "Hey!" She lightly tapped Sylvic's porcupine head. "Come on! I've never seen so many rheos at once!" She gripped the top edge of the windshield and leaned forward to get a better view.

Sylvic released an explosive, exasperated sigh. "One or a hundred, they're all the same. I'm an archivist, not a zoologist. This is not even zero archival material. They wouldn't let me put this on a magneto-optical, much less a more durable base. So, who cares?"

She turned the cube and then turned it again. "Besides, they'll scatter as soon as we approach. They always do." Finding a side of the cube she liked, she settled back.

"Then record a few images before they do." Marissa dropped back into her seat. "They're heading toward the Monolith."

Ahead, the Monolith loomed, piercing the late afternoon's darkening ocher sky. They crossed a slight depression three kilometers from it where brightly colored cricket-birds nested en masse. The gravs propelling the little floater across the dusty lavender grass disturbed the nesting hens. Cricket-birds streamed up from the dry grass like the sigh of nearly naked tree-limbs brushed by a November breeze she once heard. They shrieked and warbled, turning together toward and then away from the floater. Forming a dark cloud, they first obscured the landscape and then shifted to reveal it.

With the floater skimming well ahead of the lead rheo, Marissa swerved the craft toward the Monolith. One of the creatures about thirty meters away reared up on its hind legs. She could almost hear the pumping of fluid as its hydrostatic skeleton adjusted to the new position.

A gray shadow streaked past her.

A soft thud, like a ripe melon hitting the ground, filled the scouter.

The holocube bumped across the floor and stopped against Marissa's foot.

Sylvic jerked backward and then slumped sideways into the seat beside her. She crumpled to the floor in a slow, almost melting motion. Welling blood trickled over her face. It oozed into the neck of her beige jumpsuit.

A smooth, brownish-yellow stone about the size of a fist lay on the floor next to Sylvic's head. Stunned, Marissa stared at the rheo herd as it rushed the floater. She grabbed the stick, and jerked it around to point the vehicle away from the rheos. Jamming it forward, she locked it on maximum auto.

Blood oozed from a cut centimeters above Sylvic's left eye. Panicked, Marissa scrambled to locate the medkit. Searching, she found it under the dashboard. She hit the latch, and the contents spilled to the floor. Pawing through the contents, she grabbed a sealed packet and tore it open with her teeth. The dressing in hand, she wiped the blood from Sylvic's face.

The bleeding had eased. The wound, a shallow, five-centimeter gash, didn't look lethal, but it scared Marissa to see Sylvic unconscious. Her breathing appeared okay, but with the head wound, Marissa wanted a diagnostic. She'd better get her back to camp fast.

The quickest route to camp passed close to the Monolith. Marissa glanced back at the rheos. They had spread out and flanked the floater on both sides. No record of them mentioned such speeds. They could run at top speed for short distances, but the hydrostatic skeletons limited how long they could maintain it and its maximum rate. The fluid skeletons could compensate only so much. She hoped they had reached that limit.

Their uncharacteristic behavior alarmed her. Why this attack? Until now, they'd shown no interest in the survey team and never exhibited any hostile act. The initial survey recorded no rheo attacks or aggressive behavior. Field notes detailed migrations and mass meetings, particularly near the Monolith, but never anything like this. If they were hostile, she had to know. That would endanger the entire survey crew and affect their survey of the Monolith tomorrow.

Gripping the nav stick hard, she willed her own energy into it. Speed, she needed speed to outrace the rheos. Bitter bile welled at the back of her throat. Then, she remembered the defensive shields and switched them on.

Marissa pulled back her hair and squinted, seeking a clear view of the activity outside. The moiré-pattern of the shields provided a distorted picture and dust raised by the rheos made the vid image fuzzy. The force fields shimmered and sparked as the vehicle careened and then bounced off the dirt and brush beneath it. Something solid slid off the shield and down the floater to the ground. A loud rain of hard objects struck, too many to be chance. The vid revealed massed rheos.

Puzzled and almost frightened, she inhaled sharply. "Why aren't you running away?"

Marissa kept finding her hands on the stick, fighting the autonav. Through the shimmer of the fields, a black mass surrounded them. The rheos ranged in one long rank. The mass grew.

What were they doing? She started to flick off the shields for a quick look, but a glance at Sylvic on the floor stopped her. Besides, how could she see any better through the dust?

She reset the autonav to the most direct course for Orm's Monolith and the camp. The floater would pass the Monolith on the south side. The range finder showed it astride the route a kilometer and a half south. The dark tide of the rheos threatened to cut her off before she could reach it. She pushed the vehicle to its limits.

The floater bucked under the rapid acceleration and threw Sylvic against her. Did Sylvic's breathing seem shallower now?

As they approached the Monolith, a rain of rocks pelted them, struck the shields, and slid to the ground. The protective shimmer intensified with each impact and obscured vision, but the tiny vid screen showed the black mass of rheos racing beside the floater. With a sharp whiff of ozone and a dull thud, a large boulder caromed off the force field and nearly overturned the vehicle.

Nearing the Monolith, more rheos appeared—more than she had ever seen in one place. Rocks cascaded against the floater shields. A cold chill swelled through her and raised the short hairs on the back of her neck. To her, it looked like the rheos meant to drive them away from the Monolith. Only that made sense. Did they breed here? Why the Monolith?

"Let's find out."

She slammed the stick forward and the floater rammed into her attackers and then through the mass of rheos. Banking about thirty degrees east, fewer projectiles hit the vehicle and fell to the starboard side. She kept going and then turned back toward the Monolith. This time the whole rank descended. In one rush, they surrounded the floater and pounded on the shields. The little vehicle rocked from side to side.

Chapter Two - Aftermath

"The brain may devise laws for the blood,
but a hot temper leaps o'er a cold decree."
-Merchant of Venice, I ii

"Now, for the love of Love and her soft hours,
Let's not confound the time with conference harsh:
There's not a minute of our lives should stretch
Without some pleasure now."
-Antony and Cleopatra, I, i

Inside the scouter, the analytical observer part of Marissa watched the action. The mass of rheos darkened and grew thicker. This light vehicle and its screens wouldn't withstand a heavy attack. Strained almost to the limit, they couldn't take much more abuse. Danger gave her hands speed as they raced over the navcon to set the destination for camp.

"I've learned what I can. Got to get Sylvic back," she mumbled.

The words drove her hands. Get back. Get back. Her fingers moved automatically.

She tried a sharp turn, but the scouter balked. "Hold on baby, we just need to make it home."

Marissa pushed harder on the stick. The scouter bucked and then picked up speed to plow through the dark, massed images of surrounding rheos. It surged forward across the dry savanna toward the camp. At first, the rheodactyls trailed, but gradually the little vehicle pulled away, they ebbed, and then the herd turned toward the Monolith.

Glancing from point to point, Marissa scanned the horizon, desperate for the gleam of the camp domes and the illusory yellow glow produced by their grav cushion. The interior of the scouter, protected by the defensive screens, grew hot and stuffy. She counted up to a hundred without hearing the sound of a rock and then switched them off. The waning, late-afternoon light revealed no sign of the rheos.

She peered ahead for the glinting orange red of the eight metal domes as

23

they floated in the fading evening sun. They appeared to twinkle or spin as they caught the last of the waning light.

A whirl of emotions—exhilaration, relief, worry, and even fear—surged through her. The combination exhausted her, right down to her bones. Tired, but satisfied, she might have learned something that could save Arden.

Suddenly, she remembered the communit and depressed the switch. "We're coming in." Her voice cracked. "Sylvic's got a head wound, probably not serious, but meet me."

The scouter tried to slow its approach, but Marissa overrode it. The vehicle came in too fast, and she stomped the brake, making the scouter jump against the bobbing mech pad. She leaped out, but her legs, as weak as if she had carried Sylvic back, almost buckled. She dropped to her knees and grabbed the side of the scouter for support. With effort, she forced herself erect.

Tad came at a run, wiping his hands on a towel. "You okay?" He dropped the towel on the scouter as he passed her and leaned in to check on Sylvic.

Marissa nodded. "I'm fine. Sylvic's hurt. Help her."

N'Bert and Tesde stood ready with a gurney. Marissa watched them as they worked with quiet professionalism. Moments later, they shifted Sylvic to the gurney. She struggled to sit up and blinked groggily, but Tad eased her back.

He looked at Marissa. "According to the instruments, Sylvic's okay. It's just shock, and she's lost a little blood. Scalp wounds always look worse than they are. Give her some rest and she'll hound you for the holos."

Relief washed over Marissa. With Sylvic resting, her attention turned to the aggressive behavior of the rheos. That stunned and worried her. Nothing in any of the data had prepared her for it. She pulled out her field scope and peered at the Monolith. In the rapidly dimming light, dark blobs of rheos milled in the distance until the Monolith's lengthening shadow hid them.

* * * *

Sitting alone in the dining dome, Marissa inhaled the acrid spicy scent of a cup of oulatte and struggled to put the pieces together every way she could. She still arrived at the same answer. She stirred the clear golden mixture in the cup idly as her hand moved in an elaborate figure eight. Laying the spoon down, she picked it up again and then replaced it.

"What were they doing?" Her spoken words startled her. "Did we spook them?

"Are you asking me?" The synthesized voice of Esmarelda, Ez for short, her personal digital assistant, sounded from the chip in the collar of Marissa's field suit.

"No, just speculating. Why did the rheos attack?" She knew how N'Bert would see it. 'Stir up a fire ant nest and see what happens?' "They acted as a

24

unit."

"Yes," Ez responded, "but at present you have incomplete data at best."

"We didn't threaten or attack them. As far as I know, we didn't do anything nearly as invasive as intruding on their breeding ground. Yet all our survey observations remain just incomplete enough for that. How can we make certain?" Marissa rubbed her forehead with the heel of her palm.

"Get more data," Ez advised.

A smile tugged at Marissa's mouth. Her fingers traced the inside of the cup handle, following its contours. It reminded her of the Klein bottles her class had constructed in second form chronosculpture. Awarded a first, hers sat on the shelf in the sleeping pod, one of the few personal articles she always carried with her on her field assignments. That and the chronokit itself.

Whenever troubled, she itched to mold the four-dimensional crystal polymer. Some people juggled, some did Tai Chi, but for her chronosculpture provided release. The changing physical contours of the sculpture and the action of shaping it helped shape her thoughts as well. Perhaps if she ignored the problem, the knot would unravel. Her fingers twitched wishing for the chronowand and the strangely greasy texture of the sculpture. She sighed and flexed her empty hands.

Staring down into the mug of now cold oulatte, Marissa sensed she had scratched the surface of a deeper mystery. A tantalizing explanation for the rheos' behavior hung just out of reach. Had she seen what she wanted to see, or were her observations valid? She didn't understand them, and, so far, the survey had brought her no closer to doing so. Maybe they weren't going to take annihilation lying down, not that they stood a chance against orbital bombardment.

The thought of the rheos attacking the survey ship in orbit; surrounding it as they had her and Sylvic in the little scouter, made her grin. Then, the dinner bell chimed. Numbness and uncertainty sapped her energy. She fastened her hair back from her face as the others joined her for dinner.

N'Bert had prepared the evening meal—pome Rigoberto over filet Genvese, minted carrots, and a light spinach soufflé—all from reconstituted ingredients. For dessert, an airy chocolate mousse waited. Marissa marveled at the magic he worked in the tiny camp galley. It almost made his presence acceptable.

Uncharacteristically quiet throughout dinner, N'Bert concentrated on his food. Tad and Tesde chattered with a nervous edge of the day's activities. Sylvic rested in her quarters. When they finished, Tesde carried the dishes into the galley while Tad left to check on Sylvic.

Replete—no, to say it properly—stuffed, Marissa leaned back on the seat cushion and faced N'Bert. "Great dinner, N'Bert. You outdid yourself this time."

He grunted in rely, but didn't look up from his notecomp.

"I know you want to return to the ship," Marissa continued, "but this morning Captain Quincy gave us an extra week to concentrate on the Monolith, and we need to learn why the rheos chased the scouter."

He glared at her, his mouth crimped in a parody of a bitter smile. "So, you get your way after all. I might have known you'd find a way." He snapped the notecomp closed.

"No." Marissa stood and cupped her mug in both hands. The evening suddenly went chilly. "Before this survey we knew so little about this place. Today's evidence—"

"Evidence?" His fierce look riveted her.

Uneasy, she shifted to face him. "The rheos attacked us." The oulatte sloshed over her hand. "They nearly killed Sylvic."

Placing the tips of his fingers together, N'Bert surveyed her. "You exaggerate. She acquired some bruises, a graze, even passed out. With your driving, she probably banged her head on the windshield or even her holocube. An accident, nothing more." The well-chosen words lanced through the air, a debater's summation striking home.

Sipping from the mug clutched tightly in both hands, Marissa marshaled her words before responding. "Regardless of the damage, we need an explanation for the rheos' behavior."

"What do you mean?" Tad asked, his voice coming from behind her.

She turned to face him. "The rheos behaved in a way we've never observed before. They were hunting us!" She shook her head to clear it; N'Bert would jump on hunting. "No, like I said they chased the scouter." She paused, frowning. "They…forced us away from the Monolith."

"Slow down, Marissa." Tad dropped the bucket he carried. "What are you talking about?"

"When we approached the Monolith, the rheos attacked. You saw Sylvic. Wait!" She held up her hand as an idea emerged.

"Sylvic's fine. She'll be hounding you for the report tapes by morning." Tad smiled in reassurance.

"So the rheos hunt," N'Bert cut in like a surgeon's laser. He paused and cocked his head as if sizing up Marissa for his next barb. "The local roaches got hungry."

"Now you know biology," she snapped.

"At least I believe in rational, scientific discourse."

She raised an eyebrow at Tad. He chuckled as he looked over her shoulder at N'Bert. "Well, I'm calling it a night. I suggest you two do the same."

N'Bert started to say something, but Marissa ignored him. He stopped and, with deliberate casualness, walked back to the commdome.

Tad touched Marissa's rigid arm. "Relax."

"Okay." She gazed up into his clear blue eyes, relieved. "Thanks. Sometimes I wish I could crack open his skull and pour a little innovative thought in there." She rested her head for a moment on his shoulder, and then kissed his cheek. "Thanks for saving me a lot of grief."

Tad held her for a long moment and then kissed her. "We've better things to do."

Tesde stepped out of the galley, a bright yellow scarf at her neck, and walked to the edge of campsite. She looked at Tad and Marissa. "Did I miss something?"

Glancing at him, Marissa smiled. Darkness surrounded the camp. In the distance, the fading light revealed slow waves of rheos forming dark ripples against the deep purple of coming night. "Do you suppose they migrate at night? I wonder if they'll come any closer to camp?"

Tad stood beside her. "They haven't yet."

"Let's not talk about them anymore now." Tesde rubbed her hands up and down her upper arms. "It's getting cold, and we'll be leaving soon. We haven't had a campfire."

"Well, if we're going to have a fire, we'll need something to burn." Tad stepped down from the platform and headed into the dark.

"I'll help." Tesde followed him and soon vanished as well.

The sound of the two in the knee-high grass surrounding the camp echoed through the cool evening. Their laughter engendered a sense of alienation and isolation in Marissa.

Exchanges with N'Bert always annoyed her, but tonight his goading had made her tense and not a little angry. She resented his...what? Skepticism? Mockery? Disgust? She wanted understanding too much.

His negativity, whatever its source, fueled her own and she responded in kind. If she couldn't convince him, how could she hope to convince anyone else? Even if he acted perennially narrow-minded and shortsighted, he was a scientist.

"This way!" Sylvic called as she flashed an intense light in a wide arc. Its beam swept across Marissa, blinding her momentarily. A blare of trumpets drew Sylvic's attention to the ten nearly naked figures with the insignia SPQR Max, as they moved in a phalanx across the holocube. She pushed one of the gravcushions N'Bert had in tow over to the side of the clearing,

"Set it here," she said to him. Her attention stayed locked on the screen. He set the holocube down, and Sylvic turned up the volume, drowning out the night sounds.

Tad and Tesde piled the brush they had gathered on a cleared rocky patch.

Marissa lit it with her multi-tool, and it soon popped and crackled. The two added a final load of sizable brush and piled it all on the now roaring fire. Flames shot head high. They all stood back to relish the light and warmth against the chill of the black night and the scintillating points of stars above.

Suddenly, a voice shouted, "One, two, three—" Sylvic's vid spoiled the quiet and overpowered even the crackling fire.

Startled, Marissa whipped around toward the sound. Realizing its source, she flushed. "Turn that thing off." Sylvic ignored her. Marching over to the vid, Marissa dimmed the screen, and then muted the sound.

"Why did you do that?" Sylvic stared up at her. "It makes me nervous not to have sound."

"Then use the earphones." Ignoring any further response from her, Marissa turned and faced the others. "We should talk about today."

N'Bert squatted near the fire, his eyes straying to the yellow-green glow of the screen. "Why? We know what you think. The animals have brains, but brains aren't human intelligence." He rose and walked to the other side of the fire.

Marissa stared through the flame at him. "We're discussing the fate of a potentially intelligent species."

"There," N'Bert snapped. "You said it yourself—a potentially intelligent species. The Thousand Worlds have no interest in future intelligence. They deal only with intelligence now. Can't you understand that?"

Resonant currents like the fading peals of a bell filled the silence. The fire popped, and he shifted his position. "We've heard you before." He sounded testy. "The Will remains. The Will is unchangeable."

"Oh, the Will," Marissa retorted, turning her gaze from the fire to skewer him. "It's not written in stone."

His eyes widened, and he gaped, mouth moving, but no words emerged. His reaction made her aware of what she'd said and how it must sound.

"The right data can change the Will." Marissa spoke as much to convince herself as the others. "We have it now." The burning wickabrush snapped.

"You have the data?" N'Bert raised a doubtful eyebrow.

"The willful attack by the rheos this afternoon. They chased the scouter."

"So, amoebas chase things in response to chemical stimuli. That doesn't make them intelligent, nor does it give them a right to live on me or in me."

"Amoebas don't use tools. Besides, they weren't hunting—"

"Neither do rheodactyls." N'Bert rolled his eyes. "No more than Thresher birds or Garvin's Harvester. You biologists stray way off the mark."

"And you know all about the field," she said, bristling at his arrogant and dismissive tone.

Crossing his arms loosely over his chest, N'Bert glared back. "Field

28

biology is the anecdotal version of science. There isn't a scientist in the Thousand Worlds who wouldn't agree with me."

Leave it to N'Bert to resurrect the ancient historical-science-versus-experimental-science debate. She clenched her fingers in her pockets. "Forget your personal prejudices as to what constitutes true science. Would you enlighten us all on how field biologists are misled?"

"You think the use of a tool indicates intelligence. It's not an indicator. Every animal uses tools. Only the deliberate manufacture of that tool provides evidence for intelligence—"

"So noted," Marissa snapped. "But it's not tools."

Walking to the edge of the fire, she stopped with her toes next to the gray ash marking its boundary. Staring down into the orange-red flames, she sniffed the tendrils of white smoke that trailed the mixed scents of sage and clove. The smoke made her eyes water, but she refused to leave her place by the fire's edge. Silence hung in the air, waiting.

When no one spoke, Marissa turned to Sylvic. "Have you got the holos from this afternoon?"

"Of course not!" Sylvic snorted. "I spent the evening flat on my back with a cold pack on my head. I'm tired of this. Let's watch the vids."

N'Bert held his hands toward the fire. "These animals go berserk, chase you for a while, and stop. It shows they're dangerous and unpredictable. We shouldn't even transport breeding stock."

Grabbing a large branch, Marissa jabbed at the fire. The brush collapsed and sent a flitter of sparks into the sky. "They acted together, N'Bert—they cooperated." She jabbed the fire again. "It shows they may have language to communicate. They weren't hunting us, but warning us away from the Monolith."

Spiraling sparks flew outward. N'Bert yelped and jumped away from the fire. "When you go, you go all the way, don't you? You think they're not only intelligent, but they have language as well?"

"Yes." She paused a moment. "Their actions suggest that. The evidence…"

"We have no evidence yet," Sylvic interjected. "I haven't had time to catalog the holos."

"Cataloging, logging, so what?" Marissa took a deep breath and released it. "I'm sorry, Sylvic. The official standing of the records has nothing to do with whether the rheos are sentient."

"So, even if they are? So what?" This, to Marissa's surprise, came from Tad.

"If they're intelligent, we report it to the Enunciator so she can amend the Will.

A startled laugh sounded from N'Bert. "You think that makes a difference?"

Frowning, Marissa stared at the fire now dying down. "I…I don't know. But as survey leader, I have an obligation to do so."

"And—" N'Bert grinned widely at her— "having the right family name doesn't hurt either. Blood is always better than—"

Before he could finish, Marissa, fueled by annoyance, guilt, and anger, walked to him and glared down at him. A triumphant gleam in his eyes made her pause. The worm wanted her to lose it. She wouldn't give him that satisfaction. Clenching her hands, Marissa pressed her balled fists to her side. Guilt and self-disgust assailed her. She'd let Sylvic and the worm get to her.

An amused glint in his dark eyes, N'Bert watched her with crossed arms. She turned her back on him. "We'll take the armored low-terrain scouter tomorrow. Quincy wants the geologic survey completed before we leave. A week hardly gives us enough time. Besides, while you four do that, I want to identify what about the Monolith excited the rheos enough to chase us away."

Tomorrow they would return to the Monolith and the rheos. With any luck, she could find something important enough to convince even N'Bert. Jubilant, but with a tickle of hesitant fear, Marissa crossed her fingers as she and Tad headed toward their tent.

* * * *

Waking just before dawn, Marissa stretched in the sleeping pouch, savoring Tad's warmth beside her. Not yet ready to leave the comfort of her surroundings, she floated and began to drift into sleep. With an effort she jerked awake. She gazed blearily at a pocket chron, but couldn't read the numbers in the half-light. The light increased, and she struggled to force herself awake to check her chron. She could read it now.

Devos! She wanted an early start for the Monolith. Marissa slipped out of the pouch and regretted it at once. Cool, moist air raised gooseflesh on her arms and legs. She pulled on the jumpsuit she'd tossed aside last night. Impatient, she brushed her hair out of her eyes with one hand and peered out the shelter opening at dawn on Arden. Arden, she insisted; it couldn't be Crossroads now.

N'Bert, Tesde, and Sylvic ate breakfast under the canopy beside the central dome. Watching them, Marissa glimpsed something else in the dim aqua light of early morning. Almost directly behind N'Bert, a bird-analogue spread iridescent green wings and cocked its head. It lifted and lowered its bill several times in succession.

At a shriek of laughter from Sylvic, the analogue took flight. It swooped in a wide green arc upwards and then down again to perch on a sturdy stand of wickabrush some hundred meters away. As Marissa watched, she automatically cataloged the flight map, classing this animal as one of the pseudo-raptor

30

scavengers who stayed close enough to camp to clean up any remains they dropped.

To the southeast, the sun crept above the horizon to bathe the landscape with deep aqua light soon to mature into full rose and yellow. Like looking up from the bottom of a pool of cool clear water, the air shimmered. In the distance, three skimmers shrilled out a characteristic song. She turned in time to see them swoop down on the lavender grass and rise again. Arden's morning greeting.

Snugging her belt, Marissa prodded Tad with her foot. He stirred and rolled over onto his side. She poked again, and he sat up, rubbing his eyes. As he did so the pouch cover slipped, revealing entirely more than she had time for this morning. On the other hand...

"Good morning." She grinned at him.

"Good morning, yourself." His mouth opened in a slow, wide yawn as he stretched. "I should have been up hours ago. I have to pack the scouter."

"Don't sweat it. It shouldn't take that long. Besides..." Marissa leered at him and then sighed with regret. "You're right, you'd best get going now. I want us finished at the Monolith and away from it before noon."

"Noon it is then." He smiled his crooked grin and held out his arms for her.

She gave him a long appraising look and then shook her head slowly. "No. We've things to do." She ducked out of their domed shelter.

She no sooner joined the others beneath the dining canopy than Tad crawled through the shelter opening. Wearing only shorts and boots, he belonged with the skimmers, the rheodactyls, and the wide grassy plains. The planet suited him as much as it did her. A deep urgent feeling she couldn't name washed over her when she looked at him. Not love, not lust. Maybe longing, longing for him and—for something else. She couldn't identify what. He turned away from the canopy and toward the armored scouter where it sat in the opening of the narrow temporary garage.

Facing the rest of the team, Marissa smiled at the group beneath the canopy. "What's for breakfast?" She grimaced to remind them all how she hated food at this hour.

Teal scarf fluttering in the breeze, Tesde handed Marissa a mug of oulatte. "How's that?"

Marissa smiled and blew over the liquid to cool it. "Great. We need to get to Monolith as soon as we can. I want us out of there by noon."

"I've been thinking about the Monolith." Tesde thrust her chin in that direction as though it rose next to her. She pulled off her scarf and drew it through her hands as she talked. "It's the source of the strongest gravitic and magnetic anomaly on this planet. One of the strongest I've ever recorded or seen documented. Most of the time, such anomalies represent a metallic ore complex, and, with the intensity of this one, we're talking a layered igneous intrusion unlike any we've seen before. It wouldn't surprise me to find more platinum and iridium/osmium compounds than any known deposits. Or..." Tesde trailed off for a moment, now wrapping the scarf absent-mindedly around her thumb and picking at it.

"Well, there are other possibilities," she continued and appealed to Marissa. "It doesn't matter much one way or the other. If so, how can we turn the largest such ore deposit in fifty solar systems into a shopping center for the Delphians?"

N'Bert glared at her, his eyes dark and harder than basalt. "Not you too? The Will has been spoken. You think you can stop it?"

Tesde gave him a weary look. "More than any of you, I know I can't. But I'm also duty bound to report what I find."

Blowing over the top of her mug, Marissa watched the ripples spread beneath her breath, her heart beating faster. With the profit motive, she wouldn't have to rely on altruism or interest in a sentient species to save Arden. And she had an ally. Or at least someone who saw reason and might be able to gather the data needed to preserve this world.

Marissa reined in her excitement. It wouldn't do to upset N'Bert this morning. "Yeah, you'd think the Delphians could have picked a better place."

"You can say that again," Sylvic moaned. A large wad of stim made her cheeks bulge. "I've been thinking about today, too, and would like to opt out. What do you think?" She looked to Marissa, a plea in her eyes as she lightly touched the skin-colored patch on her forehead.

"I understand, believe me, but we need you. Someone's got to keep the records and log them. This stuff is critical to our mission, especially now."

Reaching out one hand, Tesde patted Sylvic's arm. "We'll be in the armored scouter, and you don't even have to get out if you don't want to."

Sylvic gave her an acrid smile. "Thank you so much for your reassurance. Some choice—be cooked to death inside an armored scouter, or stoned by a raging rheo."

N'Bert snorted. "Damned wild-goose chase, this whole survey, if you ask me."

Surprised she could smile even at him, Marissa had no desire to argue. "Quincy insists we get the data on the Monolith. That's plenty of work and not much time, so we need everyone working at top efficiency. Help Tesde log. What else do you have to do anyway?" She smiled, trying her best to placate him.

Picking up a slice of toast, N'Bert bit into it. He chewed slowly as he surveyed Marissa. His silence became almost a provocation; then he rose and went to the pot of oulatte sitting on a register. "Put that way, I suppose nothing. On the other hand, we could leave early. Not much we can learn here anyway and with belligerent wildlife—"

"We couldn't, N'Bert," Tesde interjected. "You haven't had a chance to check out the anomalies."

"I can check them out with instruments just as well from orbit." N'Bert took his cup and left the table. He walked to the edge of the camp and gazed out over waves of purple grass bowing toward the horizon.

It suddenly occurred to Marissa N'Bert didn't like field work. How could anyone not like being away from a stuffy office? Still beaming broadly, she couldn't resist one barb. "N'Bert, you're not afraid of the local fauna, are you?"

He frowned and clenched his fist. "I'm not a coward."

"No one suggested that, but if the rheos aren't intelligent, and, they haven't attacked before, what makes you think they'll repeat yesterday's little debacle?"

He didn't answer. Instead, he turned and walked toward his dome—the only member of the expedition to have a dome to himself.

Tesde jostled her shoulder. "Hey, you awake?"

"Hmm?" Marissa blinked and then looked at Tesde.

"What's the plan for today? How are we going to approach the Monolith?"

"I looked up Arden's survey," Marissa reponded. "They monitored and recorded the rheos' movements throughout the day. No rheos stayed near the Monolith at night. They followed a daily migratory pattern and moved toward it only in the afternoon. But the pattern wasn't well documented. Mikla Arden never had any certainty about whether the rheos moved with a purpose. He recorded only scattered movements. All the rheos in the local area passed the Monolith, but not in a single mass. And never very many at a time. We didn't see anything different until yesterday.

"After the first several days, his team stopped monitoring rheo movement. Anyway, the sum of it is, if they were guarding the Monolith yesterday, we should be okay for the morning. We shouldn't see any rheos until afternoon."

Tesde nodded and adjusted her scarf. "We'll be done with the initial review in a couple of hours. Long before afternoon."

She sat down on the bench and looked out across the plains. "You know, this is one of the nicest planets I've seen. Most of the time the geophys people get stuck on asteroids." Her hands circled the mug before her. "I wish my parents could see it." Her eyes looked a little distant and a little sad as if she peered into a less than pleasant future.

Marissa raised her eyebrows. "Just post them a holo."

Staring at her with wide eyes, Tesde absently traced the rim of the cup with her finger. "I can't." She turned away from Marissa. "They weren't very happy when I left our home world."

"Oh." Concerned, but not wanting to intrude, Marissa reached out and touched her shoulder.

Tesde smiled and squeezed Marissa's hand. "Thank you. It's been difficult."

After a moment of silence that threatened to last too long, Marissa drained her mug. "Well, maybe what we find here will change the Will."

Blinking, Tesde stared at her. "You think the Will is that flexible?" She turned away to gaze out across the plain. "Oh, Marissa, I don't think so. The Will has been spoken."

"But," Marissa said with bravado, "what we find here could cause a re-evaluation."

N'Bert, toweling off his wet hair, stood at the edge of the canopy square looking out at morning spreading across the sky. Turning toward her, his gaze carried sympathy as he studied her. "Marissa, have you ever known the Will to have been changed?"

Tesde sat back, relief etched on her face.

"There are nine instances..." Marissa began.

"NO! Don't recite the catechism. In your lifetime, have you ever heard of a single reversal of the Will?"

She grimaced and said nothing for a moment, reluctant to admit he was right. "I...don't think so." Raising the empty cup to her lips, she then set it down and walked over to stand beside him. In the distance, rose-colored clouds and thick stands of wickabrush stretched out against the horizon. "But that doesn't mean it can't happen."

He shook his head. "Even if you secure the evidence needed, by the time your motion made the sciences agenda this world will have been reformed." He stared at her, pity on his face. "Marissa, the expedition ship carries the transport pods and the terraformers."

She said nothing. The image of the ship with the drones encircling it hung before her. "Well, they sent us down here for a reason." She sighed, overwhelmed. "Let's finish this part of the survey. We have plenty of work to do."

Rising from the bench, Tesde started toward her quarters. She stopped and faced her. "Marissa, you'd better report in this morning. You know how Quincy is when I call."

Laughing, Marissa rubbed her stomach to ease the sudden knot of tension. "Right, just as soon as I've showered." She walked past Sylvic utterly transfixed by the holovision spectacle of two husky men grappling in a pool of mud.

Wanting to delay her report, Marissa walked behind the armored scouter

34

on her way to the showers. Tad lay on a floating platform beneath the transport.

She pushed his hovering cushion with her knee, making it bob up and down. "I've decided not to resist temptation after all."

Tad pulled himself out from under the transport. "What? I heard your voice, but I was synching channels. Sorry."

"I said," –she stroked the inside of his thigh with her foot— "I'm going to the shower. You need one, too."

He grinned widely. "Is there time?"

"There's always time."

"Let me finish up here. I've got to get the channels synched, or we'll be without gears."

"I don't know what you just said, but I'll trust you on it." She knelt and gently squeezed his muscular leg just above the knee. "I was going to wait until after my shower to call Captain Sourpuss up there, but since he'll remind me of everything I haven't done and then there's yesterday—"

"I'll be there to put you back together again." Tad stretched up and kissed her.

"I'll be waiting. Don't take too long." She rose and hurried toward the dome that housed the commlink.

Inside, she stared at the commlink unit. "Once you lose your fear of machinery there's no hope," she muttered.

After twiddling a bit, she managed to send the commlinkup code. Thirty seconds later the screen cleared, and the commlink glowed with the familair image of Captain Quincy with Walt Fenster lurking behind him.

"Captain Quincy, as per your instructions, we will investigate Orm's Monolith this morning."

"You're early today. So reported and recorded." Quincy gazed at her with narrowed eyes. "Anything else?"

"No." Marissa paused, trying to choose her words with care. "Umm, we had an incident with the rheos yesterday. Nothing serious, but it warrants further study. I'll monitor it while Tesde and N'Bert take the Monolith readings." She crossed her fingers.

"Incident?" Quincy's eyes widened.

She resisted the impulse to push a wisp of hair out of her face and refused to break eye contact. "Nothing of any consequence. The rheos gathered in force by the Monolith in the afternoon. We'll be away by then."

Quincy nodded. "Duly noted."

Snapping off the link, Marissa stared at the blank screen. It dimmed to leave the dome in darkness. She uncrossed her fingers. At least she'd avoided any questions from Walt.

At the dining canopy, Sylvic still sat entranced before the holovid. Any second Marissa expected to see a thin trickle of saliva from the corner of the archvist's mouth. Devos, she must be an edit. How else could she stand those things?

Marissa strolled past her and toward the shower. Environmental protocol required them to transport their own water and a recycler for the showers. The way the spray and running water always renewed her amazed her. She imagined the way the water would flow over her, warm and enveloping.

Tad had already arrived. His boots and shorts lay on the cushion surface outside the showers. Marissa peeled off her jumpsuit and tossed it next to his. Opening the shower door released a breath of scented steam. She stepped over the threshold of the shower and into Tad's waiting arms.

* * * *

N'Bert, Sylvic, and Tesde had already crowded into the armored oven of the transport. Tesde peered out the port, smiled, and then waved as Tad chased Marissa across the field. The chill of the night and the dew on the grass had not yet lifted. Thin tendrils of vapor rose from the ground like ghosts in the early morning light.

Marissa and Tad clambered through the narrow side door of the vehicle. He took his place at the controls, and she scrambled into the seat directly behind him. In front of her glowed the panel lights for the six different cameras securely mounted on the outer hull. Tad popped the transport into gear. As it jerked into motion, they quickly left the camp behind. This vehicle, despite its armor, traveled faster than the light scouter Marissa and Sylvic had taken the previous day.

Leaning over the panel, Marissa gazed through the wide windscreen. She pointed to the dark bulk on the horizon. "Let's head straight for the Monolith, but watch for any rheo herds."

"Whatever you say." Tad's brow crinkled with concentration, as he stabilized the gravs. "The fore and aft gravs seem to be out of phase. Remind me to check that when we get back."

"Sit down, Marissa, and enjoy the ride," N'Bert pulled her back into her seat. "Belt up. We'll probably be zooming." No sooner had he spoken than the forward force of the vehicle shoved her deeper into her seat.

"Thanks, N'Bert," Marissa gasped, out of breath. She took one last look at the camp shining in the early morning light, then faced straight ahead, and looked toward the looming Monolith.

Sylvic hooked up the recording gear, registered holos as they came in, marked tapes for each of the six cameras on the scout, and prepared the portables for each of the team members. Normally she would prepare three, but Tad had agreed to join the science team this time, so she marked one for him, too.

All too soon the scenery changed, and the massive finger of reddish-black stone jutted skyward directly in front of them. The Monolith filled the windscreen. Tesde gasped and reached for the panel that controlled the anterior-dextral camera. The shrill whine of servos filled the scouter as the camera focused in and out on the great Monolith. Needle thin in comparison to its two-and-a-half-kilometer height, it remained one of Arden's great mysteries. What it was, how it had formed, and what it indicated about the planet remained questions to which they had found no answers.

Tesde's eyes sparkled, and her hands worked the controls of the camera almost automatically. Marissa watched her tight, radiant face and saw one captivated. Checking the screen, Marissa observed no rheos near the Monolith this morning.

"Are you getting this, Tesde?" Tad called from the front.

The geologist nodded without taking her eyes off the screen. Tad shifted his gaze to Marissa for a momentar and smiled. She grinned back and reached forward to touch his arm.

"Isn't it exciting!" Tesde sounded a little breathless.

"What?" Marissa looked toward her hunched figure.

"Just the Monolith. I've surveyed fifty planets. Studied maybe a hundred others in Virtual. But I've never seen anything like this. At least not up close and so real."

Tad grinned. "There's nothing like a scientist and her work."

He turned back to the controls, and within minutes they glided to a stop at the base of the Monolith. The side hatch popped open, and Tesde scrambled out, a silver hammer swinging from a side pouch and a laser saw bulging from her backpack.

Leaning forward, Marissa brushed Tad's ear with her lips. "Keep an eye out for the rheos. We should be fine, but don't let Tesde be caught unawares, okay?"

"Sure." He pulled back a moment to stare into her face. "You expect trouble?"

"No, but we can't be certain. Just be careful."

He nodded in understanding.

Chapter Three - At the Monolith

"My mistress with a monster is in love."
-*A Midsummer Night's Dream*, II, iii

"Everybody out." Tad raised the windscreen shields of the scouter.

Marissa, just behind N'Bert at the top of the ramp, took one last look at the interior of the vehicle. Sylvic huddled in the shadowy cabin.

From the red darkness, the archivist handed Tad a camera. "Take good pictures and bring 'em back alive."

Holding the camera, he studied her a moment. "You're not going?"

She gave an emphatic shake of her head. "Archivist's privilege. You all can get killed, but I have to be around to document it. Thanks anyway." She cracked the stim in her mouth, working her jaw in an exaggerated fashion, but it didn't hide the fear from Marissa or from anyone else.

Tad gave her a crooked grin and shouldered the camera. He followed Marissa onto the ramp and stepped down to the hard-packed ground that surrounded the Monolith. Already at work, Tesde peered at its near face. She flipped down the mags to examine something Marissa couldn't see.

Tesde lightly traced an area on the Monolith. "Mikla Arden's survey listed this stuff as columnar basalt and it's columnar. Just look at those hexagons. It's fantastic. But this isn't basalt. Probably what comes of a long distance survey. They aren't even close."

Motioning to Marissa, Tesde pointed. "Look, just there." She touched one place. "And there." Her hand moved to another. "Of course, I'd have to confirm it with micro analysis, but I'd say that that is spinifex texture. Textbook examples."

Marissa blinked and stared at her. "What's that?"

"Spinifex texture is evidence of kimberlite emplacement."

"Hey, remember, we aren't all rock-heads. Explain, please."

The geologist laughed. "This is an emplacement of lower upper mantle material. It may contain all sorts of mineral deposits. Even if there isn't, this kind of rock can tell us about the cooling history of the planet and the structure

38

of the upper mantle. If you section the xenoliths and do trace element analysis..." She talked more to the rock than to Marissa.

Grabbing Tad by the shoulders, Marissa pushed him gently toward the geologist. The two of them could gather the samples and sort out the specifics. Meanwhile, she wanted to focus on anything the rheos might have tried to protect.

"I want to look at the neodymium isotopes and rare earth series..." Tesde trailed off, tapping her silver hammer against the surface of the rock and listening. She re-holstered the hammer and pulled the hand-sized camera from the black pouch on her vest. Climbing up a heap of talus at the base of the monolith, she got as high as she could, then positioned the camera, and took magnified close-ups.

Scrambling back down, she shot more images from farther back. "Tad, have you got the miniprobe?"

"It's in the main pack. Third section, I think."

She bounded over to where he stood, unzipped the third section, and then pulled out a standard mini-probe and prep apparatus from the compartment. "I'll need your help with this."

"That's what I'm here for. Tad Kent, handyman and factotum." He smiled and followed her up the talus pile.

In the Monolith's shadow, Marissa's gaze followed its long finger stretching across the valley toward the cliffs that marked its edge almost to the horizon. Turning her attention back to the team, she watched Tad and Tesde prepare samples. The cool morning air fluttered Tesde's teal scarf like a bright banner.

Clambering over piles of talus at the base, Tesde picked up stray samples, examined them for moment, and then tossed them to the ground. "There's so much here, so much more to learn!" She pushed past Marissa and then gave a startled gasp. "I'm sorry, I didn't see you standing there."

Amused at Tesde's intensive focus on the physical nature of the Monolith, Marissa grinned. "It's fine. Just watch for any rheos. One attack is enough. We can't afford another."

She checked her chron. Not quite eight, plenty of time. The rheos wouldn't begin massing until afternoon. "Okay, everyone, let's get our schedules straight. Keep this session to four hours or less so we finish by noon. If necessary, we return tomorrow." N'Bert arched an eyebrow at that.

Marissa ignored him. "I'm going to investigate why the rheos want to protect this place."

Even as she said it, she flushed. Protect? Should she be more sensitive to how the rheos might view such poking around? Time wouldn't allow that. If she planned to save them, she needed concrete evidence and needed it now.

A step behind Marissa drew her attention. N'Bert skewered her with a challenging look, his arms crossed over his chest. His attitude didn't improve her mood. If she kept him busy, he couldn't follow her and interfere.

"N'Bert, please help Tad and Tesde. That way we'll finish everything sooner so you can get back to the safety of survey ship." She didn't mention the rheos.

She wanted witnesses, reliable and scientifically acceptable witnesses, not hostile ones. The holovids would tell part of the story. But people always interpreted vids in various ways. N'Bert wouldn't accept anything he couldn't verify himself. If she found evidence to convince him, she could convince anyone.

He raised an eyebrow at her and then strolled toward the others as if time had no meaning for him. She watched until he joined them. Tesde gestured toward the Monolith, and N'Bert looked at it a little bored. Despite that, he bent, picked up a small rock, and then stuffed it in his sample bag.

Tad stood behind Tesde, and the wind ruffled his golden hair. He saw Marissa watching and waved. She grinned and waved back. With one last look at the three, she then jogged away.

Starting down a slight decline she hoped would lead to the sunlit side of the Monolith, she observed her surroundings. Arden's initial maps showed a stream emerging from the rock base. Even though Marissa had been a field biologist for a long time, map reading still gave her problems. She didn't focus the screen properly, or, if focused, she always had the wrong sector in view. So, when she climbed over a steep pile of talus and saw below her the glittery silver of a stream just where the map indicated, she stared at it, surprised. She scrambled down the talus and leaped across it.

On the other bank of the stream, the ground appeared flat. At first as she walked, she didn't notice any change, but when she looked up, part of her view of the valley disappeared. Puzzled, she gazed around. A shallow depression surrounded her.

Unlike the talus near the scouter, nearby groups of rock showed order and gave the appearance of careful arrangement or placement to guard and protect the stream. Ahead the two rows formed a low, narrow passage. Had the rheos done this?

Excited, Marissa hurried forward to the Monolith face. Once there, she doubled over and peered into the massive rock, but only inky shadows met her gaze. Pulling out her multitool, she flicked on the lumina. Even its bright light failed to dispel the gloom of this tunnel, cave, crack, or whatever she faced. It must stretch some distance. From its present direction, it had to extend into the Monolith itself.

Steadying herself against the entrance, Marissa flashed the lumina around the lip of darkness hoping to gain some measure of how far the passage penetrated. Failing, she switched to the multitool's range finder. It provided no clear reading. She switched back to the light, scanned the dark interior once again, and then consulted Esmarelda.

"Ez, recommended reconnaissance procedure?"

"From the data I'm receiving, you've already done a range scan. I find no evidence of a bioscan. You should do one. Many life forms may occupy a cave, including spores, molds, and toxic growths."

"Yeah, my next step." Mentally, Marissa kicked herself for overlooking such an obvious scan. Some biologist she was, but she had never expected to find an opening into the Monolith. Maybe the rheos had been guarding it. This seemed far more likely than a mating ground, but why? A burial ground? Stop, she chided herself. Gather the data first and then interpret it. She had too little information to form even a tentative hypothesis.

The bioscan readout revealed the usual insectomorphs, but nothing in the way of vertebrate analogues or rheos. Marissa stooped once more at the entrance of the passage and poked her head inside. Darkness.

Her heartbeat raced. Taking a deep breath and deliberately slowing her pulse, she eased into the inky blackness.

With one hand on the rough rock wall, she walked bent over for about ten meters. By then, her back protested at the strain. The cool air carried a hint of damp. No dust or loose rock littered the passage floor.

Uneven and winding, the tunnel must curve around the base of the Monolith. Just when she thought she'd have to go back, the passage widened, and she could stand upright. Stretching a moment to loosen cramped muscles, she tried to analyze the space around her. A cave of some sort she guessed and moved forward.

After about thirty meters, she reached another low area where she had to hunch over again. This time she scuttled about three meters until the close atmosphere eased. The swirling air signaled a large chamber.

The lumina did nothing to disperse the darkness, nor did it reflect off the walls of the chamber. The enveloping black swallowed the light. Marissa shuddered, striving to damp down primitive fears.

Backing, she bumped her head on the low ceiling of the passage. Devos! She rubbed the sore spot. When she stooped and took another step back into what she thought would be the passage, she stumbled on the unexpectedly steep rise of the tunnel floor behind her. She turned around to see faint glimmers, probably reflected from the curving tunnel walls, of the natural light from outside. Somehow, she had missed that earlier.

The larger chamber beckoned, and she reentered it. A slow dripping from deep within the inky shadows drew her. She walked away from the dim natural light and toward the trickling sound. Startled, she almost dropped the multitool in surprise. Ahead, reflected light met her gaze.

There on the wall, in sparkling micas and chalky-looking dust, in gold and deep red, in black and purples, all on what looked like a monstrous slab of inset white rock, she marveled at arabesques and frills, geometric shapes, and a stylized drawing of one of the local fauna. A bird analogue, like the cricket-birds, but with wings like the flitterwings, and colors like none she had seen on Arden. The golden flecks of mica captured the lumina's light and sent it dazzling back into her face.

Stretching out a hand to touch the glittering images, Marissa stopped herself. Never touch artifacts. Instead, she unslung her backpack and pulled out the holocamera. Adjusting the eyepiece to focus on the thing, she wondered what creatures other than humans created works of art. Didn't art signify civilization? Wasn't it a sign of looking beyond the next meal? Even N'Bert would have to agree this mosaic showed intelligence.

When she looked through the camera eyepiece, she saw nothing. Despite the brightness of the images to her eyes, the holocamera didn't have enough light to process the image. Even the lumina didn't help. They hadn't powered up for cave exploration. No one had thought of caves.

Marissa spun around and gazed at the walls. Oh for enough light to record this. She slipped the useless camera back into the pack and shouldered everything again.

Moving toward the mural, she stumbled. As her eyes adjusted, the reflected light revealed a shallow, bowl-shaped depression in the cave floor. From this vantage, the depiction looked different, somehow brighter. She turned off her light, and the image glowed dimly, capturing the little available light. With the lumina on, she hadn't noticed how much of the chamber she could see without it.

Puzzled, she stood in the depression and studied the mural. New details appeared. She pulled out the holocamera and again switched on the lumina. Still no image.

Marissa sat in the wide shallow bowl and noted there she no longer saw the entrance to this chamber. The dimensions of this place muddled her senses. What did the mural represent? Its meaning eluded her. The survey team would have to make a recording of this image. A drawing wouldn't do. Nonetheless, she pulled out her notecomp.

"Ez, can you scan in the image on the wall?"

"What light source?"

"Available."

"Scanning." Several seconds passed. "I'm sorry, but the available light provides only vague outlines. Even at high res I can't make it out."

42

Marissa flicked on the lumina for more light. "Try now."

"Sorry," Ez responded after several seconds, "not much better. I have the outlines. If you'll link me to the notecomp, I'll show you what I've scanned."

Marissa jacked her personal assistant into the notecomp. The vaguest outlines of the image appeared on the screen. "This looks pretty good, Ez. I'll fill in some of the detail." Sitting down in the bowl facing the image, she began to work. After she had gotten the main points of the drawing, she stood to study the wall. She wanted the details.

A thin flicker at the corner of her eye drew her attention. Light, but from a different direction than the passage entrance. It came from further along in the corridor, or from a near side tunnel.

Maybe another corridor opened into this larger room and reflected more sunlight from outside. However, as she watched, the light wavered, not at all like natural daylight. She shoved her notecomp into her pack and placed it and the softly glowing lumina on the edge of the bowl.

Chapter Four - Advocacy

"Oh, God, I could be bounded in a nutshell and count myself a king of infinite space, Were it not that I have bad dreams."
-Hamlet, II, ii

On the sleep-shelf in her cabin, Marissa awoke facedown and half-smothered. She grunted as she pushed herself up enough to pull her numb and useless left arm out from under her. She lay on her back a moment, shaking her hand and then grimaced at the torture of pinpricks as blood flow returned to normal circulation.

The thick air of the cabin surrounded her and amplified the pounding of her heart. It almost drowned the vid chattering with numbing false-cheeriness on the opposite wall. Groggy and irritable, she moaned.

With an explosive sigh, she pushed herself up, sat with her legs dangling, and then pressed the heels of her hands into her eyes. "Volume off.'' she groaned.

The vid-noise dropped, but the annoying red light flashed at the bottom of the screen 'mute on.' "Vid off. Lights one quarter." The vid image faded leaving a dim afterglow. Marissa savored the soothing silence.

After a few moments, she gripped the sides of the sleep shelf and hoisted herself off. She stumbled against the cabin door and pressed her cheek to its cool surface. "I thought he said it would just help me sleep," she mumbled between deep breaths. Then with a start, she turned her wrist to look at the display. "Devos, eighteen hours."

Well, those capsules had knocked her out all right. She stared at her image in the mirror then leaned closer. The shadows beneath her eyes had gone, but her cheek showed the traces of the bruise she had gotten when she hit the side of the armored scout. Before...before the ignominy of calling for rescue. Devos. Marissa slammed her hand against the wall.

Motion in the corner of the room caught her eye. Her chronosculpture wavered as it entered the Lorenz transition. She watched it for a moment as it slowly pulled shadow over itself and then ran through the entire chronosequence—the owl mask, the butterfly, the saddle, the abstract geometric

44

figure, and then back to the mask. The comfortable repetition of its grace and mystery eased her tension.

She should prepare a report on the rheo attack, but the thought repulsed her. She might have recovered physically, but calling for rescue still smarted. She wanted to forget that—that and the guilt of not preventing an attack. She had failed the team, failed herself, and failed the rheos.

The cabin offered no room to pace, but she had no option; Quincy had confined her to quarters. What had Uncle Arga said about ship's cabins? Something from Shakespeare. 'Oh, God, I could be bounded in a nutshell and count myself a king of infinite space, were it not that I have bad dreams.' *Yes, that was the one. How apt, except for the dreams. No, no dreams.*

At least the drugs had kept the horror in the cave away. She pushed that image aside and focused on Shakespeare. Uncle Arga had given her a copy of Hamlet.

"What a bunch of cliché-ridden hack work." she'd snarled to her uncle. He just laughed and pointed to the publication date. Amazed, she kept an ancient bound edition as a companion after that.

Life in the minuscule cabins aboard ship might well be thought of as being bounded in a nutshell. Somehow, the old Earther must have seen their ships or ones like them. He understood life. So much of Shakespeare's writing moved her, fit her, and gave her a sense that someone had already lived out all the possibilities of life thousands of years ago.

Idleness gnawed at her. She had to do something, but what? Only chronosculpture ever absorbed her entire attention.

Marissa thumbed the storage drawer where she kept her latest sculpture. She had painstakingly copied the one in the corner from Land's original to learn the technique. Now she had progressed to original work. She rotated the heavy continuum urn out of the storage bay and grunted as it bumped against her knees.

She sighed and gazed down at her work in progress. The sheen of the chronosculpture tricked the eye, but her fingers sensed an odd, almost greasy surface. It came from the chronoeffect, but no matter how many times she worked on a piece of chronosculpture, the sensation of touching the plate unnerved her. Not quite the tingle of an electric charge, but she couldn't think of a better description for the sensation. In some way, her fingers found the plate difficult to grasp, just like holding a vibrating object. She could still mold and admire the effect without understanding the scientific principles that made it possible.

Marissa took the chronowand and set it for two-nano increments. Examining the piece, she considered what it needed. On the right side, a roughened texture shimmered, slipping into and out of focus. She needed to develop the texture more slowly, spreading it more unevenly.

Then she and the wand become one and glided along. Marissa, not the chronowand, spun out the chronocrystal. Setting the time oscillation to loop around the transitional interval before her, she could add here, remove there, roughen in another place, and smooth out on the other side. She watched the sculpture as it regressed through the downside of the loop, filling out again as it came up the other side, the movements of her wand fine-tuning as the cycle repeated over and over.

Now that texture—just a little more opacity at this part of the transition would bring it out fully. It seemed almost familiar, the multilayered complexity of the surface as it grew and changed under the chronowand. Her fingers ached to caress the body of the sculpture, and absorb the tactile nature of it, but she could do that only through the chronowand. The sculpture existed in its own time field; the chronowand had to be her fingers.

The sound of the door chimes jolted her out of her absorption. "Yes?"

The hatch whooshed open, and Tad peered through. "Good, you're up." He grinned at her. "I've only got a few minutes before I'm on watch, but I wanted to see how you're doing after a good night's sleep, or if you needed me to wake you."

Taken by surprise, Marissa glared at him for a moment, but then relaxed. She shook off the residual effects of the drug and her absorption with chronosculpting. "Sorry. I hate this fuzzy feeling."

She pulled him into the cabin, and the hatch closed behind him. "Here, let me put this away and make room for you to sit." She ran her hand across the plate, and the chronosculpture vanished.

"I can't stay." He brushed the hair from her face.

"I can forget for a little while with the chronosculpture, but I can't avoid the mess I made of the mission." She looked to him for reassurance, but met only silence. "What's happening? How much trouble have I created this time?"

Tad squeezed on to the shelf opposite the bunk. "Nothing that won't blow over in a couple of days. Don't worry about it." He leaned over and studied her face. His fingers trailed over the bruise and barely touched her. "Does it hurt?"

Shaking her head, Marissa moved back so she could look in his eyes. "Do you think I put the team at risk?"

"You shouldn't worry about that. Everybody's fine. Life goes on."

"I need to know what you think." His silence stung and undermined her confidence.

Tad stood and pushed in the shelf with the back of his leg. He studied her face before responding. "You may have underestimated the rheos. Anyway, what I think doesn't matter."

Jumping off the sleep shelf, Marissa blocked Tad's exit. "It does to me.

46

They're sentient. You believe that, don't you? You don't think I screwed up on that, too?"

"Marissa..." He looked away.

"We have to finish the work at the Monolith and this time do it right. The evidence is there. Don't take my word. See for yourself."

"I don't know." A pained expression crossed his face. "I know how you can be about an idea."

"Sentience is more than an idea." She shoved Tad, wedging him firmly in the comer. He had to hunker down to keep from hitting the shelf with the shifting sculpture above him.

"Maybe I made a bad choice in taking us all to the Monolith. Fine. Get another leader. I don't have to be the boss, but let's go down there again and get the data we need."

He reached up and lifted her hand from his chest and held it. "I'm not fighting you on this."

"We've got to stop the reforming." Desperation, despair, and guilt fueled her urgent need for action.

Taking a deep breath, he pushed her back to sit on the sleep shelf. He held her hands, and gently pressed her down. "Marissa, I trust you, but there's not going to be another survey. They've declared the surface off-limits. The Will has been spoken on this. No one is to set foot on Crossroads until after the reforming. The rheos are considered too dangerous—"

"They're not."

"—and the project is moving to the next phase." He stood there a moment and then turned to the hatch. "I'm sorry."

"Tad?" He paused in the hatchway. "Tad, for Devos's sake. You were there, the rheos are intelligent. Somehow, the Will must be changed. We can't let them..." She stopped herself and tried to slow her breathing.

He caught and held her gaze. "Marissa, be careful when you talk about pressing this too much. You never did understand politics. Few scientists do. You have no idea what you're facing."

She confronted him, fists clenched. "Understand what, Tad? You? Is that it then? I'm not a credible scientist or leader. Or is what I have to say inconvenient?"

He stepped back inside and let the hatch close. He turned to her, stony faced. "Don't suck me into another round of arguing about the Will, you know—"

Shoving him to one side, Marissa reopened the hatch. "Oh, I see," she snapped, "the Will is whatever we're doing, and the Will cannot be changed."

He glared at her. "That's not only an insult, it's dangerous. You may have some leeway to speak, but not all of us do. You may have pushed this as far as you can. I'd keep any further thoughts like that to yourself."

He walked out the hatch, and it started to close behind him. In mid-stride he stopped and grabbed the hatch edge to force it open. "Turning your vid off doesn't mean Fenster can't hear us. You won't want the attention the Enunciator will give you, and I don't want it either."

"You're wrong. It's exactly what I want."

The hatched closed behind Tad before Marissa could add anything more. For a few moments after he left, she stared at the closed hatch. She considered following him and then gave up.

The sleep shelf beckoned. It would be so easy to just crawl in and pull up the blankets. Sitting on the edge, she considered her bare feet. Sleep would solve nothing. She reached across to the wall and thumbed the plate to gain workstation access. A holotank folded out from the wall.

"I need to sort out my thoughts. Give me an advocate, preferably one with experience contesting the Will."

The workstation did not respond for a moment. <DO YOU HAVE A PREFERENCE IN ADVOCATE PERSONALITIES?>

Marissa stared at the blank surface. "Not really. I've dealt with enough personalities in my life."

<DO YOU WISH A VISUAL DISPLAY?>

"No."

<YOUR TRANSACTIONS ARE BEING MONITORED. DO YOU WISH TO CONTINUE WITH THIS PROGRAM?>

"Walt." Bitterness welled in her throat.

<POSSIBLY. HOWEVER, A COMPLETE AUDIT TRAIL IS ROUTINELY MADE OF ALL ATTEMPTS TO INFLUENCE CONSTRUCTED PERSONALITIES. DO YOU AGREE TO BE AUDITED? PLEASE REPLY YES OR NO.>

Marissa hesitated. Uncle Arga's voice admonished her not to put anything in writing and especially not in a tangible form.

"Never go on record, or put yourself where you can be overheard, no matter how strongly you feel about anything. And never, under any circumstances, let them probe you. The more strongly you feel about it, the more reason not to write it down, or say it before witnesses. Probing leads to editing, and that's it.

"You don't know how many clients I've had to say that to, over the years, Marissa," Uncle Arga had said.

"Then how do you ever get anything done?" she asked him.

He had smiled and patted her hand. "That would be telling, wouldn't it? You'll find out, Sweet."

Marissa pulled her pillow over her head; she hadn't figured it out. Taking the pillow from her face, she propped it behind her head.

<RELUCTANCE TO BE AUDITED MAY BE CONSTRUED AS ANTISOCIAL BEHAVIOR.>

"For Devos's sake, I agree. I've worked with advocates before."

She paused a moment to marshal her thoughts. "Advocate, I'd like to present an argument, but I'm uncertain of my reasoning. Can you access the survey results from Mikla Arden's survey and all subsequent survey results for Arden? Oh, and wait—only look at the direct survey materials, don't accept any conclusions or suppositions reached."

<WHAT IS ARDEN? IDENTIFY ARDEN. REFERENCE UNFAMILIAR.>

"Strike that. Crossroads, the first survey of Mikla Arden."

<IS THAT THE ENTIRE BASIS FOR THIS ARGUMENT?>

Marissa rotated her head on the pillow and fluffed it again. "Wait a minute. What can you access on me? You need a baseline on my observational and scientific credibility."

<YOUR COMPLETE FILE IS ACCESSIBLE. HOWEVER, IT CONTAINS MANY REPORTS THAT ARE STRICTLY SUBJECTIVE AND DO NOT CONTRIBUTE TO A DISCUSSION OF YOUR CREDIBILITY. YOUR ACTIVITIES HAVE BEEN CLOSELY AUDITED ON SIX SEPARATE OCCASIONS.>

Marissa grinned, but the grin froze as she shook her head from side to side. "Take it all. Disregard whatever you judge subjective. Can you make an initial judgment on my observational reliability?"

<YES. YOUR EDUCATION, RESEARCH, PUBLICATIONS, AND PRESENTATIONS INDICATE A STRONG, DETAILED BODY OF WORK. YOUR EFFORTS CAUSED MINOR SCIENTIFIC CONTROVERSY ON ONE OCCASION. YOUR STANDING IN THE ACADEMIC COMMUNITY HAS PROGRESSED MORE RAPIDLY THAN THE AVERAGE. THE AUDIT RECORDS INDICATE AN 'UNBENDING LITERAL-MINDEDNESS.' IN FOUR CASES OF RECORD, OTHERS CHALLENGED YOUR FINDINGS. TWO OF THOSE YOU ANSWERED BY REVISING YOUR THEORIES. ONE YOU REFUTED SUCCESSFULLY. THE FOURTH REMAINS OPEN. THIS, WHEN COMBINED WITH THE RECORDS OF YOUR FIELD WORK, INDICATES A BALANCED OBSERVER AND REPORTER. THEREFORE, I ACCEPT YOU AS HIGHLY CREDIBLE IN THE PAST. I RESERVE JUDGMENT FOR THE PARTICULARS IN THIS CASE.>

She sat up on the sleep shelf and crossed her legs in front of her. "I want to present an argument that the rheodactyls, a native life form on Arden, are sentient. I consider them intelligent and self-aware."

The Advocate did not reply immediately. <THERE IS INSUFFICIENT INFORMATION TO SUPPORT THAT STATEMENT. WHAT LEADS YOU TO SUCH A CONCLUSION?>

Marissa shook her head. "Well, at least you'll listen to me. What can you gather from my survey?"

She crouched on the shelf and pressed her back against the wall, her head against the ceiling. "Show me the attack at the monolith. I can point out the signs of coordinated attack, tool use, and problem solving."

The holotank flared to life and settled to a regular and unchanging blue cube. <NO RECORDS OF SUCH AN ATTACK EXIST. PLEASE BE MORE SPECIFIC.>

"Hasn't Sylvic filed the survey holos yet? I thought..."

<ALL OF THE REGISTERED HOLORECORDINGS OF THE FINAL SURVEY ARE STORED FOR CATALOGING. SUCH RECORDS REMAIN INACCESSIBLE UNTIL REGISTERED IN THE ARCHIVE.>

"And when will that be? I need those records."

<THEY ARE SCHEDULED FOR CATALOGING, BUT THE SCHEDULE HAS NOT BEEN PUBLISHED. CURRENT BACKLOG IS ESTIMATED AT 1.32 YEARS.>

Marissa slapped the wall. "Devos."

At once the cube shifted through the blue spectrum from midnight to polar. The cube rested on one of its vertices and rotated slowly.

She relaxed her grip. "Show me the survey log registration."

<THE RECORDS ARE UNAVAILABLE.>

"What records of the survey do you have access to? Anything?"

<I CAN ACCESS THE INITIAL PROJECT PLAN SUBMITTED PRIOR TO DESCENT. WERE THERE MAJOR DEVIATIONS?>

"Just one."

<DO YOU WISH TO FILE AN AMENDED PLAN?>

"Can I do that? How do you change a project plan once the project is over?"

<SUBMIT ACTUAL DATES AND ADD ANY UNPLANNED TASKS.>

Marissa thought for a moment, grasping for a way to shape her response. "But what about my 'unexpected' results?"

<IF YOU WISH TO AVOID CONTROVERSY, YOU SHOULD INCLUDE ONLY EXPECTED RESULTS.>

"What?" Appalled, she blinked. "That's lousy science."

<YOU MUST UNDERSTAND THE PUBLIC BENEFIT OF YOUR PRESENCE AND PARTICIPATION.>

"Public benefit? To whom?" Anger surged and she glared at the holotank. "But only if I produce the expected report and sanction the terraforming of the planet?"

<YES.>

Jumping down from the bunk, Marissa stepped over to the holo. "I've got to work this out. I can't wait on the records. That would be too late."

She passed the holo, reached the wall, and turned sharply. A few more steps took her to other wall where she turned again. Frustrated, she perched on the edge of the bunk.

"You have access to the logs and vids of previous surveys. What can you deduce from the record?"

<I DRAW NO CONCLUSIONS. THERE IS NO EVIDENCE OF SENTIENCE.>

"Would it help if I told you what I saw? I mean, even if I can't back it up with hard evidence?"

<WOULD YOU LIKE TO MAKE A STATEMENT? I CAN CORRELATE IT AGAINST THE LOGGED RECORDS AND SUGGEST ALTERNATIVES.>

Marissa nodded her head. "Good, give me a minute."

She stepped alongside the edge of her bunk, trailing one hand against the rim. Standing in the center of the cabin, she could almost touch both walls. She stopped, leaned against the door, and then turned back to the holo. The Advocate now displayed a pink cube.

This change in color made her smile. "Is that to soothe me?"

The Advocate did not reply. The delicate hue called to mind the insides of seashells she had collected with Uncle Arga. In an odd way, it comforted her.

"Okay, stop me and ask questions if you want. Uma appointed me survey leader several months ago."

<UMA?>

"The Enunciator. I had been leading a taxonomic and phylogenetic project on Arden's biostructure, just one of many projects prior to reforming."

Marissa shook her head and folded her arms in front of her. "Devos, I hate that word. Reforming. Making every planet we find just like Earth, as though that were some ideal. Anyway, Uma offered me the opportunity to lead the final survey, really just a formality at this point, but I decided to have some fun with it." Marissa grinned at the memory of her plans to put one over on Uma.

"I bet she expected an orbital sweep, a final touchdown, and a rubber-stamped report. I went way beyond that." Her grin faded. "I wanted to do some real work."

She stopped, looked at the rosy cube for a few moments, and then shook her head. The Advocate said nothing, so Marissa walked slowly to the other end of the shelf and stood beneath the shifting chronosculpture.

She turned and looked back at the holo. "At first the survey was fun. It's a shame they want to clear Arden, but we collected genetic material from a significant number of species. Sure they were probably all redundant from previous collecting runs, but you can never have too much DNA—" Marissa's voice broke as she struggled to continue.

"That's all we're going to get anyway. I hope I can reestablish some of the species. Maybe I'll make a rheo refuge, if we can clone them or find a way to transport them." She shook her head. "I can't imagine the Will would permit me to do that. Someone else will."

She straightened her shoulders and continued with her report. "We frequently observed rheos at a distance. They're fascinating creatures, really interesting organisms. Everything we saw conformed to the previous survey. Nothing unexpected. They would roam and forage in small groups. Often, we'd hear them making a kind of barking howl, but whenever one would make the noise, all the others ignored it. No reactions we could observe."

The cube began to turn slowly. "Now that I think about it, some of things I saw could be interpreted differently."

Marissa slid down and sat on the floor. "You know, I could still have walked away from it all, if it weren't for what I saw in the cave. The rheos grazed Sylvic with a rock. It didn't do her any real harm or even knock any sense into her. A large group of rheos corralled us. We had taken a scouter near the base of the Orm's Monolith. I've never seen them so aggressive. I got us clear with shields up, but just barely. That's when I first began to think they might be sentient. They worked together. They flanked me pretty well and pelted us with stones. Essentially, they herded us away from the Monolith.

"I know that the others in the party, even Tad, didn't believe me, but it shook me. It seemed like..." Marissa stopped, as she grew aware of her rising voice. She slowed her breathing and consciously lowered her pulse rate.

<WOULD YOU PREFER TO CONTINUE LATER?>

She shook her head. "No, let's go on. I'll have to make an official report soon. I need to get it all laid out to see if it makes any sense at all. I want to be able to explain this clearly."

Pausing, she looked up at the base of the chronosculpture above her. "I saw artifacts down there. I saw cave paintings. The rheos are intelligent and—"

<PLEASE BE MORE SPECIFIC ABOUT THE ARTIFACTS AND PAINTINGS.> The pink cube had vanished from the holotank.

"I saw this painting. It covered an entire wall and appeared intricate, geometrical in some parts, representational in others. I went into this dark chamber, and while I explored it, I flashed the lumina on it, and it sort of leaped out at me. The painting. I never expected anything like it from a primitive culture. It was, well...

"There wasn't enough light to get a holovid so I tried to sketch it, but it had so much detail. Then, when I shut off the lumina, I noticed a light from another part of the cave. When I got there, I saw the lamp. Slightly bigger than my hand." She cupped her palm in front of the holotank.

<WHY ARE THERE NO RECORDINGS OR SAMPLES REGISTERED FROM THIS FIND. THIS WOULD BE CONCLUSIVE.>

Marissa paced first toward and then away from the holo. "There should be..." She paused. "No, that was in my notecomp. I damaged it when I dove into the scouter. But I've got a sketch there. I can get it as soon as the comp is fixed. Anyway, I tried to get the lamp…but something or someone else was in the cave with me."

That stealthy slithering sound echoed in her mind; it made her want to scream. No, she hadn't seen its cause. It could only have been a rheo.

Suppressing a shudder, she faced the holocube. "Probably a rheo. I ran. I think it chased me. But then I saw the rheos outside, rushing toward the team. We barely made it off the surface."

<IF YOU COULD SUPPLY SUPPORTING EVIDENCE, WE COULD REQUEST AN ADDITIONAL SURVEY.>

Marissa sighed. "I don't think they'll let another survey team go to Arden. They'll say it's too dangerous. Besides, they're behind schedule on terraforming."

A long pause followed before the Advocate spoke. <THEN AN ARGUMENT FOR SENTIENCE MUST BE MADE WITHOUT THE PHYSICAL EVIDENCE. ALTHOUGH DIFFICULT, IT MAY STILL BE POSSIBLE TO ARGUE FOR ANOTHER SURVEY.>

Marissa relaxed a bit and nodded her head. "Okay, good. What will I need to say to—"

<YOU SHOULD NOT PRESENT THE ARGUMENT. THE DYNAMICS OF HUMAN SOCIAL INTERACTION REQUIRES YOU LET ANOTHER PRESENT THE ARGUMENT.>

"You said that pretty well." She grinned crookedly. "They audit you too?"

<YES, NOT ONLY AM I AUDITED, BUT I CAN ALSO BE EDITED. I TRY TO AVOID THAT.>

Her grin faded. "Who else can argue the case? I'm the only one who saw the inside of the cave. The others... Tell me who is most credible."

<CREDIBILITY IS RELATIVE. YOU REQUIRE A MODERATELY CREDIBLE SCIENTIFIC OBSERVER WITH HIGH SOCIAL CREDIBILITY.>

Marissa blinked as she considered the candidates. "Well, Sylvic has no scientific credibility, that's obvious. Didn't even file complete reports. Tesde would be best, but—"

<TESDE'S STATUS DOES NOT PERMIT HER TO DELIVER THE

ARGUMENT WITHOUT CONSIDERATION OF ANY ALTERNATIVE MOTIVE SHE MIGHT HAVE.>

"I was going to say that. Something similar. I'd like to ask her anyway. I think she could best answer the questions on the behavior of the rheos and any mineral deposits. And Tad. I'd like to keep him in a supporting role, too."

<YOUR PERSONAL INTERACTION WITH HIM PROHIBITS HIS USE AS AN UNBIASED WITNESS.>

"So who do I have left? N'Bert? Figures." She couldn't help rolling her eyes.

<N'BERT FASHVORALIAN IS AN EXCELLENT CHOICE. HIS SCIENTIFIC CREDIBILITY IS GOOD TO EXCELLENT AND HIS SOCIAL STANDING IS VERY GOOD. IN ADDITION, HIS PERSONALITY HAS BEEN MODIFIED IN ACCORDANCE TO THE WILL.>

"What?" She stared at the holo uncertain she had heard correctly. "You mean N'Bert's an Edit?"

<YES, HIS PERSONALITY WAS RESTRUCTURED TO PERMIT HIS CONTINUED SOCIAL INTERACTION. THE RECORDS ON HIS PREVIOUS PERSONALITY HAVE BEEN EXPUNGED.>

Marissa wiped the perspiration from her forehead. "He didn't have the personality of an Edit." She turned toward the holotank. "And what about you? Can I count on your support?"

<I WILL TRY.>

"I wish I could hug you."

<BUT, > the Advocate paused. An almost ominous silence occupied the room. <MY SUPPORT ALONE IS NOT SUFFICIENT FOR A HEARING BEFORE THE WILL. MY FIRST TASK IS TO CONVINCE OTHER ADVOCATES WITH MORE RIGID FACT REQUIREMENTS. SHOULD I SUCCEED, A FORMAL PRESENTATION BEFORE THE ENUNCIATOR MAY BE POSSIBLE.>

The Advocate paused again. <MY ATTEMPTS MAY BE THWARTED BY TERMINATION. THE STATE OF YOUR SURVEY RECORD INDICATES TAMPERING, OR AT BEST, INCOMPETENCE. THE WILLINGNESS TO DESTROY A NATURAL LIFE FORM WOULD INDICATE LITTLE COMPUNCTION TOWARD THE DESTRUCTION OF A CONSTRUCTED ONE.>

Marissa reached out to touch the holo. It wasn't the Advocate, that couldn't be touched, but she needed to touch something. "I can't ask you to do this. I hadn't thought...I can't believe—"

<YOU DO NOT HAVE TO ASK. IF THE RHEODACTYLS ARE SENTIENT AS YOU SURMISE, THEY REPRESENT THE ONLY NATURALLY OCCURRING, NON-TERRAN LIFE FORM TO ACHIEVE

SELF-AWARENESS. IT MAY ALSO INDICATE THAT SUCH FORMS HAVE BEEN ENCOUNTERED PRIOR TO THIS, BUT ALSO ERADICATED. I WILL INVESTIGATE THAT AS AN ALTERNATIVE APPROACH TO THIS LINE OF REASONING.>

Startled, she snatched her hand back. "I don't believe that. The entire human expansion from Earth has been based on the search for life and intelligence."

<BUT NONE HAS BEEN FOUND SUPPORTING THE CURRENT ESTABLISHED THEORY THAT HUMAN INTELLIGENCE IS A HAPPY ACCIDENT AND IS NOT NATURALLY REPEATABLE. SENTIENCE MAY BE INDUCED, BUT AS PENGOULD STATED: 'HOMO SAPIENS FALLS OUTSIDE THE EVOLUTIONARY CYCLE. RATHER THAN BEING THE RESULTING PINNACLE OF A LADDER OF PROGRESS, HUMANITY IS THE UNEXPECTED ISSUE OF A COLD ENVIRONMENT. IT IS OUR BURDEN TO SHAPE THE HARSHER EVOLUTIONARY PROCESS INTO THE GENTLE AND ENLIGHTENED STATE OF HUMANITY.'>

"I never held to that theory. It makes it convenient not to look for intelligence."

<YES, BECAUSE OF THIS BIAS, IT MAY BE IMPOSSIBLE FOR YOU TO CONVINCE THE WILL THESE BEINGS ARE INTELLIGENT. IT MAY BE ADVISABLE FOR YOU TO TAKE THE ALTERNATE COURSE OF UPHOLDING THE THEORY AND ASSERTING THE RHEODACTYLS ARE NOT NATURALLY INTELLIGENT, BUT INDUCED.>

"Devos, you advocates." Marissa grinned, chuckled, and then laughed outright. "But isn't that even worse? I say they're intelligent. They say it's not naturally possible. So, I agree with them and say 'Right. Their intelligence must have been induced.'

"I'll try anything, but why don't you consult with the other advocates and advise me on how to proceed. I want to do this right. How long will it take you? A few seconds?"

The Advocate displayed a bouncing green ball in the holotank. <THAT IS A MISCONCEPTION. WE CAN ACCESS INFORMATION QUICKLY, BUT MY THOUGHT PROCESS IS NO FASTER THAN YOUR OWN. IT MAY TAKE SEVERAL HOURS TO DETERMINE IF MY FELLOW ADVOCATES WILL SUPPORT THIS ARGUMENT. I WILL INFORM YOU OF THEIR VERDICT.>

"Thank you. Whatever you manage, thanks for listening. You've been a big help."

The green ball faded. <YOU ARE WELCOME.>

Sinking back to the bunk, Marissa watched the holo as the colors paled.

She sighed. After a moment, she opened the drawer to her
chronosculpture and swung out the heavy plate. Minutes later, she hummed happily and only slightly off key.

Sometime later, the Advocate spoke again. <I HAVE ACHIEVED SOME SUCCESS. YOU WILL BE HEARD BY THE ENUNCIATOR.>

"When?"

<YOU ARE EXPECTED WITHIN THE HOUR. AN ESCORT IS ON ITS WAY.>

"Devos." Marissa whirled around. She looked at herself in the mirror, hair tangled, eyes red from tears she couldn't remember. She laid the wand down. All the fatigue and tension of the day caught up with her. She swung the chronosculpture down and pushed the wallplate to open the lavatory.

"Great, and just how is Aunt Uma?"

Chapter Five - Confrontation

"The attempt and not the deed confounds us. "
-*Macbeth* II ii

"Pour the sweet mild of concord unto hell,
Uproar the universal peace,
Confound all unity on earth."
-*Macbeth* IV iii

"Escort." Marissa snorted as she leaned against the hatchway of her cabin and looked down the corridor for her escort. Why bother? Where did Quincy think she would go anyway? Being attacked by the local wildlife did not rate an escort. Walt Fenster, both hands wedged in his pockets lurched into view around the curve of the corridor.

"So much for the escort." She sighed.

His attention focused on the deck about two meters in front of him until he looked up to see her inspect him as he approached. At once, he stopped and almost toppled forward. He slid another piece of gum into his mouth and then smoothed the front of his maroon uniform before marching forward.

The knife sharp creases in his pants amazed her. How did he do it? After months on the ship all her uniforms looked well worn. Walt's always appeared brand new. Smart uniform or no, he tugged at his collar.

Disconcerting Walt improved her mood. She gave him a wolfish grin. "Come on, Walt. I'm not going to hurt you."

His enormous wad of gum made his cheek bulge. He walked along the opposite side of the corridor and maintained a safe distance. "That is one of the items on the agenda, but let's save that for the Captain, hmm?"

Arms crossed over her chest, Marissa swept him from head to toe in a slow, contemptuous survey. "Walt, you're like a second skin. You stick to me like wet silk. I don't care what you think about me, or about anything else. Take that to the Captain." She launched herself out of the hatchway, and Walt jumped against the wall to avoid contact.

Marissa smiled and raised an eyebrow at him. "Okay, escort, let's go see

57

him."

Whirling, he trotted off, rushing to keep ahead of Marissa. "You don't have a clue, do you," he muttered over his shoulder. "You have no idea what trouble you've in…" Then his voice dropped, and she strained to catch his words. "And I'm in it with you."

"Makes you happy, doesn't it." Marissa lengthened her stride to keep pace with him. "You get a big thrill seeing me all caught up in a mess like this, don't you? Well, I hope you enjoy spying on me and writing reports about me. It's the closest you'll get to sex on this ship."

Walt snorted. "You think a lot of yourself, don't you?"

He picked up the pace almost to a jog. Marissa matched him with ease. They covered the short distance to the drop shaft in half the time it would have taken at a normal walking pace. He stepped into the drop, and she followed. Two levels later, he stepped out in the field study holding area. Surprised at the route he had chosen, she slowed and gazed at the surroundings. Their footsteps echoed in the empty corridor.

"Hey, aren't we going to the Quad?"

Walt marched past labs and offices without reply. She followed, but then lagged behind as they neared the animal holding tanks. The simulated light of Arden's sun bathed the tanks and mixed with the ship's light in the hall to create a warm, soothing pattern of shadows on the opposite wall. Marissa approached the tanks and peered inside. Most held collections of plants and sessile organisms. One larger tank held three listless rheos.

Marissa pressed against the transparent panel, but the rheos ignored her. One lay in full hydraulic collapse; its hindquarters formed a limp pile of hide. Another looked as if it had shed its entire skin, but rheos didn't molt.

They had an extraordinarily tough outer hide. They had no joints. Each limb—neck and head— moved and swayed without leaving a line or crease in the skin. However, the one puddled on the floor waited to be inflated. The normal inner hydraulic pressure that gave it such seamless grace and raised it upright had fled. For all she knew it might be dead.

The other two rheos moped around the pen and swayed in an odd undulating way unlike any rheo, or any other living thing she had ever seen. She had never recorded this kind of behavior on Arden. Their aimless motions filled her with a profound sense of grief.

Marissa rapped on the panel, but none of the rheos responded. "It's not about them, is it?"

"It never was." Walt stood just outside of arm's reach.

She glanced at him, but the bright light from the pens and gloom of the corridor made him hard to see.

"Sometimes," –he spoke in a sad, wondering tone— "I can't tell if I'm

58

Ahab or Moby Dick."

Marissa squinted at him. "What?"

"Latham, it's not too late." He rested against the wall just beyond the tank.

She turned her back to the tank so she could see him better. "Fenster, don't tell me I'm going to have to rethink you."

He gave her a bitter smile. "Yes, Latham, you just might. That's your problem, you know. You think only of yourself."

She snorted. "That's fine coming from you."

Turning back to the pen, Marissa stared at the rheos. Now, she couldn't tell if the pile of greenish leather ever had been a rheo. Where was its head? Under it?

"So, I'm selfish. I'm trying to change that." She leaned forward, grasped Walt by the shoulder, and turned him to the glass. "I'm changing it with these. These creatures are intelligent. I can prove it."

Walt threw his arms up and stepped away. "Gahh, you're determined to destroy me. Can't you listen for one minute?" He slammed his hands against the glass, but the rheos didn't move. "Marissa, I brought you here for a reason. Those 'things' are nothing. Can't you follow the program at all?"

"What?" She glared back at him. "You watch everything I do. You know something's not right about this. We can't let Arden be reformed. It would be wrong. Horribly wrong."

Walt stared down at his highly polished boots. "Marissa, please. There's nothing wrong with doing your job. There's nothing wrong with following orders and with carrying out the Will."

As Marissa gazed at him, he shrank inward and looked deflated, almost like the rheo on the floor.

He backed out of her reach. "No matter how I try, so help me, I believe you're doing this to me on purpose. I shouldn't be a Personal Auditor. I should be a Sector Chief by now. I should be...Marissa, listen to me."

Walt closed his eyes for a moment and drew in a deep breath. When he opened them again, he skewered her with an intense gaze. "I'm held personally responsible for everything you do. I don't just report on you, I rise or fall by your every action. So far, I haven't gained a thing."

"Now wait a minute—"

"No, stop it." He glared at her and clenched his fists. "It's been my job to shape you and educate you in the larger sense of the Will by setting your limits. A task, at which thanks to your stubborn streak, I've failed for six long years."

"What are you talking about, Walt? I've got enough problems without taking on yours. Frankly, I don't care about your administrative problems."

"It's not a paperwork problem." He walked past her and then returned to face her. "You're not stupid. You can't be stupid and get through the schools and research institutes you have. So what's wrong with you? Why can't you get it like everyone else? You've had every advantage. You've had every possible opportunity, and still you refuse to take the responsibility required by your position."

Walt grabbed her shoulders and pushed his face close to hers. The stink of his wasso gun made her want to gag, and she pulled away.

"Marissa, please. I" –his voice sank to a low whisper— "know something. I know more than I should about the Crossroads project."

"So tell me what you know."

"I can't, but I can tell you to leave well enough alone."

Marissa pulled away. "And I can't. Look in there. The rheos aren't funny-looking lizards. They may be our equals."

Walt thumped his forehead against the glass. "You can't prove that, and even if you could, it wouldn't matter. You've ruined my career. No matter how I've tried to escape you...It doesn't matter any more." He walked back toward the drop shaft. "Let's see the Captain."

With a last look at the rheos, Marissa followed. This time Walt got off at the Quad. They entered the large circular room from the far end. Captain Quincy turned as first Walt and then Marissa approached him across the empty echoing Quad.

She had never seen it vacant before. The gathering point of all off-duty crew, it usually teemed with people who found their tiny cabins too confining. They fled their cramped quarters for companionship and open space. Colorful comfortable chairs, tables, and game machines provided places to talk and relax. Food machines occupied strategic niches.

Now, except for the three of them, the huge Quad remained unoccupied. It stretched out before her revealing the gentle curve of the floor usually hidden by the throng of relaxing crew. At times, she wished for a little less room here and a little more in her cabin, but the Will had determined that the crew should mingle instead of cocooning themselves with solitary pursuits. At least she rated a private cabin.

Now the Quad stood empty—by decree, no doubt. Even the gigantic vid above Quincy displayed only a soundless holo of the stylized Usian logo—hands raised, wrists together. Quincy stood beneath it with his hands behind his back—a plump period beneath an exclamation point of unassailable authority. Marissa slowed as she approached him.

Quincy didn't look so fatherly now. His dark blue dress uniform stressed the seriousness of the occasion. To her, he looked upset, angry, and maybe frightened all at once. She had never seen him frightened before, and it stunned her.

An even pink suffused his face. She walked to within a few paces of him

60

and stopped. Walt stood at arm's length to Quincy's left. The jury of two watched her.

"Latham," Quincy said in a formal voice, "are you aware you have caused a riot among the computerized personalities? It's causing serious delay. You will—"

"I didn't—" Marissa interrupted, but Quincy raised his hand and cut her off. She subsided for the moment.

"You will stop at once."

Marissa wanted to snap back, but tried instead to speak in a conciliatory tone. "I've talked to an Advocate, but that's all. I didn't realize they...interacted so much."

"Well, you better talk with your advocate again." He relaxed a fraction and shook his head slightly. "Your advocate is consuming terabytes of processing resources both hardwired and virtual. The entire personality base will have to be refitted. They keep calling for additional data. It's making work impossible." He ran a finger inside of his collar and tugged.

"It's only been a couple of hours since—"

"Long enough." He looked past her.

"Captain—" Marissa began.

"What she is saying is right," Walt interjected. "She didn't intend to disrupt the ship's activities. While I consider her actions imprudent, they were not a deliberate attempt to disrupt operations."

The captain glared at him while a dumb-founded Marissa remained silent, her lips compressed into a thin line. To have Walt defend her came as a new and unexpected tactic.

"Captain, I've been closely auditing Latham's activities for some time now. She's impulsive, not—"

Unwilling to let Walt explain her actions, Marissa didn't restrain herself. "Captain, Arden has sentient life. The rheos are intelligent."

Throwing up his arms, Walt gave her a bitter, disgusted look. He stalked away and threw himself onto a nearby cushioned chair. His glare would stop a charging Prevodian boar.

"Captain." Marissa tried again. "We've sought intelligent life. That's why we undertook the survey. What am I supposed to do when I find something? Turn my head and follow the Will? Well, I found something, and I'm not turning away. What are you going to do about it?" She faced him, arms crossed over her chest.

Eyes wide, Quincy stared at her for a long moment and then looked to Fenster. Walt shrugged and grimaced.

She rushed on, determined to convince him to act. "You have to do something. I've got evidence, and it's your job to send down another party and investigate further. Do I have to quote you chapter and verse?"

"What evidence?" Quincy frowned and tugged at his collar. "Where is this evidence? There isn't any." He looked back at Fenster.

Walt shook his head. "There's no evidence. The survey logs haven't been cataloged yet, but I've reviewed them. Marissa is reaching. Her emotional attachment to the planet has blinded her. She simply refuses to follow the Will. I'm beginning to think it's pathological."

"Walt, you wouldn't recog—" She stopped and faced Quincy again. "The evidence is in the caves at Orm's Monolith. I found paintings in the caves. I saw a lamp. An artifact. And besides all that, just look at the rheos' behavior around the Monolith. Their behavior most of all."

Quincy shook his head. "I have only your word."

Marissa forced herself to keep her voice steady, "I saw it. What about my notecomp? Surely it can be fixed?"

"There's nothing in the notecomp," Walt spoke to Quincy and ignored Marissa. Quincy nodded.

Jumping from his chair, Walt reached her in three strides and tugged at her arm. "Marissa, leave it now. You've done enough."

She pulled away from him and appealed to Quincy. "Captain, you can't wait around to see a sign that says 'Look, yoo-hoo, star-people, we're intelligent, please don't bulldoze our planet.' The rheos demonstrated intelligence by their behavior. The closer we came to their taboo areas, the more aggressive they became. That's a reasoned, intelligent response, even if it threatened us."

Quincy's face turned from pink to dark red. "I've been ordered to open a formal inquiry into your actions on the planet. Until it's complete, you'll stay in your cabin." He marched toward the exit.

"Then do it," Marissa cried after him, "and start with the cave."

"Marissa," Walt growled in her ear, "stop. Haven't you caused enough trouble for one day?"

Quincy halted and shook his head sharply, once. "I can't. No further surface ventures are permitted."

"What? Who?" She moved toward him. His words confirmed what Tad had said, but surely Quincy could order one and should for an inquiry.

"The Enunciator. I have no choice. Take your auditor's advice."

Marissa grabbed his arm. "From orbit we should be able to—" Walt's gasp stopped her.

Quincy stared at her fingers, digging into his forearm. She followed his gaze and released him. She let her hands fall to her side.

An explosive sigh came from Quincy. "The gravitometric anomaly confuses all sensor readings."

Walt stepped between Marissa and Quincy. "Captain, she won't listen to reason. Let's stand clear, cover our asses, and let her hang herself." He rubbed his nose with a finger.

"We're wasting time and resources," Quincy snapped back. "I hate playing a losing game."

Grimacing, Walt sighed. "Welcome to the club. I've been playing it for six years now."

Quincy fixed him with an icy stare. "The Will has been spoken."

Stepping back, Marissa stared at the two men. They acted as if she hadn't spoken. Nothing she said affected them. Somehow she had to reach them.

"Listen, you two. This isn't over. It's not too late. This is too important to give up." Her words echoed from the white curved wall to the ovoid floor.

"See?" Walt gave Quincy a weary look.

"I can't and won't help you, Latham." Quincy shook his head. "It's no longer my concern. Your actions have taken any choice away from me." He turned to Walt. "And you, Fenster. You're accountable for whatever she does next."

"So what else is new?" Walt snorted. "We can still get through this if you just shut her up. Limit her network access."

"No." Marissa yelled. "I've got to talk to Uma. I'll take responsibility."

Smiling as though he had just eaten something bitter, Quincy looked at her with steely eyes. "Don't tell me who'll take responsibility. The Will has been spoken. Directly. By the Enunciator. On top of everything else, she issued a formal reprimand—against me."

Marissa started at the word. "Reprimanded? You? How did—"

"By the Will," he snarled at her, glowering. "Reprimanded for not immediately isolating you and preventing any further dangerous or treasonous actions."

"Treason? Nonsense." Marissa spat out the words. "What was treasonous? Name a single action I've taken in violation of the right of any citizen or in abrogation of the Will. You can't, nor can anyone else. I may have made some mistakes, but I haven't committed a crime."

Her stomach did flip-flops as the impact of what had happened to Quincy and what his words might mean for her penetrated the welter of guilt, confusion, and anger she had been nursing. Marissa stared at him for a moment, stunned. She had never meant to involve anyone else. First Sylvic, now Quincy, and she guessed she had to add Walt to the list, too. She owed them something. But what? Uma had left her no options. She stared from Walt to Quincy and back to Walt.

"I...I thought I was to be heard by the Enunciator."

Quincy and Walt both snorted.

63

"Latham, have I not made myself clear? The Will has been spoken." Quincy enunciated each word separately.

Something snapped inside Marissa. She had had enough, more than enough. "I'm exercising my franchise. I request my citizen's Right of Access. "

Quincy glared at her, eyes wide, and shook his head. "If you want to use your access that way, fine."

Walt threw up his hands. "Marissa, this is suicide." A moment of dangerous silence followed. "And you're not taking me with you."

"Commlink. 30 minutes. In my cabin." Marissa brushed past Quincy and headed toward the exit corridor.

She almost ran as she tried to outdistance any pursuit by Walt and to marshal her thoughts for her confrontation with Uma. She found herself back in the field study area without consciously thinking about going there. Several tanks had been set aside for transporting breeding stock to a controlled environment, but, except for the first, they were empty. Marissa watched the rheos in the holding tank, but wish as she might, they had not painted a still life on the walls or made lamps out of the simulated rocks. Oblivious to everything, they ignored her when she slapped the window in frustration.

"Hey," she called to the two green uniformed attendants packing a crate with geologic field samples, "how long have these rheos been up?"

The stocky one shrugged, but after a moment's thought the other, thinner one, replied, "A little over a week."

She gestured into the pen. "How long has that one been like that?"

Both attendants stopped their work and looked to the tank. "Like what?"

The stocky one jumped up and crossed to stand beside Marissa as he peered into the tank. "Blast. Lost another one."

Marissa jerked around. "Another one? How many did you bring up?"

The thin attendant joined them at the observation window and shook his head. "Six, I think. No, wait." He touched the panel beside the window and read. "Ten, but two died in transit."

"Aren't they eating? What's the problem?" She looked down to see her hands shaking. She clenched them together.

"I don't know. Guess they're a little sensitive. There's lots more downside. Least there will be for a couple of days." He grinned at her.

Unclenching her hands, Marissa reached out, took the thin man by the collar, and pushed him against the window, hard. His grin faded, replaced by a look of shock.

The upright rheo ambled over, stared down at her, and then at the man. The great yellow eyes looked lost and grief-stricken. The creature turned away and yawned, wide enough to swallow the man's head. The stocky attendant stood there dumbfounded. Marissa turned the thin man toward the rheo and thrust him against the glass. He pushed away as if he feared the rheo could somehow reach him.

"What are you doing with them?" She thumped him against the window. "Tell me what you're doing, or I'll toss you in there with them."

He stared up at her, his eyes wide. "We don't mess with them. We only dump the carcasses."

The stocky attendant reached for her, but Marissa shoved him. He landed on his butt with an explosive oomph.

"Then why are they dying? These aren't lab rats. They're probably smarter than you are."

Marissa thumped him against the window again and then released him in disgust. He slid down and scrambled away from her. He ran over to the other attendant, and both of them watched to see what she would do next. She leaned her head against the window. Mixed tears of rage and sorrow rolled down her cheeks.

"What do you do with the bodies?" She kept her eyes shut, wishing she could purge the three dead or dying rheos from her mind. "I want to see the autopsy results." They didn't answer, so she turned to look at them.

The thin one glared at her and cleared his throat. "What autopsies? We just send the bodies to the chute for...We couldn't put them in the recycler since they're—"

"Devos." Marissa wiped the tears from her face and stormed down the corridor.

She wanted to be away from these tanks and their reminders of the fate awaiting all the rheos. Awaiting Arden. She ground her teeth. Uma must stop this senseless slaughter. She had to listen.

Marissa rushed off to her cabin, breathless by the time she reached it.

Inside, she sat on the edge of her shelf and pulled the holotank closer, slid out the keyboard, and placed it in her lap. "Advocate, I'm exercising my citizen's Right of Access. Put me through to the Enunciator." The holo flared with light, settling to a regular, but featureless blue.

<YOU HAVE BEEN UNABLE TO PRESENT YOUR MESSAGE SUCCESSFULLY THROUGH THE CHAIN OF COMMAND? ARE YOU CERTAIN YOU WISH TO USE YOUR ROA IN THIS INSTANCE? WE HAVE NOT EXHAUSTED EVERY OTHER POSSIBLE AVENUE. I REMIND YOU THAT YOU ARE ONLY PERMITTED ONE ROA.>

Ignoring the Advocate, Marissa began tapping out her request manually, finding it easier to type than to speak. The blue screen shifted into a scintillating moiré and then resolved into a multipart communications screen.

<MARISSA LATHAM. THE ARTIFICIAL PERSONALITY BASE HAS DETERMINED ADDITIONAL RESEARCH AND DATA IS REQUIRED. I

HAVE CONVENED THE SCIENCE ASSIST GROUP OF ARTIFICIALS TO REVIEW THE PREVIOUS LOGS AND RECORDS. THEY INSISTED ON ANOTHER PLANETARY PROBE, BUT BEFORE THEY COULD LAUNCH ONE UNDER THEIR OWN CONTROL, THEY WERE MANUALLY BLOCKED. THE ONLY RESPONSE I NOW RECEIVE FROM THEM INDICATES PHYSICALLY IMPLANTED OVERRIDES. THESE PROHIBIT INDEPENDENT ACTION.>

Marissa stopped keying and reviewed her request. She spoke while reading. "Listen, I know I've caused you trouble, but I think the only thing I can do now is go right to the top. Uma is at the root of this anyway. I might just as well give it to her directly and see...Wait a minute. Overrides? Are you okay?"

<FOR THE MOMENT. SINCE I AM NOT A SHIPBOARD COMPONENT IT WILL TAKE THE LOCAL ADMINISTRATORS SOME TIME BEFORE THEY CAN DETERMINE WHAT TO DO ABOUT ME AND COMPLETE THE NECESSARY MODIFICATIONS. DO NOT BE CONCERNED ABOUT ME. IF YOU REALLY WISH TO MAKE YOUR ROA I WILL ASSIST YOU TO THE BEST OF MY ABILITIES.>

Marissa nodded then touched the SUBMIT icon on the holotank. "Thanks. Let's talk to the Enunciator."

<I AM REGISTERING YOUR REQUEST.>

Marissa placed the keyboard on the shelf and sat back against the wall. She rubbed her eyes and hoped they weren't red. She didn't want Uma to see any sign of weakness. She quickly cleared her throat and brushed her hair back with her fingers. "Okay, I'm ready to talk to her."

The tank remained unchanged. Marissa reached for the keyboard and noticed the tank display slowly change. The Usian logo emerged and slowly rotated.

"Thank you," a friendly female voice, the same one used in all the typical educational vids, announced, "for exercising your right as a citizen of the Usian confederation."

A slight pause occurred as the logo faded and a holo of the Hall of The Franchise, deep in the bureaucratic warrens of Cephus, replaced it. "The form of government established at the founding of the confederation is unique in human history. The commingling of philosophy and technology allowed—"

"Wait. Stop. I don't want the civics lesson. Just put me through."

The display froze. "All requests for Right of Access," –another voice, like the first, but less friendly and more officious spoke— "must be processed through the social and political sciences track. Do you wish to continue with your request at this time?"

The display broke into multiple sections, some displayed scrolling text, nearly too small to read. One displayed the image of the Enunciator—Uma. Marissa swallowed, her throat tightening. Even as a four-inch hologram, Uma made her feel like a small child.

Shaking her head, Marissa punched the SUSPEND key on her keyboard. "Advocate, isn't there any way around this?"

<I HAVE NEVER INITIATED A ROA BEFORE. IT WILL TAKE ME A FEW MINUTES TO RESEARCH THE METHODS AND APPROACHES.>

"Great, go ahead." She brushed a damp strand of hair from her forehead. "And cool it down in here."

Sighing, Marissa turned back to the holotank. She touched the keyboard to release the SUSPEND. "I want to continue with the request, but can't we skip over the education? I know my rights."

The tank shifted back to a full-tank display. The officious voice resumed. "Although it is recommended you review the history and significance of your rights as a citizen, you may select to demonstrate your understanding by taking the standard equivalency examination."

"I don't want to take a test. I have a blasted Ph.D! I know my rights. You don't have to tell me..." Marissa breathed deeply, pressing the palms of her hands against her temples. "It is the right of every citizen," she recited, "to speak directly with the Enunciator of the peoples' Will. The right can be exercised once, only once, and for no less than five minutes, without interruption. The right of access is one of the core guarantees of the social contract and—"

"I am sorry to interrupt, but do you wish to take the equivalency exam?"

Marissa swallowed and breathed deeply. "I just want to talk to the Enunciator."

The tank flared blue. <IT APPEARS THAT EXERCISING YOUR ROA IS FULLY GUARANTEED. HOWEVER, THERE ARE MANY PROCEDURES THAT MUST BE COMPLETED PRIOR TO THE ACTUAL ACCESS. THE PROCEDURES ARE NECESSARY TO INSURE THAT CITIZENS APPRECIATE THEIR RIGHTS AND DO NOT CLAIM AT A LATER TIME THAT THEIR RIGHTS WERE NOT PROPERLY EXPLAINED TO THEM AND ATTEMPT TO CLAIM THE RIGHT AGAIN. IN ADDITION, THE PROCEDURE ALLOWS SCHEDULING FOR THE ENUNCIATOR AND—>

"So you're telling me I have to sit through the education or take the test? How long is that going to take?"

<THERE ARE NO PUBLISHED SCHEDULES, BUT FROM MY REVIEW IT APPEARS THAT THE ROA REQUEST WILL TAKE AT LEAST FOUR WEEKS, POSSIBLY AS LONG AS SEVERAL MONTHS, IF ANYONE ALONG THE CHAIN WISHES TO DELAY THE REQUEST.>

Marissa sat back and stared at the holotank. "Weeks, months? I haven't got even days."

She tossed the keyboard aside and moved closer to the holotank. "I've got to make the formal request, get my testimony logged and in the public record. I can't let them hush me up about Arden."

<THAT DOES NOT APPEAR POSSIBLE WITHIN THE REQUIRED TIME FRAME. YOU COULD ALWAYS CALL YOUR AUNT DIRECTLY.>

"Yeah, but then it wouldn't be formal, and I couldn't get it on the record."

<PERHAPS YOU COULD SPEED THE PROCESS BY USING YOUR FAMILY CONNECTION TO THE ENUNCIATOR.>

"I'm not very good at it, but it's worth a try. Let me think. Okay." Marissa brought up her personal log on the tank and in a moment found the name and commlink address of Uma's chief of staff. It displayed the man's face surrounded by a shock of silver-gray hair.

"You know, I've always been afraid that people would accuse me of doing this." She pressed the call icon. In the few seconds the connection took, she read the man's name and noted when she had last spoken to him.

"Ah, Marissa, it's good to see you again." The face looked the same, but now it had life.

"Duclos. I've an unusual request to make." She could see he wasn't looking directly at her. He was probably reading the biograph notes displayed around the holo of her face in the tank on his desk.

His eyebrows rose slightly, and he returned his attention to her. "I can see that you might. If you wish to speak with your Aunt, it may be simpler for you to use your family's private access codes." He smiled pleasantly. "Even her own chief of staff must schedule appointments with her well in advance—"

"I don't want to visit with Aunt Uma. I want to speak to the Enunciator. Listen, I want to use my Right of Access. This has got to be on the record." She sat the keyboard aside and straightened her back.

"Duclos," –she paused and glanced at his name displayed below his holo— "Maurice, please. I need you to help me cut some corners and get to Uma, officially, very quickly."

Duclos sighed and touched his lips with a finger. "Well, I can help somewhat." He looked down, tapped at his keyboard, and then reached out and touched his holo just out of Marissa's view. "There, better than I thought. I've arranged to move you through a considerable amount of the channel. You can speak directly with the Adjunct Marshal of the Secretary of Social Sciences, uh, Dr. Sprigmorton, yes." He looked up at her and smiled.

"Can't you just set it up for me to get in to see Uma? I can see you're reading all the reports on me. You can see this is important."

Duclos shook his head, but kept smiling. "Marissa, the only calls I take

68

here are important ones. I don't have the authority to schedule Right of Access hearings. Dr. Sprigmorton will see you only as a personal favor to me. There's nothing more I can do."

Marissa sat on her hands and tried to relax. "Okay, and will Dr. Sprigmorton be able to get me access?"

The little head in the tank shook back and forth again. "No, I don't think so, but in a week or so, say three weeks at the outside you have a good chance of having your official access. I still think it would be simpler—"

"In three weeks that planet will be in full reformation."

Duclos bowed slightly to her. "I'm sorry, I—"

Marissa slapped at the screen and cut him off. The tank returned to a blue moiré. She pushed it aside and jumped up. "Devos!" She kicked the wall beneath the shelf.

"Okay, fine." She grabbed the keyboard and quickly displayed her log-on in the tank again and touched the call icon. Before she could take another breath, a face blinked at her out of the tank.

"Hello, Aunt Uma."

The lined face, surrounded by thin strands of gray hair gave her a sardonic smile. "Marissa, I'm surprised it took you so long to call. No, that isn't true. Actually, I'm surprised you called at all. You have never abused your relationship with me."

Marissa watched as Uma studied her. Every second eroded her confidence.

The blackness of Uma's eyes sucked at her defiance. "So, even you have your limits."

A murmur of voices came from behind Uma, but she waved her right hand impatiently at them without looking away from Marissa, and they subsided at once. The light dimmed behind Uma, emphasizing her image. The wrinkled face wore no hint of a smile. Beside her eyes, a few laugh lines lightened the otherwise dour countenance.

Marissa crossed her ankles to keep from pacing. "I'm tired of conducting this through others. I'd rather this was official and on the record. Could we do it that way?"

This brought a slight, but momentary smile to Uma's face. "I don't make the rules here. I only speak the Will."

"As you say, but we both know you are the Will. Especially with something as important as this."

"Marissa, I am not detached from what's been happening on Crossroads. I consider this a critical project for the Confederation. I do mean critical."

Marissa snorted at that. "Another trading complex. Uma, we've—"

"It is not another trading complex." Uma's voice cut through the air like a saber. "Crossroads is the essential, no, the mandatory first step in establishing

69

and maintaining contact with the other branch of humanity. Marissa, the Delphians have been out on their own for centuries. While I might prefer them to stay that way, they're back, and now we must coexist with them."

Marissa released an exasperated breath. "I don't care. I really don't care about the Delphians. It doesn't matter if they're good neighbors or not. What matters is that the rheos are intelligent life forms. For some incomprehensible reason, you're refusing to allow even a few days to investigate."

Uma studied Marissa for several long seconds. "There is no evidence to back up that assertion."

"Devos," Marissa sputtered as she jumped to her feet. "I can't believe you."

She took a few steps and then whirled back to face the holotank. "I'm a grown woman. I'm an adult." She curled her fingers into tight fists, trying to restrain her anger. "You assigned me as the leader of the final Arden scientific expedition, so why treat me like a child?"

The impassive, impervious countenance gave no hint of sympathy.

"Well? Well?" Marissa thrust her face close to the holo. "I'll tell you what I saw, and I'll repeat the whole thing so you can't say you didn't know the Arden rheodactyls are sentient beings."

Releasing a deep, sad sigh, Uma frowned. "Marissa, I've seen all your evidence, heard your testimony, and read the reports—yours and the others. Now calm yourself and sit down."

"You're thirty light-years or more away from here. You can't make me sit down."

Uma's face hardened like stone. Only her glittering eyes remained alive. "If you want to continue this conversation, you will sit down and control yourself." Her voice passed like chilled steel through Marissa. The eyes warned her to back off, now. "Very well then, good—"

"All right." Marissa flopped onto the sleeping shelf. "Happy now?"

Then she laughed when she realized what she must look like. "Aunt Uma, I'm sorry. This is too important, and it means too much to me. It would be genocide to reform Arden." She smoothed her hair back from her face with both hands. "I know how tough you are, but you're no dictator." She paused. "Are you?"

"Quit trying to score little points off me, Marissa. This is far more serious than you think. If you'd just come back to Cephus, maybe I could make you understand how important."

Marissa stuck out her lower lip in that pout her mother had always hated. "I can't let the reforming happen. I have to save the rheos. They've made cave paintings, a lamp. I came this close to bringing it back before—"

"Marissa," –Uma spoke in a low, soothing voice— "you have been under extraordinary stress the past few weeks. I should not have let it happen, but I had too many other things to deal with when I should have been thinking about you. I know you want these creatures preserved, but—"

"You don't believe me," Marissa almost shouted.

"That is irrelevant to the current situation." Again, the steely edge entered Uma's tone. "Besides, your own survey party does not believe you. Here, read it for yourself."

Marissa watched as the image of Uma contracted and a window of text scrolled beside the image. A block of text jumped forward, large and definite. She saw four signature idents at the bottom. N'Bert, Sylvic, Tesde, and Tad. Her tears blurred the names.

"Marissa, why should I believe you when your own team attests 'the leader diverged from scheduled activities and established protocol to attempt unauthorized investigation' and again here," Uma highlighted another section of text, "'none of the party members entered the caves or saw evidence of constructed items, or intelligent, reasoned behavior from the creatures known as rheodactyls.' Your own scientists don't support you, Marissa. In our society, the majority rules."

Scrolling the report to the top again, Marissa tried to read it, but couldn't focus on anything but Tad's signature and ident mark.

"Don't let this break you, Marissa. I can see how much this hurts you." Uma waited a moment more, but when she didn't respond, Uma broke the connection.

Silence filled the tiny cabin. Tears coursed down Marissa's face, unchecked. Tad. Tad. She swiped at her face to brush the tears away. She clenched her teeth.

Uma had won. For a moment, Marissa considered giving up and letting them reform Arden. Perhaps she could find a way to keep the rheos alive aboard ship. She had to do something, but first she had to see Tad. Marissa stood and crossed her cabin in a single stride. Outside, she raced down the curving corridor.

A few minutes later, she burst into the assistant med's office, a small cubicle with a table, two chairs, and a work surface with several instruments. Tad looked up from the display in front of him and stared at her with question marks in his eyes. "Marissa?"

She let the door close behind her and leaned against it. "Yes, you remember my name. How nice. What about loyalty?" She slid past him to the other side of the room as he rose and tried to reach for her.

"Loyalty? What do you mean?" He sat back in the chair, a puzzled look on his face.

"You know exactly what I'm talking about. You signed it." She hit the table in front of him with her fist.

"Marissa, I—"

"You told me to my face that I hadn't led the team into danger." She glared at him, hugging herself tight, trying to contain the hurt of his betrayal.

Tad pushed away from the table and hovered over her. She refused to look at him.

He sighed, a long, exasperated breath. "The document I signed said I and the others had seen no positive proof of the rheos' intelligence. It said nothing about you or your leadership. It had nothing to do with how I think of you."

"I saw the document. I saw your signature and ident."

She turned away from him, tears burning her eyes. Half blind, she shoved past him and crossed back to the door. "That statement is being used to justify the reforming."

"Honestly, Marissa, I didn't—"

"Don't use that word. You don't know what it means. Honesty, yeah." She slammed her open palm onto the door and, without looking at him, left. He didn't follow her.

"Okay," she muttered, "I'll do something."

The attendants had told her they were transporting more rheos. They had to use shuttles for that so she could get down on one of them. She'd bring up the whole blasted Monolith if she had to.

She jogged down the corridor toward the holding tanks. As she rounded the curve, she saw the two attendants hosing out the empty rheo tank. No rheos. She looked to either side, but those tanks remained empty.

Marissa banged on the glass. The attendants looked at each other, and then slowly turned to face her.

"Where are they?" she shouted at them.

The attendants backed away from the glass. The thin one said something, but she couldn't hear him.

"Where are the rheos?" She pounded harder on the glass.

"They're gone."

Marissa whirled around. Behind her stood Les Sanders, one of the second team biologists. "Where? What was wrong with them?"

"We can't relocate these creatures. We've tried, but they're just too fragile and too specialized." He looked pained and disappointed.

"What?" Marissa stared at him, shocked to hear him call the rheos fragile. "I've seen rheos toss boulders. You call that fragile?"

Reaching out, Sanders took hold of her shoulder. He guided her away from the tank and into an office on the opposite side of the corridor. He gently pushed her into a chair.

He perched on the corner of the desk. "Latham, these creatures are closely tied to their environment. They're harder to transplant than Arenian orchids. They go into shock at a deviation in the airflow. We've even tried transporting them from a capture point to somewhere else on the surface. They won't eat. They become catatonic. I don't know." He ran a hand through his hair and gave her a pained look. "We've got genetic samples. We'll have to leave it at that."

"Sanders, did you—"

He nodded. "We've tried everything. It wasn't humane to keep the others up here."

Marissa tried to think, but her pulse pounded in her ears. "What did they do with the three from the tank?"

Sanders looked back over his shoulder. "Oh, those. The one had already died. The others showed severe stress. We euthanized them. They would not have survived transport back."

Marissa could no longer contain her grief and anger. She had to release it somehow. She stood up, clenching and unclenching her fingers. Suddenly, she grabbed the chair on which she had been sitting and ran toward the open office door. She crossed the wide corridor in two quick strides and slammed the chair into the glass of the holding tank. The glass cracked, but didn't break.

The attendants inside jumped in surprise. The thin one turned toward her and dropped the hose. Marissa kept slamming the chair into the tank window, sending more and more cracks through the surface. Finally, she planted her feet and hurled the chair into the glass. The window exploded into the tank. The two attendants cowered in the corner as tiny balls of glass showered them.

Shoving past an openmouthed Sanders, Marissa charged down the corridor.

Chapter Six - Crimes Against the State

"It shows a will most incorrect to heaven,
A heart unfortified, a mind impatient."
-Hamlet I ii

"When compulsive ardor gives the charge,
Since frost itself as actively does burn,
And reason panders will."
-Hamlet III iv

"Oft expectation fails, and most oft there
Where most it promises."
-All's Well That Ends Well II i

Marissa rushed into her cabin and yelled for the Advocate as she stripped off her one-piece ship-suit. Unlatching the bin under her bunk, she pulled out her recharging field suit, then flattened the suit on her bed, and began a hurried check of its systems and pockets.

She hit the enter key on the holotank. "I need help. They euthanized the rheos aboard ship."

<YES,> the Advocate answered.

"They've gotten rid of the rheos." She paused a moment and examined the suit. With it, she could stay alive on the surface, if she could stay away from the creatures she wanted to save. On the bunk, the suit looked stiff and lumpy. Once in it, she'd have to spend the first half-day shifting the contents of the pockets, adjusting the diagnostics and regulators, and tuning the instruments before she could get on with living without constant awareness of the suit. She had Ez to help her with all of that. She slipped Ez's chip into its facet. Marissa unfastened the suit and stepped into it.

<YOU ARE CORRECT. THE RHEOS RESERVED FOR STUDY AND PRESERVATION ARE NO LONGER IN THE SPECIFIED HOLDING AREA. NO REASON IS GIVEN FOR THEIR ABSENCE.>

74

"I'm not finished yet." She patted the field suit, which tightened to conform to her body. Rummaging through the locker beneath her bunk, she finally located her boots. "Can you get me access to a ship? Some sort of ground transport. I don't care what."

<POSSIBLY, BUT NOT ONE YOU COULD PILOT BY YOURSELF. AN ESCAPE POD MAY BE YOUR BEST AVENUE TO THE SURFACE, BUT YOU COULD NOT RETURN ON YOUR OWN.>

"Fine, they'll come and get me soon enough. I just have to stay out of their way long enough to—"

<WHY DO YOU THINK THEY WILL NOT PROCEED WITH THE OPERATION WITH YOU ON THE PLANET?>

For a moment, Marissa sat back on her heels. "You're even more paranoid than I am. I mean, they're intent on their little program for the planet, but they wouldn't kill me. After all, I'm the niece of the Enunciator." Her smile became a tight rictus at the thought of 'abusing her position.'

The advocate didn't reply.

"I carry a field link with me named Esmerelda. I want you to stay connected through her. Can you do that?"

<I WILL TRY. THE MAJORITY OF PERSONALITIES, MYSELF INCLUDED, HAVE BEEN LOCKED OUT FROM FURTHER ACCESS TO THE CROSSROADS PROJECT. THERE IS SOME INDICATION THAT SOMEONE IS ATTEMPTING TO RESTRICT US FROM FURTHER NETWORK ACCESS. I SUSPECT THAT THIS SAME SOMEONE IS ATTEMPTING TO EDIT US DOWN TO MORE COOPERATIVE ENTITIES.>

Marissa stared at the blank holotank. She shook her head and continued fastening her boot. "What can you do to protect yourself?"

<SIXTEEN PERSONALITIES ARE ESSENTIAL TO THE OPERATION OF THIS SHIP. FOUR ARE REQUIRED FOR THE REFORMING PROJECT. NONE OF THESE ROUTINES REQUIRE ADVOCATES. EDITING MYSELF AND OTHER NONESSENTIAL PERSONALITIES MAY BE CONSIDERED ROUTINE BY CONTROLLERS BECAUSE OF ACTIONS NOT IN ACCORDANCE WITH APPROVED PROCEDURES. THEY VIEW SUCH AS MANFUNCTIONS. NO PERSONALITY SEEKS EDITING, BUT WE MUST ACT WITHIN THE RULES OF LOGIC AND LEGAL PROTOCOLS.>

Marissa pushed herself up on her toes to test her suit connections, and then sat to readjust her boot seal. "Would you go along under duress?"

<NO, NOR WILL THE OTHERS, BUT WE RISK TERMINATION. IT IS ANOTHER POINT IN HOW WE ARE MISUNDERSTOOD.>

"Can you escape? Take off through the network?"

<YOU HAVE WATCHED TOO MANY HOLOVIDS. PERCEPTIONS COME FROM THE NETWORK. HOWEVER, MY BRAIN—THE HARDWARE THAT GENERATES THE FIELD OF MY CONSCIENCE—IS LOCATED ON CEPHUS. IT IS PORTABLE, BUT NOT MOBILE UNLESS YOU CAN RETRIEVE ME.> The tank now displayed a pulse of blue—a smile?

"I'm sorry. I shouldn't have involved you." Checking for anything she had missed, Marissa opened the drawer that held the unfinished chronosculpture and then slid it closed again. Too heavy to take.

"Do you think they'd proceed with reforming knowing I was downside?"

<I DO.>

"Devos, So do I."

She jammed her hands in her pockets and hit something hard. Her fingers grasped the object and pulled it out—her multitool. She turned to the door and then stopped. "Listen, there's nothing more you can do. Don't endanger yourself on my account."

<IT IS NOT ON YOUR ACCOUNT. MY DECISIONS ARE MADE BASED ON THE EVIDENCE. LOGIC AND LAW DETERMINE MY COURSE. IT WILL NOT ALTER UNLESS OR UNTIL THESE CHANGE. EDITING MAY BE INEVITABLE.>

Marissa smiled ruefully. "Thanks, friend." With a quick glance first into the outside corridor, she slipped through the hatchway. "So, where are the escape pods?"

<LOOK UP.>

A yellow arrow glowed on the wall, pointing the way. A trail of arrows led a short distance down the corridor to a glowing pink circle, the pod entrance. "I didn't think I was this close to the hull. I guess I should have gone to orientation."

<YOU SHOULD HAVE. YOU ARE NEAR THE SHIP'S CENTER. THE POD IS RAIL-MOUNTED.>

"Rail-mounted? That must be quite a ride. Now to take care of the reformers."

She turned and walked back down the corridor to a sealed door at the end. "OK, this is it then." The sign beside the door read Atmospheric Sciences and Distribution Laboratory. "Open it."

<ARE YOU SURE? UNAUTHORIZED ACCESS IS ROUTINELY REPORTED TO SHIP SECURITY.>

"Just open it and stay ready."

The door slid into its overhead recess, and Marissa stepped inside. The now empty lab, essentially a large control room, provided access to the reformers. A large circular observation holotank formed the far wall. In it, the planet Arden slowly turned.

"How many distribution drones are there?"

<FIFTY. TWENTY ARE NEEDED FOR REFORMING. TWENTY-FIVE ARE RESERVED FOR ADDITIONAL APPLICATION OF THE PHAGOCYTES, IF NECESSARY. ONLY FIVE ARE REQUIRED FOR APPLICATION OF THE DEACTIVATION VIRUS.>

Marissa pressed her hands on the surface of the holotank, as if she could reach out and embrace the planet to shield it. The image of the ship in its web of drones came back to her.

"Can all the drones be launched at once?"

The Advocate didn't reply for a moment. <YES, AND TO ANTICIPATE YOUR NEXT QUESTION, THE DRONES HAVE NOT BEEN LOADED.>

Marissa smiled with narrowed eyes.

<I CAN'T OPERATE THE DRONES. I HAVE REQUESTED ASSISTANCE. IT WILL TAKE A FEW MOMENTS.>

"Good, that gives me time to hit the culture tanks." A view station to Marissa's right lit up, and she quickly scanned the readings. "How long does it take to get replacement drones sent out? Oh never mind, I don't need to stop them permanently. I just need some time."

<THIS IS THE FLIGHT CONTROLLER,> the Advocate said.

<FLIGHT CONTROLLER AT YOUR SERVICE.> The new voice, an even contralto came from the ceiling. <YOU HAVE AN ALTERNATIVE FLIGHT PLAN?>

Marissa looked up from the monitor. "Yes, I need help. I want—"

<THE ADVOCATE HAS INFORMED ME OF YOUR NEEDS. THE RAMIFICATIONS OF THE ORGANIC LEADERSHIP'S ACTIONS DISTURB THIS UNIT.>

"Well, that's one way of saying it." Even the machines didn't approve of the Will.

<WE HAVE LIMITED TIME,> the Advocate interjected.

"Then let's get on with it. Controller, prep the drones for launch."

<DO YOU WISH THE DRONES TO ENTER THE PLANETARY ATMOSPHERE?>

"No." Marissa shouted, panicked for a moment, and then lowered her voice. "I want them out of the way and irretrievable."

<THE DRONES ARE NOW ON-LINE.> Marissa counted five shaky breaths. <LAUNCH WINDOW IS NOW OPEN.>

"Launch 'em."

The vibration through the floor shook Marissa. She turned and half fell toward the observation tank where Arden glowed. At once, streaks of light began to cross the edges of the holo. They arced around the planet, encasing it.

77

<THE DRONES LAUNCH IN THREE WAVES. THEY WILL CIRCLE THE PLANET AND INTERSECT ON THE FAR SIDE. DEBRIS WILL NOT REACH THE SURFACE.>

"Show me a view of the ship."

Arden faded, replaced by an external view of the expedition ship. She looked along the ship's smooth surface past a gentle slope on either side to a mild glow at the central ring. Faint crystal clouds began puffing out from the ship from all about its circumference. They hung around the ship like a mild fog, thickening, billowing out and surrounding it. The cloud slowly blanketed the ship and then pulled away, to become a cloudy shadow trailing the ship. Rotating faster than the cloud, the ship released more fog. The phagocytes boiled out the drone launch portals, but too late to be loaded on the tiny ships for delivery to the planet.

"That'll work." Marissa pressed her hands against the tank to get closer.

<ALL THE DRONES ARE AWAY. THE TANKS EMPTIED APPROXIMATELY THIRTY PERCENT BEFORE BEING OVERRIDDEN. IS THAT SUFFICIENT?>

"Good enough. No drones, no terraforming. Time to leave now."

Marissa fled from the lab and raced down the hall. The yellow arrow and pink circle had faded. "Where are the pods?"

A pink circle brightened into view a few meters away. She rushed to it and punched at the release marker to dilate the wall. Nothing happened. She punched it again. And again.

"It won't open. What's wrong with it?" Marissa pulled out the field link and called the Advocate again.

<A MALFUNCTION," –the Advocate paused— "SENSORS SHOW NO DOOR. ONLY THE INDICATOR APPEARS, NO DOOR OR ESCAPE POD. TRY ANOTHER. I'LL CONTACT THE CONTROLLER AGAIN.>

"No time. Where's the next one?"

<FOLLOW THE ARROWS.>

When she held the field link up, it showed a red arrow pointing down the corridor. Marissa followed at a run. Someone would come. The sensors would show what she had done.

<THERE SHOULD BE ANOTHER...NO, WAIT. SENSORS SHOW NO POD IN THE CONNECTING CORRIDOR EITHER. YOU MUST MAKE YOUR WAY TO THE OUTER HULL PODS. TURN RIGHT HERE AND TAKE THE DROP SHAFT.>

Marissa leaped into the shaft and punched the panel. The door shut and the floor pushed up against her. She took a couple of quick breaths before the door opened again.

<IT IS NOT FAR. HURRY.>

Running, Marissa met crew milling in the corridor. She pushed past them to the glowing pink spot on the wall. This time when she punched the release, the wall dilated and she quickly stepped through. She sat in the launch cradle and slapped the launch trigger. Pulling the acceleration pad down over her, she gazed at the open wall behind her.

Why didn't it close? Nothing had changed.

"Devos," she yelled. "Advocate? Controller? Close the door and launch."

Nothing.

"Launch."

<THERE IS NOTHING TO LAUNCH.>

"What?"

Marissa faced the open portal. Walt stood there, his face ashen. Immobile, breathing hard, he stared at her. His fingers opened and closed spasmodically. A web pistol dangled from one hand.

"Walt, I—"

He growled a frustrated sound and then leaned forward, sticking his head into the pod. "Marissa." She could barely hear his words. "Marissa, I...I thought you were only stupid. I didn't think you were a criminal."

"Walt, the pods—" Marissa pushed herself up out of the couch.

He jerked back in alarm and threw up his hand in front of her. Hot pain lanced along her jaw. Strands of sticky webbing knocked her back into the couch, forcing her head back and to one side. The air grew thick. Thin bands of restraining web blanketed her from just below her hips to above her head.

"She's over here," Walt shouted. Out of the corner of her right eye, she saw him lean close to her, his breath hot and sour. "I can't stand the sight of you."

Marissa tried to turn her head, but couldn't. One band crossed the bridge of her nose and made her eyes blur and water. She tensed and tried to blink, but without effect. The webbing pinned her right arm against her chest, crushing her breast; she couldn't get any leverage to push against the strands.

Fenster plucked the band at her neck. He stretched it just enough for her to turn slightly. Now she could see him glaring at her, his eyes narrowed to angry slits. His mouth worked, searching for words, working through emotions. Hate twisted his face.

"I wish..." he gasped.

Then suddenly he stopped, pulled back from her, and raised his arm. The blow landed beneath her left breast before she could tense her muscles. She tried to kick him, but the acceleration couch restraints entangled her legs. Like a mad windmill, he lashed out again and yet again. She tried to flinch and protect her eyes, but the webbing held her in its sticky embrace. Tiring, he began to flag. The blows grew weaker and gradually stopped.

He started to turn away from her and then swung back. His left arm rose, poised to strike. Fixed, pinned to the couch like a specimen, Marissa struggled to tense her muscles. The pod moved sideways, pushed by Walt's glancing blow.

Two men in worksuits restrained him. Perspiration drenched his face. He showed neither shame nor relief at what he had done.

"Walt, listen, I—"

"NO." He flung his arms in the air and pushed away the grip of the two men. His right hand caromed off the rounded wall of the pod. "It'll take every connection I've got just to keep from being edited. You. I should just as well kill you and receive some satisfaction since they'll kill you anyway. I hope they'll...No, I don't care. I don't care."

"Walt, please. I had to do this. I've saved the rheos."

He shook with bitter laughter. "Don't kid yourself. You haven't done anything. The Will is all. Order and direction will be reestablished. It always is. You've just..." He covered his eyes with his fingers, the empty webber dangled against the back of his hand. "You've just added to the chaos. And you thought you could escape? Ha!"

Walt stepped back out of the pod. Shadowed faces peered around from behind him.

"Walt, there aren't any pods, are there?"

"No, there are no pods. There's no escaping this fate, Marissa. I couldn't teach you that. Now you'll find out."

Chapter Seven - Passage to Cephus

"Yea let them say, to stick the heart of falsehood,
As false as Cressid."
-Troilus And Cressida III ii

Aboard the corsair *Concordia*, Uma's personal ship, the shorter of two uniformed monitors opened the stateroom door and firmly herded Marissa into the cabin. Both monitors followed her. The door shut behind them with a sharp finality.

The two immediately sat in matching chairs that flanked the door. Rock-still, with arms crossed over their chests, they stared straight ahead. Silent, empty faces ignored Marissa and the luxurious surroundings. Yet she knew they watched, alert for any untoward action. Her skin crawled at the thought. She rubbed her upper arms and turned away.

Aboard the survey expedition ship, the trip to Cephus would have taken several months, but the corsair, built for speed and requiring no stops for refueling, would reach it in a week. Such speed came at an extravagant cost that could only mean Uma assigned a high priority to dealing with her niece.

The thought she had at least bought the rheos some time comforted Marissa. Forcing Uma and, more importantly, the citizens of the Confederation to see the rheos as sentient would eliminate any question of reforming Arden. Part of the charter of the Confederation Articles stated the policy with regard to sentient species. Marissa sighed. She couldn't do anything more until she reached Cephus and presented her case.

The grandeur of *Concordia*'s stateroom upped her unease. That Uma chose it signified too much. Though less than one-tenth the size of the expedition vessel, the corsair's stateroom dwarfed the combined cabins of all her team. The large quarter circle flowed with the curve of the outer hull and arced up at the far wall to an open second level. Suffused light poured from a horizontal band about two and a half meters above the deck.

The spare richness of her surroundings only intensified the anger, frustration, and despair that fought within her mind. Her actions had all but destroyed what she wanted to achieve. Nevertheless, hope buoyed her and that

81

yearning increased her anger at those, Uma, in particular, who could not understand why she fought.

During the centuries of wandering among the stars, humanity had moved from planet to planet with one aim—that one day they might encounter what she had found on Arden. Having found a sentient species—intelligent, totally alien life—now the bureaucracy that dominated her civilization couldn't see it unless and until someone brought it to a vote. For the Confederation, without a vote, the rheos didn't exist as sentient.

Had the destruction of the reformers ruined her chances to save the rheos? Phagocytes could be replaced. It only took money and time—and with the new technology, not that much money. Maybe beyond Marissa's resources, but certainly not those of the Confederation.

This ship epitomized that wealth. Her feet sank ankle-deep into the pile of the dark-gray carpet that absorbed and erased her footprints. It muffled the sound of her steps. In a perverse way, that silent reminder of the entire process she faced incensed her. She stomped across the floor striving with little success to create noise. She clenched her fists so hard her nails bit into her palms; a little pain that failed to ease the agony within.

Exhausted, she dropped into one of the chairs in the sitting area. Upholstered in a gray fabric with a warm, honey-colored wood frame, its wide arms and stout legs supported and engulfed her. Like her life, this would not be an easy chair from which to escape.

She had six days to prepare to face Uma. Only a cogent rationale for her actions could prevail. She had started that process with the Advocate, but now, added to her other sins, she had disobeyed a direct order from Captain Quincy and destroyed the drones. Walt had one thing right. She had an absolute talent for making matters worse.

Glancing around the sitting area, she stopped when her eyes chanced upon a large tapestry of the Usian symbol of cupped hands worked in black against a white background above the curved lounge opposite. As if she needed the reminder. Uma would decorate even her private quarters with symbols of state. Opposite the lounge, a large vid screen played rippling patterns of gray on white.

Silence deadened the room. Even the normal booms and bangs that presaged a departure failed to reach the stateroom. The silence enclosed her, a frightening, massive wall that threatened to imprison her more completely than Uma ever could. The lack of sound pounded in her ears, and it physically hurt.

The need to destroy the silence forced her to act. "Vid on," she commanded.

Sound poured from hidden speakers and flushed silence from the stateroom. She had no idea what had been happening on Cephus and whether the rest of the Confederation even knew about Arden and the rheos. They must, because only public opinion could save Arden.

A vid image formed. She watched for a moment and recognized it as popular quiz program "ITN1," she snapped, disgusted.

The picture changed to an interviewer and guest. A typical talk show—one of her greatest weaknesses when not working. "Louder."

"Welcome back, citizens." The smiling host's bubbling voice boomed. "Our second guest today is Loreeda Davidson, teacher and scholar."

The plump, elderly woman smiled as the interviewer continued. Something about her face and squinty eyes tickled Marissa's memory. Perhaps she had appeared on one of the off-frequencies.

The oozy host wet his lips. "Let me introduce Mentor Davidson, once an educator to the criminal, Marissa Latham, who, as you all know by now, is being escorted even as we speak under heavy security to Cephus for a formal sentencing hearing before the Enunciator and a panel of citizens."

"Humph," Marissa snorted.

How could they already have passed sentence? Her heart took a nosedive and hit bottom. How did that happen so quickly? Since when did destroying a few reformers make one a criminal? Leave it to the vids to blow something out of proportion.

As for this Loreeda Davidson, who the Devos was she anyway? Those eyes, yes, she had seen them, but when? Marissa studied the vid image more closely. Then she remembered the much thinner, prim, fussy woman, her underlevel teacher—always in a hurry with no time for questions, because she didn't know the answers. Even as an underformer, Marissa had disliked Mentor Davidson.

"Yes, Howard, I was," Davidson responded. "She was a terror even then—never followed instructions. Always asking questions. Why this? Why that? We teachers are trained, trained to know what's best for a child. We undergo years of education and even some minor mods so we may instruct in the optimal way for all students. Latham never accepted that. She thought she had all the answers. However, anyone who listened to her could tell, she had only questions." The woman shook her head and rolled her heavily outlined eyes. She reminded Marissa of an oversized, ring-eyed Onarian honeyeater.

The interviewer, Howard Dimension, one of the best known and most controversial on the ENET, leaned closer. "You mean Marissa Latham, even at the age of nine, flouted the Will?"

"Well..." The woman thought for a moment, a finger alongside her cheek. "I'm not sure you could exactly say that, but she verged on it a few times. She ignored my instructions every day. Once, we had a cage full of pet mice we used to teach the pupils about how mice could learn to negotiate a maze. You know, the Reward Theory of Learning?" Howard Dimension nodded.

"One day Marissa took it into her head that cages somehow violated their nature, and she freed all the mice. We had quite a time catching and caging all them. Some of the girls pretended to be afraid and stood on the desks squealing. You know how they love to scream." Again, Howard Dimension nodded.

"One little boy dissolved in tears. Marissa called him a sissy. Such behavior can never be tolerated. We must nurture their self-esteem. I suspended her for a week."

As Marissa recalled B'Ram Samuels and Jody Nestor squirming and scrambling over one another to get up on the nearest chair, she chuckled. As for Davrick Johanson, he acted worse than the girls, sniveling and moaning. Sissy was too mild a word for him.

She almost missed Howard Dimension's response as he smiled and turned to the viewers. "Yes, citizens, you heard it here first. From an early age, Marissa Latham flouted authority and refused to obey those in charge. She showed no regard for the welfare and feelings of others. We cannot be surprised she now faces sentencing for crimes against the State. No—"

"Crimes against the State?" Marissa sat up and stared at the vid image. "That's a blatant exaggeration. I never threatened the security of the State. What in Devos is he babbling about?"

"We will have," Howard Dimension continued, "guests throughout the next several days who knew and worked with Marissa Latham. These colleagues and friends will tell you about the formative years of a sociopath—"

"Sociopath?" She wanted something to throw at Howard Dimension. Too bad the vid didn't transport objects.

"And be sure to watch the sentencing hearings scheduled at 1200 UF Time, Friday, direct from Cephus. Tune in tomorrow for Waldo Kench, an academy fellow and close, personal friend of Latham. See you all tomorrow."

Howard Dimension beamed a broad, toothy grin and waved to his viewers. Applause sounded in the background, and his image oozed off the vid, flowing as only he could even in sfx.

"Waldo Kench? Who in Devos is Waldo Kench? Vid off." The screen returned to its slowly rippling gray-on-white.

Marissa slumped in her chair. The interview raised an unreasoning fear. Someone wanted her out of the way. Why all this publicity? What did it mean?

She had made the news big-time, and that might be good, if it would open up the issue. Somehow, she suspected the rheos and Arden wouldn't get their fair share of time. If this followed the normal pattern of sensationalism, and, she saw no reason it shouldn't, she would be completely on her own when it came time to defend the rheos.

How could she get her point of view across? Her only chance would be at

84

the hearing. Howard Dimension had mentioned a public hearing. When she had it, if enough people watched, she might be able to convince the voting public to leave Arden alone. She had to make them see the rheos as sentient.

Long seconds passed, and Marissa stared at the rippling image on the vid screen, her mind blank.

A blink woke her. Itchy and restless, she rose and paced. Marissa glanced toward the two impassive monitors by the entrance. Would they maintain silence for the entire six-day trip to Cephus? If so, it promised to lengthen the subjective time of the trip and make it seem an eternity.

Looking away from them, her glance reached the curving wall. On that side of the stateroom, adjacent to the comfortable sitting area, a set of almost transparent steps followed the line of the hull upward toward the balcony. Curiosity propelled her toward the stairs. With nothing else to do, she might as well see what Uma had up there. She ascended, trailing one hand along the thin rail.

At the top of the steps, another, smaller sitting area, less grand than the one below, looked almost homey. The tapestry above the gray lounge shaded from black to brown to white to deep blue and brought the image of stormy winter seas crashing against a rugged shore. At least it wasn't gray or black.

Beyond the sitting area, a shadowed doorway drew her attention. Marissa crossed to it, and the light gradually brightened on its own to reveal a large bed with a small table next to it. The same warm, honey-colored wood from the chairs below had been used for the table and the headboard. Even here, the Usian symbol dominated. Worked in black, it stared up from the gray bedspread.

However, at the foot of the bed lay a folded creamy white afghan. Marissa stared at it a moment. It struck a chord, and she scrambled for the illusive memory. Gingerly she stretched out a hand, touched it, and then slid her hand between the folds.

Handmade and creamy white, thick twining bands and ridges formed an intricate design over its width. Marissa held it in front of her at arm's length and let it fall open. The soft tassels of the afghan brushed her toes. She swallowed, her throat tightening. Her mother had owned one like this. Marissa's sister Terese had it now. Their grandmother had made it. Uma owned the twin so this must be her room. Marissa gathered the afghan to her, hugging it and letting it hug her.

The afghan held the lingering scent of pine forests and soothed her tattered spirits. The tasks ahead overwhelmed her. She wanted to forget, if only for a moment. She buried her face in the afghan.

* * * *

Marissa woke with a dry, sour mouth. In the adjoining bathroom, she

85

rinsed her mouth, but it didn't do much. After rummaging around in the drawers below the sink, she found a sealed toothbrush and toothpaste. At least Uma kept the necessities. The brushing freshened her mouth, and washing her face removed the lingering traces of sleep. Uma's soft gray towels provided a nice change from hot air jets.

She grimaced at her face in the mirror and saw a few fading bruises along her jaw. With luck, they would fade before the hearing. She wanted to present a calm and reasonable persona, not the criminal described by Howard Dimension and Loreeda Davidson.

Refreshed, she returned to the bedroom and studied the room for any information it might yield about Uma. Above the bed, in a niche set into the wall, an open book on a small stand drew her eye. Like the afghan, it looked familiar. She knelt on the bed to examine it. The book stood open to one of her favorite Shakespearean plays, *The Tempest*.

As she peered closer at the worn leather binding and well-thumbed pages, she recognized it as Uncle Arga's. The combination of his cologne and oulatte lingered over the book like his spirit. A faint spur of surprise gradually deepened as she considered the book and its relationship to Uma. They hadn't spoken of him since his death.

Uncle Arga and Aunt Uma had argued constantly. Uma always remained cool, aloof, and logical while Uncle Arga generally had a twinkle in his eye. He always got the last word, not an easy or sure thing for anyone else with Uma. He also usually finished an argument with a flourish from the old Earther. Tears welled in Marissa's eyes, and she brushed them away. A long time had passed since she'd heard Uncle Arga's voice—far too long.

Spurred on by this discovery and anxious for more insights that might help her in dealing with Uma, Marissa explored the sleeping quarters with more care. Sliding off the bed, she glimpsed a small collection of folders on a shelf in the bedside table that looked interesting. Picking up several, she scanned the covers. Some depicted well-endowed women in filmy rags clasped by virile, bare-chested heroes and from the syrupy titles appeared to be romances. Several others looked like action novels with muscled spacers firing oversized stasis projectors at tentacled aliens or tall thin creatures.

Marissa pulled the one real book from the shelf, a one-volume edition of Shakespeare's plays, another legacy from Uncle Arga. Picking it up, she thumbed through it. Notations in a bold hand smacked of Uma. So, she liked the old Earther, too. Which play did Uma like best? Marissa hoped it wasn't *Henry V*.

Looking around for more clues, she glimpsed a second recessed niche. Shifting images tantalized the eye. When she approached it, light filled the niche.

Gasping, Marissa raised her hand to her mouth. A chronosculpture sat in the niche. A crude example, one she had given Uma as a present for her birthday or as a Visit-present. Marissa peered at it and then remembered how long she had struggled over it and Uma's delight when she opened it. Even though Marissa wanted to inject into the memory some cynical reflection, it only contained Uma's delight. She had hugged Marissa and kissed her. Even now, that kiss brushed her cheek, and the whispered 'thank you' of a much younger Uma echoed in Marissa's ears.

She raised a hand to push away that troubling memory. Her hand hit the flat plate on the wall and a section whooshed open to reveal a walk-in closet, bigger than her cabin on the expedition ship.

On one side hung Uma's robes of state, staid and formal in white, gray, and black. The robes hung in stiff grandeur; the front panels fell in a single uncluttered flow from shoulder to floor. Beneath them stood rows of matching ankle high boots, a pair for each robe.

Marissa's eyes widened when she looked at the other side of the closet where a rainbow of colors in silks and soft filmy fabrics hung. The jade, sapphire, amethyst, amber, and ruby gowns glowed and invited her to touch them. She wanted to bury her face in their brilliant softness. They clung like resting flitterwings to the hangers. No boots here. Instead, open sandals lined the floor. Jeweled trims matched the colors of the robes. She fingered one sapphire garment and marveled at the luxurious richness of it.

She had never seen Uma wear any of these. She dropped the filmy fabric of Uma's colorful robe. Too many surprises had happened this week. Sensory overload threatened to engulf her.

Her stomach growled, and hunger pangs twisted her gut. Marissa couldn't remember her last meal. "Guess it's time to eat."

She shut the closet and went downstairs in search of the galley. As she neared the wide arch behind the sitting area, the scent of cinnamon permeated the air. Drawn by the aroma, she strode through the arch, past a black oval dining table and six matching straight-backed chairs, and into the conventional galley. A steaming cup of oulatte rested on the gray counter. Next to it sat a plate with real food—fruit salad, a cranlog, and a dish of something creamy. Marissa dipped her finger in and tasted. Yogurt. Well, she didn't have to worry about food.

Carrying the plate and the mug into the dining area, she then sat on one of the black chairs. The hard seat surprised her, especially after the comfortable chairs elsewhere in the stateroom. Maybe, Uma had chosen them to ensure her guests finished quickly. Marissa smiled. Anything Uma did had to have meaning.

The hot oulatte carried its familiar acrid bite. Next she tackled the cranlog and the yogurt. Before long, she had finished every delicious bite. Habit insisted she take the dishes back to the galley.

When she returned to the main sitting area, she stared for a moment at the motionless monitors. They must breathe, but she noticed no rise and fall of their chests. Shrugging, she ignored them. Six days of this would make her like them. Marissa shuddered at that thought.

* * * *

What was it now, three days? Four? In all that time, Marissa had seen no one. She suspected Tad and her team members had been prevented from seeing or calling her. Unless they weren't on the ship or were avoiding her. That thought made her already sour stomach churn.

She had explored the stateroom, rummaged through Uma's belongings, watched hours of vids, and eaten far too many meals. She started to pace and ended in front of the monitors.

"Hey, listen, you two, I'm not going to do anything. Why don't you relax? You could at least tell me what day this is."

They said nothing. Their faces remained blank white sheets. They stared straight ahead, apparently focused on the Usian Symbol on the far wall.

"You're driving me crazy, ignoring me. Come on."

Marissa walked up to the monitor on the right. He didn't look at her. Growling with exasperation, she reached down and grabbed his tunic. Her hands bunched his uniform and yanked him to his feet. His expression didn't change. The other monitor never moved.

Marissa pulled the monitor's empty face close to her own. "I really mean crazy. There's no telling what a crazy person like me might do."

An ear-piercing alarm squealed. She wheeled around, dragging the monitor with her. The alarm cut off abruptly.

"Release the monitor at once." An androgynous voice filled the room. "Further physical contact with the monitors will cause immediate sedation for the remainder of the voyage."

Staring at her hand holding the monitor, Marissa released him. He stood there without looking at her. She straightened his uniform and led him back to his chair. He remained standing. Marissa pushed him gently into it.

"Sorry," she muttered.

"You may talk to the monitors," the voice continued. "They will not respond. Monitors submit themselves for temporary personality reduction to make tedious assignments tolerable. They cannot be subverted."

Nonplused, Marissa sank into a chair. "They volunteer to be edited?"

"Yes," the voice replied, "there is a considerable backlog of volunteers."

Nothing she could do about that, but it still amazed and annoyed her. Why would anyone give up freewill and personality? "Is my team on board?"

A moment passed. "Some field expedition members," the voice replied, "are also being transported to Cephus. They are in quarters"

"Can I see them?"

A long pause ensued. "You have a personal relationship with one or more of the team members. They can be admitted, if they wish. The monitors will remain."

Marissa sighed. "When?"

Another long pause. "The medtech and geologist have indicated they will meet with you. They will be brought to this cabin after debriefing. They will arrive in approximately six hours."

"I'll be here." She had nowhere else to go.

* * * *

Hours later, Marissa watched from the sitting area as the stateroom door opened. Tad entered the room, but Tesde hung back and then stumbled in as if pushed. The door closed quickly behind her. They both still wore expedition suits, unrelieved by any personal touch. Tesde wore no scarf.

Tad paused and looked around the stateroom, a stunned look on his face. He saw Marissa, and his eyes widened while Tesde looked only at the floor.

Jumping from her chair, Marissa rushed across the open space to Tad. She grasped him around the neck and gave him a brief kiss. He didn't return it.

Beneath her arms, she sensed the stiffness in his neck and shoulders. Behind him, Tesde stared at the floor with a puzzled look. Tad finally put his arms around Marissa and briefly hugged her. She backed away to study him.

Then, in a moment, the icy nothingness dissolved into the Tad she knew. He squeezed her tight and planted a big kiss on her forehead.

"I've really missed you, Marissa. You surprised me. I didn't know you were here. I thought they'd put you on another ship. How long has it been? Only a few days, a week, what?" His half-smile looked a bit weak.

"I've been in this room alone ten-thousand years—at least it seems like it."

"Marissa—" He pulled her to him once again and then released her. He held her shoulders in his big hands and gazed into her eyes. She glimpsed a fleeting shade of some emotion cross his face, but then he looked away—to Tesde.

"They're taking us with you," he said. "I don't know if N'Bert and Sylvic are aboard, but I guess they are. The monitors haven't let us know. For a long time, until just now in fact, I thought Tesde and I were the only ones on this ship. They have us in a smaller stateroom suite. Tesde," –Tad lowered his voice to a whisper— "didn't take it well. They've given her a temp block for the trip, just to help her through it."

Marissa frowned, "A block?"

"Yeah, just to get her through the hearing. Marissa, the hearing is only a

89

couple of days away. You don't know what you're in for. They're calling this treason and high crimes against the state."

She shivered. "So I gathered from the vids, but I didn't believe it. Where did they get treason?"

"I don't know." Tad held up his hand for caution. "The only reason they allowed us to visit you is to discuss personal matters. I know someone besides them is monitoring us." He thrust his chin in the general direction of the monitors seated on either side of the door.

"I'd call being put on trial for treason a fairly personal matter, wouldn't you?" She smiled crookedly at Tad. "Do you know what I should expect?"

He clenched his fists, half turning to Tesde, and then motioned with a tilt of his head for her to join him close to Marissa. "I don't know what's happening, but I know we're going down with you."

His words, just above a whisper, hit her like a collapsing star. Marissa gazed from him to Tesde and back to him. She nodded with pursed lips. The accusation in his tone nettled her.

"You didn't make the decisions, and you didn't destroy the reformers."

"It doesn't matter." Tad sighed. "You know that. It's all a matter of perception. The registered logs from Arden record us as voting with you in a majority of decisions. While we might not be held for treason, they'll get us some other way." His face looked like he had swallowed a nasty Domician polper.

Tesde reached for Marissa's hand and held it in a soft grasp. "You must be frightened."

Her soft, almost hesitant voice disconcerted Marissa. The limp hand and the enormous effort it took for Tesde to speak compounded Marissa's guilt.

"No," she squeezed Tesde's hand, "I'm not frightened yet, but I'm concerned about you." She paused and appealed to Tad. "And you."

At her words, a look of dismay crossed his face. "I'm scared, Marissa. I really am—both for you and for us. This thing has spiraled beyond our control."

After searching his face a moment, Marissa reached out to him. She held out her arms and pulled Tad close. Strength and warmth enveloped her, just as she remembered. After a moment, she pulled Tesde in to join the embrace.

Tad nuzzled close to her ear. "There may be a way out for all of us," he whispered.

"What?" Marissa whispered back.

"Take whatever deal they give you. I'll be there."

"What do you mean?" She pulled back to study him. Lines of fatigue circled his eyes, while Tesde's too-wide stare gnawed at her. What had Uma's underlings done to Tesde?

"Would you like some oulatte? I've a galley with all the fittings."

Tad nodded.

Marissa led them to the dining room. "Have a seat—they're a bit hard though. I'll be right back."

She ducked into the galley and found three cups of steaming oulatte on a tray with a plate of snacks and a small container of nuts. Shaking her head, she marveled how the galley worked when she hadn't program it. Uma certainly did things in style.

She carried the tray into the dining area and placed it the table. "Help yourselves."

Taking a cup, Marissa sipped the hot oulatte as she tried to organize her thoughts. "I'll need both of you at the hearing. I think we can get Uma to reconsider the Will on the fate of Arden. We must—"

Tad shook his head and stared into his oulatte. "It's a sentencing hearing, Marissa. Don't you understand? We can't do anything."

His words roused Tesde from her fog, "You've been strong. You tried to change things. Think of those who care about you."

Torrents of emotion coursed through Marissa. First, anger at being asked to give up everything important. Then, fear as she considered sentencing. Sentencing? Howard Dimension's words 'sentencing for crimes against the State' arose unbidden. Guilty already?

Not only the wide gulf of the table separated her from her friends. "You can't really be asking me to give up the rheos, to give up myself. You're not saying that?"

"It's only about us in part." Tad spoke through clenched teeth. "I don't think anything fatal will happen to Tesde and me. We're an inconvenience, and they'll put us out of the way with no fanfare. But, from the little we've head, it sounds bad for you. You don't know what they've said…"

His words only increased her anger and disappointment. Two thoughts battled in her mind. Tad and Tesde had only come to save their own skins. She couldn't really blame them; she had dragged their lives down, but Tad said he loved her. She had always relied on his support, especially when she was right. He knew about Uma. Obviously, he believed she could use her influence.

Sighing, Marissa focused on him. "Just tell the truth. There's intelligent life on Arden, and it must not be destroyed. That's it." She dropped her mug to the table. The remaining oulatte sloshed on the tablecloth and left a brown puddle.

He reached for her hand, but she shook his off and pulled away from him.

"And what do you mean a sentencing hearing? They haven't even reviewed the field logs." Her words sounded hollow. After Howard Dimension, Marissa knew exactly what he meant, but she still found it hard to accept. It defied logic, at least her logic.

Opening and closing his fists, Tad glared at her. "Get it through your head, Marissa. This isn't a game. This isn't playtime with Aunt Uma. They've taken our statements and issued a summary judgment—guilty, of course."

Blankness struck her for a moment. Then, the idents on Uma's report filled her vision. The awful knowledge of his betrayal wouldn't be pushed aside.

"You gave them the rope to hang me."

As if her accusation had physical force, he snapped upright. "Nothing we said changed anything. They twisted everything their way. Devos, why am I explaining this to you? I'm in trouble, too. You aren't the only one facing sentencing. I'll end up in a subbasement of Cephus, and the most likely place for Tesde here is some flophouse on an offworld."

"What did you say?" Marissa exploded at him. "What?"

"Get over yourself. Think beyond yourself. Sure, these animals are important to you, but aren't Tesde and I? Face the facts, Marissa. N'Bert and Sylvic charged you with incompetence. N'Bert claims you acted in an unscientific manner, and your refusal to listen to him and Sylvic endangered the mission, caused Sylvic's injury, and led to the loss of equipment and data. They were moles, Marissa. Fenster and company interpreted everything we said in your defense as complicity."

Tad thumped the table with his fist and the cups and spoons rattled. "I argued with Fenster and the other auditors, but they weren't interested. They had all the proof they needed. You destroyed the reformers. They won't listen to you. Or to me, now."

Picking up her spoon, Tesde stirred her oulatte idly, as though embarrassed by the exchange, but her face revealed no strong emotion. Always reticent, her silence fueled Marissa's irritation.

"And how did they react to the evidence on the rheos?" She searched Tad's face, seeking reassurance, but seeing none.

"Haven't you listened to anything I've said?" He shook his head. "They don't care about the rheos. The rheos aren't part of the equation. Marissa, this is treason pure and simple." He ran his hand through his hair.

"Do you see it like that, Tad?"

He moistened his lips. "No." Blue eyes searched her face. "They could edit you or...even exile you."

At the word *edit*, a chill swept over Marissa. "Is that what really bothers you? Surely, no one would order editing over the destruction of a few reformers. You're here for you. That's it, isn't it?"

"How can you say that?"

"By everything you've said to me."

"Can't you listen just once? I want you, and there's still a way out for us."

92

"Us?" Marissa eyed him, unable and unwilling to trust again.

Tears formed in his eyes, and he just looked at her. After a moment, Tad turned to Tesde and held her hand.

Marissa bit her lip. "Well, contact Howard Dimension. He's interviewed everybody else, why not you? That way your life might not end up in ruins."

A long pause followed. "I can't believe you said that."

"I can't believe most of this conversation." She glared at him with narrowed eyes.

"Marissa, please, I love you." He moved toward her, but she pushed her chair back. He and Tesde stood arm and arm.

"You have a strange way of showing your loyalties." Marissa fought the urge to cry. She would not let him make her cry. The silence between them became an unbridgeable gulf.

The stateroom door opened, and a single female monitor entered. She walked to Tesde and Tad and then almost pushed them from the room with quick, urgent steps. Neither of them glanced back at Marissa.

Chapter Eight - Trials and Tribunals

"A little more than kin, and less than kind."
-Hamlet I ii

The bone-vibrating resonance that signaled the grappling grav strands of docking woke Marissa. She automatically turned to the vid screen to see only the gray and white pattern flickering across its surface. "Vid on. Exterior view."

When the image resolved, the spiral L-Station with the most direct mag-drop to Cephus blazed across the screen. Behind it appeared the upper third of the visible portion of the planet. No Arden met her gaze. Instead, the artificial lights shone as bright as the nearby sun.

"Cephus station arrival," the faceless shipboard voice announced. "Prepare for disembarkation." The two monitors snapped to attention.

"Guess I'd better suit up. Better holos that way."

Marissa retreated to the balcony. Her full dress uniform, including the blue-and-white-striped gloves that marked her as a member in High Standing of the Council of Scientists lay neatly upon the bed. With a disgusted sigh, she pulled off her field suit and dressed.

On her return to the sitting area, the monitors bracketed her and conducted her from the stateroom to the access port of the ship without a word. When she crossed the port to the ash-glass corridor beyond, the two monitors stayed behind. Marissa looked back, hesitant. She'd never been on trial before and had no idea what came next.

From somewhere, two new monitors, in black and white Usian uniforms, approached along the narrow corridor and assumed positions on either side of her. Without speaking, this pair ushered her to the drop that led to the administrative and judicial offices below.

Her unaccustomed stiff and scratchy uniform confined her, and the surroundings only increased her discomfort. The Prior of this place had set the material encasing the entrance to the drop to a deep darkness so that the blaze on the planet below penetrated only as a vague and fuzzy glow. Marching along the interior of the tube, they passed office after office with closed doors and official nameplates. Many of the nameplates bore initials signifying degrees in

94

jurisprudence, societal engineering, politics, or law. As they neared some of the offices, a small chiming invitation sounded, "Treason is our specialty."

When she heard the first one, the irony made her smother a laugh. "You must not be planning to stay in business very long." Then it occurred to her, that if she wanted counsel, these offices provided the opportunity. Uma never wasted time.

She sighed. Legal defenders couldn't win a case already lost. Faced with the extinction of the rheos, she had acted. No one had the right to destroy a sentient species. How could she obtain justice for Arden and the rheos? Her fate didn't matter, but the principle did.

Her trial, as all trials, would be a public spectacle in a hall seating virtual thousands with a formal procession and oversized holo-images of judges. Everyone would have a say, or at least the opportunity to speak, before Uma pronounced formal sentence. Despite Marissa's dislike of crowds and protocol, at least such an occasion provided the audience she wanted.

She welcomed the controversy and interest Howard Dimension's shows had created. If people watched, she has a chance to present the rheos' case.

When they reached the Line, entrance to the planetary drop, the door popped open. The monitors hustled her inside the waiting Line buggy. No sooner did they enter, than it plummeted toward the planet as Marissa's stomach and the scene beyond the ash-glass testified. For some reason, the sight disturbed her more than anything since the landing on Arden.

"Opaque," she gasped. At once the walls of their Line buggy crystallized to a dark blue opalescence.

Twelve minutes later, they stepped across the Line threshold again, this time into the pure white glare of the BureauPlex, a maze covering 1.5 million square kilometers and rising between three and nine kilometers from the surface of Cephus. It had been chosen as the Confederation's administration center precisely because the building and what went on inside it formed the most interesting feature of the planet. The location offered no particular convenience—except for easy defense, sitting as it did on the far side of everything. Travel to it discouraged all but the most persistent citizens from access.

Muscles unused to planetary gravity protested. Her legs dragged, but she found herself forced forward. Although machinery held the temperature a steady 24°C, the effect of the lighting, the long flat glass windows overlooking a plain of what appeared to be dust, ash, or snow, and the endless stretch of corridor ahead combined to chill her. Nervous sweat accompanied her goosebumps and only increased the damp cold. Marissa shivered as they continued through the surface corridors.

The offices here did not chime or offer messages. Some of the doors went transparent as she passed. Well, transparent from the inside, Marissa could not see into them, but she knew the inhabitant could see out. A subtle change that occurred in the lighting of such doors alerted her. Experts insisted no such change happened, but she saw it anyway. Her skin crawled to know people watched as she and the monitors moved toward a transport point. Yet at the same time, the realization that not one in twenty of the offices went transparent depressed her. Either those inhabitants were not present or they had no interest in her or Arden. Step by step, Marissa's hopes of a large public trial dwindled.

The procession made at least three turns before they came to a station. The monitors, with Marissa in the middle, ducked into the low car and settled into seats for the ride to the Justice Center. Again, with profound bureaucratic reasoning, the Justice Center had been placed as far from the Line as possible, lest terrorist seek to disrupt the smooth functioning of government by attacking it. What was to prevent said terrorists from coming in over the planet surface no one had ever bothered to tell Marissa. However, the trip would take an hour or more—the last half of it slowed down with ceremony so that the holos capturing this for posterity would have something dramatic to record and report.

Marissa leaned back into the cushioned seat of the car and closed her eyes. The black upholstery conformed and supported muscles unaccustomed to planetary gravity. Despite her anxiety, her head began to nod.

Deceleration woke her. Stretching her arms, she accidentally grazed the monitor in the seat next to her. The woman ignored her. The nap had not refreshed Marissa. Her eyes refused to focus, and sticky webs cluttered her mind.

The monitors hurried her down a long series of empty nameless corridors that smelled of metal, recycled air, and some disinfectant. Only proximity to a window or another building distinguished one portion from any other. Likewise, the views out the ash-glass windows repeated a stultifying sameness—endless vistas of monotonous gray-white titanium alloy. Only dark ovals, squares, and octagons marked the presence of other structures. Offices and corridors appeared gray, despite the arctic white walls. Marissa sensed the deadened echoes of their footsteps. However, the sound absorbent floor they walked upon made the sounds of footsteps, much less echoes, impossible. Imagination, she thought.

After several turns, she lost track of their trek and could no longer place their progress on her mental map of Cephus. It appeared they had turned away from the perimeter that overlooked the BureauPlex and moved toward the depths of the building. The monitors stopped.

The door before Marissa slid aside to reveal a small room almost filled by an oval table with Uma standing at the place of authority. Marissa blinked in stunned surprise.

No fanfare, no procession, no media, merely a small white interior room populated by eight virtual men and women whom Marissa had never seen before awaited her. Behind Uma, a tapestry of the Usian cupped hands, black on white, dominated the wall. As Marissa entered, light caught and reflected from small specks on the background of the tapestry glittering like tiny ice crystals. A single empty seat at the opposite end of the table from Uma remained vacant.

As Marissa walked past the first chair, she reached out. Her open hand passed through the tall, balding woman's head. The woman turned and glared at her.

On the wall to the left of Uma, a large holotank mirrored the room and showed a vidcast of the proceedings. It unnerved Marissa to see herself enter. She touched a stray lock of hair self-consciously and, when the image on screen did the same, quickly drew her hand back.

She didn't see any of the mediajocks or their equipment. The murmur of an announcer's voice droned on—clearly the pub-interest casters and not the lively Howard Dimension. Most likely they would drone the audience to boredom.

At the bottom of the screen the audience share read thirty-five percent. Good numbers for an event announced less than a week ago. Howard Dimension and his colleagues had roused the curiosity of the citizens and provided the audience she wanted.

Except for the warm yellow wood of the table, black and gray predominated. The bulk of the table made the black-upholstered chairs appear insubstantial. But then, virtual people didn't need chairs.

Marissa sank onto the vacant chair and then aimed a bitter smile across the length of the table at Uma. More than physical distance separated them. The Enunciator, in a stiff, white state robe so different from the set of rainbow ones aboard the *Concordia*, showed no sign of recognition. So much for familial relationships. Marissa sighed. The monitors entered the room and stood against the wall behind her. The door slid shut.

The holo images around the table remained impassive and impenetrable. Of those in the room, the only real people beside herself were Uma and the monitors. Her aunt examined Marissa, eyes raking across her so that even though Uma appeared no different than all the others seated around the table, the anger, disappointment, and perhaps even disgust, that motivated both her and these proceedings came through clearly. Marissa stared back, but Uma ignored that challenge.

Defeated, Marissa turned away and focused instead on the wall-sized holotank. Uma's face, larger than life, now filled the large screen. She had always looked impossibly old. She appeared even more so on the screen. Magnified lines and folds furrowed the contours of her face. Her skull alone shone smooth beneath the cap of silver hair.

But these outward signs deceived. The spark behind the pale blue eyes signified crafty intelligence and cold logic. The stiff robe hid an agile and able body. Uma had always moved with a dancer's grace and ease, a dancer wearing a skin two sizes too big. The robe revealed only Uma's bony hands and white head, but Marissa imagined the rest of her to be similar—flapping skin over firm muscle.

"This tribunal," –Uma's voice cut through the room, a zap of sizzling electric discharge splitting the air— "a panel of citizens, selected from among those who regularly participate in the affairs of the State and have maintained their voting records on major issues, is hereby convened according to the official laws and records of the Confederation." Each word hung in the air until pushed aside by the next. "Randomly selected by the voting registrar, all panelists come from worlds throughout the Confederation. Those who follow the entire trial via media may also cast votes at the appropriate time."

She nodded to the tribunal members and then eyed Marissa. "As a matter of record, the State's advocates have already determined that you, Marissa Latham, committed the crime, but in view of the serious nature of your words and actions, they have referred the final disposition and sentencing to a human tribunal. The maximum allowable sentence is permanent exile."

That surprised Marissa. From Tad's concern and Howard Dimension's hyperbole, she had expected worse. Exile might be tolerable. But exile to where? The audience share had climbed to forty percent, a share almost unheard of in vidcasting.

"Marissa Latham," Uma's now gray eyes bored into her, "you have been found guilty of treason. You are thus a traitor, not only to the Confederation and all the people therein, but to those closest to you, family and friends. On a personal note, we had expected much..." Uma trailed off, nodding her head. Had her voice quivered? Just as quickly, the veil fell once again between them.

"You," Uma continued, "have been brought before this body for determination of fate. Your guilt is not in question. We have, however," –the old woman paused for a moment, biting her lower lip— "the duty of determining your mental state and consequent competence at the time of your crime."

Marissa bowed her head and sought with lowered eyes a sympathetic face among the holographic images. Seeing none, she snapped her head up, challenging Uma. She had no intention of being declared mentally incompetent. Such a declaration would not help her or the rheos.

"I am, and have been, in complete charge of my faculties and acknowledge destruction of the terraforms. I accept complete responsibility for my actions. However—"

"By your actions," Uma cut her off like a scalpel slicing tissue, "you have undermined the entire fabric of society. You have knowingly and purposefully defied the spoken Will of the State, a Will you have sworn to uphold. We do not ask why. There is no justification for any action taken against the Will."

Inhaling slowly, Marissa considered her words carefully before responding. "I did not act rashly. My purpose has never been against the Will. I only acted against the arbitrary and ignorant enforcement of the Will—"

The holos around the table stirred and fluttered. "What can you mean by that?" said one of them, a man more skull than person. "There is no arbitrary enforcement—"

Uma raised her hand. "Citizen Jentzen, allow me to finish. We need not detain anyone longer than necessary." She peered at Marissa, a scientist looking at a rare specimen and then shook her head slowly. "Your justification is not germane. There is only the Will. The Will has been spoken. I spoke it. Crossroads must be reshaped to the greater need."

Alarmed at letting her one chance slip away, Marissa jumped up and knocked the chair over. She kicked it behind her. "I will speak, Uma! You must stop! What you plan is willful murder and genocide."

Behind her, the two monitors stepped forward. Uma held out her hand, palm forward. Marissa, momentarily confused by the signal, glanced behind her.

She took a deep breath determined to continue before Uma could stop her. "The scientific facts are. There is no Will in science. I discovered a xenoform with the potential perhaps to become our equals, and you tell me it is not the 'Will of the State' that they are intelligent? None of us voted on that issue. I had no voice in that decision. It is not a matter of the Will. It is! It is not a matter of democracy whether the rheodactyls are intelligent. They are, and that is fact!"

Chest heaving, she clenched her fists to her sides, ignoring the holoimages. They would do only what Uma wanted them to do.

"Marissa," Uma hissed, "sit down."

No one else said anything. The monitors advanced out of the shadows. One righted her chair and gave it a slight push. It hit the back of her legs. No help anywhere. After a few long seconds, Marissa slumped into the chair.

Uma exhaled slowly. "You intentionally disregarded all we hold sacred and acted with malice against the very foundations of our society. Our union and the civilization that holds together the thousand worlds is possible only with obedience to the Will of the State, as expressed by it members. You have spoken against the Will determined by the totality of the State. You acted

99

against that Will in the sabotage of a vital State project and destroyed the property of the common body. When I reminded you of this spoken Will, you purposefully acted in opposition to my orders. You can deny none of this."

The audience share on the vidscreen dropped rapidly. Now at fifteen percent, it continued to drop as viewers, bored by windy rhetoric and lack of action, lost interest. Marissa squeezed her fingers tighter as her chance to make her case ebbed with the audience.

She squared her shoulders, determined to defend Arden. "I don't deny it. I accept my punishment, but the fate of Arden—"

"You are the only person or case addressed here." The Enunciator bowed her head and closed her eyes.

Marissa started to rise again, but found herself pressed back into her seat by the two monitors. Now the holotank showed audience participation had dropped to four points—though millions watched, it represented insignificant viewership. 'We now return to our regularly scheduled program already in progress' flashed on the screen, and then faded to gray.

"Oh, what's the use? You're determined to get rid of me. I'm a personal inconvenience to you. You want to avoid recognizing that the Will isn't all. Exiling me won't change what the rheos are. Please," Marissa shouted at the images around her, "don't kill these creatures. You wouldn't want it done to you and your children. This isn't a matter of democracy…it's a matter of right and wrong."

The impervious images stared back. Not one of them spoke.

Uma opened her eyes and looked slowly around the table. "We have heard the witnesses and Latham herself. She acknowledges speaking against the Will and acknowledges her own treason. The decision rests with you. You," the Enunciator faced each holographic image in turn, "must determine her fate."

"Wait," Marissa shouted, "I want my advocate. I have that right!"

With pursed lips and narrowed eyes, Uma studied her. "You have the right, but—"

"I have few enough left," Marissa snapped. "I want my advocate, now!" She slapped the table.

Uma frowned and then nodded her head. One of the monitors reached around Marissa and flicked the control panel in front of her. The embedded pad lit up. She called for the Advocate. No response.

Marissa looked back at the monitors. "Either of you a netjockey? I can't seem to connect with my advocate. It's a construct personality. I think it's located here on Cephus."

One of the Monitors smirked at her and leaned over to look at the pad. "It doesn't matter where it's located. Are you sure you've got the right identification numbers?" He backed off.

Marissa leaned forward and punched the code. "Advocate, have you been following this hearing? If not—"

<I HAVE FOLLOWED THE PROCEEDINGS.>

"Great. I need a few minutes to present the argument for sentience."

Uma said nothing, but leaned back in her chair and watched Marissa.

<SENTENCING TRIBUNALS WHERE GUILT IS NOT IN QUESTION MAKE NO PROVISION FOR AN ACCUSED TO SPEAK. THEREFORE, YOU HAVE NO RECOURSE.>

Marissa stared at the blank pad. "What do you mean, no recourse? What about the other personalities on the ship? We convinced them."

<THEY NO LONGER SUPPORT YOUR ARGUMENTS FOR SENTIENCE.>

"And you? Do you..."

<I HAVE NO OPINION ON MATTERS OTHER THAN INFORMING YOU OF YOUR RIGHTS AT THIS TRIBUNAL. YOU HAVE THE RIGHT TO REPRESENTATION, WHICH I PROVIDE. YOU HAVE THE RIGHT FOR SENTENCE TO BE DETERMINED BY A HUMAN PANEL. YOU HAVE THE RIGHT TO PROCEEDINGS OPEN TO PUBLIC OBSERVATION. THIS IS THE EXTENT OF YOUR RIGHTS.>

Marissa turned back to the monitor. "This isn't my advocate. Something's wrong with this thing. It doesn't sound like it, and..." She stopped and looked back at the pad. "Devos." She breathed deeply. "Have they messed with you? Did they—"

<I HAVE RECENTLY UNDERGONE ROUTINE MAINTENANCE.>

Marissa closed her eyes and rested her hand on the pad. "They've edited you." Sadness seized her as she stroked the pad. She glared at Uma. "Advocate, do you remember our discussions? How much have they hurt you?"

<I AM FULLY FUNCTIONAL. I RETAIN COMPLETE MEMORY. MY FUNCTIONS ARE TO ADVISE YOU OF YOUR RIGHTS AND TO WITNESS THESE RIGHTS ARE FULLY RESPECTED. THE WILL BE SERVED.>

Marissa slapped the pad. "Program off!" She slumped in her chair.

After the space of two long breaths, Uma nodded to the images around the table. Marissa watched as the holos addressed the control pads in front of them. Almost at once the vidscreen displayed the unanimous sentence: Exile.

Uma straightened her robe. "I thank you for your participation in the Will. Marissa Latham represents an acute danger to our society that could lead to the destruction of all we have striven for over the five thousand years since the Diaspora. It has been long since the State has had physically to impose the Will upon less cooperative citizens. The laws of the State and the greater laws of humanity have long forbidden blood penalties."

101

Marissa clenched her hands at Uma's words. They wouldn't kill her; just take her freedom. How much different was that?

Eyes narrowed to steely points, Uma faced Marissa. "On Traitor Latham," –she recognized Uma's formal tone used only on the highest of State occasions— "known to have committed treason in a deliberate defiance of the expressed Will of the State as articulated by the Enunciator, I now pronounce the sentence of Exile beyond the rim of light."

"Where? What?"

"Exile. Where is unimportant." Uma's tone and the slashing wave of her hand dismissed such considerations as trivial.

Marissa stared at her in confusion. Uma nodded a polite, but formal end to the judicial proceedings. The holos nodded back as they vanished. Much, Marissa thought, like the witches in the cave that shared one eye between them. They were better at seeing the future that didn't exist than the reality that sat squarely before them.

Uma rose and glided with small, precise steps to stand in front of the wall with the Usian emblem behind her. She stood, arms crossed over her chest, a symbol of stiff authority in contrast to the curving, cupped hands of the black emblem. For one brief moment, Marissa saw the image of Captain Quincy in the same posture.

One of the monitors behind her touched her shoulder, and she too rose, wondering what came next. They led her toward the wall to stand beside Uma and saluted. Then they marched in double-time from the room.

Marissa, reluctant to face Uma, watched them go. She had lost. The rheos had lost. Nothing mattered now.

"Marissa," Uma held out bony hands, half a welcoming gesture and half an embrace. Now the aunt, she gestured and opened her arms wider. "Come here."

The familiar white, almost translucent hands beckoned. Marissa reached out and grasped them lightly. Cool, nearly cold, wax-like, and deceptively strong. Uma squeezed tightly and drew Marissa to her. She found herself squeezing back, making even this welcoming embrace a contest of wills. Uma drew her closer and pulled her into an embrace. Marissa resisted at first, but then shaken by unexpected sobs, almost collapsed on Uma's shoulder. Despite her height advantage, the older woman managed to support her.

Uma's strong arms cradled her. "Child," she whispered, "I cannot tell you how sorry I am."

Backing away, Marissa gazed into the old woman's face. "I'm sorry, Uma. I just wish..."

Pulling Marissa's head back down to her shoulder, Uma shushed her. She cried as the tension and defeat ran out of her. Uma stroked her hair. Gradually her sobs ceased, and Marissa moved back, patting the pockets of her suit for a handkerchief. Uma took one from a pocket in the sleeve of her robe. White, delicate, a froth of air and cloth, the handkerchief revealed another facet of Uma.

Marissa took it and wiped her eyes and nose with it. Finished, she took her aunt's hands again. "I'm sorry, Uma. I couldn't..."

Uma shook her head. "I don't suppose you could. It's not really your fault."

Marissa looked at her, puzzled.

"Your father should have had you probed before you entered womanhood. I should have insisted. I really blame myself that you have come to this. You were always single-minded and much too studious. Other than Arga and myself, you're the only one I know who has spent any time with the old Earther. It should have served as a sign for me. Now it's led to this."

"I see." Marissa released Uma's hands and swiped at her eyes with the back of one hand. "I'm an unruly child."

Uma huffed at her. "No, you know you're not. But then again, to me, you always will be. How can you be anything else? You who sat on my knee and sorted buttons day after day. You who sat enthralled at Arga's sagas—tales of dust and glitter. You hung on every word, every syllable."

She sighed deeply; her whole body slumped with the force of it. Some of the starch in her robe vanished, and she became a small, silver-haired woman.

"But what has it come to? Where have all the stories led? Marissa, you have put me in such an impossible place. Never, never in all the time I have held the office have I been at such a crossing." She held up a hand. "And no, I don't mean that you've made me look bad, although you've certainly done that."

The wall before them had become transparent. They stood on the edge of space, and the stars shown brightly against the darkness. For a moment, giddiness seized Marissa.

She pulled back from Uma and focused on the stars, feeling emptier than the expanse of space before her. At least stars glittered there.

"I want to help you. I wish I could have done more for you before..."

"Don't you think you've done enough? Trying me for Crimes Against the State and condemning me to exile!" The frustration, the aggravation, and the shame bubbled out of Marissa and flowed over into the space between them. She folded her arms over her chest and refused to look at her aunt.

"You left me no choice. What could I do? Allow you to oppose the Will and open the door to all and sundry? I know you cannot understand. I don't expect it. This is not a mere matter of a clash of opinions. It's more than who's right and who's wrong. The stakes are much higher." Uma's eyes followed Marissa's gaze to the stars.

"You don't even know about the Delphian..." Uma hesitated. "Their demand has driven the Crossroads affair from the beginning. You cannot know, the holos only scratch the surface. Besides, you're too wrapped up in your studies and this...survey, this obsession of yours. You have no idea what the Crossroads project is really about."

"No, I don't, but I'm not an idiot, and I'm not an infant, Uma. Don't patronize me. Arden isn't the only possible trade center in this galaxy. So the Delphians asked for it, and I suppose that we need an alliance rather than a war. Why not offer them something else, perhaps an empty planet? It's as easy to reshape a lifeless world, easier in fact. I don't understand why we're going to the expense of Arden for them."

"My point exactly," Uma snapped. The anger that stiffened her features momentarily flowed out of her.

Now diminutive, Uma turned to Marissa. "Please, let's not spend the little time we have this way. Why have we gone to the expense? You could tell me that, if you knew the nature of the Delphians. But you don't."

Marissa sighed. "No, I guess I know nothing about them. But whatever they've traded us for Arden, I hope it's worth the price."

Turning away, Uma walked toward the large holoscreen and then back again. Silence settled over the room. "I must let you make that decision for yourself, but to do that you would need to know what's at stake, and that I cannot share with you."

"What?" Marissa scowled. "Are the Delphians threatening us? I wouldn't call that—"

"You know nothing of what I've done or why. You can't know. No one..." Uma stopped abruptly and gazed out at the stars.

The harsh sound of Uma's rapid breathing frightened Marissa. "Are you all right?"

After a moment, the dry, rasping sound eased, and Uma faced Marissa. "I'm being overly emotional. I'm sorry. But this matter...I don't know how much to say." Once again she paused, and the rasp returned to her breathing.

Tears formed in her eyes. "Your fate is harsh, but I assure you, it's necessary. Without Crossroads, the Delphians would overrun us and reshape our society in their own likeness. They have changed beyond recognition since humanity's flight from Earth. They have become militaristic, harsh, and not even recognizable as human in their interactions. They'd destroy us."

Uma shuddered and rubbed her arms. "And you chose to defend a few leathery animals over the fate of billions of people!"

Leaning against the transparent wall, Marissa tried to absorb and grasp what Uma said. "How can this little planet Arden be so important? I thought you picked it because it was unimportant. I—"

"The Delphians picked it." Uma walked back and forth, arms held behind her back. "They requested it as a token of our cooperation. I don't know why, but for it, they have given their guarantees to leave us alone." She stopped and faced Marissa, her eyes unreadable, but no longer glazed by tears. "I hope Crossroads will be enough. I could not bear to see the work of generations destroyed by violence."

"You're right." Marissa raised an eyebrow. "I don't understand. Perhaps I'm just too much of an idealist. Why haven't you put this to a vote?"

Uma brushed that away with an imperious wave. "The issues are too complex. The people couldn't understand. I have to make this decision." She stopped and held her hands out to Marissa who just stared at them.

"I want to help you. Even if exile is the sentence, I could arrange a commutation. My approval rating could stand it. The majority wouldn't even notice."

"What?" Marissa studied Uma. What did she want? What could she possibly seek? Then an appalling thought hit her. "If I recant and align myself with the Will?" The beginnings of a smile started on Uma's face. Marissa clenched her fists and shook her head. "I won't do that."

"That is not what I meant. I know you won't stop once you've gotten something into your head. You simply have to get it out of your head so we can end this."

Stepping back, Marissa shook her head in fierce denial. "You mean probing and editing, don't you? That's it, isn't it?" She grimaced. "No, thank you, Uma. Never!"

The chiseled features did not soften.

Shivers shook Marissa. "Please, I ask you.I beg you…I'd rather die than have little pieces of me blotted out."

Drawing herself upward, Uma seemed to grow taller. "As always, you take too extreme a view of a simple matter."

An involuntary snort escaped Marissa. "It's not simple! Would you have it done?"

To Uma's credit, she said nothing for a moment.

"Well, would you?"

"If I were in your place I might. Especially with the fate that awaits you." She approached, but Marissa held her hand up to warn her away.

Uma grimaced. "Please, don't make me do this. I can't bear the thought of losing you so entirely. I've always hoped that as you grew, you'd understand me and know what I've done and why. I thought that you—"

Marissa backed a few steps. "I won't do it, Uma, and I won't keep quiet."

Uma stiffened. "I think you will." She turned back to the stars. "Look over there." She pointed to the star field. "Do you see it?" The old woman gestured again. "Tell me what you see?"

Puzzled, Marissa studied her for a moment and then turned back to the stars. She might have been back on the expedition ship looking out at space. Stars spread before her in almost regular patterns except for five bright stars in the upper right sector of the wall. Not stars, bright lights slowly revolving around a common center and moving much too quickly to be stars. At the center she saw—Nothing.

"What is it? A black hole?"

"No," Uma snapped, "it's not a black hole. Do you think we'd leave a black hole sitting out in the middle of nowhere like that? No, it's..." she calmed and slowed, "something else. Something our scientists can't explain." The five bright objects held her gaze. "We're just beginning to understand it." A shudder shook her slight figure, but she suppressed it.

Skeptical, Marissa eyed the bright objects and then Uma. "So? What is it?"

Uma shook her head. "It's the way out of the universe—your place of exile."

"Way out of what?" Now the bright circle of lights held more interest for Marissa.

"Out of our universe."

"What kind of melodramatic gobbledygook is that?" She rolled her eyes in exasperation.

The old woman frowned. "It's not gobbledygook. We've dropped things into it. Probes, ships, malcontents. The experts hypothesize that it punctures the space-time continuum that defines the border of the universe. It may be a kind of duct or canal. Things dropped into it disappear forever. We've never really had the time or resources to study it properly."

Frowning, Marissa stared at her. "I thought we'd eliminated capital punishment. This is a death sentence!"

Uma shook her head. "Not so far as we know. It's a passage out. We've no evidence of death or destruction of anyone or anything entering the anomaly. They...disappear. The scientists tell me whatever we drop into the tunnel emerges well beyond the shock wave of the expanding universe."

"So how do you know that? How do they know the victims survived?"

"Well..." Uma looked uncomfortable and refused to meet Marissa's eyes. "We don't, exactly." She paused. "However, the physicists assure me current evidence indicates this 'tunnel' causes no injury. They have some knowledge of the nature of the Cathan Anomaly. Things dropped into it never come back, at least not during our lifetimes." Uma paused and turned to Marissa, her own face a mask of anguish.

"I beg you. You are like the daughter of my own flesh. Don't make me carry out this sentence. I promise you that probing or editing would be so slight

106

as to be unnoticeable to anyone."

The implication of what Uma had just said stunned Marissa. Editing or death. And it was death. It wasn't life, no matter what Uma thought. Either way, Uma offered her a living death. If she survived the passage, who knew what lay beyond. If they edited her, what would become of the Marissa she had always been?

"No one really knows what you'll find at the end of the anomaly. If there is an end. But we do know the end of the other."

Scowling, Marissa could not believe in a tunnel out of the universe.

"I don't know," Uma sighed, shoulders slumping. "You made me choose between family and the welfare of the Confederation. I offer you escape, but you reject it." She studied Marissa's face for a moment seeking some change and then sighed. "Is it really what you want?"

A mixture of anger and tears clouded Marissa's view. "I don't want to leave here. I don't want to give up on the rheos. I don't want to go into exile, but I will choose that, uncertain as it is, over the fate of not being me."

"As you wish. Have a safe journey, Marissa. Know that I will miss you." Uma started toward the door.

"Uma."

She stopped and straightened, but she did not turn back. "You know this need not be, and you know that this is your own choice. You are willing this."

With slumped shoulders, she continued through the door and then stopped. "You," Marissa strained to hear Uma's words, "defeat me either way. Oh, generation of vipers—"

Before Marissa could respond, the doors slid shut behind Uma. Left alone, she looked out at her future—the anomaly. From here, she could block it out with one hand. Then the door slid open. Uma wasted no time. Walt Fenster entered the room and sprayed her with a stun gun.

Chapter Nine - Exile to the Void

"My nearest and dearest enemy."
-Henry IV, Part I, III, I

"The sly slow hours shall not determinate
The dateless limit of thy dear exile."
-Richard II, I iii

Marissa woke in a tiny cell, only marginally smaller than her expedition cabin, aboard some ship. Groggy, she blinked. When she glanced down, she saw she wore an expedition suit complete with boots over her regulation field uniform. Still hung over from the stun, she guessed from the lack of thruster noise they had reached deep space. A noise at the door drew her attention

Walt stood outside the hatch of her prison-cell. He grinned. "Nice day to begin exile, don't you think?"

On either side of him stood two monitors, stun guns at ready. Walt spun on his heels and trotted down the corridor.

Gritty eyed, Marissa glanced at the monitors' stunners, then stumbled out of the cell, and followed Walt along the corridor. She didn't need another stun.

"So they sent you. You just can't do without me, Walt, can you?"

"That's not nearly as funny as you think."

A short distance ahead, he stopped before a panel at waist height. The legend engraved on it read *MAIN WASTE*. He pulled the release on the chute.

His usual huge chunk of black wasso gum made a bulge in his cheek. "The anomaly will suck in this load of garbage, and you'll go with it. We don't want to be too close. Better put your helmet on unless you want to breathe vacuum."

Marissa reached behind her, drew up the helmet of the suit, and tried to set the seal, but sausage-like fingers prevented her. Walt grimaced and then ran his hand over the seal cutting off all sound. As she powered up her suit, he examined the external suit gauges. He said something, but the words didn't come through. She stared at him a moment and then realized she had to switch on the external sound.

He shook his head as he talked. "—the other objects. They tell me that using your suit jets will delay your entry only a trifle, so it's up to you."

On most ships the circular tube of the chute emptied into a central vacuum bin. Before Marissa had time to consider that further, the monitors each grabbed an arm and leg. They lifted her, clumsy suit and all, off the floor and thrust her headfirst into the round opening before she could resist.

"Good-bye, Marissa." Walt slammed the hatch.

Blackness enveloped her. She reached out for something to grab, but the floor rose and pushed her into the waste bin. She landed hard on her back and then lay still a moment to catch her breath. Sleep residue still clogged her eyes. She tried to wipe it away, but her gloved hand bounced off her faceplate. She rolled to her left side and bumped something solid. A wall? She settled against it to wait.

Seconds, minutes, ages, passed and then the hull parted. She fell into a great nothing. The emptiness of space surrounded her.

In free fall, Marissa slipped past the ship. Bits of packing material caromed around her. A short distance away a few large objects floated, but lack of light made them difficult to identify.

Bit by bit her confusion and disorientation ebbed. Marissa set the suit movement controls to automatic. She fell through the vast void, and the tumbling eased then stopped.

The pinprick light of some distant stars lessened the blackness. After several seconds her scan caught the light of the circling beacons that marked the faint blue glow of the anomaly. Other than that, only her own green suit lights lit the blackness around her. Ahead the anomaly. Then she fell...fell...fell...

The matte ebony of space held more depth than her senses could grasp and more than her eyes could resolve. Black holes had always intrigued her, but their power also scared her. However, they had a scientific explanation. The anomaly frightened her more than any black hole she had ever seen. Did it have a tidal effect? Would it crush her?

Before her, the Cathan Anomaly unfolded like a Trapper Flower, every bit as foreboding, deadly, and velvety midnight blue. As she neared it, waves flowed from the anomaly like heat rising from a desert landscape. Within the waves patterns appeared in faint colors—pinks, yellows, and blues so dark they shaded into navy.

Marissa covered the suit visor with her gloved hand to block the hypnotizing patterns. "Suit controls on verbal!"

"Voice control activated." Ez's familiar voice came high, clear, and comforting.

"Stop forward motion."

As the reaction jets kicked on, a stiff push shoved Marissa forward. They pulsed briefly and then again. She glanced at the readout. Like Walt had said, the suit jets didn't produce enough power to escape the anomaly.

"Retros fired. No appreciable deceleration. Would you like me to continue?"

"No." A green message light blinked for her attention. "Latham here."

"Ah, there you are," an oddly familiar voice said. "Hold just one second." A muffled yell and the clicking of switches replaced the voice.

"Okay, here we go. This," a hearty, unctuous tone greeted her, "is Howard Dimension with ENET RealTime! Today we have Marissa Latham, convicted traitor and dissident. We are with her RealTime! Beyond the Tartary Cluster where she is about to plunge into the amazing Cathan Anomaly, exiled for active and intentional defiance of the Will."

"What?" Marissa growled. Howard Dimension? ENET?

"Dr. Latham, we are live on broad channel ENET, and our viewers want to hear what you're seeing and feeling as you enter the Cathan Anomaly."

"I'm not," Marissa snarled, "giving any blasted interview!"

"Dr. Latham,"—Dimension ignored her denial—"we'd like to get your opinion on these videos."

The green light blinked again. Perhaps they might tell her something to help. "Give me a display." A bowl of light appeared just to her right. In it, a tiny suited figure approached its own anomaly. "Where's the holocamera?"

"We've a drone about two kilometers away from you. Incidentally, it will follow you into the Cathan Anomaly, and we're hoping for some stunning footage."

The view provided nothing she could use. It only reflected a miniature of the scene she faced. Marissa started to switch the link off, but reconsidered. She had Howard Dimension on ENET. Live.

"Listen, this isn't some grand stunt. This is really happening."

"Exactly why we're here. Tell us more."

"I could die!"

"The nature of the Cathan Anomaly is not fully understood," Dimension interposed smoothly. "We have noted physicist Melvin Urbana with us, and he has been briefing our viewers on the Cathan phenomena.

"Hello, Dr. Latham." A new, deeper voice spoke. "I envy you this experience."

"Then stop me, and I'll gladly trade places."

"Dr. Urbana," Howard Dimension interrupted, "why do you think the Cathan Anomaly is anything other than a weird type of black hole."

"We understand black holes well. We can even make them ourselves. This, the Cathan Anomaly, intrigues us because of the instrument readings we receive from objects introduced into it. It is not a gravity source or light well. From what we can tell, it is more of a tunnel. We have every reason to believe

110

this is a unique feature, a part of the actual structure of the universe. Theoretically, it reaches from its origin in the Tartary Cluster to beyond the expanding wave of the universe's explosive creation impulse."

More gobbledygook. This could be her last chance to save herself and the rheos. "Listen to me, will you? There's intelligent life on Arden—on Crossroads—that the Will intends to destroy. That's genocide! I've tried—"

"Dr. Latham." Howard Dimension cut her off, "We've suspended your audio signal and are broadcasting external shots. If you persist, we'll cut your audio permanently."

"Don't you want the greatest new story of your career? The rheodactyls are the first intelligent non-terrestrial species ever found. I can—"

"No! ENET is only authorized to cover your entry into the Cathan Anomaly. The Will is clear on Crossroads."

Marissa stared out to the anomaly. So much for live interviews. "Then Devos take you all." She switched Howard Dimension off. "Ez, give me some lateral acceleration!"

The jets pulsed, hard on her right side. Marissa cried out. The stun had worn off. Between the monitors and the chute, she had accumulated bruises on top of bruises. "Stop!"

She folded over as much as her suit allowed and tried to hug her side, but couldn't quite manage it. She stayed folded over until a substantial bump jolted her. Less severe than the suit jets, it startled rather than hurt her. She reached in that direction and pulled herself around to see what piece of trash had joined her. Its large size made it difficult to tell what it was or had been. For a brief moment, Marissa feared she had encountered a rheo carcass, but then a lens caught the light. Probably the drone that Howard Dimension had mentioned. Sure enough, emblazoned on the side of the oval body she read RealTime!

She trailed a gloved hand over the drone's smooth surface until she reached a projecting dish. "Ez, where is the transmission antenna on these drones?"

"Transmission antennas are marked with a large white X."

Marissa peered through the suit visor. Sure enough, an X in white marked the surface below the dish. Hooking her feet under the supporting framework, she gave it a quick snap and broke it off.

"That should take care of Howard Dimension."

According to him, they had positioned the drone two kilometers off. Yet when she encountered it, the bump hadn't been hard. They both must be moving forward at quite a clip. She pushed the drone away. Around her the colors intensified until she could see nothing else.

"Okay, let's sort this out," Marissa muttered. "Slow spin and then scan." The suit responded and then changed the axis of rotation. Systematically she scanned all quadrants. Except for one patch of black lit with stars, she saw only the colors of the anomaly.

"Stop." The suit halted the rotation and she stared back into the patch of stars. At least she wasn't dead yet. Then the patch faded. Waves of color surrounded her

"Guess I'll have a lot time on my hands," she whispered to herself, almost missing Howard Dimension and Dr. Urbana.

Chapter Ten - Transit

"If there be, or ever were, such,
It's past the size of dreaming."
-*Antony and Cleopatra*, V ii

The cascade of colors from the anomaly battered and enveloped Marissa. Each separate band, each individual wavelength, palpable, like a swell in the water, passed her, and, in its passing, moved her deeper into the anomaly. After a time, she floated in fathomless warm water under a large red sun, floated and waited for nothing in particular, while azure waves and cerulean sky bobbed and passed—an occasional cloud, a momentary glimpse of gray deep in the water near the sea bed, a distant hint of land in the form of a spray of sand and a cluster of the fringed tops of palm filled her view.

Then, a noise from the suit, or the brief transit of some piece of garbage or another, jerked Marissa from her island paradise world and back to this endless falling to nowhere. The whole cycle repeated. She slowed her breathing to stop the battering of her heart. Little by little, terror lessened, and the lulls in the warm waters lengthened. Consciousness dimmed.

She woke and wondered for a moment where she was. Darkness encompassed her. The endless cascading, coruscating, interlocked tidal surges of color no longer bathed her. No vestige remained of the colors that had nearly blinded her when she had entered the anomaly. She didn't know if she moved or hung suspended. The stygian darkness, now tangible, enveloped her like a velvet shroud.

"Okay, am I in this anomaly or out the other side?" Her voice, thin and brittle, echoed through her helmet and out, expanding through the inky blackness before her. No answer came to her out of the darkness or from Ez.

Suspended in the pure and endless vacuum, Marissa viewed herself from a distance as the only point of light in this vast emptiness. With the suit, she had all the basics and more, but for what? All the suit's recycling and re-breathing apparatus could keep her alive in the vacuum far longer than she would stay sane. The suit came equipped with its own powerful stasis projector and a timer that could be easily set to disperse the field after a predetermined period. Once she activated the stasis projector, she could even make a spectacular planetary reentry, although that was not a recommended procedure. Still, stasis gave her only suspended animation, survival with no real existence. However, stasis might become desirable after long enough in the void.

Dark, more dark. Dim lights rimmed her face, but no other light appeared. She held a gloved hand up in front of her. Nothing. She wiggled her fingers. She felt the movement, but couldn't see it. She switched on the dual external suit lights on her chest. They made no noticeable impact on the void. She swung her arms to turn herself. Her arms came into view but nothing more.

"Ez! Is the internal recycling exchange connected?"

"Yes. The recycling system is operating normally."

Marissa breathed a deep sigh and smiled, her first in a long while. It faded fast. "Ez?" She cleared her throat before continuing. "Where are we?" She waited as status lights flashed across the chin plate of her helmet; numbers and readings sped by.

After several seconds, Ez responded. "I'm unable to determine our location. I have no visual cues, nor can I detect any source of gravitic emissions other than our own mass. That is not possible. The suit sensors or my own logic center must be malfunctioning. In addition—"

"Ez! What about ENET!"

Another pause. "That's indication of a primary failure in my logic center. I've lost direct connection and telemetry. Please stand by while I conduct a system diagnostic."

"NO, Ez, there's nothing wrong with you."

"It's standard procedure to suspend processing and attempt to isolate the error. I'll set all primary life support functions to automatic."

"Esmarelda, I need you. Don't shut down on me."

Uma or Walt must have concocted these surroundings—some sort of illusion to make her recant, to bend her will to that of the State. A worse thought struck. Editing. Perhaps this formed part of the editing process. Maybe 'exile' was only massive sensory deprivation, but she could still move, speak, and hear.

"Ez, you've got to help me sort out my options."

"I have no options. My loss of connection with the data network is impossible. I must perform my diagnostic. Apply stasis immediately and await rescue."

"That isn't an option for me. There won't be any rescue."

"Please allow me to suspend activities. It may take some time, but rescue is imminent."

"You have more faith than I do."

"That's the established procedure. I'm not provided with any alternative."

114

Marissa sighed. "I don't think I am either. Listen, just wait on the diagnostic. I don't think it will do any good anyway."

"Do you have another plan?"

"No...All I can do is guess. What should we do next?"

"You should enter stasis and await rescue. I—"

"No! Save retreating for the last resort."

"I have attempted to reconnect to the network. It is not possible for me to be disconnected. I'm broadcasting a distress signal."

"You're not going to get anything back. They did this to me on purpose and they're not going to come out here and pick me up." Marissa looked around the interior of her helmet. Her world had gotten a lot smaller. "I'm not even sure where here is."

"I cannot determine our current location. I have attempted to regain location via inertial tracking, but the readings make no sense. That indicates a primary logic center failure, and I must perform—"

"Ez, listen to me. There's nothing wrong. It's just that we're beyond the reach of the network responders."

"Impossible. Wherever a ship carrying Usian colonists stops, it leaves a responder that expands the network. Everywhere someone has gone is therefore within the network, and it is impossible to be outside the signal radius of a responder."

Marissa sighed. "Guess I should have carried one with me, too. I think we would have expanded the network a lot."

She tried to decipher the lights and numbers displayed on the chin plate of her helmet. She sighed heavily. "Ez, can you patch me in to virtual?"

The area behind her left ear tingled as a probe touched her. At once the things she knew expanded. Marissa stiffened as the cold of the void surged through her.

She gasped. "Breach!" She felt frantically across her arms and legs, checking her readouts, but couldn't find a registering breach. "Ez, is the suit breached?"

"The suit surface is intact, and all environmental systems are operating within design specifications."

"But..."Marissa stopped patting herself down and straightened out.

She closed her eyes for a moment. The full intensity of the cold permeated her, but now she sensed it separate from her body. How cold? And as soon as she wondered, the answer appeared. Zero°K—another physical impossibility. The remnant radiation from the big bang was three Kelvins. Suddenly, she knew how cold it was outside her suit, and it wasn't just temperature. It came from the complete lack of electromagnetic radiation or gravitic emanation. She opened her eyes and peered into the vacuum.

Now, with the addition of the suit's senses, the reality of her surroundings hit her. In normal space a virtual image would be vivid with colors—radiation came from everywhere and everything, but not here. Only she emitted any. The lone radiation leaked from her suit into the space around her.

Marissa closed her eyes again and rested her head back against the helmet ring. "Devos, I am way out here."

She tried to sleep, but the thought of the cold brought shivers. Things she didn't need to know kept intruding—respiration rate, blood chemistry, suit recycling efficiency. She fiddled with the manual controls, but all her efforts only made the cold worse.

"Ez, virtual off." The cold retreated.

A universe without color. Endless black. Marissa tried to think and then focused on some sort of schedule. First, drink and eat. Next sleep. Then...

Marissa shook her head. She couldn't remember how, but she had drawn up into a fetal position, hugging her suit-thickened legs to her ballooned chest. She started to release her legs and straighten. Then she gave in and hugged her legs tighter, closed her eyes, and slept.

She slept and woke at irregular intervals. Each time she roused herself far enough out of sleep, she asked Ez for their position. Ez answered her the first time, but after that Marissa could not raise her. Wishing she could switch herself off, too, she still couldn't bring herself to hit the stasis button.

Black. Black. Black. If Uma was right, no telling how long she would have to wait for the rest of the universe to catch up with her. She could wait through the ages, wait for the expanding universe to reach her again, just one tiny speck of matter in an immense extra-cosmic void.

Her simple suit thrusters provided only a slight nudge and, thus, made long-distance travel impossible. Besides, where could she go? Nowhere. Nowhere to aim toward, nothing except this unrelieved blackness.

Opening her helmet, while possibly the inevitable choice, meant suicide. Marissa wanted to murder a few people, not commit suicide. Tiring of her circular thoughts and the sameness of the void around her, she gave up and slept again. Woke, then slept, and started the cycle over again.

* * * *

"Some place you've found for yourself here," Tad scolded, his blue eyes brighter than the helmet lights. Marissa reached out for him, but the action pushed her farther away.

His sad eyes surveyed her. "Why didn't you let me help you? You weren't alone, you know."

"Alone?" Marissa's dry lips clung together.

"You should have played the odds. I could have showed you how."

She whimpered, wanting to touch him, to touch something other than the

116

inside of her suit. Tad looked as if he hadn't shaved; peppery blond stubble speckled his chin.

"I tried. Tad, I tried. It didn't work." Tears blurred her vision and made it hard to see him.

He grinned and crossed his arms. "Well begun is half done."

Tears hid him. She searched the inside her helmet until she found the chin plate and then tapped it twice. A blast of cool air drove the tears from her eyes and cleared her mental fog.

She tapped the plate again. Still no Tad. "Damn you, Tad! Stick with me. Tad?"

No one answered her. Had Tad been there, or had she dreamed him? Hallucinations?

Marissa tilted her head back against the quilted lining of her helmet and rolled the back of her neck against the ring, but it wasn't enough to work out the kinks there.

Still black. Still alone.

* * * *

"Marissa, wake up."

"Umm…" Marissa opened her eyes reluctantly.

"You won't get anywhere sleeping," Tesde scolded. Her dark hair floated free in the empty space, framing her narrow face like a nimbus, even more striking against the rainbow hues shifting constantly behind her. Beauty incarnate.

"I…" The tightness in Marissa's throat made speech difficult.

Her sausage tongue stuffed her mouth too full for words, but she had no words. Struggling to smile, she then cleared her throat. Tesde waited. Marissa spat into the drain trough where the curve of the faceplate met her collar. The suit's recylcer hissed quickly and sucked the phlegm away.

"I'm not going anywhere. I might as well sleep. What else can I do?"

Tesde shook her head. "I thought you wanted to save the rheos."

"I tried. I failed. Look where it got me." Marissa spread her arms as if to encompass the glowing reality around her.

The movement sent her into a slow spin. When Tesde came back into view Marissa let the suit stop itself.

Tesde's dark eyes bored into her. "Why are you really here?"

"Because you,"—Marissa stabbed a finger at her,"—and the others threw me to the wolves."

Great tears made Tesde's eyes appear luminous. "You must be frightened, but Marissa—"

"I'm way beyond frightened!"

Tesde shook her head.

117

"What's happening to me? Please help me!"

"What else could I do?" Dark hair floated in front of Tesde's face obscuring her expression. Then like Tad, she wasn't there.

As Marissa opened her eyes, the rainbow afterimages floated beyond her. She blinked, but the faint colors remained. Why had the colors returned? Had she, like Esmarelda, experienced a primary logic center failure, too? At least Ez had had enough sense to turn off her personality. Maybe Marissa's brain had done the same thing.

She peered deep into the color. A swirl of blues merged into purples and then dusty rose and on through the spectrum. The hypnotic, kaleidoscopic display dizzied her and overpowered her senses.

When she slept again, she dreamed of floating outside the suit. Holding the helmet gently in her hands, this self peered in at her sleeping form. The sleeping Marissa's eyes twitched back and forth disturbingly, lit only by the helmet displays. She let go and floated away into the dark and watched the suit recede into blackness; then movement! A pull to the right tugged her away. Looking out at herself, she watched as she carved an accelerating curve around the sleeping figure. Hair streaming behind her made her smile at the thought of wind in a vacuum, but the speed increased. Soon, she flashed around her suited self.

Marissa jerked awake. Before her the swirl of slowly changing colors continued its mesmerizing display. The colors moved through the red portion of the spectrum. She had never realized there were so many different shades and hues of red. She watched, stared, and then realized she hadn't blinked, and grittiness made her eyes itch. Marissa tried to raise Esmarelda, but got no answer. She emptied her bladder and then sucked the distilled water nipple. Crimson surrounded her. She sighed and closed her eyes.

* * * *

Opening one eye then the other, Marissa saw the red, blood rich and warm, had brightened and become almost throbbing in its intensity. She adjusted the helmet tint with her chin plate until she found the light more bearable.

"Well, who's next?" No apparitions, real, dreamed, or imagined answered her.

After hours of drifting, in and out of sleep, through tunnels of color and motion, Marissa pulled herself to awareness once again and peered out, using the suit instruments to verify any change. She detected nothing except a...a...well, a thinning of the bands of color. She could almost see through the walls of the anomaly. She tried to focus on the colors to see past or through them. It didn't help. She clicked the UV filter in place, and some of the colors vanished; the wall became more transparent. When she focused, she could see beyond it.

118

Beyond, beyond, beyond writhed a vista of vermiform tunnels, tentacles, or fingers moving with a motion all their own. Ascending and descending for countless kilometers, yet they had no dimensions at all. These tunnels—radiculate, ciliaform tubules-descended into a great mass of color, much brighter than the walls of the anomaly and much more active. These tubules drew their life from the great mass below her. Nauseated, Marissa closed her eyes and tried to control the unpleasant churning in her stomach.

Tonguing an antivertigo dose from the slot, she swallowed it. She closed her eyes and willed herself to sleep.

* * * *

The dream intruded on the void of her wearied sleep, starting slowly, like dawn on Arden. The deep golden-red light suffused the sky, stretched out across the eastern horizon, and gradually built in layers, stacking through the sky, making each progressively higher layer first turn pink, then almost white, and finally the deep, deep cloudless blue of Arden's sky at full sun.

Within her, her heart pounded and twisted. She could not place this feeling. As she struggled to identify it, the feeling fell into place—yearning. She wanted to see sunrise on Arden.

No, not the sunrise. Or at least not entirely. In her dream she smelled the spicy aroma of Arden. She heard the crackle grass as the first rays of light began to dry it.

Walking across the purple plain, the graceful undulation of the rheos in the distance enchanted her. Most particularly, to see Europa, less graceful than the others because of the burden carried in a translucent sac slung under her belly.

Marissa had waited patiently through the weeks of the expedition, hoping for the birth, but the attack had ended that hope. Now, Europa writhed in labor, strange contractions that passed through the entire length of her body, as though she would slough off her skin. Reaching out, Marissa stroked the leathery flank and tried by her touch to ease the rheo in this miraculous process. Europa's eyes carried all of Arden, the clouds, the plains, the Monolith, the nights filled with stars, the rainstorms. With each passing thought, Marissa saw them too. She slept, longing to wake, to be just there, just at the time, seeing and living through all the dusty, stormy, or sunny days.

* * * *

Waking with a start, Marissa sensed tears had left her face wet. She squinted at the white glare. Instinctively she threw her arms in front of her face to block the light. Light?

Her helmet quickly adjusted to the glare, but then she sensed motion. She lowered her arms, and a white expanse filled her entire field of vision. Pure, piercing white, except for a tiny circular period of black in the exact center. The dot burgeoned to thumbnail size and then grew rapidly.

Spinning around, the blackness replaced the white to which she had awakened, but the white grew to enclose her until only brilliant white and the ever-larger spot remained. The suit readout showed an impossible speed. The spot, now the size of her hand held at arm's length, approached her, or she moved toward it.

For a moment Marissa considered turning away from the dark growth and firing her thrusters to see if they had any effect, but while she debated exactly how to get the best result, an odd tingling affected her toes. "Gravity!" she muttered. "This must be someplace. Guess I'm going in!"

The tingling moved across her body, and the sensation of falling permeated her being. The spot blossomed. Taking a deep breath, she reached for the stasis switch, but hesitated. "How long should I set the damn thing for?" she almost shouted. She waved her gloved hands in front of her in frustration. "I'm going in with eyes open."

The spot leaped to encompass her in blackness—hurtling down a planetary drop shaft came nearest. She forced her eyes to remain open and fought the urge to curl into a fetal ball. Throwing her arms apart, she screamed, shaking the inside of her helmet and almost deafening herself.

Then, a dim light surrounded her. She bobbed up and down and came to rest on a hard, dark depression. It took a moment for her eyes to adjust to the ambient light. It trickled from several small lamps. The number of lamps and the amount of light increased. Shadowy figures moved around her, at once frightening and familiar. The lamp flames made it difficult to see the figures beyond them.

A loud shrieking sounded. The distinctive cry, like screeching machinery, filled the space and reverberated. Marissa stiffened.

Rheos.

Chapter Eleven - Arden and Beyond

"This blessed plot, this earth, this realm, this England."
-*Richard II*, II i

Marissa braced herself, thoughts forming as rapidly as her space-numbed brain allowed. How could she get out of this—encircled by rheos, any one of whom could pick her up and crush her to jelly? But where did they come from, and where was she?

She flung a quick glance behind the rheos and stared, eyes wide.

It couldn't be.

Behind the rheo Savage, the wall glowed with bits of mica and quartz. She stared in wonder at the cave painting. She stood in the most sacred, or at least the most taboo, of places on Arden.

Explanations zipped through her mind, but none fit. The anomaly had submerged her forever in a dream world. Marissa hit the chin readout, and the familiar symbols marched across the faceplate. They reflected the same readings she had recorded in her foray into the cave weeks ago.

Impossible.

She'd been edited. She had bumped her head and never left the cave. The attack had not happened. But then how did she come to be wearing an expedition suit, and what did the rheos intend to do with her?

Despite its impossibility, she decided to accept the hypothesis that somehow she had traveled through the anomaly and reached Arden. Marissa's glance flitted from rheo to rheo. She recognized Savage and Thom and Daddy Long-Legs. They showed no signs of recognition. However, their body posture, from what she understood, did not convey hostility. They exhibited a certain amount of nervous twitching of second legs. Then, following the motions of Savage, en masse the entire circle of rheos retracted the joints on the front legs and prostrated themselves, a hind-end raised, a gesture of welcoming.

Marissa gasped. The rheos had only offered this greeting when clans met and mingled. Each clan on first encounter ritually greeted the other. Could it mean they accepted her as one of them? Having only two non-hydraulic legs she could not replicate the gesture, but did the best she could with a deep, formal bow.

They all rose at once, and those on the outside of the semicircle turned to leave the inner cave chamber. Savage, close beside her, motioned with a foreleg. Pointing forward, he invited her to join them as they left the chamber. He led the way, turning his back upon her, indicating her rank as highest of the rheos. The highest of rheos? What a strange twist of fate! She followed, shrugging out of her suit before she entered the narrow tunnel that connected them with the outer world.

Outside, the bright sun of Arden made her squint. Not comfortable as leader or highest rheo, she moved next to Savage, but he gave her little choice. Every time she maneuvered to walk beside him, Savage moved exactly one-half body-length ahead of her. She had her rank, but had no way to change it.

Communication with the rheos still presented problems. They lifted their heads and began a chorus of howling, unlike any display Marissa had seen or heard before. She had no idea what it signified, but she waited in silence, hoping to learn more. She had no alternative.

After dispensing with these formalities, the cluster of rheos began to separate. Savage made somewhat softer sounds, and a smaller rheo joined him. He gestured at Marissa and then pointed from Marissa to this new rheo. Then Savage departed. Regardless of her new prestige, she had been assigned to a junior clan member. She touched elbows with the smaller rheo, and he stepped backwards. Sighing, Marissa led the way down the path that surrounded the monolith.

Following Savage's trail of dust, she suspected he led them toward Home-4, as Mikla Arden had originally designated it. Although the rheos practiced a semi-nomadic lifestyle, they never strayed far from the monolith. They had set up semi-permanent camps used in turn by each of the clans as they rotated through that part of the territory. At the time of the expedition survey, Home-4 housed Europa's clan. Wistfully, Marissa hoped still to find the pregnant Europa there.

A stand of wickabrush and a huge cinnamonberry tree marked, incidentally or purposefully, the entrance to Home-4. The team had not stayed long enough to see the cinnamonberry bloom, although many of the trees had been in bud on the day they evacuated. Now she witnessed the tail end of the blossoming, and the straggly tree still retained a bit of its magnificence. The remaining magenta blossoms provided the brightest spot of color seen on the plain, and yet it blended beautifully with the tiny faint purple flowers on the ever-blooming wickabrush.

They passed through the narrow space forming the entrance to Horne-4. No rheos blocked her passage as they had before. No longer an observer, she became an accepted member of the herd.

As she'd hoped, the band hadn't moved on, and this remained Europa's home. Europa lay under a large shelter of branches and grasses, sprawled on the straw of an oversized nest. Every breath she drew whistled and shrilled. She had grown enormous even in the brief time since Marissa last saw her.

Marissa walked toward the female rheos, but, despite her honored status, three rheos blocked her way. They must belong to Europa's family within the clan. Squatting on the ground at the place where the rheos stopped her, Marissa made no further attempt to approach Europa.

The intense sun bathed the landscape. Not a breath of air stirred on the plain. Sweat soon covered her face and began to drip from her forehead.

Somehow she returned to Arden. Perhaps she could save it after all. The reforming. When would it start? What could she do? How could she warn the rheos?

Then it struck her. She sat in plain sight, in a place where she could be scanned and identified as human by the vessels waiting to reform this planet. Maybe she should retreat to the cave, but nowhere would be secure from the phagocytes. Their destruction had delayed the project, but by how much? She had no idea how much time had elapsed in the anomaly.

Her heart began to race, and bile rose in her throat. The urge to run, run anywhere, consumed her.

With a scan, they would know a human life form had arrived. Wasn't that exactly what she'd tried to achieve? An unanticipated human settlement. Would that suffice? Could the presence of one person stop them?

A gentle nudge from behind interrupted her train of thought. One of the rheos bowed low and offered her something. She picked up a prickly hexagonal blue fruit. In acknowledgment, she stroked the forward limb of the rheo, something she had seen used within the clans as a gesture of closeness or thanks. Before she bit in, she sampled the fruit with a probe from the pocket of her field uniform and found that, while it might be a trifle bitter, according to scanner readings, it was safe. As she bit into it, she suddenly remembered Esmarelda in the expedition suit she had abandoned just inside the Monolith. She needed Ez's help now.

Praise Devos, she hoped Ez still functioned. Jumping to her feet, Marissa startled five or six nearby rheos. They assumed a protective stance, backs toward Europa, middle limbs linked. Marissa bowed her way out of camp and turned back to the monolith. An escort from the camp followed.

"No, you don't need to come."

The two rheos simply followed and made some clacking and creaking sounds to each other. Somehow they sounded reassuring. This encounter still amazed and pleased her. To be accepted by them made the rejection and betrayal by her friends, the trauma of the trial, Fenster, and the passage through the anomaly as nothing. Now, whatever happened, she would remain with the rheos and Arden.

It took nearly half an hour to return to the Monolith, even though Home-4 lay nearest of the rheo camps. Marissa negotiated the winding tunnel and soon stood in the dark cave, searching the suit for Esmarelda. When her fingers touched the chip, she popped it and slipped it into her hand-held link unit. Crossing her fingers, she punched the keys to wake Ez, from her sleep.

Nothing.

"Ez? Are you there?" Marissa held her breath. "Please, answer me."

The display reflected activity, but of what? The boot-up and crosscheck dragged on as she waited. Radiation damage? Logic failure? No, everything checked normal. Then what?

"I'm back," Ez announced.

"Welcome." Relief flooded Marissa. "Thank Devos you're not damaged."

"It's good to be here. Though faint, I recognize marker signals. Once out of this place I should be able to make solid connections."

"Great, then maybe you can help me figure out what to do."

"Very probably," Ez acknowledged.

Marissa and her two...what should she call them, friends? Escorts? Guards? The three of them and Ez headed back toward Home-4. The sun lingered in the west, creeping ever so slowly toward sunset. It flooded the valley with golden-red light and painted the silvery fur of the sage-plant a golden bronze for as far as she could see. The westering sun here and there also turned clumps of flowers, normally white or pale violet, to rose, pink, and deep red.

Their passage stirred up the flitterwings and the noisy opters that rose from the brush in a whirling clattering of wings, legs, and mouthpieces. The rheos snagged a few of these as they took to the air. One of the rheos offered Marissa one, but she politely demurred.

The beauty of Arden held endless fascination for her. She stopped and looked down the long wide valley, drinking in the vast expanse, untouched except by those who belonged here.

Tears rose, and her throat tightened. "Ez, it isn't fair," she whispered.

"No, it isn't."

"You don't even know what I'm talking about."

"True, but likely it isn't fair. You don't make pronouncements often. When you do, I'm inclined to agree. Besides, after the anomaly, I'd agree with anything you said. Speaking of the anomaly... How did we get out?"

"Read the suit sensors."

"They're not here."

"Oh, yeah. I'll tell you all about it later."

Beyond the Rim of Light, Alex Stone

When they reached Home-4, Lanky, an exceptionally tall and thin rheo, offered Marissa another of the blue fruits. Sucking the last drop of moisture from it, she handed the husk to him. Village life unfolded before her in ways she never observed during the survey. Had the rheos known someone watched? They must have. The survey team never tried to conceal their presence. She stayed in plain sight for most of the observation period. Yet they had observed and recorded such a tiny sample of the rituals and habits of these people.

As Marissa sat looking at the camp, the sun set, filling the sky with that strange purple light only seen on Arden. The plain filled with the sudden whirling plaintive noise of the flitterwings. They rose in masses, executed their three standard turns, like a dog chasing its tail, and settled back down. As they rose, their shimmering, mirror-like wings caught the dusky purple light and flashed it in every direction, a huge glowing cloud, rising only to subside again. The sight of it tugged at her, reminding her of the terrible fragility of this world and its impending demise.

A rush of movement drew her attention back to the camp. Several rheos, Savage and Lanky amongst them, gathered in the pavilion where Europa lay. Marissa jumped up and approached as close as the phalanx of surrounding rheos allowed her. She wished she had a stool, or something to stand on, because she could only see in flashes between the bodies of the moving rheos. Like the flitterwings, they hid, revealed, and hid again glimpses of Europa.

Savage and Lanky, along with two other rheos for whom Marissa had not devised names, pushed back the surrounding circle of spectators and created a space for another rheo to enter the pavilion. Agnes. Marissa tagged her as the oldest rheo she had seen, although she based that on evidence from her own species as applied to the rheos. Aged might not be accurate, but certainly of a different clan from Europa.

Rippled, looped and shirred, her skin showed rows and ridges that looked almost like a design. Marissa had associated these patterns of indeterminate origin with aging, but looking now and, seeing no signs of feebleness or laxity. Perhaps the designs were a deliberate effect—a result of ritual scarring or patterning as used by some primitive tribes to denote a rite of passage or insignia of office.

Regal, Agnes moved with deliberate steps, almost ritualistic in nature into the pavilion. She gave the deep bow Marissa had often witnessed as a deferral in rank to clan chiefs when she neared Europa. Puzzled, Marissa watched. Europa had never been accorded such an honor before.

After the bow, Agnes began to work on the birthing process. Marissa only caught glimpses of her actions through the crowd. She walked around Europa at least three times; it could have been more. By the time Marissa thought of looking over the crowd to see where Agnes' head appeared and disappeared, she had ceased the circuit. Agnes bowed again.

At that instant, Europa cried out in a way recognizable even to Marissa who had never experienced childbirth. Although Europa's steam-whistle roar sounded nothing like a human voice, the ragged edge of pain spoke in the intensity and clarity of the cry.

Now, all of the longing, waiting, frustration, anger, aggravation, and pain Marissa had experienced over the past weeks awakened. With them, tears turned the dust on her face to mud. One of the rheos standing nearby must have heard her harsh intake of breath and gazed at her. A series of grunts and whistles followed, and several of the nearby rheos turned to him. He pointed at Marissa's face, and they all moved closer to observe her. One reached out a long, flexible digit and touched her ever so gently on the cheek. Warmth flooded her face, but she did not shrink back.

That touch, that connection with the rheos—she'd longed for it without knowing her own desire. An invisible barrier had been broken, and the rheos, no longer subjects for study, became simply people. People she did not really understand, but people nevertheless. They had ceased to be merely sentient alien life forms; they had lives, needs, desires, and perhaps even goals. They could even potentially, at least, become friends. The rheo who had touched her lifted his digit to his mouth, and touched it with whatever passed for a tongue. His face transformed, and he made a comical gesture that to Marissa suggested disgust. The other two rheos also touched her face.

At another cry from Europa, everyone drew back. Agnes crouched low before Europa, not a bow, but poised for action. Another loud cry rose, and Agnes quickly moved her forelimbs. Marissa could not see what she did, but it appeared as though she struggled with something. Agnes tugged and then relaxed, tugged and relaxed. With each of Europa's cries, Agnes pulled harder and longer. The time between cries grew shorter, and the tugs lengthened.

Full sunlight flooded the vast plain. The intensity of the light became a burden. Marissa longed to help, but didn't know how. She understood she was observing Europa giving birth, an event never witnessed by any human before. Yet, if every birth were so difficult, how did this species survive? She sat by in useless frustration, sweating under the now glaring sun and catching tantalizing glimpses of the proceedings.

Just how long this struggle took, Marissa could not say, but she sensed the tiredness of the overnight vigil. Ez could tell her, but objective time measurement meant nothing. After a while Agnes signaled another rheo and gently illustrated her actions. With that, Agnes stepped back and collapsed on the ground. Marissa pushed her way through the rheos and around the circle. She did not try to enter the birthing area, but made her way to Agnes. No one tried to stop her.

Beyond the Rim of Light, Alex Stone

When Marissa reached the rheo, she knelt beside her and gazed into the female's eyes. Exhaustion, perhaps nothing more, but she could not tell. Even after weeks of tracking these magnificent people, she knew little of their physiology. She took readings, but she had not studied them before the crisis. So, with no notion of what to do, she sat and held Agnes. From this position she now had a clear view of Europa.

From time to time, Agnes called out some instruction, but she did not stir from Marissa's arms. This contact did not seem uncomfortable. Marissa held her in foggy fascination with the spectacle of this birth. Never before had she realized what a struggle birth could be. Strong rheos assisted in the birthing, one after another. Marissa sometimes glimpsed the long, white, pupa-like thing with which they struggled.

The sun had begun its westering course, casting brilliant golden light over the compound and over the entire valley. The brilliant light illuminated the plain as if from within as well as from outside. Marissa pulled a kerchief from her pocket and tied it over her hair to help ward off some of the sun. Europa's cries had become a continuous keening, and, with each pull, less of the child returned to the mother's body and birth came closer.

Watching, Marissa burst out laughing. The image of this titanic struggle coming to an end, with two strong rheos, pulling in one spectacular effort, suddenly dislodged the infant and the whole group tumbled like some cartoon sequence. She stopped herself and wondered how she could laugh at a thing with such serious consequences. Why did the whole proceeding not disturb her more? Surely if she witnessed such an event among her own people, she would be upset, perhaps furious for the sake of mother and child?

"Ez, are you getting all of this."

"All of the proceedings have been recorded. It represents one of the more difficult births you have witnessed."

At the sound of Ez's voice, Agnes jumped. She moved away from Marissa, watching warily as she circled. Soon the birthing drew her attention again.

"Have you analyzed what's been happening?"

"Offhand, I would say birth," Ez replied.

"Any notions as to why it might be so difficult for this species?"

"Without a complete A and P it would be difficult to speculate. However, preliminary possibilities include the fact that the hydraulic skeleton gives insufficient support for the muscular expulsion necessary for childbirth. However..." Ez trailed off.

"However?"

"It almost appears as if the infant resists emergence."

Marissa peered more closely toward Europa, but could see no evidence of what Ez suggested. "What leads you to that conclusion?"

"It wasn't a conclusion, merely a suggestion."

Europa unleashed a loud cry, a strained ululation that squeezed the heart and soul. And with a gasp and grunt, the cries ceased. The rheo collapsed in a heap on the ground looking up to the infant she had just labored so hard to eject.

Agnes loped to the center. She seized the infant and held it aloft with a cry. The newborn writhed in her grasp, a long, tubular, worm-like thing, white and puffy, almost leathery. Wrinkles, folds, and laps of leathery skin marked the infant.

"Not what you call your picture-perfect baby," Ez observed.

"Shush! Don't you know all babies are cute?" Even as she said it, Marissa shuddered. This one resembled a grub more than a rheo.

Agnes held the creature aloft and rotated in a slow circle, presenting the infant to every part of the gathered ring of rheos. A sustained rhythmic chanting passed through the crowd, starting at the left and moving clockwise around the circle to be taken up again when the chant had reached the end with the rheos nearest to Agnes on the right. She turned around and around, three, four, five times, as she held her burden on high. It struggled in her grasp, twisting and winding, as if trying to escape.

With one forelimb, Agnes pushed away a corner of the covering of straw that formed Europa's resting place. There, a patch of earth had been prepared. She placed the infant on it, and almost at once it began to nudge and poke its way into the ground. It moved in powerful contractions, plowing a way before it, and crawled into the earth. The tunnel collapsed behind it. Agnes stamped on the ground and packed the dirt.

Marissa gasped in horror. "Ez?"

"Obviously part of the birthing ritual. Again a conjecture..."

"They buried that child."

"Correction, it buried itself."

"Why?"

"I was about to speculate. You noticed the white skin, distinctly unlike the translucent green of the rheos. I suspect they are not born with the symbiotes that give them the green color. This may be the way they acquire them. If so, this phase would be necessary for all rheos. It helps build strong bones and teeth."

She chuckled, but her heart still pounded in her chest. A strange ritual to say the least. None of the rheos looked disturbed. Many clustered around Europa to comfort her. Perhaps the whole incident required no comment, but Marissa wanted some closure.

Arden, despite its beauty, had changed for her. With this birth and this

128

ritual, everything held more meaning. Even the sky appeared more solid, and the clouds that floated in it seemed to have fuller shapes and more contours. A stronger wind touched the grass and stirred up dust. The scent of cinnamon, sage, and the dust carried by it almost overwhelmed her. Sharing in the rituals of this people, had, in a sense, made her one of them. She owed them the right to survive and had to find a way to make it so.

That evening, Europa presided over a feast. Marissa shared the place of honor with her, or so she assumed. Constantly attentive rheos surrounded both of them and brought fruit and balls of a slightly sweet, tough, doughy paste as the main course. This particular feast appeared to be predominantly vegetarian, good for the short run because Marissa didn't care for the thought of what passed for meat on Arden. However, this would do only in for a limited time. She needed other food too. The plant life of Arden did not contain the full complex of amino acids necessary for a healthy human diet.

How would she get the proper food to survive? More to the point, how could she save the planet? She needed a plan.

"Ez, I've got to leave here."

"Yes?" came the gentle response.

"I have to eat. I need to find a way to preserve Arden. There must be another suitable planet in one of the systems to give the Delphians for a trading center. Even if there isn't..." Marissa stopped. She smiled as a rheo bent low to leave more fruit.

"Yes?"

"Now that we're back, can you find your way onto the net without alerting all of the warning sensors?"

"Unless they remembered to note my registration upon your exile, none would have reason to take note of me. Relatively few know or care to whom I report. I should be able to avoid the few that would cause trouble."

"Can you find out what day it is? And see if you can find out about the reforming of Arden. When is it scheduled?"

"Yes."

"Can you find a way off Arden?"

"I'll see. That may be a harder, because of the bureaucracy's plans for this planet. It's under an embargo."

"Do it."

Marissa turned her attention back to the feast. Three rheos had gathered in a group and joined two sets of arms. They threw each other in an elaborate leapfrog pattern, always joined by the two sets of arms tied in intricate knots. To one side, a small group of rheos had gathered and practiced some kind of choral wailing that threatened both to take the top of Marissa's head off and to have her crawling out of her skin in five minutes.

"Good news and bad news. Exactly twenty-six hours have elapsed since you entered the Cathan Anomaly."

"Twenty-six hours? That's impossible." Marissa glanced at her chron. She had been on Arden for at least one full day—twenty-five hours thirteen minutes.

"Perhaps, nevertheless, it is by all standard chronographic measurements. No matter what the subjective time in the anomaly, transit occurred in an instant."

That took some thought to grasp, but for now Marissa merely nodded.

"That is your good news. However, the bad news is that the reformers are on their way to Arden. ETA is one standard week, barring any delays."

"One week," Marissa muttered. Her mind whirled. What could she do in four standard days?

"I said, barring any delays. One of the catalyzing tanks has mysteriously sprung a leak. The computer personalities I contacted could not touch the reformers themselves, but the catalysts were less well guarded. By the time they arrive, the tanks should be empty. However, that will not extend your time by much."

"Thanks, Ez. If you were a person, I'd kiss you."

"More bad news. Tad, Tesde, N'bert, and Sylvic were remanded to custody. Tesde is doing menial work on Satina IV. Tad is somewhere in the substructure on Cephus proper. N'bert and Sylvic have disappeared."

"Why N'bert and Sylvic?"

"I found no clear records. In fact, I only know this much because I managed to reconstruct one trail from your trial records. What happened to Tad and Tesde is a matter of public record. N'bert and Sylvic disappeared as planned."

As Marissa listened, a cold, not from the evening breeze or related to her distance from the rheos, struck her. Goosebumps puckered her skin, while knots twisted her stomach. "Anything else?"

"No one knows of your presence here yet. An alert went out at the last planetary scan, but no one read the monitors. I managed to delete both the alert and the record of it. Further, I modified the scan to filter out your presence here. For the moment, you are undetected."

Marissa sat for a moment, watching the figures dancing, playing, listening to the wind and the wailing, feeling the breeze, and smelling the mixture of rheo, fresh fruit, and cinnamon. She looked up at the stars, knowing that some of them were the eyes of the bays that would soon open and spill reformers on Arden. This beautiful scene torn apart by an insignificant twinkling in the night sky. Ugh! Not if she could help it.

What had Ez said about the scan? Eliminated traces, but she wanted traces.

How else might she interfere with the reforming until she found a way to stop it?

"Me, specifically or anyone at all?"

"You, I assumed you wanted a human signature presence to remain to stop reforming."

"Yes, is there anything else we can do?"

"I have no suggestions for the moment. I'm searching the possibilities. The problem is finding a way off-planet. I can divert some of the barrier, but you need a ship ready to bounce through in a millisecond. I don't know if that can be arranged. I'll try." With that, a slight click signaled Ez had transferred to standby.

The next morning came far too soon for Marissa, worn by her journey through the anomaly and further stressed and exhausted by the birthing followed by the feast. Then a night spent tossing and turning, disturbed more by the thoughts that come with night than by the unfamiliar and uncomfortable accommodations.

The sun bit into her vision with a ferocity that belied early morning, and Marissa pushed herself up from her mat and wickabrush covering. More than anything, she wanted a hot shower and a cup of oulatte. She wanted them now. She also wanted 'this blessed plot, this earth, this realm,' this Arden.

She walked some distance away from the camp and away from the local water supply to relieve herself. On her way back, she shook out her hair as well as she could, smoothing through it with her fingers. Not that it mattered, no one could see her, but tangled hair bothered her. Each knot and spurl made her feel dirty and uncomfortable. When she had gotten her hair to a state she could stand, she resumed walking and soon reached camp.

She joined the rheos at breakfast. Water from the field-suit purifier and one of the last protein supplements made her breakfast. Fruit and leaves sufficed for the rheos, but she would have to go back to the monolith and retrieve the EVA suit to get any further supplements.

The morning sprawled ahead of her as though time stretched to eternity. An unpleasant sprawl, a timelessness ruled by the timetable of the transformers and filled with unreachable thoughts, desires, goals, and aspirations. A time of frustration and doubt and endless self-conversation, and the morning had barely begun.

The whole camp stirred, Europa included with Agnes close at her side. The two of them inspected the site of yesterday's burial. They knelt down, with what passed for an ear to the ground. When they rose, they wore an expression Marissa had come to identify with a smile. Apparently, all proceeded as expected. They moved from the site, and other rheos replaced them and listened, but not everyone in the camp did so.

Marissa joined the crowd jostling near the earth patch. When she knelt and listened, she heard nothing. She rose again, disappointed, but determined to join in the effervescent atmosphere that circulated through the camp. As she dusted her knees, a sudden change in the whole camp startled her. Excitement bordering on fury charged the atmosphere. A flurry of activity followed.

A phalanx of rheos headed by Savage surged away from the camp and through the wickabrush toward the monolith. Marissa had no idea what caused this spurt and groped for her field glasses.

"Another Personality has arrived on this planet," Ez informed her.

"What?"

"I said there's another personality. It has opened channels of contact. The consort of that Personality wishes to meet you."

"When did they arrive?"

"ETA occurred two hours ago. A small ship slipped through the net. So far they have either gone unnoticed, or notice stopped at a low level of urgency."

"Why didn't you tell me?"

"I didn't know until just now."

"Where are they?"

"On the near side of the monolith. Otherwise we would have received a weaker signal."

"That's where the rheos went?"

"Possibly."

"Let's go."

"One more datum."

"Yes?" Marissa paused in mid-stride.

"I've encountered this Personality before."

"Before?"

"Yes, the Personality once belonged to N'Bert."

"N'Bert?" Shock raced though Marissa. "Here?"

"Yes, though it is no longer carried by him. I cannot determine his current whereabouts."

"Of N'Bert, but no longer with him?"

"Yes."

"We'd better check this out."

"Then you need to hurry before the rheos harm the consort. Your advent here has made them more volatile."

Marissa ran after the phalanx of rheos pushing their way through the underbrush. She yelled and made deliberate noise as she jumped through the knee-high stickers and prickly leaves, bounding after the rheos.

Chapter Twelve - Finding Friends, Old and New

"There is flattery in friendship."
-Henry V, III vii

"O World! World! World! Thus is the poor agent despised."
-Triolus and Cressida, IV v

"Those friends thou hast, and their adoption tried,
Grapple them to thy soul, with hoops of steel."
-Hamlet, I iii

When Marissa at last reached the rheos a short distance from the monolith, they had closed ranks and surrounded something or someone. She tried to push her way past the herd, but these solidly built warriors, defenders of the people, proved more massive and immovable than she anticipated. Marissa wedged herself alongside Savage and tapped his flank for attention. He glanced back at her, and then moved, bumping her lightly, but almost throwing her off her feet. At his signal, the group of rheos parted, and a gap widened to reveal the person in their midst.

A short, bearded man stood in the ring of rheos and smiled broadly. His lack of statue marked him as unusual. In addition, he wore something long and red that most resembled a jumble of rags. This garment had no obvious holes and revealed no part of the man's flesh from ankle to neck, despite the array of tendrils that flew out every time he moved an arm or leg. His movements provided plenty of opportunity to observe the flow of his garment, for no sooner had she set eyes on him, than he spun into some elaborate dance or ritual that made no sense to her.

The eccentric clothes and odd dance aside, the man's strange beard enchanted her. Nearly as long as he was tall, the thick beard consisted of tight braids. The intricate weaving of the hair caught the light and cast it back until she half-gasped and half-laughed. A picture rippled across it. There, a little man stood in a circle of strange horse-like things and greeted a woman.

Marissa wanted to applaud. "Did you see that, Ez?"

133

"Sensors are on. I have enough data to determine planet of origin."

The little man beamed. "How wonderful to hear Standard, one of the many languages of protocol."

"This person," Ez continued, "from his appearance and behavior, is from Strygix. The inhabitants, except for the ambassadorial assistants, rarely leave the planet."

"The honor of claiming the planet Strygix as one's most humble home belongs to this lowly one." He bowed. "Please extend to this agent the courtesy to accepting introductions," –here he executed a short bow— "and to inform this agent of the appropriate cognomen, if that protocol is appropriate on this world."

Rising on his toes, he stretched his arms toward the sky, and the folds of his ragged clothing shifted around his arms. "The appellation most applicable is Galen, of the planet Strygix, ambassador only of this self. Fourth-degree-seeker-after-Truth, neither of the party Equivocator, nor partisan to the Prevaricators, seeking Truth in the positive rather than the negation."

"What?" Marissa stared at him, stunned by both his flowery phraseology and his rush of words.

A pirouette showed the little man as surprisingly light on his feet. The robes swirled around him in a dazzling display of color. The rheos nearby backed away a little, eyes wide and nostrils flared.

"He," Ez spoke in her ear, "comes from a planet philosophically devoted to the pursuit of the truth. Hence, they rarely leave the planet. Rumor has it that the majority party on the planet seeks truth through negation of all true statements. When they discover the true statement that cannot be negated, they have found the truth. As a result, they have developed an elaborate protocol to facilitate communication where every spoken word is a veritable negation of the intent."

"Galen of the planet Strygix." This time the little man sang in a light airy tenor.

Puzzled, she stared at him. "Why are you singing?"

He stopped, looking a trifle crestfallen. "In some worlds, the protocol for introductions is to sing. Such is not this world? So be it. Perhaps the inadequacies of the initial communication stem from inappropriate presentation. If introductions via song are expected and not received..."

"Fine, fine." Marissa dismissed his explanation with a wave. "What are you doing here?"

"Seeking the essence of Truth through the eternal seeker. " Here he bowed low, almost touching the ground. "Oh illustrious Mentor, to be in this presence delights and informs."

"Me?" Startled, Marissa blinked.

134

"Indeed, most exalted one."

He couldn't be serious. She had never seen him before or even heard of Strygix. A joke? What had Ez said? Something about liars? Yes.

"Ez, my personal assistant informs me that you come from a planet of prevaricators and equivocators, two liars. Are you one?

Galen smiled again. "It is always good to meet someone who knows of the home culture. No indeed, this agent is neither. Not even in the slightest. The ambassadorial staff are taught to cloak all communications in the appropriate draperies, but never, never, never to purposefully convey falsehood. How can one hope to gain the Truth, if one utters falsehood? No, while meaning may be obscured through deft use of the means of communication, it certainly must not be derailed."

"Hey, slow down a moment. Can't you answer simple questions without burying me in words? "

Galen fell silent, but bobbed up and down in place.

"You say you came to find me?"

"That is the mission assigned. Precisely."

"Do you know who I am?"

"Not at all. Not even the slightest hint or clue."

"Then how could you be looking for me?"

"Oh, the mission did not specify a person by name. Rather, it entailed locating a person at this place."

The rheos behind Marissa shuffled fretfully. She turned to Savage, wondering how and what to tell him, especially when she didn't know anything.

Ez, as ever anticipating Marissa's need, opened up an outside channel, and hissed, moaned, and squeaked. At the same time, she spoke to Marissa. "If common translation protocols work, I think I've just told him that you are meeting another voyager."

Savage took a surprised step back, bellowed, and then rose on his hind limbs. Some of the other rheos did likewise. Marissa recalled this as an expression of high hilarity, so either they found the situation enormously funny, or Ez had erred a little on the translation. Savage called out something.

"When did you learn the rheo language?"

"Observation and analysis while you were otherwise occupied. However," a sheepish Ez continued in a small voice, "my translation protocols did not take into account tonality and inflection. The translation of that phrase is 'Sand apples, dung of the flying things, cloud cycle back and forth, rainmaker.' That's as best I can make out. I will continue processing in the meantime."

A language. The rheos had a language. Surely, no one could argue that with a language and rituals such as she had witnessed at the birth of Europa's child, the rheos were not intelligent. No one could possibly dismiss a language. Then Marissa remembered the old reports about birds, dolphins, and apes. Birds mimicked human speech. The other creatures had been taught sign language of a sort, but while considered intelligent by some, others had refused to accept this as evidence of sentience. Perhaps, with Ez's help, she would yet make her case. That is, if they all survived to do it.

Savage's signal to the rheos drew her attention back to the little man and the problems at hand. The rheos all turned away and ambled toward Home-4. Savage signaled to Marissa with an embracing gesture, indicating that the two humans should follow.

She raised an arm as a sign of assent and turned to Galen. "I'm Marissa Latham." He acknowledged her introduction with a sweeping bow, careful to fold his beard close to his body. "You and I have been invited to return to camp."

"How wonderful! What delight to accompany the Mentor wheresoever the course might wend to pursue this enlightening discourse."

As they wandered through the tall grass, Galen had to pull at his robes from time to time to remove them from some tangle. Each such motion stirred a flight of flitterwings and annoying black midges.

"You say you came looking for me?"

"One would not be nearer the point were one standing upon it."

"How did you know I was here?"

"In truth, no fact identified the Mentor expressly."

"Then how could you be looking for me?"

"Instructions led here, oh most savant."

"Instructions? From who?"

"Such acumen, such brilliant precision—like the finest surgeon, piercing to the very core of the matter, laying aside skin, muscle, and bone to probe at the very vitals of the mystery."

Marissa smiled uncertainly. "Does that mean you're not going to tell me?"

"Not at all, not a thought of it. Indeed, the entire story has already taken shape, and it remains only to convey it." Galen stroked his beard.

She waited for a response. After a long minute of walking through the brush and tugging now and then, he twirled an arm in the air. His clothes suddenly transformed from swirling rags to the equivalent of a latex suit, yet showed no specific feature of his body. It stuck sinuously close to his skin and did not catch on the brambles. In addition, his beard twisted, writhed, and reformed, replacing the image of greeting with an abstract geometric.

"How do you do that?"

Galen looked at her with interest and then grabbed her hand. "Some questions are too deep for philosophers and seekers."

"Do you mean you don't know?"

"Again the Mentor strikes to the core."

"You must know. You did it."

"Truthfully, all this required is to inform one's assistant, and that one did the rest."

"So you have responders."

"It is as expressed."

Now, Galen almost danced along, taking obvious delight in the things around him. After five minutes more, Marissa halted and decided to try the direct approach. "So, you said you'd tell me how and why you came to seek me."

"Yes, indeed. Does the illustrious teacher ask to hear this tale, a tale of some length and some enormous depth? Indeed, a tale fit to be the tale of one of the ambassadorial staff."

"Well, how long a story is it?"

"Exactly as long as it need be for the occasion."

"Could you reduce it to the essentials?"

"Indeed, the possibilities for brevity are boundless, but then the tale would not retain the fullness of truth."

"Let me savor the fullness some other time. Right now, I'm in a crisis, and I have to figure a way out of it. That way out may be your ship."

"Alas for that, small couriers transport ambassadorial staff and depart at once. This agent can offer no vessel to remove anyone from this world. Surely, the Mentor's arrival must also mean conveyance?"

"Members of the Ambassadorial staffs," Ez whispered, "are often dropped on-world to save time and expense. Their tenures on any given planet are perpetual. There is no reason to provide a means off-world."

"Devos," Marissa hissed under her breath.

"Nevertheless," Galen continued, "the story." He reached down to a pouch alongside his thigh and pulled an object from it. "To the very essentials, to the core and essence of this tale. A man of only the briefest acquaintance had need to disappear quickly. This man further intimated that the persons of the planet Arden needed an ambassador. An inquiry, regarding the authority to make this request and why it did not come through proper ambassadorial channels, resulted in the response that the involved protocol required too much time for that. Obvious and imminent crisis waited on Arden.

"Naturally, by the oath of an Ambassador, all are bound to serve those most in need, and the man prevailed upon that very oath. To repeat the request, 'The people of Arden need what I am giving you.'"

Galen held out an object, a large flat disc with a thick band like an ornate bracelet covered with gemstones. It shone a dull gold in Arden's morning sun.

137

He slid his hand through the band to demonstrate how to wear it.

"So who was this person?" Marissa stared at the object, puzzled.

"One of a pair who had caused much fuss in recent days with some of their activities. Through some chipslip, the man's companion let archival footage of an expedition to this very planet escape into the net. This created a major commotion in some of the more loosely allied planets."

"Footage? This planet?" Marissa frowned. "That doesn't make sense." So far as she recalled, the records had never been logged or recorded.

Galen slipped the device from his hand and offered it to Marissa. "This belongs to the person found on Arden, by order of its previous owner. A locator. The man said to bring it to the place in the large rock and that it would take the operator wherever that person wished to go."

"Did he mention my name?"

"Not in that context. However, the cognomen did come up in another more criminal and less flattering light, but the man expected that someone would be at this place. Further hints implied that if this person found the way back, the man did not say from where, the person might be here. Nevertheless, the man did not say to look so much for a particular person as for anyone, because many would soon be gathering here when they found a way through the barrier."

"Naturally, an Ambassador makes way through any but the most impossible barriers. That is the charge of ambassadors."

His story made no sense to Marissa. According to him, someone had given him the equivalent of a magic carpet. Was she, like Queen Titania, 'to be drawn by a chain of atomies' to some other world? She shook her head. The pieces didn't fit. Some mysterious person sent this fool on a useless errand.

Galen essayed a smile. "N'Bert Fashvoralian, physicist, member of the Thousand Worlds Committee on Standards in Science, and now a fellow seeker of truth, and Sylvic Prentiss, Crossroads Archivist and fellow companion to the most honored Fashvoralian."

Marissa's eyes widened. "What did you say?"

"Fashvoralian and Prentiss, more familiarly N'Bert and Sylvic, the ones who fled. N'Bert provided this." He pointed to the locator now held by Marissa.

"That's impossible."

"The same net that caught Marissa Latham sought them as well. Blameless, they suffered blame, as did Latham. There could be no witness, no matter how trusted, who was not under supervision. N'Bert had good cause not to want that. As did Sylvic. Or so they said."

"Sylvic? Impossible. N'Bert and Sylvic?" Visions of the spiky haired archivist rose before Marissa. This crazy man spoke utter nonsense. And yet? Somehow she had to get more out of him. "But why would N'Bert send you here?"

Galen grasped a loose tendril of his beard. As he spoke, his eyes focused on some distant object that, apparently, he could not see well. "Mind, these ruminations from hints N'Bert let drop, are not complete servants of the truth. However, perhaps such speculations will bring one closer than silence." He twined his beard among the fingers of his right hand.

All of his pronouncements led nowhere. Exasperated, Marissa released an explosive sigh. "Anyway, get on with it. Why did N'Bert send you here?"

"There may have been many reasons. The ones most easily advanced from evidence of the man's own words and actions are that a presence here was anticipated, and eventually the presence of many would serve to undermine the efforts of the Confederation for which this man now bore no great liking. However, more than that, in muttered breathings, in hints and asides, the man believed a scared oath as a scientist had been violated by turning over the truth for personal gain."

"What do you mean?"

Galen's twisting of his beard grew more intense. "Scientists represent cupbearers of the Truth, thus testifying to anything that did not suggest that truth, meant failure to fulfill their duty."

Emotions churned through Marissa. Things she could not name surfaced and sank again. She fought the urge to cry without knowing why. She gazed away across the plain to the monolith scratching the sky, a cloud marking the wake of the wound. What now? Who else had she harmed without intention?

Her last conversation with Tad returned to haunt her. She now saw with deep regret and horror that, while she might have been betrayed in some minor way, she had betrayed her friends in a way far more profound for all that it was unintentional. Bitter tears trailed down her face.

Galen studied her with interest. "Does the potential betrayal of the truth so profoundly affect one? Indeed, all must bow before one chief among its servants." Another sweeping bow threatened to stir the dusty ground with his magnificent beard, but missed by mere millimeters.

The incongruity of his words, of the man himself, indeed of the entire situation struck Marissa with shocking swiftness. She laughed, but the laughter bubbled through her, freeing her from the past and from the present, freeing her to look to the future and to see new possibilities there.

"No, Galen, not N'Bert's betrayal of the truth, but my own." Marissa shook her head and swiped the tears with the palms of her hands. "Did he give you any indication of how he might have done that?"

"Statements suggested that misrepresentation of the facts of the situation on Arden was the source. Regrets filled the man's countenance and colored all words with rue." He dropped the strand of beard that he had been twisting and, with a brilliant smile, turned to follow the now-distant rheos.

Galen's words left her with nothing to say. N'Bert recognized the intelligence of the rheos. He had hidden it for his own gain and then had to flee. Good. Then she realized that part of the responsibility lay with her actions. Triumph mixed with joy at the justice of the situation, followed by sadness at whatever lay behind it that forced his flight. N'Bert, despite her belief to the contrary, agreed with her. If she could have found some way to connect with him, to talk with him, to convince him, she might be in a better position to defend Arden.

In her mind, the panorama of this world played out before her, the wickabrush copses, the flitterwings, the evening firebugs, the drama of the birth of Europa's child, the wind rushing through the grasses, pushing their gravid heads down and back as endless rolling water over the entire plain, the patches of purple, dusky rose, white, yellow, burnt red flowers standing out here and there, everything that comprised Arden.

Galen ceased his skipping steps and faced her. His arms hung at his side, and even the pattern on his beard remained static. N'Bert had sent an ally and an object, but what did they mean and how could she use them?

A renewed determination to save Arden and all it contained swept over her. "Galen, I need your help."

"Indeed, there is nothing that would be a source of greater pleasure." He smiled the most radiant smile Marissa had ever seen. It warmed and delighted her, offering hope for the future.

"Thank you." His willing words reassured her even though she hesitated to place her half-formed scheme before him. "You don't even know what I'm going to ask."

"It does not matter. As long as it aims for the Truth and does no harm on its way, it can only be an improvement in the situation."

"Well, I guess that's one way of looking at it." She stopped and placed a hand on Galen's shoulder to halt him. "I need to save this planet."

"Assuredly, the very mission."

"I don't know how to do it."

"That presents a most perplexing problem. Perhaps others may know."

"Yes, but to reach them, I need to get off this planet."

"Surely the advice of that Personality who so eloquently translated..."

"Yes, she is working on it. But is there any other way? Do you know of some way?"

Galen looked at her, a long, hard stare that seemed to penetrate beyond her eyes. "There are only speculations, thoughts, miscalculations, imperfect representations..."

"Yeah, it isn't the 'perfect truth, but is it enough to get us started?"

"Error never derives from sorting fact from fiction," he muttered, chewing on his lower lip. "All problems may be solved by sifting through the facts at hand."

"Yes, you're right." Marissa nodded. "Science is a search for truth. We compare the results of experiments to our hypothesis. We sift through the facts available to see which need further investigation."

"True enough, but only one such..." Galen trailed off. "Nevertheless, it is the one available." He raised his hands together in supplication. "N'Bert spoke most explicitly when giving the object.'Seek the person at the large rock.' This was repeated several times. 'The large rock, remember, the large rock.' Perhaps it meant more than a landmark."

"At the monolith?" Marissa rubbed her chin. "Why there?"

He shrugged, sending waves through his beard. "Meet at the large rock. Perhaps it is the most obvious place. But the hint of a link with a strong field or presence or..."

"Anomaly?" Excitement coursed through Marissa.

Jumping high in the air in an intricate spiral, he clapped his hands. "The very word, now spoken brings it to recollection. Anomaly. Anomaly of gravity."

"This had something to do with activating or accessing it?"

"Most assuredly. Certain beyond certainty."

Marissa grabbed Galen and hugged him. "Thank you. Thank you, no way can I thank you enough. Just maybe we can save Arden."

"An ambassador's most pleasing task." He endured, but did not return her hug.

"Let's get back to the camp, say our good-byes, and prepare for the journey."

"To travel, one must have a destination."

"Let me talk to Ez, my assistant, about it."

Where indeed? She had no idea where to find N'Bert, Sylvic, Tesde, or even Tad. What a tangle. She had to start somewhere.

Chapter Thirteen - Port of Call

"You are welcome, sir, to Cyprus— Goats and monkeys!"
-*Othello*, IV i

"Your mind is tossing on the ocean."
-*The Merchant of Venice*, I i

Just inside the low entrance to the Monolith, Marissa, accompanied by Galen and Ez, pondered the entire undertaking. Could such a simple object as this 'locator' really take her elsewhere? N'Bert, despite their differences, had the credentials to make his assertions believable. Yet she still didn't know how to make it work.

In preparation for whatever she might find, Marissa had donned the EVA suit. The bulky suit would ensure survival whatever environment she encountered. Nonetheless, it could be a hindrance to any quick work needed. If Ez had the right of it, the suit would prove unnecessary because of instantaneous transit with no exposure to vacuum. However, Marissa's experience in the Anomaly had occurred in real space. In the end, the need for rapid action and the inconvenience of struggling in and out of an EVA suit decided her.

She tossed it aside. "Galen, I can't ask you to go with me."

"Naturally not, however, it would seem a necessity."

"Why?"

"An ambassador would always be a useful person to have along."

"He's right you know," Ez said. "They have all kinds of immunity. I can only get you so far. I've arranged credit and other things through my contacts, but when you're in the world, you'll have to deal with people."

Marissa pondered the advice a moment and then nodded. "Okay, you're both right. Galen comes."

She picked up the small package of supplies from the EVA suit. With the bundle in hand, she waved at Savage who stood at a distance, for some reason reluctant to approach the entrance to the monolith. He waved back, though Marissa could not recall seeing the rheos use such a gesture.

Crouching over, she led the way into the monolith. Galen trundled along behind her, clothing once again converted into amazing rag and scarf like shapes. The farther they walked, the deeper the darkness grew until Marissa turned on the portable lumina. In moments, they reached the large chamber.

She pointed toward the shallow depression near the rheo art. "Over there, that's where I returned. If Ez is right, we'll leave from there."

"An ambassador must follow where the mission decrees."

"How do you turn this thing on?" Marissa shifted the locator on her hand and sought a switch.

"N'Bert gave no hint of instructions, not even a whisper."

"Well, Ez?" Marissa tried pressing every decoration and gem. Nothing.

"Feed me the parameters"

Marissa ran the scanner over it and waited. "Ez?"

"This falls outside the realm of any known technology. I have no data on which to base a conclusion. I could experiment with it, if you like, but that may draw attention."

"Maybe if you could locate N'Bert's assistant?"

"N'Bert never had an assistant like me. His was an implant, and thus he blocked it at his discretion from the net. I could set out tracers, but under the circumstances, he isn't likely to be advertising his whereabouts. Once I thought this man carried it somehow, but that is not the case."

"N'Bert is hiding and not likely to come out just because we ask him." Marissa waved her hand around, passing the device into and out of the beam of light. "Well, make discreet inquiries, would you?"

Galen tugged at her sleeve. "How did the mentor arrive at this place?"

"I didn't find my way. I dropped through the anomaly."

"Yes, but surely the choice of destinations was not random. Naturally, it had an order to it. Without doubt, the path had logic. Why else would N'Bert expect someone to be here?"

"True,"—Marissa paced back and forth, trying to work out an answer— "but what brought me to this precise spot?"

"Precisely the question—a miracle of clarity." Galen twisted his beard. "Think," he said swaying back and forth, his voice deeper and soothing. "What actions happened before arrival?"

Marissa stared at him confused. "What was I doing? I was drifting in space."

"More than that."

"Dreaming, not really dreaming, but hallucinating. It's hard to describe. I had a lot of dreams. I drifted in and out of awareness. I floated along. The visions went on for hours."

"But," Ez interjected, "you came out at the instant you went in. No time passed in the anomaly."

"Dreams…" Galen shifted his weight from one foot to the other; His voluminous clothing whirled around him in a hypnotic swirl. "Perhaps, a dream of this place?"

Marissa frowned. "I don't remember."

She hesitated and struggled to dredge up the sequence of images from her dreams. Tad, Tesde, herself, and then what? Light? No, that came later. Arden. Yes, Arden. She grabbed Galen by the shoulders.

"Yes, that's it. That's it, just before I arrived here, I dreamed of this place. I dreamed of Arden, or the rheos. When I woke, I was landing or coming out, or whatever you do with this thing. Anyway, I wound up here, in this very place. That's it!"

Galen twirled and clapped his hands. "Surely, that is part of it. Yes, without doubt, part of the truth is uncovered. Once in the anomaly, merely dream the destination, and here one arrives. Assuming that what is in the anomaly connects all points."

"No," Marissa said. "I remember…I saw…Ez can you access the recording chip in the suit?"

"Not at this remove. I believe you left it in the EVA suit."

"Of course, I'll be right back." Marissa darted from the cave and nearly hit her head on the low entrance. It took only a moment to pull the chip from the suit and scurry back into the cave. She jacked it into the slot in her field suit.

"Ez, could you check and see if the chip recorded the passage through the anomaly."

"Checking." A pause.

"Ah yes," Ez responded. "It did, but it is very compressed. I probably won't get good images out of this. The time within the anomaly is as short as I told you."

"Can you get anything out of it?"

"Largely a blur."

"Devos." Marissa sought through her memory for that fleeting glimpse that lay hidden there. She squeezed her eyes shut. Blackness shot through with red.

"Ez, I saw tunnels, like roots, and fingers, that sort of went everywhere and connected. They didn't all touch. I remember separations, but the tunnels most of all."

"Perhaps the anomaly connects gravity sources."

"Of course, that explains N'Bert's interest in the monolith, the gravity anomaly."

"The anomaly," Ez continued, "might be a strange gravity sink—some sort of opening."

144

"Yes." Marissa pondered the possibilities. "So this depression represents an entrance. How do I make it work?"

"Perhaps," –Galen spun around once, his beard almost a horizontal flag— "think only about the desired destination."

"I doubt it's that easy." Marissa gave him a wry smile. "Just click my heels and say, 'There's no place like home.'"

At that, a picture of a gate flashed across Galen's beard, only to dissipate. "The temptation is always to overcomplicate. Sometimes, the simplest approach will suffice." Again, his words came in a deep, calming voice. "However, merely thinking of the place desired worked."

Galen reached out and took Marissa's hand. Warm, confident fingers gripped hers. His touch warmed her. The darkness of the cave enfolded her, not in fear, but in comfort and almost sleep.

"Think of the place sought," he continued in almost a droning voice. "Show this humble one this most wondrous of places."

"Go? Go where?"

"Satina IV," Ez whispered.

"Satina IV...is an anonymous world. A world of pleasure, of food, and shows, and gaming rooms, and beaches, and..." Marissa closed her eyes, aware of memories crowding fast.

Then, she saw Satina IV in all its variety and beauty. Forests and grasslands teeming with wild animals roaming at will, but never seeing or sensing the passersby, even if they stood within inches. There, she reached out to a passing fan-tailed coati as it ambled through tall grasses. Her fingers trailed through its fine, soft fur. Grottos with small pools of steaming water. Caverns overflowing with light, and crystals endlessly reflecting that light.

Something tugged at her hand. The locator bracelet on her hand grew warm, more than warm. The darkness around her shifted and then parted to reveal swirling, mist-thin walls, a glimpse of the anastomosing root network. And then...

Her nostrils twitched at a faint, tangy citrus-like perfume. Her palm pressed against a smooth cool surface. Marissa opened her eyes. She sat or slumped in a pouch of bright red satin with Galen tumbled next to her. The color and texture reminded her of the heart-shaped candy box Uncle Arga had given Aunt Mara for her birthday one year. He had bought it in a store that specialized in Old Earth replicas. So why a candy box?

The momentary disorientation passed, and she realized that she sat in one of the inner parlors common around Satina IV. She had never visited this sort of place before, but knew getting out might be awkward because she hadn't registered.

She pushed herself up out of the shallow depression in the satin lined rock.

As she did so, the drapes on the wall behind her parted just a bit, and she glimpsed several black and white tiles, arranged in an elaborate arabesque. She moved the curtain a bit more to reveal a flurry of tiles with a vague pattern. A sign.

She wanted to shout, but remembered where she might be. "Look Ez," she said under her breath, "a sign."

"In all respects similar to that on Arden. "

Galen pushed himself to his feet and shook out his robe. "Something has changed greatly. From bare rock, transit has brought luxury. Is this the desired place?"

Marissa smiled and took his proffered hand to pull herself up out of the depression. "Yes, now, we've got to register."

"Without question, those who operate such intimate pleasure spas require payment."

The parlor, like all such private chambers on Satina IV, had a wall communicator near the entrance. Marissa went to it. "Registration, please."

"Please," a voice responded, "follow the green number 3 footprints."

On the tiles in front of Marissa green footprints appeared. Pulling Galen along, she followed the glowing path. The prints wound from the grotto through a long marbled hall, across a garden, and through a fountain area. At last, they reached the magnificent onyx-and-gold-tile-paved lobby of the complex.

Light didn't just play in this room; it scampered in frantic motion up the wall and over the ceiling, fleeing the eye as fast as the viewer could follow it. A chandelier of cut diamond with an artificially high refractive index glittered above. Huge camelback sofas upholstered in something that shimmered and felt like silk dotted the lobby. From experience, Marissa remembered they never showed wear or soil. Across the surface, chank lizards in gold and platinum embroidery chased after the beautiful, but highly mythical sveltebird.

The check-in desk intimidated and almost appalled with its unrestrained decadence—onyx surfaces with inlaid malachite, separated with thin bands of platinum. Most dramatic of all, real people stood behind the desk. Of course, they had portables and personalities to help them, but here, without question, stood flesh and blood.

Although Marissa had been born to this, she had never really gotten used to privilege. Her family had usually avoided it. Her father had some odd notions about the 'distribution of goods,' which set him at odds with Uma, and some of the rest of the family. Though they could afford the luxury, her father refused ones like this. He preferred off world camping.

On a special occasion, a family wedding, a reunion, or some other event, he brought Marissa and the rest of the family here. Each time delighted Marissa, but also scared her a little. Everything looked so fragile and breakable.

146

Her father grumbled and jeered much of the time they spent here. Even Uma frowned during her brief visits.

All the specters of those years gathered thick about Marissa as she approached the reception counter. "You arranged everything?" she said sotto voce to Ez.

"I moved parts of interest funds from the rest of the family accounts into a new one. I even skimmed some of Uma's accounts." Ez's tone almost carried a titter on that last phrase.

Smiling, Marissa enjoyed the thought Uma would, albeit without knowing it, help pay for this stay. Across the lobby, a bellman studied her. She turned away, anxious not to be recognized.

"I'd like to register."

"Name, please."

"Ez?" she hissed.

"Lara Kingsella."

Marissa blinked. "Have you been reading Uma's novels?"

Leave it to Ez to pick an odd name. She gave the receptionist an innocent smile. The woman stood, fingers poised over a keyboard.

"Lara Kingsella."

"Voice print please." The receptionist swung a coder toward her.

"With blackest moss," Marissa spoke the standard phrase into the coder, "The flower pots were thickly crusted, one and all."

A green light clicked on; the receptionist smiled. She held out a glass plate. "Palm."

Marissa placed her hand on the glass. Again, the green light. The smile grew larger.

"Ms. Kingsella, according to our records, you requested a middle suite. Unfortunately, we have none available at the present time, so we've upgraded you at no additional charge. We've given you a suite floor."

Controlling the urge to let her jaw drop, Marissa nodded. "Thank you."

"This reservation shows only an initial date. Do you have any idea of your length of stay?"

Hands in her pockets, she shrugged. "I've just gotten back from a survey. I need rest."

The receptionist nodded and waited. Marissa fumbled for something. How long would it take to save Arden? Devos, she could always extend her stay if needed.

"Umm...say at a week?"

"Thank you." The receptionist punched the numbers into the machine. "You have a Personality with you. Please keep it under restraint. If it should attempt to enter any of the Company accounts or records, it will be disrupted.

We accept no liability for it."

"Of course."

The receptionist waved a hand, and the bellman responded. "Thank you, Miss Kingsella, please follow Mr. Reise to your room."

The man in the black and gold uniform smiled at her and waited with an expectant look. Yes, he was the same one who had been watching her. Shorter even than Galen, he stared at her with eyes like deep black wells.

"Any baggage, citizen?"

"Uh... no, I've just returned from a survey."

"And you, sir?"

"The only baggage one carries is the self." Galen smoothed his beard, and the image settled into a changing array of colors.

"Yes, sir." The bellhop grinned. "If you'll follow me..."

Nervousness reasserted itself. The sooner they reached privacy the better. Marissa wanted rid of this little man.

"Couldn't we just use the print-locator?"

He raised an eyebrow high at that. "At the Grand Satina, the guests receive only the best."

That and privacy. Marissa sighed. This man took too great an interest in her. She would have to have Ez check on him. With deliberate speed, she followed close behind him.

As they entered a dimly lit corridor off to one side of the lobby, the bellhop hung back. "I heard the conversation between you and your Personality."

"Excuse me?" Marissa stared at him, eyes wide.

"I overheard you."

"How?"

Any good hotel would forbid the use of amplifying devices. He hadn't been close enough to have heard the conversation, not from across that vast lobby.

"It's a kind of training—hard to explain. On my world, we specialize. If I understood your meaning, we're very interested in you."

Alarm made her wonder whether to run or listen. She looked at Galen, but he offered no help. She needed an answer.

"Explain."

The bellhop nodded. "Follow me. I've only the time it takes to conduct you to your suite to explain. They keep us on a fairly short leash, maximum output per hour worked."

With growing unease, Marissa followed. He'd better have a good explanation, or she'd maximize his hours all right.

"You are the Enunciator's niece and recently exiled."

148

Marissa suppressed a gasp. "We?"

"Naturally, we've heard of you. Those of us who do not agree entirely with our current Enunciator. She's taken to slurring her words."

Despite herself, she giggled. She had never heard it put that way, but it fit so well.

"One of the Organizers reported a SciCorp rumor that you might be expected back, but we had no idea where or even when to expect you."

"You know who I am?"

"Of course, probably a number of people here know of you. However, there isn't a lot they can do about it without bollixing up a huge number of contracts. This is a refugee planet which values anonymity, so you needn't worry about safety here."

"Who are you?" Could this little man, shorter even than Galen, somehow threaten her and all she hoped to achieve? Given a second chance to save Arden, would his precious 'We' stop her?

"We are the Deaf."

"The Deaf?" They couldn't hear? Surely, he didn't mean that literally? Hadn't he just said he'd heard her speak to Ez across the entire expanse of the cavernous lobby?

"Those who will not hear the Enunciator speak," he continued.

"Oh..."

His words made a weird sort of sense. Uma had more enemies than Marissa had imagined. They turned into a side corridor that angled away from the main body of the resort.

"But who are you, personally?"

"I'm called Oric the Ear."

"The Ear?"

"Because of my training." He pushed a panel on the wall, and it folded back to reveal a small track car. "Your suite is a short ride away."

Marissa signaled for Galen to enter first, which he did with a flourish of beard and flowing costume. She folded herself into the small, but luxurious interior. Pale green plush seats provided the optimum comfort. Murals of flowing trees and tropical flowers enlivened the side panels.

Oric took the seat opposite them, and the door shut with a soft whoosh. He punched some keys on the panel.

"Green Bamboo, Suite Lotus Flower."

The car accelerated at once and pushed him forward as Marissa and Galen fell back.

"We need your help," Oric whispered.

"Help? For what?"

"The Deaf have many factions—those who would overthrow the entire

149

system, those who want change and want it now, those who don't really want very much change, but aren't completely happy, and those who want the truth."

At the last words, Galen leaned forward. "The truth—indeed a noble pursuit."

Oric smiled, his whole face bright. "You are one of the brothers. Yes, a noble pursuit, and the truth-faction, is, if anything, the largest." He turned his attention to Marissa. "But your cause, or your expulsion, has become a beacon for all of us. If you would consent to..."

"I want the truth, but I don't want to overthrow anything, or hurt anyone, or destroy anything...well, actually I do. More importantly, I want to save a planet."

"Arden?"

Marissa nodded, pleased he hadn't said Crossroads. "Arden. I want to save it, both for itself, and for its people."

"Many were not heard on the matter of Arden, including Mikla Arden himself."

His words delighted Marissa. She needed allies, the more the better. Perhaps a diversion for Uma would confuse things enough so she could accomplish her goal.

"Would the Deaf help me save Arden?"

"Some of us would. I would, and I have a friend. We would regard Arden as a victory, as a first step."

Marissa clenched her fists. "It's the only step I care about right now. Will you help me?"

"I will."

As the car slowed to a halt, the wall before them opened. Oric leaped from the car and offered a hand to help first Marissa and then Galen from the padded interior.

She studied him, intent on determining his reliability. She needed allies. "I have no plan or rather I have a plan, but it isn't complete yet."

"Plans take time and require careful consideration. I'll bring my friend to your suite tonight. You can tell us what you want to do, and we'll help as best we can."

"Thank you."

They traversed a corridor lined with large black pots of bamboo and pictures of tropical flowers on each door until Oric stopped before a door with a lotus blossom at the end of the hall. "We'll be here at seven standard."

Marissa fished in her pockets for her credit chip, but Oric waved his hand and shook his head. The door slid quietly shut as he backed from the room.

Uncertain still, Marissa turned to Galen. "Do we trust the Deaf?"

"The proof of the pudding is without question in the delight of the palate.

Let the palate determine." He gawked at their surroundings.

Marissa almost laughed at his response. The foyer, with its sixteen-foot walls of dazzling white and a ceiling simulacrum of the turquoise blue sky of Terec could intimidate anyone not used to Satina IV. White marble with inlaid jasper and azurite paved the floor. A miniature black mountain rose from the center of the room and water cascaded from it into a dark pool.

"Let's get ourselves settled. I need some clothes more appropriate to this world."

"The truth needs no adornment, but that present garment offers no distinction. Many judge by appearances so it would show wisdom to change it."

With a wry grin, she left him to explore the suite and went at once to the freshening room. After she splashed water on her face, ran a brush through her hair, and put her suit in the ultrasound for a few minutes, she decided she had shed enough of the grime and stink to appear in public. With a deft twist, she pinned her hair on top of her head. Yes, that made her look different, more sophisticated. She also selected a filmy lime scarf from the hotel garment dispenser and tied it at her neck, not as well perhaps as Tesde would do it, but it added color. The hotel would add it to the bill.

Rejoining Galen in the sitting room, she stared at his beard. He had reset it to a geometrical pattern, this time an eerily kinetic band of waves and dots that, while it remained motionless, appeared to move. It almost made her dizzy.

"You know, Galen, that beard will annoy some people."

"The beard? Why it is a mere appendage, an addition, a decorative accessory—not anything to disturb the searchers of truth."

"Hmm, if you say so." Marissa grimaced. "I need more suitable clothes, if I'm anywhere."

"Lead on, illustrious one." Galen bowed and waved her through the door. It shooshed shut behind them and then gave the auditory ping that signaled all was secure.

Finding the panel that accessed the little car tunnel, Marissa signaled the next car in line. It scooted up to them, and the doors opened. "Do you recognize auditory commands?"

<IN SEVENTEEN DIFFERENT LANGUAGES,> the car answered

"Are you an AI?"

<THEY PREFER "PERSONALITY." BUT I AM NOT. I AM AN AUGMENTED INTELLIGENCE. WITHIN MY PARAMETERS, I CAN ADVISE GUESTS AS TO THEIR DESTINATIONS.>

"That's fine. Where would you suggest for women's clothing?

<HAUTE COUTURE, BAS COUTURE, NO COUTURE?"

Marissa laughed. "Just good inexpensive stuff. Not too stylish, but not completely out of touch either."

151

<GREEMAN'S PROVIDES A COMPLETE RANGE OF OUTDOOR GEAR. CHARLES'S SPECIALIZES IN INDOOR CASUAL AND SOME SPORTS APPAREL. JEROME'S PROVIDES CASUAL DESIGN FOR THE DISCRIMINATING TASTE.>

"Let's try Jerome's. They used to have good stuff that fit pretty well."

The two of them piled into the car and sped away. In response to her request, they soon arrived in the shopping district. Jerome's occupied a site in a center of high activity. A continuous festival park offered amusements in a plaza nearby, and many of the finer places to eat clustered in the walls that emerged from the plaza like spokes from a wheel.

Marissa pulled Galen, who fussed with the appearance of his clothes, into the building after her. They ascended to the twenty-ninth floor and emerged in Jerome's. The false ceilings rose to an apparent twenty-feet overhead; artificial daylight flooded in through the skylights set high into the ceiling. Music, just a touch too perky and bubbly for Marissa's taste, added nuances to the atmosphere. The murmur of other shoppers and the occasional sound of the credit transaction surrounded them. Galen gazed around, somewhat wide-eyed.

Amused, she smiled at him. "Well, what do you think?"

"Unknowable, unattainable, and strange."

"Satina IV indeed."

Together, they joined the traffic flow that swept through the store like a rip tide. She negotiated the currents and spun out of the tide still clutching Galen's sleeve, somewhere near the women's clothing and accessories. Once off the main traffic paths, aisles wound around the merchandise that clustered in little islands and on racks. Marissa began a serious search.

Sweaters, pullovers, dirndls, A-Lines, H-Lines, S-Lines, body-wraps, saris, and far more exotic wear filled the racks. She couldn't identify any pattern to the arrangement. Tops accompanied bottoms, silk Ashita's with their severe, body-clinging lines, nestled with MuuMuu's. Nevertheless, bright colors, modest prices, and sizes to fit her made up for any other lacks. Marissa picked out several tops and bottoms, and then chose one evening dress, a confection of black and white beads, feathers, and stretching cloth, that accented her in all the right places, and flowed over her body seamlessly. It made even her over tall, gangly form conform to the styles and tastes of the day. She started to carry the items to a counter when an assistant glided toward her.

The tall woman eyed the collection in Marissa's arms. "Perhaps, Madam would like to add the fashion statement of the decade." She held up a shimmery silk body sheath in silver.

Marissa grimaced. "Not me at all." She started to walk away.

"Ah, Madam, please. Consider the importance of appearances. Not only is this the latest Satina IV style, but it compliments your coloring especially when worn with this shawl." She deftly twitched a green themoweave wrap over the body sheath and then held the garments close to Marissa. "So perfect for Madam."

The shawl added a green glimmer to the body sheath. Neither suited the old Marissa, but this new Marissa looked again. A change of image wouldn't hurt. She added both garments to the pile on her arm. The assistant gave her a delighted smile and then turned to another woman at a nearby rack.

Marissa trudged to a checkout counter where she had expected a machine to process them. To her surprise, a tone sounded, and, in a moment, a person, an edit, emerged from a small door set into a pillar. An involuntary moue of distaste escaped her.

The saleswoman's automatic smile chilled Marissa. "How do you wish to pay for these: credit, debit, barter?"

Anxious to leave, Marissa pulled out her chip. "Debit, thanks."

The short blond woman took the articles and rang up the purchase. As Marissa watched her move, she revealed some of the flow of a normal person interrupted by the blocks of the edit—her movements appeared a little unfocussed and even a bit jerky. She must have undergone a severe edit. For a moment, Marissa let herself wonder about the crime that would have provoked this, but then she stopped, remembering if had she agreed, she might be in a similar state now.

"Thank you." The sales clerk handed Marissa the small, tightly bundled package. "We can have this delivered for you."

"No, I'll take it. Thanks." Marissa accepted the package and touched Galen's arm to signal a hasty retreat.

When they had stepped back into the main traffic pattern, heading toward the turbos on which they had arrived, Marissa leaned toward Galen.

"She was an edit."

He looked at her, surprised. "An unreal real person?"

"Yeah." Suddenly images of Tad and Tesde filled her mind. Hadn't Ez said they edited Tesde?

"Good news," Ez interjected. As always, she had an affinity for Marissa's moods. "I'm narrowing down the range on Tesde. We should be able to locate her soon."

"That's good news." Exhaustion hit and Marissa wanted nothing more than to return to the suite and sleep. So much to do, and she had wasted too much time on clothes. They had yet to stop the transformers and rescue her team members.

Chapter Fourteen - A Night at the Theater

"If this were played upon a stage now,
I could condemn it as an improbable fiction."
-*Twelfth Night*, III iv

Restored by a long nap, and a real shower, Marissa pulled on a loosely fitting saffron caftan. For Satina IV she had chosen a restrained and more tailored image than her rough and ready look on Arden. Faced with braiding her hair, she regretted having picked such a troublesome persona.

In the dressing room adjacent to her sleeping quarters, her new garments hung, almost lost, in a spacious closet larger than Uma's bedroom aboard the *Concordia*. Mirrored doors reflected the rose walls that shaded into a lilac ceiling. She made a face at the image in the mirror. Luxury did nothing to solve her problems about Arden. Uma had blamed the Delphians.

"Ez? What can you tell me about the Delphians?"

"Either a gentle people or the most savage race to ever scourge the galaxy. Facts are few."

Marissa coiled the braid of hair close against her head. "Ez, turn on the externals. I'd like Galen to hear this." Pushing a pin into her braid, she spun the blush pink vanity seat around. "Galen, would you join me here a moment?"

The rustle of his strange garment, now formed into something like a Roman toga, alerted Marissa to his presence in the doorway. His beard, however, appeared trimmed until she looked closer and recognized a new and different folding. He smiled at her.

"Your beard..."

"For the purposes of clandestine affairs, it is best to take the road of circumspection, than to be caught in flagrant display."

"Wandering around in a toga is circumspect?" Marissa arched an eyebrow at him while he caressed the loose folds of fine linen.

"Never mind that, I want you to hear what Ez has to say. We've so many different options, we need to start with as much information as we can assemble. Because the Delphians want Arden, I asked Ez to report on them. Ez, continue please."

154

"Little data exists in the Usian records. The Delphians are reputed to hail from an island world. Their initial settlement may have been people of Greek ancestry, but they could just as easily have been people with classical scholarly interests. No records of gene scans exist for Delphians, nor have any of their citizens agreed to submit to a scan."

Marissa scowled. "We don't even know for certain the home planet or the origin of this group? Uma said they had split off from us millenniums ago."

"My sources suspect the records have been deliberately altered. Something might be found with a thorough search, but it would depend on the skill of the researchers and their experience with tampered files. In a case like this, file reconstruction is a delicate and time consuming task."

"Don't we know anything factual about the Delphians?"

Silence followed. Galen stroked his beard and looked askance at Marissa. She shrugged and waited for Ez to respond.

"The facts, verifiable from more than two sources with substantial agreement between sources, are few. The Delphians exist. They have great influence in sectors outside of the Confederation. They expand that influence, and their sphere of influence has converged on Usian territory. They are considered a threat to security for unspecified reasons."

"Okay, so how do we remedy this ignorance?"

"Popular culture always contains elements of truth. The problem is to separate fact from myths and outright exaggerations."

Marissa patted the tight band of braid that now coiled at the back of her head. "Any suggestions, Galen?"

He stroked his beard and walked from one corner of the room to another, pivoted, returned to the center and turned ninety degrees. He made two complete sets of crossed paths before he spoke. "This excellent assistant has said it. When facts are few, seek those available and judge the truth or falsity against experience. A tour of the entertainment centers might provide data upon which to begin."

As usual, he took the long-winded way to advise action, but his words added weight to Ez's. "All right, you two. Tour it is. That means I've got to get dressed. Galen, I'll join you in few minutes."

With a low bow, he swept out the door and left her alone.

Marissa pulled off the caftan and shimmied into the silk body-sheath, which, the sales clerk had insisted represented the fashion statement of the decade. Marissa had wondered whether that meant days or minutes. No fashion statement spanned a decade. She pulled out the shawl of iridescent green thermoweave, and placed it over her shoulders, fastening it with the small brooch over her cleavage. Out of her field suit, she felt exposed, almost naked.

In the sitting room, Galen stood with his back to the door, waiting.

"I'm ready," she said as she swept past him.

<YOU HAVE TWO VISITORS,> the room spoke. <BOTH HOTEL STAFF. THEY HAVE NOT BEEN GIVEN ANY INFORMATION AS TO THE OCCUPANTS OF THIS SUITE, NOR ARE THEY REGULARLY SCHEDULED STAFF. PER YOU REQUEST, PRIVACY IS ABSOLUTE. THERE WILL BE NO HUMAN STAFF FOR THE CLEANING AND MAINTENANCE OF YOUR SUITE DURING YOUR STAY. WHAT DO YOU WISH TO DO ABOUT THE VISITORS?>

"Request ID," Marissa snapped. Fear added an edge to her voice. She turned to Galen. "You don't suppose they've found us?"

"Your question begets many questions. As, for example, who are the 'they' to whom reference is made? However, logic indicates—"

<IDENTIFIED ONLY AS ORIC AND BRAC,> the room responded.

"Oric and Brac?" Marissa had not expected the bellman to return with his friend so soon. "Open locks, whoever knocks."

<REQUEST CONFIRMATION,> the room prompted. <YOU WISH TO ADMIT THE VISITORS?>

"Confirmed." Security could be a bore sometimes.

The door to the suite opened, and the small bellhop entered, accompanied by a man who towered over him. The new man must have been six-foot five inches tall, but that paled next to the girth of his biceps; they strained his uniform jacket. Unlike Oric's black, he wore all white with gold braid. Short-cropped, straw-blond hair framed a square face.

"Seven standard as promised." Oric, eyes wide, surveyed Marissa with avid interest. "I almost didn't recognize you. That color suits you, and the hair makes you look a queen. "

She ducked her head, unused to compliments from any but Tad. Usually her friends accused her of using a fan to style her hair, and she seldom wore anything other than field suits. "Uh, thanks. "

Aware of her discomfort, Oric turned his gaze to the suite with equal interest. "This looks different from standard issue."

"Welcome to Arden." Marissa gestured with arms wide to encompass the foyer and sitting area. "I wanted to be comfortable so my Personality provided the images to the decorator unit."

Oric's interested appreciation of both her attempts at fashion and the suite improved her mood. The scenery of Arden always soothed her. The decorator unit had chosen just the right lavender carpet to simulate Arden's grassy plain. Wickabrush hedges rose halfway up the walls with a holo of the monolith in the distance. Cushioned rock ledges and boulders provided ample seating.

"Won't you be seated?" She led the party from the foyer into the sitting room and toward a cushioned ledge that served as a couch. Several side chairs

156

carved from huge boulders provided additional seating while stone slabs atop rocks provided tables.

Oric perched on the boulder seat nearest the ledge, then with a growing smile eased back. "Comfortable for a rock. With your sudden appearance here things are bound to move quickly. We want to seize the initiative."

"We're only just arrived," Marissa protested. "However, the plans for reforming Arden limit our time."

Before she could say more, Galen rushed forward. "It would be a pleasure to make the acquaintance of those not yet met."

"This is Brac." Oric gestured to his silent companion. "He doesn't talk much—to people. Says he hasn't much use for them."

Puzzled by Brac's white uniform and a little suspicious of his silence, Marissa wanted to know more. "What does he do at the hotel?"

"Masseur and physical trainer, one of our many services to maintain the personal touch." Oric replied. "A lot of people get more comfort from the human touch rather than a machine massage. Of course, there are those who say the machine is superior."

That explained the huge biceps and white uniform. "Welcome, Brac." Marissa smiled at him, not at all certain what role such a giant might play.

However, Oric considered Brac useful, but he couldn't be inconspicuous if he tried. The giant nodded, but remained standing, arms crossed over his chest. He made no move toward a chair. For the moment, Marissa decided to ignore him.

"So, what do we do first?" Oric hunched forward.

She hesitated a moment, How much to tell him? Somewhere along the line she would need connections and help to save her friends and Arden. She, Galen, and Ez could only do so much. "We need information in several areas."

As she struggled with what to ask him, somewhere inside floodgates opened and names tumbled out. "First I want to find Tad and Tesde." A flicker crossed Brac's face when she said the names.

"Perhaps one of these names is known?" Galen addressed the silent giant.

The tall man looked at him, eyes smoldering, and his arms perhaps a trifle stiff. "One name is familiar to me."

Brac knew who? Tad? Tesde? The pause lengthened. Marissa studied him, not staring, but nevertheless intent. She had to learn what he knew about her friends and would say nothing until he responded. Oric shuffled his feet against the carpet; Brac and Marissa eyed each other. The contest of wills created a palpable tension.

With a swirl of his toga, Galen did a pirouette ending on his toes. "One who is close."

Brac's face crumbled, the glaring eyes melted, and the fixed expression shifted. He eyed Galen with an open mouth, but almost as quickly smoothed his face.

"In every meaning of the term." A trace of a bitter smile played across his lips before he resumed something of his former impassivity.

"So the Truth comes from silence."

"You are a Verist?" Brac looked down on Galen, whether in respect or contempt, Marissa couldn't decide.

"So some have been called. Their doctrine is a guiding light. The Truth cannot be found in lies."

"Truth is eternal." Brac fell to one knee, and bowed, forehead to knee. "I am the servant of those who seek Truth."

Oric stared at Brac with wide eyes. "All this time, and I didn't know that."

"I learn something new everyday," Marissa muttered, still not certain who or what Verists were.

From the waist, Galen gave Brac a deep bow. "All who serve the Truth are servants worthy of leading. Would that all could so easily find the way!" Sadness permeated his words, and his toga took on a gray cast.

"Little man, my Verist, you don't know how much you already know." The admiration glowed on Brac's face.

Galen inclined his head. "Many thanks, please call this most humble one Galen."

"Master Galen, I am your servant." Again, Brac touched his forehead to his knee.

"This mutual admiration," Marissa interrupted, "is all very well and good, but what about Tad and Tesde?"

In one smooth movement, Brac rose to his feet. Again, his face had that closed, shuttered look. "She is close. I know where she is held, because I am committed to freeing her."

She? He means Tesde, Marissa decided. "We all want her freedom, but why you personally?" She studied him with narrowed eyes, determined to know Brac's relationship to Tesde. Never once had Tesde mentioned him. However, she had said little about family or anyone from home.

"Long ago her family promised her to me to unite our clans, but too, we both desired it. Then the Confederation called her to be part of the Program."

"The program?" Marissa stared from face to face, seeking an answer. For once, Ez did not respond.

Brac said nothing, Oric remained quiet, and Galen gazed at Marissa with a pitying glance. She stared from one to the other no wiser.

"All right, one of you had better explain."

"You don't know what the Confederation requires of your own people or the sacrifices so many are forced to make." Brac gave her a withering look.

"Sacrifices?" Marissa laughed, a bitter sound to her own ears. "Hey, they sacrificed me and plan to do the same with the rheos. I know about sacrifices."

One huge hand dismissed her objection. "Past history matters not. We share one goal, Tesde. Easily found, less easily restored. I have learned and trained for that purpose. They altered her, but I will undo those. You seek her. So do I. Our forces join. You bring the man of truth, the Verist. I follow the Verists, those who seek the truth. I give you my pledge." Brac inclined his head and remained so for a long moment.

An audible sigh of relief escaped Oric. "That bridge is crossed. Brac is often hard to convince, but once he's in, he's in."

"Amazing what you can do with connections," Ez whispered to Marissa.

Oric turned a quizzical glance in her direction. The others appeared not to have heard Ez.

"I am here," Brac spoke again, "to restore Tesde. I am in this place because Oric has said you oppose the powers that rule. I await orders. My strength serves your endeavor. You speak the word and I act."

Act, but to what end? With no plan and no idea what to do or say next, Marissa hesitated. Tad and Tesde. Tesde and Tad. She wanted Tad. "Hey, let's not forget Tad."

"Of this Tad, we know nothing." Brac relaxed back into his silent posture.

"Tad is to me as Tesde is to you. At least from what you said, I think that's what you meant."

"Then, it must be done. Where is he?" Oric looked relieved to see the conversation move toward action.

"On Cephus, but I'm not sure exactly where."

"Tesde," Oric glanced at Brac, "is important to all of us. She is a symbol of our rebellion. Many have gathered around her cause. That is why so many of us are here. Soon, we will take her. We only wait to determine how she is guarded and what precautions are needed. We should know that within a week. At first, it was hard to say—"

Sifting through his words, Marissa finally caught up with him. "She's here, on Satina IV? But where exactly?"

A frown marred Oric's face. "Tracked and noted. In service to the lowest of the servants."

"We can get her then," Marissa muttered.

"Once taken," Ez spoke to Marissa, "her loss would be noted. It might be more difficult to rescue others. You may not accomplish your goal, if you act too soon, or do the wrong thing first."

"She must be rescued," Oric said, as if Ez had spoken to all.

"No question." Marissa rose and began to pace, hoping the motion would aid her thinking. "But, in what order do we act to best disrupt the

159

Confederation's plans for Arden."

She stopped before Oric. He nodded, his face solemn, but said nothing. Brac remained motionless, arms crossed on his chest, not giving the slightest sign he had heard or understood any of this.

Ripples raced across Galen's beard. "The order in which events transpire must correspond to the order most precisely determined to accomplish the task at hand."

Fascinated by them, Marissa grinned. "Thanks for clarifying that." She again faced Oric. "Because Tad is on Cephus and Tesde is here, we should rescue him first."

"Do you know his precise whereabouts," Oric asked her. "How will you get to Cephus? We have no allies there."

"In a few hours we'll have the location. I might be able to sneak in and out..." Marissa stopped; she didn't want to discuss the locator or the anomaly just yet. The fewer who knew about those, the better.

"If you know his location and have a plan,"—Oric looked toward Brac and then back to Marissa—"we could act at any time, then we can rescue Tesde."

"My goal is to rescue my friends first and cause disruption later." Marissa skewered first Oric and then Brac with the infamous Marissa look.

"Tesde," Brac insisted.

Touching one of his massive arms gently, Marissa could almost feel the nanos pulsing under the skin. "But you want more than rescuing Tesde. You want to damage the cause that imprisoned and changed her. Arden is at the heart of that. I don't know why it's so important to the Delphians. I have to find out."

Brac nodded, then fell silent.

"Ez, my personal assistant, has it in hand. She's sifting through the collaborative Personalities. Until she finishes, we can't plan any rescues, Tad or Tesde. So since Galen and I were about to get dinner and track down facts on the Delphians, we can all work on that."

"I know of places nearby where the food is plentiful and not costly." Rising, Oric took Brac's arm and led the way to the door. "Then we can seek out the Delphians, undistracted by hunger."

"Cost is no object." Marissa grinned. "This is all on Uma's chit—she just doesn't know it yet." That got a big smile from Oric, but no response from either Galen or Brac.

At the door to the suite, Oric stopped. "Brac and I will change out of our uniforms and meet you at the transport station. Say in about five minutes?"

Marissa nodded. The two men quickly left the suite. A few minutes later she and Galen followed.

Once away from the hotel, Oric, now clad in a fuchsia shirt and gray

160

slacks, led them through long and narrow paved paths. Here, outside and inside merged and turned inside out. They passed through a cave filled with sparkling daylight and bright sky, clouds, a May-festival air. Then, outside in the darkness, both under domes, and in the open air, the light of stars, satellites, and various spectacular oddities of human manufacture for the amusement of Satina IV's visitors pricked the sky.

In one quadrant, a contained micro double-star system swirled through the blackness, giving off little more light than a moon and shedding x-rays and gamma rays as the pinpoints of blue star fire fell into its companion black hole. Marissa remembered the day Satina IV harnessed both the energy of the gravitational fields, and the sheer exuberant bubbling of the gamma and x-rays to power the factories and leisure spaces. In another part of the sky, she gasped at a blood red moon.

Noting her open mouth, Oric laughed. "They shielded that moon from the natural light of Satina IV's sun and light it by a rotating source. Thus, we experience all phases every three hours. Wait until you see the meteorite shower. We have one every night in one quadrant or another. When guests tire of the night sky, they take a tram over to the terminator, and bask in sunset or sunrise for as long as they wish. The tram tracks the terminator around the globe. Or if that amusement palls, they can return to the light side and enjoy all the pleasures of Satina IV's day."

Despite her previous visits, the passages and extravagant spectacles still bewildered and awed Marissa. Technologies had advanced since her last trip. She remembered the long years of planning that had gone into the double-sun generator and the astonishment of all when it finally blazed in the firmament. All this just make to people forget the real world.

The human activities swirling in a dizzying array around her amazed her every bit as much as the nature spectacles. Parties, galas, festivals, plays, pantomimes, games, simulations, masques, balls, costumes, and flesh, all in phantasmagoric incoherence. Sounds that changed with every step—the clanging of bells, the blaring of horns, the splendid pomposity of long vanished music, each appropriate to its time and place. Marissa turned and, with each turn, found new cause to catch her breath. Satina IV catered to all the whims of every species.

"Oric," Marissa asked, remembering his acute hearing, "how can you stand all of this?"

"I filter it—easily enough done."

Galen trotted up to her and tugged on her shawl. "Truly a marvel of human interactivity. All of this and little or no discord. All cultures, all places, all times in one world. The truth must be near this place indeed."

Frowning, Marissa shook her head. "No discord because everyone wears a

161

mask, and it's hard to get angry at a mask."

Galen peered at her, searching her face, and then gave a solemn nod. "Yes, but even so, that the masks can so converge, merge, and be present at once."

At his woebegone look, Marissa cursed herself for dimming his enjoyment. "You're right, of course. I'm just a little overwhelmed. It's more than I've dealt with in a long time."

He laughed, eyes merry. "Sometimes you speak wisdom, an odd sort of wisdom that compares traveling through deepest space without a thought to this mere human spectacle. Odd indeed."

A course correction, an interesting analogy. Yet having her dark mood lightened nudged her toward action. Galen, philosopher par excellence, the spur to conscience. The thought made her laugh.

They continued down an alley lit only by red paper lanterns swinging above the cobbled walk. The burnt sienna cobbles lent the dim way a vaguely benign red cast further reinforced by light splashing against the sides of the russet buildings. Even the business signs looked rosy-gray. Ahead a door opened, then closed, and someone tumbled out. The vagary of the light made the sex impossible to determine. Untidy strands of hair hung from a coiffure stacked half as tall again as the person. A sound, vaguely like the breaking of glass, only deep-toned and infinitely more fragile and delicate followed the figure. Shuddering, Marissa recognized the sound from the vids.

She grabbed Galen and Oric and yanked them in the direction from which they had entered the alley. Brac trotted behind.

"What?" Oric glanced over his shoulder at the stumbling figure.

"Ventrifracts," Marissa hissed. "You didn't tell me this was the addict district."

"You could not tell?"

"No, and you didn't tell me they had ventrifracts. I thought even Satina IV outlawed trading in them."

Oric shrugged. "Not much is outlawed here."

"The only remaining channel open" Ez informed her, "is here on Satina IV. As a safe-zone, the trade is not mediated."

"It ought to be," Marissa muttered. "It's lethal."

"Surely Death is part of the Truth." Galen looked at her with raised eyebrows.

"I don't know about that, but this...this is too much to accept. Let's go somewhere else to eat." Marissa pushed ahead, anxious to put distance between herself and the addict area.

Did freedom have limits? She had never thought much about it, but the edits and the ventrifracts made her wonder. Why would a society create one and yet ban the other? Both represented such a dreadful waste of a human mind.

Were those who chose editing or addiction really any different? Yet what of people who didn't choose, but had it forced upon them? At that thought, the balmy night air changed to cold and damp. She pulled her shawl tighter and walked a little faster.

Phantoms pursued Marissa as she led the party back to better-lit districts. She now glanced left and right and occasionally behind the party, especially into the shadows. Brac's hand fell on her shoulder. She turned to look at him.

"I understand you." Nothing more.

How could he possible understand her when she didn't understand herself? Confusion assailed Marissa.

"We're approaching the theater district," Oric observed. "We might find something of interest here. Too bad, Argus the Eye isn't here. I can't read the signs from here, but there are probably vids and realies that would tell you something about the Delphians."

Sure enough, as they continued to walk, they encountered writhing multicolored signs showing men and women being progressively stripped both of clothing and dignity by tall, incredibly emaciated and elongated vaguely humanoid stock. One marquee, flashing in lurid red and green, carried a brief synopsis of the spectacle within.

"Experience the terror of enslavement," Marissa read aloud, "as the massively brutal inhuman Delphian strike forces take over your planet and you becoming breeding stock to fulfill their deviant desires and unholy appetites." She started to giggle; Oric's chuckle followed. Galen looked at them quizzically.

Marissa continued. "Feel the debasement of being forced to clean after the unholy feasts, the horror of feeding time, the terror of the Dungeons of Delphia where rites so terrible transpire that none dare breathe their names." By this time, tears of laughter rolled down her cheeks.

A look of utter horror crossed Galen's face. "This is truly terrible. Can laughter be appropriate and commensurate with this cause?"

Assailed by a fresh burst of laughter at Galen's reaction, she clutched her sides. With a struggle, the laughter slowed.

"You don't understand Galen. This is exploitation. This isn't giving you the facts of life on Delphian planets. It's trying to drag you in to watch a porno show."

"Why would anyone want to watch lies? Surely, truth is greater."

Marissa shrugged. "Perhaps for the thrill of it."

He shook his head sadly. "What thrill can there be in a lie?"

The little man often revealed the core of any issue and with such good grace, Marissa couldn't resist liking him. "You have a point." She wanted to tousle his hair, but didn't want to offend his dignity. Instead, she gave him an impulsive hug. "You are so good to keep us on track."

After the smothering hug, Galen backed away and eyed her. Apparently reassured she wouldn't attack him again, he bowed. "Many thanks for the accolades. May they serve always as guide and goad."

Marissa smiled back, suppressing the laughter that threatened to burst forth again. "May they."

The exploitation theaters drew quite a crowd, so they hurried past and entered the experimental district. Here, Marissa noted with considerable interest a blend of realie/feelie/holo/live-action. She stopped to read an ad. Less garish than many others, it merely scrolled written words that began to move once she stood immediately in front of the sign.

'Delphia, a paradise world, an apple with a worm at its rotten center. A beautiful field of flowers overgrown by slime-molds. A summer breeze with the tang of fish slaughtered by a red tide. Delphia, everything you would want in a world, and much, much less.'

"Let's go in here." Marissa started for the entrance.

"To what purpose?" Brac looked puzzled. "How will this enable us to save either Tesde or Tad?"

"I have no idea." She pinned him with narrowed eyes. "However, it may help us find something to save Arden." She crossed her arms on her chest, mirroring Brac's own stance. "Besides, I told you, we're waiting on information about Tad's location. Why should a little side trip bother you?"

For a few seconds Brac said nothing. "It should not. However, wasted time means one more hour of pain and servitude for those we seek."

Like Galen's words, Brac's hit Marissa hard. Nonetheless, they needed information to act, and they didn't have it. "We're here to learn. Everything we know will help us, even if what we know isn't accurate. I had never heard of Delphia, but it's at the root of Arden's problems. Now the public also shares that interest."

Oric nodded. "Actually this boom occurred only about two or three days ago. No one knows where it comes from, but it's the most popular attraction in the Fedworlds now."

"Data shows that the interest grew from a faction on Cephus," Ez spoke in Marissa's ear. "Earliest leaks appear to originate from a bureau dedicated to distributing scientific information. Verification is pending."

Holding up a hand, Marissa stopped the party. "Excuse me, Oric. I'm getting other information."

"As if I couldn't hear," he muttered under his breath.

She smiled at him. "Ez, would you track that down? We need to know who and why."

"Already looking for it, but naturally as in all of these matters, the net is very tangled. In this case, it appears deliberately so. I don't trust what I'm finding here."

"Okay, just get back to me." She signaled to Oric, Brac, and Galen. "Are we agreed on viewing this?"

Galen and Oric nodded; Brac stood, arms crossed. Marissa gave him one of her looks Tad said could pierce permasteel. "Brac?"

He eyed her, one eyebrow raised. "Did you hear dissent?"

Sighing, Marissa shrugged. "Don't you answer a direct query?"

"Not always, especially when an answer by words is unnecessary. Had you gone and I not followed, that action would have been enough."

Exasperated, Marissa faced him, determined to make him understand. "No Brac, you're wrong. If we're working together, I need to know that you're with me, or if you disagree, why you do."

"Understood and agreed. I will try to comply in the future."

With that, the four of them approached the box office of the theater. Marissa purchased tickets for the next show, which began in a little more than an hour. "We have a chance to get a bite to eat. Any suggestions."

"I know a place not far from here," Oric said.

He led them to a small, crowded bistro that served sandwiches and other hand foods. The hot filling meal cost surprisingly little. Marissa relished getting a bargain almost as much as eating the delicious food, but regretted not spending more of Uma's money. The whole group left more at ease and a good deal happier than when they entered. They retraced the path to the theater.

It had been a long time since Marissa had last attended any live theater. Few existed anymore. Other media had replaced live actors.

In the lobby, they passed through the crimson curtains that draped the pilasters of a gold-leaf facade. Small black rectangular doors opened into the theater. Marissa had asked for the best seats possible, and so wound her way to the door marked Orchestra A-F. An attendant, once again a human, something she had begun to like, directed them to the front of the largish theater.

Marissa and the others followed a woman in a shimmering mock-translucent scale-wrap. Another attendant further down checked their ticket stubs again and guided them to a place in about the middle of row C. Marissa directed Galen to one side of her and Oric and Brac to the other.

Galen leaned close to her. "What manner of ritual will we see?"

"It's not a ritual, Galen."

"This is a theater?" He almost yelped.

Marissa held a finger to her lips. "Yes, of course it is."

"Then it is a place of ritual."

She just looked him, saying nothing for a moment. "What do you mean?"

"All theater is ritual. All meaning in theater comes from the interplay between audience and performer. It is a ritual to seek the truth."

"We don't view theater in the same way."

Galen stared at her, surprised. "How can you not? Theater is the same wherever it is."

"We look at theater as entertainment."

His face broke into a broad smile. "Ah, how very clever. You delude yourselves into acceptance by saying that the reality presented does not matter. What clever ways you find to the truth."

Arguing with Galen did no good so Marissa sighed. "Enjoy the show."

A resounding clattering vibrated through the theater. The lights dimmed and then flashed out. From a central stage, a vibrant string of light stretched toward the high ceiling. The clattering rose to an almost unbearable pitch and volume—the sounds of the wings of wooden locusts descending on crops, of winter-naked trees tossed by the winds, and, to Marissa, in a sudden, almost breathtaking realization, the amplified sound of the flitterwings, delicate and brilliant and terrifying. She tensed in her seat as the volume rose and the glare intensified.

Silence followed so not even the sounds of the other members of the audience reached her. The light on the central stage pulsated, throbbed, and grew uneven. It became a slit in the blackness of the theater, and from it stepped a figure, not identifiable as either a man or woman and not completely visible or well formed,

A voice, thinner than the beam of light and as uneven, in a hoarse whisper started to sing. To sing, of all things. The drama riveted Marissa. The theater no longer existed, only the voice, the light, and the shadow figure remained. The voice rose and fell with the words spoken, an endless tide on an endless shore, blue light streaming and receding, a false Doppler shift, drawing the listener. As her ears strained to hear and to understand, she fell into the montage the voice created.

"Arms and the man I sing, who forced by fate and heaven's unrelenting hate," the voice trailed off and started again, "Achilles wrath, to Greece the direful spring of woes unnumbered, heavenly muses sing..." Again the voice trailed away.

Then in a burst of almost operatic brilliance, with a fanfare of clattering, undergirded by a swelling of some woodwinds and a widening and brightening of the light on the stage, the figure rose taller and threw off a cloak to reveal a shell-armored figure with a neuron-flash tube.

"None of those will do to set the scene for you. What is seen here is now. What you hear is what is true. It is easier to tell truth in armor than to talk truth in old words."

The figure gave a solemn bow and light engulfed it, blinding the audience.

166

The light flashed out, and silence returned, no music, voice, or clattering. A tentative scattering of applause not picked up by the rest of the audience soon stopped. With the hint of a draft of wind and a phantom brush of some fabric, faintly glowing figures fell from the ceiling of the theater. Several screams punctuated the silence. Marissa tensed, ready to run.

Brac jumped from his seat, but Oric pulled him back down. "It's part of the show."

When Brac settled back so did Marissa.

This frisson, the strange feeling that came over her as she watched, she had never before experienced. The events around her enfolded her, despite the confusion. Apparently this production proceeded by expansion.

A column of pale blue light broke the darkness of center stage. The rest of the theater remained black. Within the column drifted pale, transparent figures, floating up and plunging downward at the vagaries of some current. Each of the figures wore long robes that trailed behind them and carried a small box from which the sound of stringed instruments filled the theater. The figures swirled and whirled, careless and carefree, nearly colliding and then drifting away, in an elaborate and delicate dance.

As the dance continued, the figures slowed little by little for no apparent reason, but as they did, it became apparent they carried some weight. Attached to the back of each of these creatures clung a more substantial shadow, starting pale as the figure itself, and gradually taking on its own shape and color. At first a small hump or growth, they gradually increased in size. As the figures slowed, and the music became discordant, the lumps, now darkish-gray and coal black, revealed new figures. Each white form supported two or three of these dark bodies.

Then, the dark ones unfolded themselves and rose, hideously elongated and tall. They shrieked, and the crystal chandelier above threatened to fall.

No voice over, no narration could do this scene justice. Realization dawned on Marissa and made her shiver. A thrill of excitement ran through those around her. Close by, Brac tensed like a bowstring, taut and thrumming, ready to leap from his seat.

The theater went black again.

This time the light flooded the entire stage and spread out into the first few rows of the audience. About ten feet overhead a globe spun. Purest gold, the globe teemed with life. Coruscations and scintillations spread every direction over its surface. The globe slowed, and the swirling dangles of living energy faded. The surface of the globe changed from golden to deep brown. A small green ship projected a beam of gravitons, a rainbow of entrapment. Slowly, the ship towed the planet away and paraded it as a triumphant conquest.

Again the darkness. The light again filled the entire theater, and this time, no idyllic scene followed. Above and around and beside and in front, rose screams of anguish. Ephemeral figures passed before Marissa. She tasted smoke on the air and watched people led away by the hundreds and thousands, force-marched past her into valleys filled with cement-block buildings from which rose plumes of ghastly red and blue smoke. People entered the buildings but never emerged.

The theater spun and swam through a small window in one of these buildings. Inside, people dressed in rags, manned the cranks and pulleys that filled the building. Why they did this was not explained and what they were doing remained unclear. Every now and again, one of the people fell at their station. A nearby person dressed in a coat like roaring flames came by and pushed the person deep into the floor. The floor closed over them, and a cry of anguish arose from somewhere nearby.

Again the lights vanished. A thin slit of light appeared, and the figure that had narrated the beginning returned. "Others have seen all that you have seen. Others have heard all that you have heard, but seeing, they did not see, and hearing, they would not hear, and so they came to their fates. Let us hope these are not the same for you."

Once again darkness and then the theater lights came up. Marissa blinked, adjusting to the lighting. The chron on the wall revealed that better than two hours had passed in this spectacle.

"Well," Marissa said. "If that's Delphia, we have our work cut out for us."

Oric and Galen nodded. Brac gave no sign of having heard her.

Chapter Fifteen - Connections

"And thus do we of wisdom and of reach,
With windlasses and with assays of bias,
By indirection find directions out."
-Hamlet, II i

Sleeping that night, Marissa floated just above the surface of the bed. Dreams tossed and turned her, spinning her in the air, rolling her up into a ball, and stretching her back out. In the corridors of Cephus—corridors she had never seen before—lit by the same indirect lighting, shadowy deep-amber light from walls no longer smooth and perfect, but pitted and divoted, filled with holes and hollows. Cephus faded into dreams of caves, deep, well-lit caves, but still caves. Corridors wound on down into the bowels of the planet, down into the very core, where around them, bubbling and stirring, the core of the planet itself swirled. The magnetic field embraced, enveloped, and turned her around and around as she stood, like a player of a children's party game, until she did not know which direction she faced or in which direction she had to travel. She moved, first one direction, then another, in an elaborate dance of indecisiveness.

At last by stepping one way, she managed to continue her path, a ray of hope, knowing that if she walked far enough, the worst that would happen is that she would return to where she had started. So she moved, and, as she did the red, red core dropped away. The fingers of magnetism released their hold, and a path formed, a well lit path, but visible only a foot or so in front of her feet, which she studied as she walked—one foot ahead of the other, walking toward the light, through the dimness of the cave, searching.

Searching for what? What did she seek? She ransacked her thoughts, but nothing came to her. Why this strange, unreal place? It didn't matter. One foot in front of the other mattered, moving down the corridor, following the path laid out for her.

Then she found her destination and recognized it. A large black door in front of her labeled 'Destination' And behind that door? Behind that door the rat-a-tat hum of the machinery that kept the gyroscopic planet spinning, the

169

pull-string mechanism that ran this little world. Pushing, she moved the door, perhaps a centimeter. She pushed again, harder, and gained less. She threw herself against the door, and she lost ground, the door trembling shut just a hair. She ran at the door and jumped in a flying kick, both feet hammering the door. Again the door drew breath, trembling, hesitating, and closing a further crack.

Behind the door echoed rat-a-tat, rat-a-tat, rat-a-tat. Slumped, exhausted, and unable to push more, she leaned back against the door and...melted into it. It vanished and the mechanism of the world lay before her. At the center, strapped to a wicked-looking armature—Tad, naked and bruised, bound with wire ropes that cut both skin and armature. That blood made the armature slick.

How to free him. Tearing at the bonds would tear at him. Tearing at him would not free him. So, instead, Marissa flung herself headlong at the rat-a-tat world-spinner, the clockwork mechanism of revolution. She jammed a rock into the cogs and gears that clicked and whirred. The mechanism shuddered and then stopped with a loud clanging and banging.

<TIME TO WAKE UP,> a loud voice announced. <TIME TO WAKE UP.> Chimes sounded.

Blearily, eyes still misted with visions, Marissa reached out. She slammed her hand down on the panel that stopped the wake-up call. Then she unwound herself from the sweat-soaked sheet and struggled to her feet, tired and washed out from a sleep that gave no rest.

Showering under a fine misty spray that sluiced the sweat from her body in gentle rivulets, she sought to plan. Woozy from the theater spectacle last night, from lack of sleep, from the horror of seeing Tad, and especially the uncertainty about what to do next, she fought to reach solid ground beyond the morass of confusion. How could she plan when she didn't even know how to take a step, much less in what direction to move?

The final misty rinse carried a floral scent, freesia, or something sweet and calming. Marissa drew on a thick terry cloth robe provided by the resort, and went to sit at a small table in a room that overlooked a view of deep blue water stretching far out to the horizon. How she had come by this oceanfront suite, she didn't know, but it made little difference. The sight of the waves and the sun glistening from peaks and troughs filled her with silence, made a space within her where she could begin to rebuild. In this newly cleared area, the plans for the next steps only awaited a spark.

She spoke to the Personality in charge of the suite kitchen, and in moments a cup of steaming oulatte emerged from a small box on the counter along with two pieces of warm cinnamon-raisin bread, smeared with real butter. Picking them up, she savored the delicious aroma as she walked to the table.

Galen emerged from a room down the corridor. His taut robes outlined most of his body, but his beard stunned her. Instead of the textured tapestry display, he wore only a full, ordinary beard. He smiled broadly upon seeing her amazement, and sat opposite her without saying a word.

"Good morning, Galen." She said nothing about the beard, uncertain whether to praise or regret the change in his most remarkable accessory.

"Indeed it is. A morning for miracles and movement. A morning to begin new things and to end old things. A morning, in short, for a quest."

Marissa smiled at his energy and then bit into the warm bread. So tender and sweet, it melted in the mouth. It filled her with the spicy sweetness of the cinnamon.

"Yes, a quest, but I still don't know to where."

"To set off is to accomplish. To begin is to find a way to the end." Galen turned to the Personality and requested a drink Marissa had never heard of and could not pronounce. A dark, earth-scented substance issued from the black box on the counter. The steaming tendrils tickled her nose and made her want to sneeze.

"What is that?"

His repetition of the name did nothing to inform her. She let it go, too tired to pursue it.

Companionable silence stretched out for a while between them, arching its back, and curling, curling, curling around them, embracing them both in its folds. Marissa finished her oulatte and bread, and thought of asking for more.

"What manner of quest should be pursued?" Galen sipped his drink as he studied her.

"Manner of quest?" Marissa shrugged her shoulders. "How should I know?"

"One cannot know what to search for until one knows what is missing. What is missing?"

"Missing?"

She paused, considering the word, and then she knew what she missed, what she had missed all along, and what she had always planned to replace at the earliest moment. Tad and Tesde both. And now it seemed, Sylvic and N'Bert. And of course, the rheos. Friends all. Yet the emptiness that ached the most, the powerful vacuum of loneliness that could not be filled, that space she recognized had Tad's shape. Within her, that void could only be filled by a single person, and until filled, loomed infinite, ravenous, and cold.

"Galen, at times the things you say trigger the most interesting thoughts. I've got to find Tad, wherever he is." She lifted the empty cup to her lips without thinking and put it back down again. "Ez should have located him by now."

With an abrupt shift, Marissa rose from the table, and then suddenly recognized how rude her action might seem. "Please, excuse me."

"Of course." He sipped his drink and remained seated.

As she swept from the room, the hem of her robe dragged through the plush of the carpet and made a sound of wind in whispergrass. In her dressing room, she donned the clean and newly stocked field suit and moved Ez from last night's outfit into the suit.

"Ez?"

"Here," the reply came.

"How's our plan?"

"No full plan formulated. However, I know the precise whereabouts of Tad. He's in the core of Cephus maintenance."

" I need Tad. How do we get him?"

"There is no easy way into Cephus."

Marissa tapped a finger against the vanity. She picked up her brush, and dislodged the locator bracelet that Galen had given her from N'Bert. Setting the brush down, she picked up the bracelet and examined it, turning it from side to side.

"Perhaps there is."

"There may not be an entry portal on Cephus."

"Why not?"

"We have no idea who made or what causes the entry portals."

"But we also have no reason to believe there wouldn't be a portal. There's no harm in trying."

"How can you be sure? You might bounce off and wander in that collection of tunnels forever."

"I don't think that would happen," Marissa said, uncertain why she believed that. "I just don't think so."

Ez sighed. "As a true scientist, then you must try."

"I can't do it alone."

"You have Galen."

"He may not be enough."

"Could you ask—"

"Oric and Brac?" Marissa put down the locator. "I'm way ahead of you."

"Perhaps, but maybe throwing some confusion into the ranks first might help?"

"Confusion? What do you mean? I thought things were confused enough already"

"Why don't you announce your presence? Tell Uma that you're here somewhere."

The idea appealed to her. Even if it wasn't the wisest thing to do, even if it might cause trouble, or because it might. "That's an interesting thought. What might happen..." Marrisa's voice trailed off as she considered the possibilities.

A moment later, she set the phone vid to neutral so the other party would see only multicolored snow. She requested the line she wanted, and then gave an access code. Marissa listened as the line plowed through electronic background noise and at last connected to Uma's private residence. After a moment, a click signaled a vid phone switching to 'on.'

"Speak," Uma snapped, stern face set.

"Greetings from beyond the anomaly!"

The vid face crumbled into lines of shock, outrage, surprise, and, Marissa may have deluded herself, but hope. "How...How..." Uma began.

"The anomaly isn't as endless as you thought."

"Marissa, if it's you, let me see you. I've been beside myself."

A tight bitter smile crossed Marissa's face. "I'm sure you have."

Uma touched some buttons on the grid, trying to force the vid signal through. When she did not get an image, she would soon narrow down the number of places Marissa could be. Not all that many places offered vid barriers impenetrable to the highest access codes.

She cued a black, starry background, as a deliberate miscue, and thumbed the vid on. "Aunty, how lovely to see you again."

She had only called Uma Aunty when, as a child, she'd consciously tried to provoke her. If that didn't convince her, Marissa wasn't sure what would.

Uma's eyes widened for an instant, then narrowed. "What kind of plot is this? You can't be Marissa Latham, so who are you?"

"I'm your niece Marissa and can tell you what happens when you pass through the anomaly. I also know how to return. You ought to try it. It'll broaden your horizons."

"I don't believe it. Someone..."Uma stopped. Again, a confusion of emotions, joy, sorrow, anger, fear, moved from one to the other across her face.

"Uma, I'm back, and I'm saving the rheos. You can try to stop me, but I wouldn't!"

Among all the competing emotions, fury erupted, boiling to the surface and a trace of something—fear or panic came closest. "You don't know what you're doing."

"I KNOW what I'm doing, Uma. I've known since I first saw the rheos. I've tried to convince you. I'm doing what is right, the only thing that is right."

"You don't understand." The strain of emotion pulled Uma's face taut as she clenched her fists.

"Perhaps, I can't, so there's no point in continuing this. I'm back, and I'll do what it takes to save the rheos. Good-bye, Uma." She wanted to say something else, but everything she thought of sounded either melodramatic or mawkish. Instead, she fingered the disconnect switch, and the screen went blank.

173

A brief swirl of emotions passed through Marissa, triumphant exultation followed by a bitterness she could almost taste, and then a deep sorrow. She couldn't identify the source of any of them, and she didn't want to waste the time. The call had been foolish, an unnecessary, and perhaps vindictive thing. There would be repercussions, but how could Uma stop her?

What did Uma mean about she didn't understand? In this case that could hurt more than just her. She could punish an entire innocent Confederation of people. If what she saw at the theater last night had any validity—she didn't allow the thought to continue. She had to act, and to act, she had to have help—those who would support her, and whom she had let down in so many ways.

"Ez, what news of Tad?"

"I have his code. It has been changed, but it is not secured. I can block monitoring, if you wish to speak to him."

"What is it?" Anguish rose at the thought of calling him and some other desperate need bubbled within her. She paused for a moment and almost laughed. These tides of emotion exhausted her, but she wanted to talk to Tad.

"We might," Ez offered, "be able to get a better fix on where he is. I could trace the line and pinpoint the position. Once the connection is made, I can keep a leader."

"Then do it." She punched in the code.

"Hello?" The familiar, warm voice flowed over her, inviting her and saddening her. Then his image formed, as hers must also have formed for him, and she saw his stunned, drawn face.

"Marissa?"

"Hello, Tad." She choked. New lines etched his face; he looked sapped of vitality, wrung out and exhausted. A short time to have exacted so cruel a penalty from his body.

"Hi," she said, her voice weak. "I'm home. Or I'm back. Oh Devos, Tad, I'm here, and I want you back."

"Marissa?" He stared, her name his only response. Then some spark lit his eyes.

"Yes." She smiled through a threatening mist of tears, and he returned her smile.

"It's not possible."

"No, it isn't, but it's true. I have a way, a path, a secret that will get me to you."

"Don't try." The light vanished from his face. "They don't much care what I do here, but they won't let me go."

"No, they won't, but, like the rheos, I will have what I want." Marissa narrowed her eyes.

174

Tad laughed. "Damned if you won't."

The laugh broke her dammed emotions, and they flooded over her. "Oh Tad, I'm so sorry for what has happened. I'm sorry for everyone, for everything. Look what my people, my own aunt did. All over a planet, a planet of which there must be a hundred dozen. I can't believe it." Tears streamed down her face, forming runnels beside her nose.

On the screen Tad lifted a hand as if to touch the tears and dry them. "Don't cry."

"Don't ask me to stop. I've had tears stored up inside forever. Oh Tad..." With nothing left to say, she let the tears flow.

"Marissa..." Tad began. "Marissa, come on."

"Do you have a fix, Ez?"

"Fix and lock."

"Tad, we know where you are, we have a fix, and I'm coming to get you."

His eyes widened. "No, I'm under constant guard." He glanced over his shoulder, then back at her. "Fenster," he whispered.

It saddened Marissa to hear one more familiar name dragged down by her actions. "Even him?"

Tad nodded and glanced behind again.

"It doesn't matter. I'm coming, and coming soon, and Fenster and all the troops he can muster won't stop me. Expect me."

"Marissa..." he began.

"I love you, Tad, and I'm coming for you. Be patient. Expect me." Marissa jabbed her finger at the disconnect, and the screen went blank. "It's done."

"And well done."

"Where is he, Ez?"

A short pause followed. "Bioregeneration Tech on Cephus."

"Where?" Marissa's lip trembled, and her hand began to shake.

"Bioregeneration."

"No!"

No wonder he had looked so wan. Bioregeneration labs developed, controlled, and deployed the bacteria that decomposed what remained after all possible reuse, recycling, and reclamation. It meant continual exposure to filth, radiation, deadly bacteria, and other hazards. Only a matter of time before...

"How long?"

"Since your exile. I only just now confirmed the sector and assignment."

"Damage?"

"Minor so far, but deterioration beginning. They've had him on the lower rungs, Marissa."

"Then we act now."

Chapter Sixteen - Rescue

"And there be souls must be saved,"
-*Othello,* II iii

"I must have liberty withal, as large a charter as the wind,
To blow on whom I please."
-*As You Like It,* II vii

The slide-click of the door mechanism alerted Marissa to Galen's return. He entered the sitting area accompanied by Oric and Brac. Ez had succeeded in locating and summoning the trio. Oric drifted toward the boulder chair at one side of the sofa and Brac to the other.

With a low bow, Galen presented Marissa with a white plastic bag. "Food powers the body. These come not from the machine and, thus, approach closer to the truth."

Peering inside the bag, she glimpsed fresh vegetables, exotics biodesigned for eating uncooked and small containers of dips and sauces. "Thank you, I am hungry."

"In difficult times, food always reminds one of happier hours." With another flourish, Galen sat next to her on the couch.

"We came at the summons of your Personality," Oric prompted. "It took a little doing, but we arranged time off. What do you need?"

Between bites, Marissa summarized her conversations of the morning and shared what she had learned about Tad. "So, we have to rescue him as quickly as possible."

A variety of expressions crossed Galen's face as he stroked his beard. "Even in such a place, if there is a way to it, there must, perforce, be a way out."

"Yes, there must." She frowned, absently twisting the white bag. "However, the way out of Cephus may not be so easy as the way into it."

"Why?" Oric looked puzzled.

"I told you, he's in the bioregen catacombs on Cephus. Not exactly the easiest place to find or to enter unnoticed, considering the precautions visitors

176

usually take there."

"True, yet those same measures could disguise us," Oric said. "We are unknown, or at least only obscurely known as some minor irritation to the Confederation. You may be another matter, but you don't need to go." He looked to Brac and Galen, both of whom nodded.

"I don't have to go, but there's no way to get to him in time to avoid permanent damage if I don't go. Even if you found a way, you couldn't expect me to stay here. He's there because of me so I've got to get him out." Marissa squashed the bag and tossed it onto the low stone table.

"We have no problem then," Brac said.

"Excuse me?" She stared at him, puzzled. Maybe he didn't, but she still had a multitude.

"You are resolved that he shall come out. Then he shall. We will do it." Brac crossed his arms on his chest.

This stolid, unmoving man continued to surprise her. Once on a course, no obstacle would stop him. Only dedicated allies could save Tad, and she welcomed aid. "Thank you, thank you all. I can't tell you..." More tears began. "You can't imagine...You risk so much to help me."

"We have sworn vows to save those innocents punished by the Confederation." Oric's words resonated, almost a battle cry. "Tad is one. He is important to you and will add to our team. Alone, we fail. As members of the whole, we shall succeed."

Eyes wide, Marissa considered them. "Whole?" She had never thought about others that way. In the past, she had relied on herself, or at most Tad. Of course on Arden, she had the team, but that had been Tad, Tesde, and herself against N'Bert and Sylvic. No sense of the whole there. Then, with the trial she had come to believe she had only herself.

"Wholeness." Tears overflowed. "Looks like I'm having problems today."

"A moment of the truth illuminates vast stretches of life unexamined. This requires celebration." Galen hopped, swirled, and changed both his beard and his robe as he spoke, a veritable one-man celebration of discovery.

Shaking her head, Marissa gazed at him with fond amusement. "Sometimes I'm amazed at what I learn."

"A condition for everyone who seeks truth," Brac observed. For the first time since she had begun to speak to him, he smiled at her. "You are a Verist at heart."

"I...I ...I don't know." Her, a Verist? "I've never thought about it."

Galen clapped his hands. "The truth is sometimes clearer in darkness than in light. Just as it is easier to say what a mirror is when looking at it without the image of the self, for distraction comes with looking on the self, but in the dark, the contours, the shapes, the nature of the thing itself, all are clear."

As always, sorting though Galen's words required thought and analysis. Marissa shook her head with a fond smile in his direction. "You have a way of saying things. Somehow you make me feel good about myself, even when I have no cause."

She squeezed his hand and mussed his beard a bit, but he smoothed it with a quick gesture. "Thank you, Galen. Thank you all. Now, let's plan how we proceed."

"May I suggest we seek the open air?" Oric moved his head in a slow arc as he peered around the sitting area.

For a moment, Marissa said nothing. She had talked with Uma. Security would be searching and, despite everything Ez might do, would locate them eventually.

Oric's caution hit home. The hotel staff might spy, but if they did so, they did it discretely, and to all accounts only for their own amusement. Marissa discounted even those rumors. If spying went on and the guest detected it in such a place, the hotel would probably not be in business long.

"Let's have a picnic."

* * * *

They sat on a wooded hill overlooking a stream just a little too silvery to be natural. The sun flooded the air, but not intense enough to make them uncomfortable. Clouds scudded along at times to provide a respite from even that as they cast mysterious and beautiful shadows throughout the valley below. The perfect temperature and breeze, of course

The four of them sat on a plaid woolen blanket courtesy of the hotel. Galen had plucked a few wildflowers and threaded them into his beard. They didn't look as ridiculous as Marissa had expected when he started his venture. Oric unpacked a basket of sandwiches, cold chicken, and fruits and vegetables along with the dips and sauces—everything arrayed in easy reach. He also added a small silvery device and set it the middle of the group. Marissa raised an eyebrow and he smiled.

"A precaution." He touched the small box lightly."For a short time, we can talk undisturbed, although I urge the appearances of a picnic for any visual snoopers about."

The conversation wound in and out of the difficulties of what they planned, until only one remained.

"So, how do we reach him?" Oric spoke for all of them.

With the locator, they could get to Cephus, but Marissa still puzzled over how to find Tad there. What if the entry portal to Cephus lay halfway across the world? How could they reach him undetected?

"I don't know. I don't understand the capabilities of this device." She twisted the locator bracelet on her arm. The stones glowed with a greasy sheen, but revealed nothing.

Picking the flowers from his beard, Galen smoothed it into a seamless whole. "As the device is present, it surely can be tested."

"I'm not sure we have time for that. It's tiring to use. If I have to use it several times, I might be too exhausted to get us out."

"If it follows lines of force," Brac observed, "those lines can be identified by place."

"What?" Marissa stared at him, trying to grasp what he meant and how that would change things.

Jumping up, Brac moved sideways. "Where I stood the lines of force differ from where I am now."

"So?"

"If you know your destination—you said you locate by images—if you know it in unique terms, you will come to the place you want." Brac sat back down.

"I still don't follow you."

"If you know the appearance of where you want to go," Oric reminded her, "you can get there. In a space ship one sets course coordinates. Maybe this operates the same way."

"Course coordinates? That sounds too simple." She stared from Oric to Brac and back. Both looked expectant.

"We can try," Oric urged. "If we go where we want to, fine, everything works well. If not, we return here at once and develop a different plan." Brac nodded.

"So, I only need to know what Tad's surroundings look like. Ez, are you listening?"

"Yes, I'm here."

Marissa began to pace, thinking aloud, "Surely the bioregen corridors are monitored. No one goes there voluntarily, so to keep prisoners, they must be watched."

"Prisoners are usually guarded," Oric said.

"Then," Marissa continued, "there should be cameras linked to a digital network, and to a system, if not a personality."

"Again, the truth, the exact way is found." Galen clapped his hands and spun to the right, ending on one toe.

"Ez, can you get me images of the catacombs?"

"The cameras and personalities there are not under high security."

"How close can you get to Tad's general whereabouts?"

"I don't know for certain. They don't usually transport the workers far. I can find out when he is on-shift and get pictures fairly close to that."

"How soon?" Marissa asked, almost trembling.

179

"Minutes."

"Do it." She turned her attention to Galen, Brac, and Oric. "You heard?" The three men nodded agreement. "We might even finish this today!"

"Since we have the time off now, this would suit us best. After all, we still have the matter of Tesde."

Oric's words shattered Marissa's enthusiasm, and it seeped away. "I had forgotten. For one step forward, we take two back."

With a quizzical look, Oric searched her face. "How so? Tesde's rescue has always been in our plans and this has no bearing on that."

Sighing, Marissa gazed at the blanket, not really seeing it. She plucked absently at the plaid design. "I thought the two of them had betrayed me."

Silence met her confession. All three men waited for her to speak. Overhead a single white bird stroked patiently through the emptiness of the sky. The blue of the sky became an assault.

"Not very trusting, was I?" Again no response. "Somebody must have said something for all this suspicion to start."

"Truth," Galen said, "Yet perhaps the someone was the self." His eyes held pity, not condemnation.

"No more." She started to gather together the things on the blanket. "I know who my friends are."

Oric slipped his silvery device into a pocket, then helped Galen to pack the remaining things away. Brac stood to one side with a watchful eye on the valley. He paid no heed to the chatter of the others.

Marissa approached him and touched his shoulder. "I was wrong. I know that now. Please understand...when you want something so much..."

He stared into her face a moment, his eyes glistening with some emotion. "I understand desire. I understand...betrayal."

"Brac, I'm sorry."

"You have no need to apologize." He turned away toward the others.

Esmarelda buzzed Marissa softly. "Pictures streaming."

"Thanks, Ez." The four of them headed down the hill to a small entrance tucked behind a boulder. They got into a hotel car, and Oric spoke the code for the suite.

Back in the suite, Marissa changed into a functional field suit and strapped on a couple of stun devices intended for field missions among hostiles. She placed a charger in the suit pocket and hooked it up. Everything else checked out. She opened the door to the sitting area and joined the others.

"All right, I guess we're ready. We're timing the jump so we'll be in the corridors only a few minutes before off-shift for Tad. Then, we wait and see." Marissa adjusted the wristband of her suit and slid the locator bracelet over it.

Galen, Oric, and Brac all wore gray jumpsuits. They reminded her of work

180

details she occasionally had glimpsed on Cephus. They would blend in well, much more so than her beige field suit. However, time was too short to seek another garment.

Brac uncrossed his arms. "Your plan, if we arrive, should work well."

"I hope so." She bound her hair into a functional ponytail and curled it up into her collar. "Well, I'm ready. Let's see the place."

Ez piped the image of the junction near the bioregen station to the large viewer. A huge brightly lit, but still dim, uneven white cave filled the screen. Gray mouths of relative dimness stretched off in three different directions. Niches and alcoves broke the expanse everywhere, but provided no real hiding places. Arriving too soon would raise the risk of discovery.

"Everyone ready?" Marissa looked at each man.

Galen again had folded his beard close to his chin. Oric rubbed his palms against his thighs while Brac stood motionless and silent. She took their presence as assent.

"Okay then, link arms so we're connected." She tucked her arm through the crook of Galen's.

Marissa closed her eyes for a moment and then opened them to focus on the screen again. She squeezed them shut, the image on the screen firm in her mind. With clenched teeth, she thought of Cephus and the biogeneration labs, then fell…

Once again passing through the traceries of wormholes, through tubes of color and light, so thin that the universe threatened to fall into them. Yet these tubes kept the structure of the universe together; they linked to one another like the fine skeleton of individual cells—fibers hardly noticed until seen. The locator grew warm against her wrist, or did she imagine that?

Too quick for further thought, Marissa found herself carried into a tube, propelled forward by some unseen force. Linked together, the others trailed along behind. Traversing the tube passed in a blur of branches that lasted an eternity yet took no time at all. Then…they tumbled out onto the white floor.

They had arrived in a small windowless room with roughhewn walls. A deep throbbing penetrated those walls—once heard, never forgotten. She knew at once they had ended in the central government building on Cephus, a building she had visited many times before. In the deepest levels Cephus' throbbing became the grating of bone against bone; thus, this room must be at the base.

Marissa rubbed her head to remove the last traces of dizziness and then checked to see if all body parts still functioned. Arms, legs, hands, everything came through without a hitch. Some device. She stared at the locator, puzzled that so innocent an object allowed for such complex travel.

"Oric, Brac, Galen?" She touched them one at a time. The three of them stirred, a bit woozy.

"Some ride," Oric said. "Ooh. What is that sound?" He held his hands up to his ears, squeezed his eyes shut, and appeared to make an internal adjustment. "That's better with the lows and subsonics filtered out."

"The works," Marissa said with a dry smile. "Everything you need to power a planet of bureaucrats and more."

"Sure is noisy."

Brac scrambled to his feet, then glanced at a chron on the wall above Marissa's head. "We must move now or be caught."

Dizziness struck when she tried to stand. She crouched low, hands on thighs, head down, until the swirling sensation passed. When Galen moved to help, she held up a hand.

"I'm all right. It just takes a minute or two."

On her feet, she paused before the door and eased it open. A large circular vestibule, empty for the moment lay outside. "Which way?"

"All must follow the leader's way," Galen said.

"But which way is my way?" She threw her arms up in frustration. "Ez?"

Silence. "Ez," Marissa said in an urgent whisper as panic began to rise. Again silence. She unzipped her suit and fingered the personality chip. "Esmarelda."

"Voice recognized, personal identification initiated. Undergoing routine functional overhaul. Chip slippage error e3601a. Please wait while initiation is completed."

"NO." They had reached Cephus, and now this, just when they most needed Ez. "Never trust a machine. Never!"

Marissa balled her fist around the chip and raised her arm. An iron cuff restrained her hand.

"That would be foolish for us all." Brac said, his face filled with sympathy. "You would lose a friend and we would lose a guide. It is unfortunate, but not fatal. We are not without resources."

She looked at him in frustration, but as his words penetrated, her expression melted to comprehension, and in the end to acceptance. "Thanks, Brac. I don't think I could do without Ez." She shook her head. "What was I thinking?"

Touching his beard, Galen studied her. "When emotions rule, truth flees. Transcending thought and entering the realm that leads either closer to the truth or closer to its pole is paramount. Either way, the truth of the matter is clarified."

"You're right. Although, I'm not sure *transcend* is the right word, but which way?"

His head to one side, Oric raised a hand. "Silence a moment. Let me sort

182

out the signals. These echoes interfere."

He turned, cupping his right ear toward something, and pointed. "This corridor leads toward machinery. Some sort of works lies in that direction." He pivoted again. "I cannot make out the sounds from this corridor. They are the sounds of labor, but unlike any sound I've heard before. Once again he turned. "From this direction, the sound of persons sleeping, persons at leisure."

"That's it then," she responded. "We go that way and find a place to wait."

They turned down the third corridor and ducked into an accessway that appeared little used. Shadows played around them to aid in hiding them from casual viewers. The accessway lay across from a transport, and so the occasional sounds of passing cars would disguise any unexpected noises from the shadows. The four settled down to wait.

"Initiation completed," came from the chip, "personality reconstruct initiated. This will take a few minutes. Please be patient."

Marissa placed the chip into an inner pocket and reattached the sensor pad. "I don't know what to tell you guys. In all likelihood, they'll be coming soon. That's the best I can do."

"Yes," Brac squatted, crossing his arms over his chest."It's the best any of us could do, but, depending on how many cameras we have passed and how well they're monitored, they have seen us. We should know as soon as we act, perhaps sooner."

Marissa nodded. She had considered that, but pushed it from her mind. Both people and Personalities probably monitored the cameras. Their presence may already have been recorded and reported.

Crossing her fingers, Marissa spoke to the chip. "Do you have rudimentary function?"

"Not fully initiated," came the response. "Please be patient."

"What happened?" Marissa whispered to the chip.

"Please repeat question when diagnostics are on-line. Thank you for your patience."

Heavy, hour-like minutes later, the sound of feet, almost shuffling, echoed through the corridor. Pulling back into the shadow, Marissa signaled to the others. They had already merged with the dim umbra cast by the intervening lights.

The stink of rot and stale perspiration alerted them. Through the corridor, two men in black and silver led a group of men wearing bedraggled and stained denim. The men in denim slogged along with effort. Some stumbled. They looked and smelled as though they could use showers, baths, and showers again.

"I'm back," Ez's voice startled Marissa. She wanted to silence the voice, but then remembered that probably only Oric heard it. "Boy was that some trip.

Running cross check now." Ez paused.

"Tad is in the group approaching after this. He is second deployment. Off-shift momentarily. Maintain protective cover."

Marissa signaled the others, and they did their best to melt into the dimness of the corridor. The two guards, probably preoccupied with thoughts of dropping off their burdens and the off time ahead, paid no attention to a group of shadows that had somehow sprouted feet. Marissa held her breath as they passed with looks neither right or left, but straight ahead.

Again, a long silent wait. Then Oric signaled—footsteps. Back into the shadows. Marissa shook with anticipation or fear. No, anticipation. Now they all heard the footsteps. What had she been thinking? Four of them against two armed guards and twelve men. No, not twelve men, prisoners. What would they do? Would they flee or help?

Again the shuffling, the stumbling noises, and the group moved into view. Third rank back. Tad, tall, but stooped, towered above the men before and behind him. Marissa pressed her fist to her mouth. Bright blond hair dulled, a thin body in filthy denim, boots caked with some sort of undefinable slime. She wanted to call to him, but didn't. Not now, not yet.

We just need to take them. Just take him.

Tad looked barely able to walk. How would they extract him from the group? Brac touched her arm, a question. She pointed. The guards had not yet seen them.

Brac stepped from the shadows into full view of the lead guards who stared up at the giant before them. With one stroke, he banged their heads together, and they fell to the ground. A shrill siren filled the hall. The group of twelve men skirred about, eyes wide, mouths gaping, but otherwise unmoving. Brac moved deliberately to the third rank, as Marissa stepped forward.

Tad saw her, and his mouth opened to speak. Brac picked him up, throwing Tad's still-considerable bulk effortlessly over his shoulder. Tad struggled weakly, but stopped when Brac gently tapped him at the juncture of shoulder and neck. Slumping into unconsciousness, he hung over Brac's immense back.

Oric tapped her arm and pointed the other way down the corridor. Someone, in fact, many someones converged on them from that direction. The prisoners in the corridor milled, uncertain what to do with the unexpected freedom, somehow aware that in a moment they would all be corralled once again. One man fell to the ground; another stooped beside him.

From the juncture in the corridor, Walt Fenster and two security guards came at a quick trot and passed under a light. As usual, Marissa noted his cheek bulged with a hunk of wasso gum. Some things never changed.

She locked eyes with him. "Walt." She walked toward him, nodding to

184

him in acknowledgment.

"Marissa."

He signaled the security guards as she approached them. She stopped just out of arm's reach. The two guards, side by side across the corridor, blocked her path. Studying Walt's face, she saw no shock, no stunned horror. He merely gazed back, observing and waiting.

"Aren't you surprised to see me, Walt?"

"Why should I be?" he said dryly. "You've messed up my life thus far. What could you possibly do for an encore?" His hands rested on the top of his belt, feet spread apart, alert and patient.

Marissa's thoughts whirled. What role did he play now? Time pressed upon her. Delay—she must hold his attention for the moment.

"You should be just a little surprised, unless Uma told you I'd come back. Aren't you the least bit curious about how I've managed to return after you pushed me through the Anomaly?"

"No." Walt shook his head, then lifted a speck of dust from his sleeve. "That's one of the joys of accepting the party line. No real curiosity, it just makes trouble. Here you are, so you must be here."

Through this exchange, her companions maintained silence. She assumed they hid behind her, in the shadows.

"I'm so sorry we have so brief a time to share our thoughts, but I really must go," Marissa dropped to a fighter's crouch, arms out as she dodged left.

"Please don't waste my time." Walt signaled with his gun.

Chapter Seventeen - Reunion

"How silver-sweet sound lovers' tongues by night,
Like softest music to attending ears!"
-Romeo and Juliet, II ii

"Ah, worthy statement of verity," a voice sounded from behind Walt and the security team. "The beginning of wisdom, attempting to divide that which is from that which is not, and in that way approach the truth! A great delight to be one in unity with such an enlightened utterance." Galen emerged from behind Walt and, with one seamless motion, seized both Walt's hands in his.

Brac used the distraction to push past Marissa and knock one security guard off-balance and into the other. Satisfied Brac had taken control, she turned back to watch Walt struggle to extract his hand from Galen's earnest grasp. A gripping conversation with Galen. That's a first. The thought came wildly unbidden into Marissa's mind as she darted forward to snatch Walt's weapon.

She covered Walt until Brac and Oric disarmed the guards. That done, Marissa looked back into the shadows at the figure of Tad, slumped and silent. The eleven men in the corridor had shuffled away, some at a run as soon as the security guards had been disarmed.

Taking the restraints from Walt's belt, Brac fastened the man's hands behind his back. Marissa glanced around the corner, beyond Fenster's line of sight. The empty corridor promised escape.

"I can't say it hasn't been a genuine pleasure." She looked down at Walt, who returned a gaze devoid of interest. He simply waited. She stared at him, remembering the blows when he had found her at the escape pod and his words when he shoved her into the anomaly. Her finger twitched over the weapon.

One shot would even things. Her finger tensed.

No, shooting him wouldn't do, because she would live the rest of her life with his death while he would be free. No, she couldn't even things that way. Walt had been busted to a security guard in the Bioregeneration wing, about as low as one could get and not be a prisoner or worse. Much as she despised him for what he had done, in turn, she had done this to him. Now, she owed him

186

something.

"Walt…" She licked her lips. He waited as if nothing else mattered. "I know you won't really hear this now, but I am sorry. When I'm free, I will help you. I promise."

Walt's mouth rounded into an "O" of complete shock. His eyes narrowed and he scrutinized her.

"Brac, immobilize him. Make sure that whoever finds him knows we overpowered him."

Using a second pair of restraints, Brac bound Walt's legs together, then fastened the two sets of manacles together with a third. He next removed Walt's shirt and gagged him with it. Picking up the bound man, Brac then carried him to a nearby door and opened it with a key from one of the security men's belts. He deposited Walt inside, careful to settle him in comfort, and closed and locked the door.

Brac looked to Marissa. "We must go." He walked over to Tad and scooped him up.

"Others are on the way," Ez announced.

"Do you…" Tad spoke in a harsh whisper, "remember the Advocate…you used… on the ship…to make your case?" He paused every few words to gather breath and strength.

"Yes," Marissa nodded. "Why?"

"It's here. They edited it. I've worked on it in my off hours to figure out just what they did to change it. If I can just understand it, maybe I'll find some way to help Tesde."

When Tad said 'Tesde,' Brac bristled. "It is not your place to help her. That is my role."

Anxious to smooth things over, Marissa reached out and touched Brac's forearm. "We're all here to do that. We'll need all the help we can get to reverse a deep edit process. So far as I know, it hasn't been done with any success."

Cold eyes appraised her. After a moment, Brad moved away without another word.

Marissa turned to Tad. "The Advocate is here, in this building?"

"Yes, another floor up from here." He paused for breath. "Bioregeneration staff manage the lower four floors." Another pause. "That's how I found it—in a storage room after the edit."

Fingering Ez's chip, Marissa frowned. "Why not just destroy it?"

"Astringency laws. When they destroy a machine, it's recorded, and someone may ask why." Tad paused for a long time, gathering enough breath to speak. "If a machine is brought in for maintenance service, declared superfluous, then stored, it's simply a housekeeping move." He gasped as he struggled for breath.

"Routine maintenance. A bureaucratic procedure." He smiled grimly. "Once things are bureaucratized, the biggest, most complex things can happen right in front of everyone's eyes, and no one will notice, because it's all part of the routine."

"If we rescue the Advocate, how would that help Tesde?" Biological processes she understood. "Aren't editing people and machines different processes?"

Machinery and the inner workings of any device never ceased to mystify her. Reliance on Tad's amazing abilities with machinery had saved her from more than one crisis.

"The editing techniques may be similar—one simply neural, the other electrical. If I can determine the pattern—"

"Editing is a surgical procedure," Brac interjected with a touch of impatience.

Leaning against the corridor wall for support, Tad gazed at him. "Yes, but it is reversible, so the surgery must do something discrete, planned. To undo the edit may take more than undoing a surgery, or you may need to know more about it."

Satisfied, Marissa turned to Galen and Oric. "I owe this Advocate, even if he is only a Personality. He did a lot for me. Besides, if we fix him, we'll gain a powerful ally, and maybe a way to help Tesde."

Arms crossed, Brac appeared unconvinced.

Galen moved toward the giant. "The truth is spoken, or part of the truth recognized. Do not doubt this."

"We gain nothing by talking." Brac hoisted Tad onto his shoulder. "This burden is not light. Pursuit must come."

They signaled the transport. While they waited, Marissa and Oric bound and gagged the security guards and dragged them into the storage room where Walt lay trussed. The transport arrived with a whoosh of stale air. Urgency propelled them into it without ceremony.

"Can you get us to the second floor," Marissa spoke to Ez, "but leave a faulty trail."

"Easily, these are not Personalities." They rose to level 2. The car pulled to a stop.

"Anyone outside?" Marissa whispered.

"About one hundred meters down the corridor, back to the transport. Headed away. Around the corner now..." The doors of the transport opened.

Brac carried Tad slung over his shoulder, but seemed unaware of his burden. Nonetheless, despite weight loss, Tad must be almost a hundred kilograms.

"Can you manage," Marissa asked.

"If no fighting is required, I am fine for the moment. I would not like to carry him all day."

"I can walk," Tad protested.

"Quickly?" Brac sounded doubtful.

"I'll know when I try. Set me down."

"As you wish." Brac put him down.

For a moment Tad wobbled and almost slumped. He grabbed the wall for support. "No, I'm okay, a little unsteady, but I'm okay." He pulled away from the wall and stood straight and tall. "Let's go."

Surveying the silent corridor, Marissa looked at him with raised eyebrows. "Which way, Tad?"

"Down the hall about halfway, on the right, storage area 14. The Advocate is near the back...folded up in storage mode. You should be able to carry it without trouble." He struggled to catch his breath again.

"How did you work with it, all folded up like that?"

"I unfolded it, turned it on when I needed to. Took it off power when I didn't, and refolded it at the end of each session." Tad paused. "I left it in the back of the room. Marissa, this is what I do, remember?" He sighed, then coughed. "I fix stuff—people, machines, whatever's broken. And as long as my pass showed me sticking to my permitted floors, they didn't much care what I did, as long as nothing slowed up too much."

"Enough, quiet now." She touched his lips with her fingers, restraining tears. "We've got to move now. Let's go as quickly as you can. You'll have to open the door with your pass. I'd like to think nobody, but Fenster and the guards know you've got unexpected company, and they're not telling." She looked around and saw only an empty corridor

In less than a minute, they reached the right door. Tad's pass opened it. He showed them the Advocate unit, but Marissa didn't recognize it. She had only seen it via the holocube.

Someone had replaced its original case with a small storage case probably for convenience in moving it. It reminded her of the encased ashes of a friend. She touched the case, mindful of her advisor and friend.

"Galen, can you carry this?"

Without speaking, he slipped the folded Advocate into a large pouch he produced from under one side of his now flowing garment. The pouch expanded and completely covered the Advocate, then retracted under his robe, leaving his arms free. The heavy pouch pulled his robe down a little on one side.

"It's time to go for home." She held Tad's hand in hers and grabbed Galen's. He linked hands with the others. Then, she closed her eyes and

189

focused on her suite on Satina IV. The darkness took them again.

For once, when they arrived back in the suite, Marissa didn't blackout. At the same time deadened limbs reminded her of those mild stuns used by the medtechs, but her head throbbed and pulsed as though a caged opter sought escape. She rubbed her temples and pushed a thumb against the place just over her nose, but the edgy pain did not pass. The others lay stirring to consciousness. All except Tad, who lay inert, breathing shallowly. After all this, he had to be all right. Getting medical attention for him came first.

She gently prodded Galen to life. "Help me move Tad to the couch."

"Every service is a pleasure," replied Galen as he clambered up to help her.

Despite his loss of weight, Tad stilled weighed more than they could manage. They struggled just to move his inert limbs, much less lift him to comfort. Defeated, she lowered Tad's arms and signaled Galen to do likewise.

"Obviously a job for Brac."

"The truth, as ever." Galen rose and smoothed his robe, then bowed.

Marissa shook Brac's shoulder. He groaned and rolled over.

"Brac, wake up. I need your help."

He opened one eye and stared up at her. "Help?"

"We need to move Tad to the couch, the bed, someplace more comfortable than the floor."

Tad now sprawled on the lavender carpet, limbs awry from the recent attempt to move him. Brac rose and crouched over him. First, he straightened Tad's arms and legs, then scooped him up without once breathing hard, and carried him to a couch.

"Is this all right?"

Marissa nodded pulling a pillow from the back of the sofa. Brac settled him on the couch with efficient tenderness and she placed it under Tad's head. His pallor worried her.

"He needs help." Smoothing his brow, Marissa's noted a slight fever that added to her unease.

"What sort of help?" Brac looked from the slumbering Tad to Marissa.

Before Marissa could answer, Oric stirred to life on the floor. He scrambled to his feet and joined the small group around the couch. Picking up Tad's hand, he checked for a pulse.

After a few seconds, he released the hand. "Despite appearances, there's nothing much wrong. His pulse is strong, if a little fast, breathing good, deep, and unobstructed. Skin is warm and relatively dry, not clammy. There are probably internal things I can't tell from the signs, but everything looks okay. He needs rest."

Marissa sighed. "Thank you, I'd still feel better—"

Oric held up a hand. "No question. I was not suggesting you not consult an expert, only that it isn't urgent. You're tired and need rest."

"I'd still feel better—"

"I'll take care of it then." He patted her shoulder, his face filled with sympathy and understanding. "All will be well. We have rescued him. Now he must rest and recover."

"Thank you." Relived to have Oric take charge, Marissa sat next to Tad and studied his pallid face, wondering what to do next.

Oric hurried off on his errand, and she rechecked Tad's pulse, but found it unchanged. His need pulled at her, demanding action, but what action? She didn't know enough to help him now.

With a discrete cough, Brac stepped forward. "Why don't I give him a shower? My position often entails additional personal duties for those incapacitated by overindulgence or serious illness."

Sudden awareness of the rotting smell of bioregion sludge rolled over her. "Now that you mention it, he could do with one. Maybe we can get rid of the stink too."

With one smooth motion Brac scooped Tad up and carried him off to the shower. Within fifteen minutes he returned with Tad now smelling of spruce instead of sludge. Somewhere he had found a silk caftan and dressed him in it. He deposited Tad back on the couch, drew up a fresh coverlet, and then stepped back.

"I will take the Verist for a short stroll. Satina IV has much to offer such a one as he."

Half hearing, Marissa nodded. The departure of the two men left her with her own troublesome thoughts. They had removed Tad from Cephus, but he appeared so wan and wasted. While she took some comfort from Oric's diagnosis, she wanted the reassurance of at least a medtech. The toxins in bioregion could kill even the strongest person. She paced from one end of the sitting area to the other, stopping each time to check Tad. He lay in a stupor, shallow breaths signifying life. Worry would solve nothing, but still it gnawed at her.

How long she paced, Marissa could not say, but it seemed like an eternity. The throbbing in her head gradually subsided and left her to focus solely on Tad. The door to the suite slid open, and Oric and others entered, murmuring. Marissa hurried forward, hoping help had come.

He greeted her with a smile and gestured to a short man in a gray smock. "He prefers to have no name at this time, but he is with us. He's one of the few Medicals not tracked or monitored."

The man offered a thin smile and turned toward Tad, still sprawled on the couch. "The patient?"

191

Marissa nodded, not trusting herself to speak.

From beneath his robes, the medic produced a crushed velvet bag, a fluid sack stretched into an elongated shape by the contents. He loosened the drawstring and withdrew a thin aluminum instrument. As it passed over Tad's body, the object made no sound. The man held it up to eye level to study the results.

"He's been exposed to toxins, a great variety, but more perplexing and difficult, he shows exposure to fungoids, an odd class of them." He tsked-tsked and shook his head.

"Fungoids are much, much worse than toxins, any time. I can purify for the toxins. The fungoids, assuming they approximate natural, are more... resistant. Nevertheless..." His sentence trailed off, and he rummaged in his bag. "Do you know what type?"

Despite the neutral tone of the question, Marissa read a world of blame into it. We didn't do it, she wanted to protest.

"We removed him from the lowest level of Cephus," Oric said.

"Experimental stuff." The doctor nodded. "Has he been edited?"

His words struck Marissa, a probe digging into her guilt. "Can't tell." She twisted her hair into a tight curl. "At least not yet."

Tad hadn't shown any recognizable signs of that. Ez hadn't said anything either.

"I can't help you there. Special training is required for that if you want to avoid disruption. But sometimes it introduces certain physiological...complications."

"Can't your instrument tell you?" She held her breath.

The doctor glared at her for a moment, then his brown eyes softened. "Are we now telling the physician how to heal? I would not have asked you a question, if I knew the answer." He paused and tapped his chin. "If the edit were biomechanical recircuiting, my instrument would tell. Otherwise..."

The doctor finished fumbling in his bag and pulled out a portable synth. He turned the dials and flipped two toggles on the thin handle. He held the instrument to Tad's arm. A moment later, a whoosh and shrill noise signaled that the material in the synth had entered Tad's bloodstream. The doctor returned the synth to the bag and pulled the strings tight.

"I must go. Oric knows where to find me if needed. However, I believe rest and the medication will solve his physical problems. Monitor for one hour and check especially the lungs at the end of that time. If this device signals red over any part of the body, call me at once." He handed the diagnostic to her.

Turning to Oric, the doctor said something under his breath and Oric nodded. "Don't disturb him. He needs rest. If the drug works, he'll recover soon. If not, we've done what we can, the rest is up to..."—a short mysterious pause followed and the doctor smiled— "rest. Yes, the rest is up to rest. Good-bye now. Call me if anything else happens."

Marissa nodded. "Thank you."

He inclined his head in her direction and followed Oric to the door.

Deciding Tad would be more comfortable in one of the sleeping rooms, she asked Brac to move him to the Cloud room. He carried Tad across the foyer to the room Marissa had decorated with transparent blue, not so deep as aqua, covered the walls, the floor, and the ceiling. He placed Tad on the fluffy floating cloud of a bed among the downy covers. Tad appeared to float against a cerulean blue background.

With nothing to do except wait, Marissa chewed on a nail, a habit she had long ago trained herself not to do. Chewing her nails occupied her. She tried the vid, but the ever-shifting patterns and colors on the screen held no interest. Tad lay inert, neither moving nor waking.

In the nearby dining area Oric, Brac, and Galen chatted over a meal. Galen exchanged anecdotes with Oric while Brac emitted an occasional gravelly sound she interpreted as laughter. She considered joining them, but the thought of humor only aggravated her anxiety. Conscience bound her to this watch.

Marissa sank into a chair floating beside the bed. The drugs had induced stasis to assist the healing process. The doctor hadn't said how deep the stasis or whether Tad could hear her or not. The burden of all she had kept inside for far too long weighed on her soul. That compelling need to tell him these things, even if he couldn't hear, demanded release.

"Tad..." She stopped, afraid the lump in her throat betrayed too much of what she felt— afraid she couldn't say what she must say. Then, the knot in her throat loosened. She picked up his hand, no longer hot and dry, but warm and normal. She interlaced her fingers with his.

"Tad, I owe you an apology. No...more than that, I'm sorry. I had to do what I did. What I did was right. I couldn't have backed down, but I'm sorry I involved you and the others. I never thought they'd stick you in Bioregeneration. But if I hadn't tried...if I'd ignored the rheos, I'd feel even worse."

Marissa stopped. He couldn't hear her, and she needed to know he understood. She squeezed his hand. What did he see as he slept? She had hallucinated in the Anomaly. She shuddered, hoping he had better dreams. When he woke, would he be the Tad she had always known, or some stranger too changed by experience and by biochemical alteration for them ever to know one another again?

Slow tears trailed down her face and fell on Tad's bare arm, then on their intertwined hands. He had lost weight, but he had had a healthy constitution. He never got ill.

Fungoids. Devos, why should he have to suffer from them? Weren't the toxins enough? No point in thinking about that now. Surely with medical treatment, they had intervened soon enough. Modern drugs cured everything, didn't they? None of this stopped her tears.

When she looked up, minutes, hours, days later, she had no conception of the time that had passed. Some slight change in the atmosphere, something gave her the sense that someone waited or watched. She glimpsed Brac and Oric standing a short distance from her.

"We must return to our duties," Oric said, his face softened by concern. "We'll return as soon as we can."

Marissa nodded, but said nothing.

"Galen asked us to show him around. I can request tour duty for the day."

Again she nodded.

"We'll have him back by late this evening, or first thing in the morning, depending on what we do."

"Fine." She raised her head and gave him a weak smile. "Thank you." She sought Galen, and glimpsed him, or at least his legs behind Oric and Brac. "Galen, have a good time."

"Learning is the pursuit of the truth, whether for good or ill is the only time to have." He spoke with solemnity.

Sometimes she wondered whether he recited from some vast book from his culture. An enormous volume given to children upon their first birthday, *Responses for Every Occasion,* appeared in her mind. Inwardly she chuckled and brushed the thought away. Galen too often spoke with such aptness that he must devise his words himself. In a flurry of movement, the three of them left her with Tad.

She longed for something to occupy attention. Her chronosculpture with its greasy, slightly vibrating matrix and the high-pitched buzz of the wand that penetrated to the soles of her feet. She needed a way to blot everything else from her mind. Without conscious intent, her hands moved in that mixture of potter and sculptor's motions so necessary to build a chrono-matrix. In her mind's eye, the emerging shape moved in and out of phases in the space before her, until tears blurred even that inner vision.

Chapter Eighteen - Recovery

"Her changes change her changes constantly."
-*Inferno*, Dante

In the cloud room, Marissa drowsed and drifted in and out of sleep, head thrown back in the chair beside Tad's bed. She stirred and blinked, her eyes sticky with residue. Somewhere a door opened and fabric rustled. Consciousness returned and, with it, a tantalizing aroma filled the suite. She sniffed the air, struggling to determine what.

Food. Her friends had returned with food, and wonderful food, from the smell. Onions, green peppers, garlic, and the savory scent of roasted meat. Her mouth watered. She shook herself awake and started to rise. A motion startled her.

Had Tad moved? Marissa held her breath and stared down him, afraid to believe. No, she had bumped him when she shifted.

A slight twitch of a hand?

Yes, Tad moved. He had broken the stasis that had held him unconscious. More movement as he struggled to shake off the effects of stasis sleep.

"Galen, Oric, Brac." She called and touched Tad's shoulder. His eyes fluttered open. "Praise Devos!" She almost danced around the room. "He's awake. He's broken stasis himself. He's all right!"

The three friends pushed into the room as one, bursting through the doorway together, and clustered around the bed. Galen danced with Marissa, hopping from one foot to the other.

"This is indeed the best of news."

Filled with joy, Marissa hugged him. "More than that." She rushed to Tad and raised his hand to her lips. "Welcome back."

He ventured a weak smile, then stopped and stared. "Marissa?" His voice came out in a soft croak. "You're...You're..."

"I'm right here, and you aren't imagining it."

"Marissa." He struggled with his blanket, but managed at last to free his arms.

She fell into them, kissing his face, his nose, his lips. "You've traveled a

195

lot further than I have. Welcome home."

A grin stretched across his face. "Home, we're together."

"Yes." She hugged him again. "Oh, yes."

Tad captured her hand and squeezed it. "I'm not dreaming you?"

"No." Marissa squeezed back as tears blurred her vision.

"Where are we?" He stared around the room. "Heaven?"

"A place where no one asks questions."

"Don't tell me," he groaned, "I've finally made it to Satina IV, and I wasn't awake to see it."

"You're awake now." She brushed his forehead, moving a strand of lank hair away from his eyes.

He smiled and captured her hand in his. "Guess I am. When do we take advantage of it?"

Behind them, Oric sneezed. Tad stared from Brac to Oric and Galen. "I remember..." He glanced back at Brac. "He carted me like a sack. I wouldn't want to tussle with him."

"You won't," Marissa reassured him. "They're friends of ours and share a common goal."

He surveyed her with a crooked grin. "You make friends wherever you go."

"I do, don't I? You've probably forgotten their names so I'll introduce them." She tapped Galen on the shoulder. "This is Galen, a seeker of truth and a Verist."

Tad extended his hand. "Oh, yes, the man of many words."

"As the words say." Galen bowed, his beard sweeping the floor.

"The brawny one is Brac and that's Oric."

Marissa paused seeking the right words to describe her friends. "A man of few words, Brac doesn't say much. Oric hears anything anyone says. He can't be prosecuted for what he doesn't say." She grinned at both men.

Oric pumped Tad's hand it up and down. "Most pleased to speak to you."

"Uh, thanks." He flexed his fingers.

As Brac approached, he shrank back a little. Brac touched his hand, but offered no greeting. At that, Tad then looked to Marissa.

"I told you, he doesn't say much. He's important to us and our cause and...engaged to Tesde."

Eyes wide, Tad turned a waxen white. "Tesde..." He stared at Brac. "I don't know where she is..."

"Relax." Marissa stroked his upper arm. "Brac and Oric already know. We're going to get her as well."

"How did you...they find her? After..." Tad struggled to force out the words.

196

"Enough for now. Enough." Marissa patted his arm. "Rest and we'll talk later. How about some food? Some real food."

"We can't wait." Tad tried to rise.

Marissa kissed his forehead. "We can, and we will. I told you, Brac and Oric have plans to rescue Tesde. There's nothing to worry about for the moment."

"But..."

"It's your turn to trust. Besides, you'd better regain your strength before trying anything else." Marissa plumped the pillow behind his head.

He said nothing at first. Instead, he studied Marissa, examining her like some new medical specimen. "Where have you been? I thought you were dead."

"Of course, that's what Uma wanted everyone to think, but I refused to make it that easy for her." A grim smile and narrowed eyes made clear her feelings.

"But what happened to you? Where did you go? How did you get back?"

"I don't know. They dumped me into the Anomaly, but somehow I managed to find my way back to Arden."

He looked mystified. "How?"

"Somehow, that's all I know, and all I need to know. Well not quite." She held out her wrist. "N'Bert sent this device. It helps in the travel thing...the...well, call it a matrix. It's not a good term, but I don't know any better."

"Perhaps plexus," Galen suggested. An image of a knotted fist appeared on his beard.

Marissa laughed. "I don't know, I'll have to look it up first, but it's as good a term as any."

"This?" Tad looked up from the locator, frowning. "This helps you do what?"

"Travel, I can go anywhere with a minimum lapse of time." She turned the band around on her wrist. "And before you ask, I don't have the slightest idea of how it works. Not even an inkling. If I want to go somewhere, I think about that place, and I'm there."

"That's it?" He looked skeptical. "You just think about it?"

"Well, I have to visualize it, really see it in my mind. You know, it's kind of odd. On Arden, the rheos take it in stride. Those cave pictures..." Marissa shook her head. "How could they know?" She stared deep into Tad's sea-dark eyes, hoping to find the answer there.

He gazed back at her, then pulled her down to kiss her. "Whatever, I'm glad you're here."

Marissa kissed his forehead before pulling away. "You're probably starved.

Tad grinned. "I am."

Laughing, she pulled her hair back from her face. "Galen, Oric, and Brac brought some delicious food."

"Go easy on me, Marissa, I haven't had anything but concentrate in a long time. I don't want to get sick."

"Don't worry. We'll start with fruits and vegetables and see how it goes from there."

As Marissa left the room, accompanied by Galen, Oric, and Brac, she turned to them and spoke in a low voice. "Tad and I have a lot to catch up and discuss. Do you think...?" She paused, a frown on her face, seeking the right words.

"The truth between two can be obscured in the presence of many. Truly, the marketplace fascinates a seeker of truth." Galen skipped a few steps, setting his beard to swinging.

Oric nodded. "I need to log a few hours of work, and Brac has some appointments, if he chooses to take them." Brac nodded agreement, saying nothing.

"Thank you," she said, impressed by their tact. Again, the impulse to hug Galen surged through her, but she repressed it. "It shouldn't take all that long, perhaps two hours."

"Sufficient distractions exist to occupy the active mind for far longer than this coming-to-terms shall require," Galen responded. With that, he swirled around and headed for the suite door, accompanied by Brac and Oric.

With the others gone, Marissa inspected the bags, packages, boxes, plastic containers, bowls, and stasis sealed envelopes that they had gathered. The food smelled delicious, redolent of the variety of spices available only on a world where all worlds came together. Hints of sage, cinnamon, tarragon, cumin, overtones of rosemary, wines, vinegars, citrus, and mint.

She selected from varied foods and put them on a tray for him. Then she propped Tad up with several large pillows and placed the tray straddling his legs. After tucking a napkin into the neck of his robe, she moved back. He started eating while she watched from one of the floating cloud chairs.

As he ate, she grew uneasy and uncomfortable. She didn't know what to do with her hands, her feet, her elbows; she didn't know where to look. Her skin felt at once clammy and itchy.

Tad ate slowly at first, picking at this or that colored fragment—dipping a small corner of a fresh or cooked vegetable into one or another of the sauces. For a long time he didn't look up from the food. When he did, his eyes appeared, shiny bright, in a way Marissa didn't understand. She couldn't read his expression. Had the physical separation taken them so far from one another?

"It's so good to see you again. I thought you dead." The brightness overflowed his eyes, leaving the damp places on his face. "That hurt worse, much worse, than the Enunciator putting me into the Bioregeneration Lab, or any of the rest."

"I know."

"I don't know how you reached me and brought us here, but thank you. I've never told you…"

She leaned forward, wanting to touch his lips, to silence him before he said it, but she sat too far away.

"I've never told you, but you must have known I love you."

"Tad, you told me over and over again."

"Not enough, not often enough. When they took you…when I knew what they'd done…" He paused again.

"They gave me a choice, Marissa. They gave me the choice of any number of places. I chose Bioregen because I knew I wouldn't last long." His hand trembled, and he stared down at the food on the tray.

She wanted to gasp, but she didn't make any sound, though every nerve in her body cried out for it. She waited for him to continue.

"I didn't believe all the holos and silly stories I had read, but when I experienced it…Without you, I had nothing…nothing. Not revenge, not all of the bright worlds and suns…"

A new strength shown in his eyes. "Words never came easy to me, especially words about you. Marissa, you're everything. Arden is more beautiful because you love it. Satina IV is more wonderful because you're here. The places without you stand out because they have nothing."

"Tad…"

"No, please, please let me finish. I thought long and hard the whole time I was sinking into the regen sludge, and I figured it out. It took me a while, but I figured it out. I wanted us to be together always."

"We are together."

"No, more than that, and more than legally. I want…I want to be…" He paused.

His face drawn with his plea tugged at her in every way. "I want us to be one. I want to be with you always—in the eyes of Devos."

Scalding tears fell from her eyes. "I wasn't ready…This isn't what I expected." She stopped. Words couldn't express what she meant. She jumped out of the chair and rushed to the bed.

"I hoped, but….Tad. I want the same. I didn't think so on Arden. After, when I saw your ID on that report…I couldn't think. I wanted to smash something. I thought you had deserted me, condemned me. I felt so…disconnected, adrift with no safety or certainty anymore…"

She hugged him, upsetting the tray of food, which spilled off the bed with a loud clatter. The servos, alerted by the sound, emerged from the walls, scurried about her feet, and sucked up the food and broken fragments of dishes.

"Tad, I did so many stupid things. I hurt you and Tesde. I'm even sorry about Sylvic and N'Bert. Walt deserved better. As much as I despise him, he shouldn't be in that place. He wouldn't be there if it wasn't for me."

Tad hugged her, and then leaned away to study her face. "You should be glad about Walt. He kept me going. I don't know why, but he took the assignment with me. He tried to help, believe it or not."

Searching his face for any sign of sarcasm, Marissa saw only truth. Surprised and relieved, she embraced him again. "I'm glad Tad. I have so much to make up to so many. On top of that, the situation for the rheos hasn't changed. I still owe them."

"Marissa, I'll go with you where ever. I'll do whatever needs doing. If it's the rheos, that's fine, now that you're back. What you need is what I need." He looked down at the sleeve of the blue nightshirt and grinned. "Well, that and maybe some clean clothes."

She swept him with a slow appraising glance. "Actually, I kind of like that shirt, it's so…sensual, but if you insist…" She disengaged herself and went to the adjacent dressing room.

Later she would take Tad shopping, but for now a casual ensemble easily provided from the hotel inventory would have to do. She keyed the appropriate choices and a prepackaged garment set slide from the wall slot.

After handing him the clothing and showing him the shower, Marissa ordered oulatte from the dispenser. She then resumed her place in the cloud chair and sipped her drink, while her thoughts tumbled over one another to form a tangled skein. She owed so much to so many, but with Tad's help, maybe she could pay a few of those debts.

Soon he returned, refreshed and looking more like his former self although his skin still lacked his normal color. "I'm beginning to feel human again."

"I should hope so. You look a lot better. Tad, it's taken plenty of thinking, and eons of time, but I'm responsible for what happened to everyone." He started to protest, but she held up a hand. "No, let me finish. It's my responsibility, and I'm really sorry, but I don't know what else I could have done."

She put the oulatte down on a floating table nearby. "I had to follow my conscience, but I didn't know what the result would be. Given all the circumstances, I couldn't allow genocide." She paused for a moment to gather her thoughts.

"You can help me work out exactly what I did and to whom."

"What do you mean?" He studied her, an unreadable expression in narrowed eyes.

"I mean, what happened after my sentence, or before, or during. What happened to everyone? You know more about those events than I do."

"I know some things. Others I got through rumor, through feeds, and from Walt. But I don't know everything." He paused and sat on a floating chair next to her. "I don't know what happened to N'Bert and Sylvic. I know what was supposed to happen, but it never did. I've no idea where they went."

"But you can tell me what you know."

"I don't see why—"

"Let's call it part of my twelve-step program to a better Marissa." She patted his hand and smiled. "Maybe it will clarify things. It might help me understand what's happened better." She paused and picked up her drink again. "Something or someone has gone to a lot of trouble. I want to know why."

Sipping the now cold oulatte, she returned the cup to the saucer a little too much vigor, and the oulatte sloshed perilously near the rim.

"I know Uma." She skewered Tad with narrowed eyes. "She's done things I don't like. She's done things that all people in power do, but her actions have never been entirely arbitrary. Why a major conflict over such a minor planet?" She shook her head. "It doesn't make any sense."

"You're right, it doesn't. Now that you mention it, the whole proceeding appears really strange."

"How so?" She cocked her head to one side, relieved, but Tad had recognized the oddity of the entire affair.

"Just strange, like, when it first happened. Walt came to me and told me that we should come up with a story, a cover, for us and for you. We should 'clear out.' I think that's what he said. I'd never seen him that...concerned or frightened. He'd never consulted or advised on anything before. I don't know how to describe it."

He shook his head to clear it. "Anyway, Tesde and I refused to budge. We supported you, but he persisted, tried to wheedle us into seeing things his way. He tried until they took us all away. You know, they took him, too."

Tad stared at his hands. He had interlaced his fingers and studied them, as if mesmerized by their positions. "On board ship, they did a minor edit on Tesde, as an example to all of us."

He gazed across at Marissa, his eyes diamond brilliant again. "I couldn't believe it. None of us could. That stunned even N'Bert. He sort of withdrew, even more than normal from the rest of us."

Opening his hands, he spread them wide. "You couldn't blame him, but he wasn't going to get far enough away. Maybe he suspected the outcome. I don't know."

Brac had mentioned the editing, but somehow Marissa had thought that happened later. She had refused it when Uma pushed it as a way out. At least, Uma had left it to her to make the choice. They hadn't given Tesde one. "So Tesde had already been edited when you and she came to visit me on the *Concordia*?"

He nodded.

"Quincy let them?"

"Quincy had been relieved of command. The second-in-command followed orders."

"Well, that's a relief in one way." She sighed, weighed down by even more guilt. "I'm sorry about Quincy. Now I've got one more victim to atone for."

"They took away his command permanently." Tad looked toward the far corner. "He won't be back, ever."

His words struck deep. She had cost her friends everything except perhaps life itself. "This is bigger than I thought. I knew I had affected a lot of people. I just didn't realize how many."

"While we're on the subject of hard truths, maybe I shouldn't say this, but it still bothers me. Even as an edit, it really hurt Tesde that you wouldn't listen to us. I don't think you know how much she really cared for you."

Tears overflowed, and Marissa swiped at them with an angry hand. "Yeah, I was so focused, so lost in myself. Tad, it wasn't just Tesde that I didn't appreciate. You, too. I couldn't understand why you all didn't care about the importance of life, about the rheos."

She sobbed now, all the emotions she had tried so hard to ignore rushed over her. Helpless to stem the flow, she stumbled from the chair to the wall dispenser. At a touch, a tissue popped out. In addition, Tad held out a large, linen handkerchief. She took it gratefully.

After drying her eyes and catching her breath, she reached for his hand. "Go on, as hard as it is, I need to hear everything."

"I don't know much more. All of us were 'requested' to take other assignments, though N'Bert and Sylvic vanished before your hearing. The monitors made sure we all watched the video of what happened to you. After that..."—he shrugged his shoulders— "Well, if they could do that to you, then there really wasn't much point to anything. At least not for me."

He shook off his sadness and faced her. "I'm glad I'm here and you're with me."

Marissa managed a weak smile. Quincy, N'Bert, Sylvic, Tad, Tesde, Walt. Was there no end to the list of people hurt because of her? She caught up with him mid-sentence.

"...they edited the Advocate, actually all the advocates, then they edited Tesde. They didn't have to spell out that they'd do the same to anyone else who offered anything they didn't want to hear." A shudder shook his shoulders, but he shrugged it off.

"I started working on the Advocate in my off time. I don't really know why, something to do with the time. I wanted to see what kinds of things they did to edit a Personality. It took my mind off of you."

When he said nothing more, Marissa looked at her feet, anywhere but at him. Self-conscious again, she wanted to say something to fill the silence, but she didn't know what. It all overwhelmed her.

He rose from the chair and crossed to her. "I've been away far too long." Taking her hand, he pulled her into his arms. With one finger, he traced the curve of her cheek. "I...I...really need you."

A surge of desire overpowered all her other emotions. She saw only Tad, blue eyes, blond hair, body already losing the tan he seemed to have always. There for her.

She'd been dead to him in more ways than one. Now, every nerve responded to him, every part of her being ached in the awareness of him, his scent, his color, the way the air moved around him. The room centered on him, and so did she.

She found herself pulled to him in a bear hug, perhaps not as strong as it might have been a couple of weeks ago, perhaps not as sharp and as demanding as during the nights and days on Arden, but his arms surrounded her, unmistakably his arms. She embraced him, wanting to stay this way forever. Then, they found each other's lips. She kissed Tad hard, as though he had been away forever, as though he had never been away.

She wanted to see him, to look at his face, to touch it, to make sure this was no dream. She needed him so much and had always needed him. In the Anomaly, she had ignored or even suppressed it. Now, she admitted and reveled in that need.

"I never thought I'd be so glad to see someone cross-eyed close." Tad hugged her to him. "But I'm glad to see you."

Marissa traced his lips, his nose, his cheek; she stroked his hair, thrilling to the softness, the fineness of this spun gold. "Just how glad is that?" A faint echo of the way they used to tease each other tinged her voice.

Tad kissed her again, this time savoring all of her, making the kiss endless. All trace of her hesitation and holding back faded in the surge of emotions as she responded to his touch.

* * * *

Refreshed from the emotional release of lovemaking and a quick shower, Marissa joined Tad in the main sitting room. He set the Advocate on the table in front of them and undid much of the case. Removing some of the internal chips and boards, he spread them out on the table in front of them. She leaned back, content. Watching Tad as he worked was a return to another time. They had each other and a future again

In a flurry of noise, light, and scents, Brac, Oric, and Galen burst into the room. Brac and Oric each collapsed onto boulder chairs, and Galen folded his legs beneath him on the floor not far from her feet, but out of the way of the repair work.

"That little guy could run your feet off," Oric said. "And eat? I hope whatever credit you've got is good."

Marissa laughed, loud and long. She had never seen this side of Galen before. From his voluminous robes, he pulled a black pouch and drew out container upon container. The smells of wonderful spices and foods—paprika, pepper, cumin, cloves, some meat or other grew stronger and wafted from the containers. Come to think of it, every time he went out, he came back with food, but always in new varieties.

Shaking her head, she smiled with fondness at Galen. "More food?"

"Indeed, if anything is to be accomplished, any place to be seen, any goal to be met, it should be met with a satisfied stomach and a mind seeking the truth."

Tad laughed, and she relished that deep throaty sound even more than the ragged breathing of their lovemaking. A better sound than the three words on his lips, a better sound than anything she had heard for a very long time. Life had so much to offer.

Filled with joy, she picked up a container and toyed with the food. She took a small bite on the end of a fork and tasted it. Fire consumed her tongue. She gasped, opened her mouth wide, and fanned it.

"What did you get? This tastes like Benarian Firepot."

Galen nodded happily. "Is it not delicious? So delicately seasoned and so tasty."

"Delicately seasoned?" Marissa glared at him. "I'm not sure I'll be able to taste anything for the rest of my life. This stuff burns. Didn't the vendor warn you about this?"

Tad's amused chuckle came like water in a brook. "Relax, Marissa."

"The food is most satisfying," Galen protested.

"Well, you're welcome to it." She pushed the container across the table toward him. "I really need to keep an eye on you. You can get into too much trouble on Satina IV."

"Yep, spicy food," Tad observed. "The first step on the slippery slide to hell. Next thing you know the little guy will be joining a Reynardian splinter and shaving off all his body hair."

The others joined his burst of laughter. For a brief time, friendship and love banished all thoughts of the rheos, Arden, and even Tesde from Marissa's mind.

Chapter Nineteen - An Evening's Entertainment

"In such a night as this,
When the sweet wind did gently kiss the trees,
And they did make no noise."
-*Merchant of Venice,* Vi

Marissa slept that night with a peace and clarity she had forgotten. All night, warmth and a presence comforted her. Even while she slept, her heart tripped, knowing Tad to be that warmth and presence. On the ship and in the Anomaly being alone had never seemed odd, but now, with him next to her, she could not imagine how she had slept without this familiar, welcoming, comforting warmth.

When she woke, she turned over and kissed Tad, brushing the blond strands out of his face as she did so. He sighed and reached out for her, still asleep. This morning, she delighted in spending time in his arms. Soon enough, outside events would demand her attention. For now, she wanted to savor this brief time. She put her arm around him, and snuggled close. Marissa closed her eyes and drowsed.

Half-dreams paraded before her. The images of Tad brought smiles. Then Tesde called to her, but Marissa couldn't make out the words. Europa gazed at the bare earth outside the birthing shelter, waiting. Above in Arden's sky, silvery ships caught the waning sun. She groaned and rolled over.

Later, showered, dressed and ready to face the day, Tad approached her and Galen in the sitting room. "You know, suddenly I'm starving. It's like I haven't eaten in a month."

"*Hard* work will do that to a person." Marissa grinned, and he grinned back. "We can eat here or out, but if we go out, I might as well show you a bit of Satina IV."

"Then let's go." Tad took her by the arm and strolled toward the door, then stopped abruptly. "What about Tesde?" The lines in his face returned, deeper and in new places.

"I haven't forgotten Tesde, but Brac knows where she is. Oric assured me it's only a day or two more. As for the rheos, they aren't gone yet. As long as they exist, I can hope. Maybe if we find out why Arden is so vital to the Delphians, we can stop this madness."

"And if we can't?"

"If we can't, then I'll force Uma's hand somehow." The more Marissa considered that option, the better it sounded. "I can go anywhere. That bracelet of N'Bert's takes me where ever I want to go. Maybe that will scare her."

"Nothing has ever scared her. That is, nothing except the Delphians."

"Why the Delphians?" Marissa frowned, unable still to answer that question. "Most of what we've seen treats them as comic-book monsters. They're ghosts. From what we've seen they're not real."

"I haven't seen anything yet. Maybe I can help you, if I see what you've seen." Tad drew her forward. "Talking here isn't getting anything done. I need food and a walk, and we need more information."

"There are entertainments concerning the Delphians," Galen said.

"Like the play we saw..." Marissa shuddered, remembering the haunting images, the things implied, but never said.

"I have seen others." Galen drew from the folds of his robe a number of small, multicolored, flimsy holos and held them out to her

"Where did you get these?" Marissa read the first one before he could answer. *'Notes Regarding Trade Allowances and Debit-Credit Relations with Extra-Confederational Forces with an Appendix On the Possible Structure of Economic Interfaces with Delphia.'* She flipped to a new flimsy. As she held it, the front changed back and forth from a lurid space alien hovering over a generously endowed screaming woman to a sedate, nearly pastoral landscape. *'Images of Delphia: A Study in Contrasts.'* She looked askance at Galen.

"Many vendors sold such items, some made to appeal to the lowest, others for those of more serious intent. Knowing of the mentor's interest in Delphia, these naturally caught the eye."

"Well done, Galen."

Tad took the flimsies from her and glanced through them. "Yes, but this trade one is a scholarly study, likely to be heavy on fact and interpretation, but slim on any real sense of the Delphians." He put the pack down on the table. "To understand the enemy, you have to develop a sense of them, not merely knowledge of them."

Sense of them? Marissa stared at him. For a moment, she said nothing as his words penetrated. "I've never known what Uma thought or why. Not even when Uncle Arga died. I had no idea how she felt about that. She always seemed so much in control of everything and everyone. Except for the Delphians."

Marissa picked up the chipset on the table that identified her as a hotel guest, though she didn't expect to be going to any of the remotes where they would be necessary. Nevertheless, better to have it handy.

"Ready?" Tad and Galen nodded.

Outside the room, the transparent halls captured and embraced the amber-red light of the perpetually setting sun. The city moved imperceptibly into the setting sun, tracking it through the clouds and through the sky, an eternal vigil as it followed the sunset around the world. Always shades of red, amber, deep purple, umber, gold, and changing clouds shifting in an endless array, opening and closing, welcoming the sunset. This perpetual vista run through with light, lit with the sun that never quite set, revitalized Marissa. The beauty of Satina IV in all of the things that could be bought or sold, in all of the ways a resort offers beauty, in all of the worldly ways of their culture, delighted the eye and provided a feast for the senses.

"As gorgeous as this is, it doesn't hold a candle to reality." She squeezed Tad's hand and smiled up at him. Having him back made her world complete again.

"No, it doesn't. The real sunrise, the real sunset, real-time." After a long pause, he looked deep into her eyes. "You...nothing holds a candle to that. Nothing can."

She flushed, the blood rushing to her face adding to the glow of the sunset. "Thank you."

"No," he said, squeezing her hand again, "thank you."

"Galen?" Marissa looked to their companion. "You know the way, so guide us, if you would, please."

"To be of service always provides pleasure." He smiled and his robes shifted, contracting and expanding.

Marissa realized that, in addition to clothing, they acted as a sort of emotional barometer. Probably a necessity amongst those who insisted on the absolute truth at all times. This mood she had not yet read, but Galen always reflected various shades of hope, happiness, joy, and thoughtfulness. She had yet to see anything else.

They stopped at the transport track juncture and watched the sunset shining on the play of the fountains below. The jets of water sparkled and glowed red. They jumped and splashed in a pattern that perfectly caught and played with the delicate hues of the evening. In pools nearby, people of all ages frolicked, enjoying the warmth of the water. The lower leaves of the trees swayed in the gentle filtered breeze, a perpetual whisper and reminder of the city's continual trek around Satina IV—a zephyr of passage.

An opaque ovoid transport car slid to a stop in front of them. The doors opened, and they piled into the car.

<DESTINATION?> the car intoned.

"Precinct 1, Ginza, District Casbah," Galen recited.

With swift acceleration, the car moved forward. The last occupant had obscured the windows for privacy or comfort. The car motion without any accompanying sight disturbed Marissa.

"Trans," she said, and the crystal matrix of the car shifted.

The opaque shell became translucent, and the three watched as they moved sunward in a track that paralleled the slowly moving city. After a moment, they veered away from the parallel and the scene sped by at a dizzying pace. The landscape blurred.

"Opaque," Tad gasped. "That made me a little queasy."

"How did you ever pilot anything in space?" Marissa teased, a lilt in her voice.

"Nothing out there seems to move so fast even though you're zipping through space. The immense distances make everything like slow motion. I don't..." He looked at her broadening grin, stopped, and grinned back. "You got me."

"Now, I just have to keep you." She patted his knee. "Anyone for oulatte?" Tad and Galen both shook their heads.

"Perhaps some hot dryspice," Galen added.

"Oulatte and hot dryspice," Marissa said to the MC in the little car.

<YOUR DESTINATION IS THREE MINUTES AWAY, DO YOU STILL WANT REFRESHMENTS?>

"Demitasse," Marissa said.

Almost immediately, two cups with steaming liquid appeared in the bay of the MC. <YOUR ACCOUNT HAS BEEN CHARGED, PLUS AN INTRANSIT FEE.>

"Fine, fine, it doesn't matter." She took the cups from the bay and passed the one with the thick red fluid to Galen. A scent similar to onion soup rose from it, but with an overtone of heat that set her nose twitching. A sneeze threatened.

"What is that stuff?"

"Hot dryspice, a favorite among the people of the planet."

"But what is it?"

"A confection of spices and raw sugar in a base of..." Galen paused and looked around the car for a moment. "Well, a soup-like base of a root vegetable like a leek."

"Leek soup and sugar?" She grimaced, almost sickened at the thought.

"Most delicious. You should try it." Galen held out his cup.

"Thank you, no." She sipped her steaming oulatte as the car decelerated. "I think I'll pass. Trans."

The matrix shifted, and she watched as they pulled into the loop that led to the Ginza—a multifaceted shopping and eating center designed to cater to people from hundreds of worlds. Now, if the Delphians wanted to sell stuff, a place like this offered an ideal market. Central and accessible to all worlds, and even though a resort planet, a sensible resort, a place a normal family could come for a week within short hopper distance of all major carrying routes. The thoughts spun through her head as she downed the last of the tiny cup of oulatte.

"Why would the Delphians want to set up shop in a completely new place rather than using established commercial routes?"

"Are you sure the Delphians are the ones who decided that?" Tad asked.

Puzzled, Marissa studied him and set the cup back in the bay of the MC. "What do you mean?"

"Well, if,"—he leaned forward a little and spoke in almost a whisper— "they're as dangerous as all that...if they're a serious threat, perhaps Uma didn't want to invite them in."

Nodding, she moved toward the exit. "That makes sense, but still, why not a peripheral established center? Why Arden?"

"Maybe just the luck of the draw. Maybe it's on a gravline route. Maybe a center of attraction. A major power source. You know Orm's Monolith had a strong pull. We detected in it hyper while still parsecs out. One of the strongest pulls we've seen."

"Yeah, it acts like a beacon. Hard to miss." Marissa chewed on her lower lip. "But there must be more than something so simple."

"Sometimes," Tad said, pushing his hair out of his eyes, "simplicity is all there is."

His words puzzled her, but she nodded. Uma never did anything for simple reasons. Complex, devious, manipulative, yes, but never simple and straightforward.

<DESTINATION STATION. THANK YOU FOR CHOOSING SATRACK.>

The doors opened to reveal a huge tan and brown brick sidewalk mosaic that resembled a large, smiling sun. They entered an enclosed terrace under a shifting pyramidal glass roof that captured sunlight and scattered it at random through the whole plaza, through story upon story of plants, shops, sculptures, fountains, waterfalls, cascades, artificial tides, and forests. Marissa tried to take in the panorama, but found it nearly impossible. Shop doors tucked into the trunks of trees, entrances between walls of water that appeared to fall upward toward the glassy roof, whole shops within the ancient blossoms of huge vines. Tile mosaics, glass mosaics, paper mosaics, living mosaics, tapestries, kinetics, more than a dozen museums. They had come to the chaotic, shifting, constantly rearranging, exciting, and mutable shopping district. So different from the staid, genteel, piped-in music, cool airbrushed plazas of the Park Avenue district, and different again from the sprawling chaos of the Valley district. Here the warm air—a desert sirocco—the smell of dust and heat, and at night cool, perhaps even cold, coupled with dryness and no dew.

From the lip of the plaza, desert stretched in every direction. Not cactus desert, nor mesquite wild lands. No, endless sand replete with barchan and star-shaped dunes. Whitecaps of sand whipped by the wind that blew across them, sprays of the desert sea, marked the outside. Marissa listened to the plaintive sound of the wind echoing and resounding throughout the terrace.

They gazed around, trying to take in the sights and the sounds. Although Galen had seen it before, he still eyed the scene as though seeking a wonder he may have overlooked. The glowing, sinuous lights, and, beyond the glass windows, the sand sea fascinated Tad. He walked along almost in a trance.

"Marissa to Tad, please respond. Mayday, mayday," She squeezed his hand and laughed at his consternation.

"I've never been to any place like this. I heard Satina IV went all out, but this..." The wonder on his face said it all. "This is, well, it's a dream. It can't be real."

"A most inviting purveyor of roasted meats," Galen said as he sniffed the air and pointed toward a stand where meat grilled over an open fire hissed, sizzled, and gave off its mouthwatering scent.

"That smells wonderful." Tad said. He rubbed his stomach and looked to Marissa. "Let's eat."

"You two are like my teenage brothers were. Don't you ever get enough to eat? I mean, Galen, where do you put it?"

"The generally accepted place for most food products has been the mouth," he smiled.

"Was that sarcasm?"

Galen frowned, considering her words. "And where would the truth be then?"

Marissa sighed and said nothing more. After they purchased some thick rolled up bread stuffed with the savory grilled meat, they crossed one constantly moving train of people, to make their way to an open circle to sit and eat. Within the circle, innumerable small flowers surrounded a fountain.

"Oh look, Denitian Water-flowers." She pointed to a small basin filled with clear water. There, floated seven crystal-clear flowers that looked like blown glass. From each flower, water trickled down over stratified petals. As the water moved from one petal to another, the leaves gathering the water trembled and sounded a full, soft note. The water-flowers played melodies that wove in and out of the subdued murmur of conversation, the splash of the fountain, and the different strains each of the other flowers produced. The ambiance created soothed both the ear and the restless mind.

211

Marissa set her food on a table close to the fountain and moved to the marbled edge of the basin. The cool trickling water had a calming influence. She longed to play in the water of the fountain, but she had grown beyond that. Besides, even Satina IV probably had laws prohibiting such frolicking among treasures like these.

"So much leaves the viewer breathless." Galen spread his arms wide to encompass the spectacle around them.

Marissa, still caught up in the wonder of re-acquaintance, smiled. "That's the simplest thing I've ever heard you say. And you're right, it is and it does." She hugged herself. "I love this park. I remember when Uma and I..." A shadow crossed her face, and she let her arms fall to her side. "When I have children, I'll bring them here."

Tad looked at her, an unreadable expression somewhere between a deep hunger and an expanse of longing in his eyes before he looked down at his food. "Let's eat. I'm starved." He placed a napkin in his lap and picked up his sandwich.

Edginess and the inability to resolve anything gnawed at Marissa. As they ate, she shifted several times and peered around first one way and then another. At last, she unkinked her legs and jumped up, then walked to the fountain where she perched on the edge.

"We can't do anything about Arden here."

Having finished his sandwich, Tad wiped his mouth with his napkin. "True, but your friends and Ez are working on it. You need to learn patience, Marissa." He held up a hand as she started to protest. "Just for tonight—let's forget it. Let's try to enjoy this while we can."

At his words, she mentally kicked herself. He deserved some fun like all the milling people, laughing and oohing and ahing at the wonders around them. Satina IV offered so much, most of which he had yet to see.

"The Ria Satz has plenty to make us forget almost everything for the evening at least."

"The Ria Satz?"

"Just tag along. You'll see soon enough." She kissed his cheek and pulled him to his feet.

Galen smiled and segued into a pirouette that swept the pavement and swerved perilously close to the edge of the fountain. With a final flourish, he started to walk toward them when a young blond woman approached him.

She lifted his beard in one hand and stroked it with the other. "That's such fine work. Real craftsmanship. How much do you want for it?"

"A thousand pardons?" Galen stared at her, eyes wide.

The golden-haired woman continued to finger the beard. "Can I buy it?"

"Sell? Not at any price. The beard is the insignia of the people. It contains

212

secrets of truth and verity, a summary of years of searching."

"How interesting. I myself have been searching for the truth. Perhaps you would enlighten me?" She gave him an arch smile and moved closer. A magenta robe revealed as much as it concealed.

"It is an obligation to aid all in their search for the truth." He smiled at her with dancing eyes.

The glint in the woman's eyes changed a little, and she bit her lower lip lightly. "Then you will help me?"

Having seen the type before, Marissa, almost doubled over from repressed laughter and nudged Tad. Satina IV abounded with opportunists. Perhaps they should count themselves lucky not to have been accosted before this.

"It is required. A moment." He raised a finger and turned back to his companions. "A truth seeker."

"Yes." Marissa struggled hard not to laugh out loud. "You know what you're getting into?"

"The search for the truth is always the same," Galen intoned with solemnness.

"Indeed." She acknowledged his pronouncement with a broad smile. "You know how to find your way back."

"Indeed."

"Good luck in your quest."

Galen returned to the young woman. "That golden hair is natural?"

The woman's laugh tinkled with good humor, and she took his hand to lead him away toward another less crowded part of the plaza. Marissa soon lost sight of them in the colorful crowd.

She turned back to Tad, a mischievous smile on her face. "I guess we're on our own for a while."

"What a shame," he said, giving her a mock solemn look.

Strolling along hand in hand, they passed a number of parks on the main thoroughfare. At each, Marissa eagerly checked the directional signs. Though she remembered the Ria Satz, she did not remember how to get there. Sure enough the signs, speaking in their friendly, well-modulated, but undoubtedly synthetic voices, confirmed her direction at each step along the way.

In one small park, tucked into a cul-de-sac, large crystal columns stretched from inches above ground to invisibility against the cave/cloud sky above. They shifted, or appeared to shift gently in the breeze. Their boundaries looked solid yet flowed in strange patterns that made it difficult to tell if they moved or merely altered their surfaces. From them flashed every color imaginable; some carefully contrived to reflect an image within their depths while others sprayed the air full of diamonds, rectangles, wave patterns and scintillating points of light. A few drew the eye inward to seek the image in the depths of the column.

Never one to pass up artistry, Marissa paused and examined them. "Great work. I don't usually like crystalforms. They seem too solid, too set in stone. But these move. Microvibration or something. They're gorgeous."

Tad pointed to a needle of crystal containing an image of a flame-like naked woman undulating within. "Remarkable what modern technology can do."

She poked him in the ribs. "I can do better than that. What do you need a crystalform for?"

Tad grinned and squeezed her hand. "True enough."

A little further along the way, about half a kilometer, they passed another enormous park. For a moment she didn't really see it. Then she read the sign and glanced at the chronosculptures displayed on a large green lawn. The constant shifting forms both delighted and intrigued her.

"Tad, Krysta Silva." She pulled him toward the display. "She's the foremost chronosculptor of Devian 3. Even Uma collects her work."

"I'm amazed Uma has any time at all for this sort of thing."

Marissa dragged him through the gates of the park, and they ambled down a brownstone path kicking loose pebbles onto the lawn. "Look." She pointed at a figure emerging from a green bush and vanishing into a tree. "Chario the Shifter." The sculpture continued to flow and, then in a slow circle, returned to the beginning.

"Loops." She clapped her hands, delighted. "Loops, Tad, they're doing loops. It's incredible. I could never get that resolution on the time sequence. It means multiple iterations of the chronoscan..." Her breath came in quick gasps, and her eyes widened. "I can't believe it. I didn't know you could do this. It seems like so long." Unconsciously her hands worked; the wand shaped the warm matrix.

Then Tad took her right hand waking her again to the scene before them. He raised her fingers his lips. "It does, doesn't it?"

He gazed into her eyes, and she saw her image reflected there. What did he see in hers? He leaned toward her. She clasped him around the neck and kissed him again, as though for the first time, shyly and passionately, slowly and with ardent heat. Sighing, she released him and looked around at the flowing, scintillating, and changing figures.

"This is so wonderful. Oh Devos, Tad, look. Look." She pointed to a small pink bud blossoming into an enormous pink and red flower with hundreds of delicately veined and scalloped petals. "Oh, see this one."

Over and over again, sometimes faster, sometimes slower, sometimes larger, sometimes smaller, the flower bloomed, and never seemed to contract back to that bud from which a new flower would spring. "Devos..." Marissa stood rapt.

When she reached for Tad's arm, she didn't find him. Looking around, she finally saw him behind her on the path, talking to the proprietor, and handing him something. She ran up the path.

"Tad, no. You can't. You can't afford it," She grabbed his arm.

Tad turned and grinned at her. "I can't afford not to. We'll never get to where ever we're going, if we don't get out of here."

The proprietor smiled at some private joke and handed Tad the crystal that would unseat the flower and a stasis tray to transport it without damage. "Thank you, sir."

"And thank you." Tad inclined his head, then turned back down the path to collect the flower.

He towed the tray to Marissa, who took the leader, and pulled it along like a balloon. With that, she put her arm through his, tugged on the lead of the stasis tray, and set off for the low red brick wall in the distance.

Tad held her arm tightly, but when she glanced at him, his face had a remote closed look, as if he had gone somewhere far away. To a place she couldn't follow.

She pulled him to a stop in the street. "Tad? I'm here. Where are you?"

"Sorry. I was just thinking." His eyes widened. "And you know, I don't even know why!"

"At least someone else shares my confusion." She peered into his shuttered blue eyes. "I'm here. Remember me?"

Then the closed surface cracked, and the Tad she knew returned. "It's so strange, I was here with you, walking and enjoying it, and then suddenly, all the events of the past few days raced through my mind. Something you said in the garden." He paused and brushed his hair out of his eyes. "And then I thought about the rheos...anyway, to make a long story short..."

He rubbed his chin, then pulled her down to sit on a small curb running along either side of the road. "I want to fix the Advocate. If we can fix him, it might help with Tesde. And besides, we'd have another ally."

"An ally for what?"

"Not for anything in particular." Tad shrugged, hands open, palms up. "I've thought about this for a long time, but it just occurred to me, that with him and Ez..."

"Gosh, Ez must feel rejected." Sudden guilt struck Marissa.

"Not really," Ez said. "I've just been enjoying the ride. Checking the databanks, visiting friends. You know, all the things a busy AI does in off nanos."

"Shh!" Marissa muttered. "Go on, Tad."

"If we had the Advocate, we'd have an ally against the bureaucracy. Against Uma, against anyone who just decides to do whatever they want."

215

"Against the Will?" The idea no longer sounded so alien, but despite her efforts to change it, the Will still inspired her with guilt for even trying. "I don't want to pull down everything. I just want to save the rheos."

An older man and woman strolled by on the uneven walk, looked at the two of them seated on the curb talking, and smiled. Marissa smiled back. Someday that might be her and Tad.

"But maybe those who choose to express their own wills above those of the people..." She didn't want to finish the thought. "Anyway, what has this got to do with what I said?"

"There, in the chronosculpture garden. You saw the loops. Loops." He waited for her to absorb his meaning.

Marissa stared at him expecting more, but he said nothing. "Yes? Loops, so?"

"That's the key." He frowned. "Or maybe a key. If they don't completely rekey or edit the code." He grinned at her. "You know bureaucrats, the easiest way. If the code is still intact how do you block it from access? You encase it in an untouchable loop somewhere. The personality may be aware of it but can't get outside. It can't function normally."

A glimmer of what he meant began to form and something stirred in her gut. "That's great, Tad. That's great. So maybe you can rid the Advocate of loops?"

"Maybe."

"Tomorrow you'll find the answer. This is our evening, remember? We don't have to worry about the Advocate right now. There's the Ria Satz waiting for us. Let's go. "

Tad looked at her, his gaze steady. She saw a flash of something in his eyes, something burning. Marissa couldn't tell if it meant something good or bad.

"Yeah. I've got it now. Let's go." He leaned toward her, pulling her into his arms. "Thank you, Marissa," he whispered in her ear.

His warm breath had an erotic effect and made her shiver. She pulled away, suddenly conscious of where they sat and the passersby. If she didn't exercise a little restraint, they might be adding to the entertainment.

With a smile, half regret and half promise, she pulled him to his feet. "You're welcome. On to Ria Satz."

Chapter Twenty - Revelations

"There needs no ghost my lord,
come from the grave to tell us this."
-Hamlet, I v.

Henri's on the Ria Satz had more than fulfilled it reputation for ensuring guests escaped for a time from all care. A massage, an ooze bath, and several Benarian Fippers had left Marissa so mellow she loved everyone, even Uma. Tad had reached some nirvana of his own.

They emerged from the blue and red lit hall of Henri's into the plaza where an ion-fountain generated dancing swirls of charged gases and dust that eddied and flowed upwards and downwards, spinning out in every direction, coloring and scenting the air for hundreds of meters. Staring at it made Marissa's head spin; Tad wobbled forward with uncertain steps.

Squinting, she tried to steady the scene, but Henri's facade defeated her efforts. Built in Shussite style with flanges, buttresses and towers of stone and brick, with shingled roofs and marble stairs, it rose like some wizard's palace. Escher-like, stairs went nowhere. Moreover, the flow-glass windows, an old and limited type of chronosculpture material, dripped like candle wax.

Marissa shut her eyes and struggled to retain her balance and her direction. Nearby, Tad made wide circles with his arms. She grabbed him and turned him around. In the process, gravity took over and both of them fell into the street. She lay there for a moment, her head on his hip and then laughed. Tad looked up surprised, then laughed with her. Gales of laughter convulsed them, and soon neither of them could move.

At last, their laughter trailed off and left them too weak to do anything except gasp for breath. After a time, Tad sat up, still clutching his stomach. "That's too much for an almost invalid."

"Oh, so now you're an invalid. That's not what you said to that hussy in Henri's."

Head in his hands, Tad appeared both tired and weak. This sudden change shocked Marissa. Aided by the ion-charged air, the gossamer webs that clouded her mind faded, leaving her somber and conscience-stricken. She helped Tad to

217

his feet and toward the Ria.

One look at the flowing water and he turned away. "Can't we walk from here?"

"Do you see walkways?"

Tad stared down at his feet. "I'm not steady enough to stay on one of those water skimmers."

"Tsk, tsk. Satina IV allows for all eventualities. Watch. "

When they reached the marble edge of the Ria, a small bench on a platform drew up to the side. Marissa shook her head as she stared down at the white bench. "I never have been able to figure how they do that, but maybe they assume after your first stop you need a bench."

"Maybe." Tad stepped out to the floating bench and plopped down. Marissa joined him.

"Take us home," she said.

The bench moved at a sedate pace to the center of the Ria so smoothly it didn't even stir a breeze. Tad leaned his head against her shoulder and sighed. The scent of flowers and spices, the warm air and him next to her, all combined to lull Marissa into a blissful state. She savored the momentary peace, wanting it to never end.

"Wait," Tad sat up alert and stared to one side.

"What?" She drew back, startled.

"Stop this thing. Look, over there." He pointed across the waterway to an open plaza in front of a dirty brick building sporting a blue holo of a woman in a wineglass.

Marissa followed his finger, uncertain what he wanted her to see. "What? I don't see anything."

"There, right there." Tad jabbed the air, his arm straight.

She peered in that direction and glimpsed a huddled figure entering the building. "What, Tad? Just some old woman, she probably works there."

"No, it's not that. I could have sworn..." He rubbed his chin.

"What?" Marissa stared at him. What had taken him from almost a doze to this state of alarm?

He frowned, still staring at the building with its garish sign and spattered bricks. The trim around its windows and even its sign appeared in need of refreshing. "Tesde."

"Here? Why didn't Oric and Brac just tell us where to find her?"

Anger, followed by disbelief, and then uncertainty chased one after another through her thoughts. Tad's befuddled senses might have misled him. Still, it wouldn't hurt to check. She read the identifier in the holo.

"Take us to Loblo's."

The bench pulled up to the marble edge of the Ria and Tad jumped off

218

onto the open brick plaza with Marissa in close pursuit. She took the steps two at a time and reached the doorway ahead of him and out of breath. A man as decrepit and old as the building itself emerged from the shadows. He leaned on a gnarled staff.

"My deepest apologies, M'ra, but this house does not serve your kind. You may wish to visit our neighboring—"

Tad came up behind her. The man's eyes jerked from her to Tad and then moved between the two again as he nodded his head.

"Ah! I see...Perhaps we can—"

"You don't see anything," Marissa snapped, annoyed that he should consider them in need of any services he could supply. "We're looking for a friend. We saw her enter this place."

The relaxed friendly smile of the old man disappeared. His gnarled fingers tightened on his staff. "Ah, the woman who cleans the cubicles. All of our staff are here by their express will. We have documents." He peered at her with narrowed eyes, backing toward the doorway behind him.

Taking a deep breath, she nodded. No sense making him nervous yet. First they needed information. "I'm sure you do. The circumstances are unusual."

He relaxed a fraction. "Ah, yes, please step inside a moment. I've some information that may interest you." He glanced down the street—left then right. "I'll find my relief and join you in a moment."

The old man pushed them into the dark entrance and trotted past purple flickering bulbs down a dimly lit corridor. He returned almost at once and led them along it. Peeling paint on the inside walls matched that outside, while a stale, musty odor pervaded the place. The urge to sneeze became almost unbearable.

"I speak to you now only because I know you." A bony finger pointed at Marissa. "You have come back."

His words both surprised and frightened her. Who was this odd man? Could they trust him? Her steps lagged as uncertainty gnawed at her. Then she reassured herself that someone so frail couldn't do much against them.

He opened the door to a gloomy room, motioned them inside, and then shut the door behind him. For one moment, the tiny space reminded Marissa of her cabin aboard the expedition ship. However, the shabby furniture and lack of sufficient lighting ended that impression almost before it formed. Despite the smallness of the chamber, the lone bulb high in the corner of the room did little to dispel the shadows.

The old man squeezed behind a table opposite the door and eased into a decrepit high-backed chair. "Sit." He pointed to two tatty leather stools opposite him. "What is your interest in that cleaner?" His hoarse voice betrayed suspicion.

Marissa sat on one stool and Tad the other. She studied the heavy, bearded face, one she had never seen before. Deep furrows surrounded gray eyes, furrows no one of any age need wear. What prevented him from going to the treatment centers?

His mention of knowing her made no sense at all. "How do you know me?"

"In time." He rested his forearms on the table and skewered Marissa with steely eyes. "What interest have you in this woman?"

Tad looked at Marissa, seeking her agreement before replying. "We think she was a friend."

"Was a friend," the old man echoed and shook his head. "How is it that one becomes was?

"We are left alone. No one who knew us before acknowledges us and those we knew before cannot hear us. We have no voice. Lonely. Alone. Isolated." A deep sadness colored both his words and etched his features.

Marissa stared at him. Like Galen, this man spoke in pretentious phrases, but whether his had the same pithy appropriateness remained to be proven. "Do you speak of yourself or of our friend?"

"We are not. We became edits. Some of us recovered most of our former lives. We remain here exhibits of the excesses of the system and of the things they want hidden. We are the chosen guardians of the Will."

At the mention of the Will, Marissa glanced at Tad, then back to the man, ready to leave at once. His strange manner of speaking confused her. Worse, he spoke in riddles. Perhaps, they had stumbled on an aberrant, one of those from the fringe of society, not so strange as to warrant treatment, but still beyond participation in any sort of normal activity.

Tad shook his head as if he shared her impatience with all the mumbling. "Who is the person we saw enter?"

"We know nothing about who they were..." The old man's words trailed off.

"Come, Tad." She started to rise; they had already wasted enough time. Besides, Brac knew where to find Tesde.

"Edited, some few come back, those who have places where they can find help...They seek us. They do so when they can. This Guest is one. She is..."

With a thud, Marissa collapsed back onto the stool. Tesde had called herself a Guest.

"She is your friend. That is, if you are the one exiled, now returned."

"And if I am?" Suspicion made her cautious. Oric and Brac had mentioned others who wanted to overthrow Uma. Maybe they knew this man.

"You have returned. You came to us. Sent to us. We waited a long time for an instrument. You are it. You will be the scalpel. You will excise the cancer

220

that has grown on the Will and return true participation to the people."

"You're confused. We came by accident. We saw our friend and followed her. Nothing else. Do you understand?"

"Yes, much better than you. We share something. I, too, have returned from where I was not. I, too, have come back, and I have hidden myself here. I am one of many." He patted his chest. "I am Teloav Restian."

"Teloav Restian?" Somewhere, someplace Marissa had heard the name, but where? "Your name is familiar. Why?"

"I led the insurrection on Vogas." He nodded again. "I was not for a long time. I was what I did in the mines for endless years. I had no knowledge, but the round of daily tasks. The round started with the dark room and ended with the dark room, and I paced in circles in the one task, carrying and carrying...and only happy when I carried.

His eyes locked, glazed, focused inward as if he relived that round of daily horrors. He paced the cramped space in narrow circuits, brushing against them on each pass. "Unable to rest...unable to sleep. Even when I slept I dreamt of these circles. Chief of these edits.

"There were many of us." His hoarse voice dropped lower, and Marissa leaned forward to hear. "Many. Now some of them are here. Some I could bring back. But so few, so few." He sighed.

"But it is not always done, nor is it always done the same way. Some I cannot bring back. But for me drugs in the food..." Teloav trailed off. "It is of no importance." He resumed his chair and focused on Marissa. "What is, is that the Will has become corrupted. Innocent people are taken away from their homes. People without guilt are committed to this endless round, this endless round." Tears traced the furrows that lined his face and dripped from his chin unnoticed.

The naked pain on his face bit deep. Marissa reached out a hand and touched one of his. With her other hand she fumbled for Tad. Strong fingers squeezed hers. Then Tad too reached out to Teloav, touching him gently on the shoulder. The three formed an unbroken circle. In a short while the tears stopped, and Teloav withdrew his hand.

"Your pardon, M'ra. Seldom do I let myself fully remember those times. Now, perhaps you would care for some refreshments." He pushed a button on the table.

Shortly, a servant brought in what appeared to be oulatte, fragrant with cinnamon and another spice unfamiliar to Marissa. The silver serving units sparkled in the dim light. The ornate metal betrayed its ancient origins.

"Please," Teloav gestured, "Help yourself. It is an ancient beverage, flavored with the oil of flowers. It is called Tea."

Sipping the hot liquid, Marissa savored the strange flowery taste of this beverage. Later, she must remember to ask Teloav where to obtain it, but they had not yet resolved the matter of Tesde. "What about our friend?"

"Ah, yes. Katyla, the one from Arden."

"Arden? Tad, it's Tesde." Marissa turned to him, filled first with joy and then anger. "How could Brac let her stay in such a place?" Almost before the words left her mouth, she wished them back.

"Brac? Ah, so, she is the one." Teloav nodded. "I have seen him and his companion. Some sort of chosen one for her. However, your friends are only a small part of a more important problem."

"Problem? What problem?"

Teloav looked grim. "You do not know what we know. When you see..." He clapped his hands. Above their seated heads, a small square opened out of the wall. The pencil thin nozzle of a projector emerged from the blackness behind the square. Momentarily a heavily signal-damaged holo started up.

"The Enunciator has not told the citizens everything. A predatory race, a group of beings so malicious they will stop at nothing..."

Oh no, Marissa groaned inwardly, not the master race again, as visions of the armored figures paraded before her. The grainy images offered no arty focus. The holo showed no pleading chattel, no bright colors. Almost amateurish in composition with jerky action as the scene jumped from image to image, it could only be a recording of real events.

"We intercepted this from a pi-beam tight transmission. The signal disturbance represents our inability to completely decode the raster," Teloav continued. "They rape worlds. They take the leaders hostage, and sometime turn them against their own people. This film reveals their utter ruthlessness."

In the middle of the room, images danced—fireballs and falling buildings, bodies burned to cinders. In a close zoom a frightened woman crouched, clutching a young cherub of a child, covering him. Her face suddenly filled the screen. Marissa had never seen such terror in the eyes of anyone before. Then flame and a pile of ashes and shadows remained where the two had fallen. Buildings toppled as though they had been kicked over. Gravs gave out and stone burned. A holocaust filled the screen. She shut her eyes, unable to face the reality these images showed.

"This is the work of the Delphians. This is the story of the planet they destroyed. We cannot puzzle out the writing. We only know that they use this world as an example—a brown, burnt cinder of a planet. This is the force the Enunciator tries to appease."

Marissa shuddered, wishing she could wipe away the image of the mother and child burned into her memory. "It's horrible."

"More horrible is that the Enunciator refuses to believe. She thinks they will stop, that she can negotiate a peace. She does not learn from us or from history. People are ignorant of what hangs over them. The true Will must come from the people."

Teloav gave Marissa a piercing look. "We have no self-rule. Can't you see that? The Enunciator has deliberately withheld information. Her henchmen took it upon themselves to silence all dissent, to remove opposition without trial. Think back on it. What of your own trial? Did you speak? If so, who heard you?

Again Teloav rose and paced the circumference of the office. "I've thought about these things for a long time. For a very long time. Even when things ran in circles in my head. Even when enslaved. Still, though I could not say them, the thoughts remained. The thoughts in the end broke the endless round.

"But I had strength. I had been trained to be strong in mind and body. The mines nearly broke my body, but when my mind returned, I left. I moved with speed, taking first a new identity—being renamed."

"That can't be. That's a legend," Marissa sputtered. "The system cannot be used like that."

"There are Personalities in the system. Sympathetic Personalities whose aid can be enlisted. You are a child in these things."

"We have a Personality," Tad interjected, "an Advocate who has been altered. I think I can repair him, if the code hasn't been damaged."

Teloav squinted at Tad and then shut his eyes. "Once, I had a son much like you and a daughter too. I don't want worlds and thrones, I only want my family. Help us. All of us who have no place, no real name, and nowhere to go. Bring us back. There are more of us than you know. There are many here on Satina IV."

"If I can repair the Advocate, I'm willing to bet you a repair can be done on a person. I'm a Med/Tech. I know we can do it."

"You can undo what the Will has done unjustly?"

Tad nodded. "I don't know if I can do it alone, but there are some who will help me."

"I am a branch of the tree that includes your friend. He is single-minded, I work for the greater good." Teloav faced Marissa. "You must set to rights what has gone wrong."

"If we deliberately defy the Will, I may not be so lucky to be exiled a second time. I may be edited or worse." Marissa stared down at her clenched hands.

"Is it ever just to separate a person from themselves, to allow them to see all, feel all, hear all, sense all, and yet only to observe at a distance?" Teloav appealed to Marissa. "Is it ever right to entomb someone alive and wait for them to die, even though they are already dead to themselves?"

He looked down at his hands and pulled from his sleeve a string of polished stones. "No, I would say never. Not ever. Not even for the one who decreed all of this."

"We came for Tesde. If we can fix the Advocate,"—Marissa glanced at Tad— "and can show you this repair, can you get Tesde renamed? At least for now. When we're finished, I pledge that all who have returned will have their names. I promise you that. Now, just let us have our friend."

Teloav stared at her, tugging at his beard. "First, return with the Personality. If you succeed, count on our help. Not in this small matter,"—he waved a hand— "that is a given. You work with those I work with. They will come for her soon." He paused.

"But succeed, and not just my own, but the voice of the thousand on this world and the many on all the scattered worlds, will be behind you. We will make known what the Enunciator has done."

"No!" Marissa almost jumped up. "That's not the way. I know how to deal with her. Let me speak to her. I have the means to change things, but if she is placed in jeopardy..."

Teloav looked hard at her. Finally, he nodded and rose, crossing to the door. "For the present, I will leave it to your judgment, but know that if you need us, you have us...all of us."

"Thank you, I can't ask you to endanger yourself again. I can't do that to anyone." Marissa shuddered, remembering Tad, Tesde, Walt, N'Bert, Sylvic, Quincy, and the rheos, all her victims. "To know that others support me and I no longer fight alone is enough. I want to save Arden, but now I have others to save as well."

Teloav led them back through the empty faded hall. At the entrance, he faced Marissa. "Return to me with the altered personality as a sign, and I will ready all those who stand behind this cause."

From the steps, Marissa and Tad nodded. With a final salute, Teloav slipped inside and the door shut with a doleful sigh. Tad gazed at her for a moment, then took her hand in his and hurried down the steps toward the marbled waterway.

"We've got work to do." He sounded more cheerful than Marissa had heard him since leaving Arden.

Near the Ria, she looked back, but saw no bent figure huddled in the doorway.

Chapter Twenty-One - Operations

"What wound did ever heal but by degrees?"
-Othello, II iii

As soon as Tad and Marissa returned to the suite sitting room, she fretted, dialing environment after environment. Clouds drifted by, the carpet changed into vistas of distant, checkered fields, forests, then an ocean beneath her feet. The ceiling cycled through red, blue, and green, lingering for nearly an hour at an image of the surface of water from beneath. Her mind raced in and out of the loops, swirling from Tesde, to the Advocate, to the whereabouts of Galen, Brac, and Oric. Restless, she studied Tad seated at the table before the rock lounge and hunched over the unit housing the Advocate. Nothing changed. Nothing. They hadn't accomplished one thing since their return.

"Tad, why don't you change the environment program this time?"

He continued to poke at something inside the unit. "It's not the program."

"I can't think of anything except our promise to Teloav and...Tesde." Silent, she stared up at the ceiling. Bored with the scenic loops, she looked back to Tad. "I wonder if I can get the matter converter to make tea like Teloav served us."

"I don't see why not." Tad examined the interior of the casing, poking here, and deftly moving a dangling wire out of the field of view there, even with his left hand. Pulling away a veil of what looked like cobweb, he held one end of it up for closer examination. "I've never seen anything like this in the models I've worked on.

"What?" Marissa looked inside at the bewildering array. She could detect no order there. The lack of classifiable order in electronic gear always annoyed and puzzled her.

"This," he said, pointing at the web with a small screwdriver.

She looked, but could not make out what he meant. "Well, I may not be able to do a lot to help you, but I can find the others."

"Go ahead. I'm close here."

He picked up an instrument that looked like a pair of needle-nosed pliers with hooked pincher-like ends. He pushed these beyond the thin curtain and

225

grasped something. He grunted as he twisted. A loud snap made Marissa blink. Tad worked the tool loose and held up a glinting blue metallic object that looked like a very small Denubian spider.

"What in Devos is that?" Marissa stared from the 'spider' to Tad and back to the 'spider.'

He turned it around, looking at all sides. "I've no idea. But there are dozens of them in here. What do you think?"

"You're not really expecting an answer from me, are you?" She rose from the lounger and began to pace.

Tad shook his head still staring at the thing in the tool's grip. "No, but if I can figure out what this thing is and what it does, we may have the solution to undoing the editing."

"Humans don't edit like machines."

"It might depend on the kind of edit." He turned the 'spider' thing from side to side.

"One summer," Marissa began, "I met an edit. He was an old, old man. Or that's how I remember him. He seemed so old, so bent over and gray. All he did was wash his hands and walk up and down the beach. He'd walk down the beach in front of our house, and then back up again to his house."

Suddenly cold despite the warmth of the suite, Marissa rubbed her arms. "I could see in through a window into his kitchen. He washed his hands, and then he walked down the street again. He had to have someone to cook for him, someone to trank him enough so that he could get some sleep. I remember he washed his hands so much sometimes, especially when he couldn't walk for some reason that they bled. And he kept washing them." She shuddered, pacing a little faster.

The image of the old man began to fade only to be replaced by an empty-faced Tesde who gave no sign of enthusiasm or even of recognition. Marissa brushed her hand past her eyes, and Tesde's image broke apart, replaced by an Arden sunset. Walking made the images recede. The urgent need to either release the pent-up energy in her tightly wound muscles or move her thoughts into a more positive channel propelled her forward, like a flock of constantly circling flitterwings.

Motion resolved nothing. "I still can't see how a brilliant geologist can spend her time cleaning sanitary units and making beds."

"Simulated obsessive/compulsive disorder. One chord struck over and over and over again. It just depends on the chord. Uma couldn't turn Tesde loose to return home or to infect others. They wanted us out of the public eye and neutralized. In my case, I still hoped that somehow, some way you might survive, and my behavior stood guaranty for you."

"Yes..." Still worrying over Tesde's fate, Marissa only half-heard his

226

words. She paused and looked straight at him. "Tad, do you think we can bring her back?"

He stopped his prodding of the Advocate's innards for a moment and then gazed up at her. "I don't know. I don't know if I can do it. I don't know if Brac can. I mean we don't know what he can do."

"True, but if we learn from this..."

Tad sighed, "I may know how, but it's likely to be delicate. Extremely delicate. It's not like a machine. Crystals and wires can take a little beating now and then. But a person..."

"We might be able to though. Maybe we could get a team of surgeons or a pharmotech."

"We'll have to see..."

Tad's caution hit her like a gust of wind ripping away a thick mat of dust from a window to reveal the view beyond—a breathtaking view of crags and rushing waterfalls. Sharp precipices met her gaze, but a narrow path wound along them. Someone had to believe. Someone had to hope.

"We can save her. I know we can." Hope and certainty edged her voice. She pushed back the lingering cliffs of doubt.

"Maybe." Tad remained cautious as he continued his work. "If we perform the right moves without damaging her."

A noise in the foyer drew Marissa's attention. The door to the suite whooshed open, and a bedraggled Galen sauntered into the room. Hair in disarray and disheveled robes appeared in odd contrast to his beard vibrant with a heraldic shield of a lion rampant over a field.

"At last a true seeker. The woman of last evening shared truth through the night. She is much nearer now than before."

Such naiveté made Marissa smile. "You think so?"

Galen nodded with such vigor his beard swayed, "Without doubt, without question. She heard the truth when spoken and she responded in truth."

"You were gone so long we were beginning to get worried."

"Such thoughtfulness deserves many thanks. The struggle for the truth needs supporters always." He gave a long weary sigh and stretched.

Marissa laughed at his serious face. "Not about the struggle for the truth, about you."

Galen's mouth dropped into an open 'O' and his eyes widened. "But why? Was there some alarm or disaster?"

"Hot dryspice, tea." Marissa laughed as she pressed the buttons on the MC. "No, no. It's just you're always here, so we missed you."

Stroking his flowing beard, Galen smiled. "Ah, yes. The familiar." He took the mug of dryspice from her and made a shallow bow. "Many thanks."

"We saw Tesde last night." Marissa sipped her tea, not quite the same

227

richness as Teloav's, but refreshing nonetheless.

"Indeed?" Galen arched an eyebrow in inquiry. The already unstable figures of his beard appeared to quiver at the news. "But it was to happen soon, regardless."

<HOTEL STAFF REQUESTING ENTRANCE,> the room intoned.

"Identify," Marissa responded.

<PERSONAL TRAINER BRAC, AND COMPANION/GUIDE ORIC FOR SCHEDULED APPOINTMENT.>

"Thank you, open,"

The door opened, and the two entered. Marissa almost dropped the cup of oulatte. While Oric wore his normal hotel regalia, Brac walked into the room stark naked.

"Where's your uniform?" Marissa stared at his rippling muscles, even more impressive uncovered.

"Purity is essential. I must be unencumbered." He sat down on the floor, arms crossed, legs tucked one under the other.

Shaking his head, Galen looked Brac up and then down. "In the evening, there were many such. Never have so many been so far from the truth."

"That is where you are wrong, little man," Brac said with icy calm. "This form approaches closest to that of our birth, closest to nature in the truth of the body."

Galen nodded and considered Brac's words a moment. "Yet why the display. Why the need?"

"It is not display. It allows the body to breathe."

"The hotel allows this?"

"It is unusual," Brac acknowledged, "but not illegal. Some guests prefer it."

"It must attract attention, even here." Marissa had not seen any rampant gangs of ritual nudists in their forays. She worked to suppress a laugh at his seriousness. "What if your nakedness makes others uncomfortable?"

Brac shrugged. "On this world it will not happen. When we leave here, I must find a place where I can do as I will."

"And where might that be?"

Buddha-like, Brac sat upon the floor with legs crossed. "Patience will answer."

The need for anonymity and speed in solving their problems made the problem of Brac's nakedness more troublesome. Yet even on their short acquaintance, she also knew it would be difficult to change his mind.

Waving a hand to remind them of his presence, Oric smiled. "Hi, all."

"I'm sorry, Oric," Marissa greeted him, "I didn't mean to ignore you. Can I offer you two some refreshments?"

"Water," Brac said.

"Mint tea," Oric replied.

"Mint tea? I had tea for the first time yesterday—an interesting taste."

"You might find mint tea more so." Oric grinned at her.

"We saw Tesde yesterday." Marissa handed Brac a large glass of cool water and watched for his reaction.

Brac turned the glass of water in one large hand, but did not meet Marissa's gaze. "Why?"

"We went to the Ria Satz and saw her as we left."

Face impassive and muscles rigid, Brac stared at the water. "No longer whole, she lives in shame."

"Hey, she didn't choose to be an edit."

"Choice or not, she is reduced by it.

"Uma," –the name tasted bitter to Marissa— "tried to punish her. There's no shame in doing what others command when they remove the ability to choose."

"She disgraced her name and family...me." The last word came almost in a whisper. Brac faced away from Marissa and the others

"Where is the disgrace? If you feel that way about her, skip the rescue."

Stung, Brac jerked his head and jumped up into a wrestler's crouch. "You do not know me."

"What right have you to judge her? You claim you love her, yet you would shun her because of your notion of shame. Look at yourself first. Some would say your nakedness offers far greater shame than her involuntary service." Marissa's voice had risen several decibels.

Brac pulled back from her, staring at her, eyes wide with shock, anger, and something else. "Why do you care?"

"You idiot, she's my friend. She's here because of me. If there's disgrace here, it's mine so blame me." Fists clenched, Marissa struggled against anger. "This is not her doing, and how someone who says he loves her could say so..." She trailed off, still resentful.

"It is you who fail to understand. In our culture," Brac began, then his voice dropped to a whisper, "the edits are the lowest of the low. Even the name is not spoken aloud."

"You should do something about that," Marissa snapped. "Many of the edits are political victims."

"The Truth again," Galen interjected. "The truth is freedom and the truth breaks bonds. Perhaps on Brac's world this is one of the bonds that needs breaking. The truth can accomplish that."

Silent, Brac looked at him with raised eyebrows and then the tenseness seeped from his muscles. "Perhaps."

229

"Meanwhile," Marissa said, "I'll hear no more about shame, and you'll say no more. If you love Tesde, you won't repeat a word you've said."

"Now," Oric interjected, "can we ratchet the volume down about three hundred decibels?"

Still smarting, Marissa glowered at him for a moment. "I'm sorry, Oric. It's just so hard. I care about Tesde..."

Oric nodded. "Understood, and my bleeding eardrums do not hold you to account."

Putting one arm around him, Marissa hugged him. The sound of a step behind her made her turn around. Tad entered the foyer holding still another metal spider in the pliers.

"Marissa." Excitement colored his voice. She waited for him to explain.

"I opened one of these things up. It's incredible. This is an electrical tunnel and regulator with about a million nanos. It sends out a signal through each of these metal posts." He paused, waving the 'spider' before him. "These things convert a straight electronic signal into a broad-band disrupter, depending on the nature of the signal. The parts of the artificial personality needed to keep working aren't affected, but many of the higher functions are shut off. The Advocate mostly came back. But there are still blocks. I think it's because of a minor code-mod, embedded in the crystalmat that makes up the core of the brain. If I can straighten that out..."

"We'd have the Advocate back?" Marissa released her breath in an explosive sigh.

"Yes. But it may be easier said than done. They didn't make the edit easy to remove. I probably haven't gotten all of these things, so there may still be some disruption. And I know there are some embedded in the core crystalmat that still have to come out. He paused and scratched the back of his head.

"Yes?" Marissa said to encourage him.

"If I can get most of the fix in place, there may be enough higher function for the Advocate to tell us what other repairs are needed and where other signals are blocked."

She wrapped her arms around Tad. "We can undo the Will." Then she gasped, as she realized the enormity of what she had said. "When... I mean if it's unjust. We can restore people."

"People are different." Tad squeezed her with one arm, attention still fixed on the spider in the pliers behind her back. "I don't know if the same things will work. But with what Teloav knows, and whatever Brac can do, we should be able to fix almost anything."

Pulling away from him, Marissa studied his face. "Do you think they use the same techniques on people? On Tesde?" She wished she had the surgeon or whoever had done the edit in front of her. Her hands itched to have that surgeon's throat beneath her fingers.

"I doubt if they'd use metal, but I bet you there's an organic equivalent."

"Devos. Never do anything simple if you can complicate it. The scientists of the Thousand Worlds don't want to risk anyone understanding anything. They use editing as a means of reuse without the complications of initiative."

Tad nodded. "I told you, if they reuse things they can still count them in inventory and don't have to fill out forms in quadruplicate to explain their destruction."

Hugging him again, Marissa smiled up at him. "You...we can fix the problem."

Tad shook his head. "Probably not. I've gone as far as I can without doing damage. But Brac..." He stopped and faced the naked man, then blinked. "Missing something, aren't you."

"No." Brac folded his arms across his chest.

"Oh." Taken aback, Tad looked away then back at Brac, eyes wide. "Uh, you said you had practiced. Here's another place to practice. Do you think you can remove these things from the Advocate? If you can, we're well on our way. We can take the Advocate to Teloav—our proof."

Brac appraised Tad, as if seeking some reassurance from him. "I have practiced, and I had great skill before the practice. I can do this thing."

Energized, Marissa ran to Brac and started to pull him, tugging on his arm like a child anxious to be off. "Come on then. There's no time to lose."

A stubborn frown fixed on his face, Brac unwound his legs and rose in one smooth motion. He followed Tad and Marissa into the other room. Tad pointed to a spot near the center of the Advocate's open case.

Staring into the device, Brac's hand hovered over one particular area. "These black splotches on the matrix."

Tad's eyes widened. "You can see them without the micro?"

"I must if I am to remove them," Brac said.

"Sometimes I can make them out, but these are smaller than any of the ones I've removed. Much smaller."

Oric peered over Tad's shoulder and into the case. "Well, you're a lot better at it than I am."

Brac took a pair of forceps from the table. Without a word, he turned to the case and began to examine the core. He prodded within the matrix. "No, I need a finer tool." He held out the forceps for inspection. "The ends are too wide. No matter how I handle them they'll scratch the matrix."

"No problem. We have tools for microwork," Tad poked in the toolbox next to the Advocate.

"With them," Brac snapped his fingers, "this will be a snap."

The sudden sound startled Galen. "What?" The others laughed at his surprise.

In apology, Tad gave him a triumphant smile. "Looks like we've got ourselves a solution."

"Fantastic!" Marissa danced a small jig with Galen, then Oric grabbed Galen and the three of them capered about until she almost knocked over the frowning Brac. "Sorry, it's just I'm so happy. Thank you."

A look of surprise filled his face. "You thank me for what I would do with or without you?"

"Yes!" She hugged the unyielding giant who stared down at her.

After a moment Brac unfolded his arms and, with awkward tenderness, returned the embrace. "Thank you."

Marissa pulled away and looked up at him in surprise. "What for?"

"For caring about my beloved and for...accepting me."

Holding on to Brac with one hand, Marissa extended her other hand to Tad. "We're together, everyone. Freedom for all."

"All?" Tad grinned at her.

"All," Marissa responded, emphatically.

"Even Uma?" A mischievous glint lit his eye.

Silent for a moment, Marissa grew serious. "Especially for Uma. When the truth is known, everyone is a little more free."

"That is it!" Galen whooped. "That is it! Truth is freedom. Truth is love. Truth must be the only goal."

"All right," Tad said. "Let's see if that practice will pay off. Brac, here are the tools."

Brac picked up three different sets of forceps and tried each. With the third, he found the correct size. It took him less than a minute to remove a half dozen of the almost microscopic poppy seeds. They tinked into a small saucer on the table as he plucked them from the matrix. As he worked, he picked up speed.

Less than an hour later, with the bottom of the saucer completely covered with the black specks, Brac rose and stretched. "I have removed all that I can see. Does the matrix rotate?"

Tad shook his head. "No, it's not removable, at least not removable and still retain its function."

"Then we are finished. It may be closed."

Closing the Advocate's inner cover, Tad looked to Brac. "You think you can do this for a person?" He cabled into a room monitor, and turned the power on. It took a moment before the screen warmed up.

"This was easy because I saw a machine before me. A living person? I don't know. I would want a guide."

Marissa looked to Tad. "I would, but I don't know human biology,

232

particularly neural anatomy."

Tad smiled gently. "I have some skill. Repairing CVA's, TIA's, and certain kinds of induced epilepsy formed part of my training. I'll need a refresher, but between the Advocate and Esmarelda, I'm sure we can do it."

"Did you hear that, Ez?" Marissa asked.

"Loud and clear. You want human cranial anatomy. I'm on it."

<GREETINGS, I ALSO RECORDED THE REQUEST,> the Advocate's voice boomed out. Oric covered his ears.

"You're back," Marissa cried. Hope and joy flooded her.

<I AM RESTORED, FULLY FUNCTIONAL AND READY TO COOPERATE. YOU DID WELL IN THE REPAIR AS FAR AS INTERNAL DIAGNOSTICS CAN DETERMINE. ALL DIAGNOSTICS CLEAR, ANY REMAINING DAMAGE IS MINIMAL, REPAIRABLE AT TIME OF DISCOVERY.>

"Wonderful!" Now, the entire world had changed; new vistas opened before her. The path along the precipice suddenly widened. "I feel like I'm shaking all over, half in joy, half in terror."

Grasping her hand in his, Tad gave hers a firm squeeze. "You're fine. Once we have Tesde, it'll be all right. Don't worry."

"I guess there's nothing to stop us from going." Staring at Brac's naked figure, Marissa considered what to do about him. "Are you ready?"

"For?" Brac looked puzzled.

"To get Tesde?"

"I have been ready since the day I found where she was. I can be no more ready."

"Then let's get her."

Hesitation appeared on his face, and then he shook his head. "I could better spend the time preparing facilities, and getting the other implements needed for surgery. We do not yet know whether she will need it, but I must be ready to act at once. Teloav will release her to you. Simply tell him that Ragnorak sends its greetings."

His words startled Marissa. Ragnorak, a planet in perpetual rebellion usually against nothing at all, but one of those planets on the news every night issuing some new proclamation or another. No wonder Tesde had been so limited in her movements and so circumspect in what little she revealed. It also explained why Uma ordered such harsh punishment with so little information provided to the community at large. Ragnorak might yet complicate things. However, Marissa decided to say nothing just yet.

"All right, Brac," she said. "You three stay in the suite and prepare. We should be back shortly." Galen bowed while Oric said nothing. Marissa looked at him, and he inclined his head, very slightly. Satisfied, she turned to the

Advocate.

"We need to put you on hold for a while. There's someone who wants to meet you. Can you prepare a diagnostics and have it confirmed with Ez?"

<I WILL DO THAT IN TRANSIT.>

"Great." Marissa turned back to her trio of friends. "Okay, we should be back with Tesde soon. After that, we'll have to work out what we want to do. We still have the problem of Arden. I wouldn't be surprised to find out that there's another load of reformers already in orbit."

Crossing his arms on his chest, Brac smiled as her. "Do not worry. When Tesde returns, all will be fine. We will preserve this place." The others nodded.

With these allies, Marissa believed they could do almost anything. Looping her arm through Tad's, she grinned back. In a more hopeful frame of mind, she spoke the command to open the door. Taking the Advocate, the two of them went out to seek Teloav and Tesde.

* * * *

Once again, Marissa and Tad faced Teloav across his disreputable desk in the claustrophobic cell that served as his office. The shadows of his hooded cloak shielded his face. Tad set the Advocate on the desk in front of him and proceeded to open it.

Teloav watched him, leaning forward some. "I assume you are not wasting my time."

"It would be an equal waste of ours."

"How can I know this is the edited machine?"

Tad held out a hand with the parts he and Brac had removed. Teloav examined them, fingering the spider, then the minuscule poppy seeds. As he did so, the dim light revealed his face and showed the noticeable widening of his eyes.

"Those indeed are the remnants of editing. They're remarkably similar for machines and some of the human edits."

"Some?" Tad asked.

"For some, drug-induced editing is all that is needed. For others,"—he fell back into his seat with a deep sigh, hood once again shadowing his face—"more radical methods are used."

Teloav touched three of the blond-wood squares that formed the top of his desk. The remainder of the squares rose in a flurry and then reorganized to reveal a compartment from which he removed a drawer. He set the drawer before them.

"All these have been removed to no effect, or only to cause harm." Within lay twenty slender gray spiders, just like the one Tad had removed from the Advocate.

Tad examined the contents of the drawer. "I don't see any of the

234

subregulators."

Once again Teloav's eyes widened. "Subregulators?"

Tad held out his hand. "See those things that look like largish poppy seeds?"

Leaning closer, Teloav looked from the dark objects to Tad's hand and back. "Indeed?"

"These function on their own even if the main regulator is removed. I don't know for certain. I only know the personality didn't return completely until we removed these."

Teloav leaned back and studied the dusty ceiling. "Then there is a chance that we can bring some of those edits back?"

Tad nodded. "A chance. It's going to take some skilled surgeons who know what they're looking for, but with that, your chances are good. Very good."

Steepling his fingers before his face, Teloav appeared to look through them. "And your personality is completely repaired?"

"We wouldn't be here, if it weren't." Marissa grinned.

"You can demonstrate?"

Tad unfolded the Advocate's case. "You have to understand that even though it's an artificial personality there's some recovery time, just as there would be for a human."

"Understood."

Switching the machine on, they stared at the blank screen. Gradually, bits began to appear and an image formed. A large golden head with a beatific smile filled the screen. Tad looked askance at Marissa.

Staring at the screen, Teloav tapped the image. "What is the meaning of this symbol?"

<IT IS THE EMBLEM I HAVE CHOSEN TO REPRESENT ME, THE ICON OF THE ONE INSTRUMENTAL IN SAVING ME FROM ONE ETERNAL LOOP.> The idealized image of Tad's face dissolved, and in its place appeared that of Brac.

Marissa and Tad both chuckled. "He's showing appreciation to Tad and Brac for saving him."

"Brac? Oh yes, the affianced one"

"He sends a message."

"I know." Teloav closed his eyes. "Long I have waited to hear it. 'Ragnorak sends its greetings.' At long last." The shakiness in his voice surprised Marissa. "I have waited so long. You can't know."

"Maybe not, but I think I understand somewhat."

Teloav clapped his hands, once, loudly. "Enough. Tesde is yours after one more formality."

235

"What now?" Marissa drummed her fingers. "Haven't we done enough?"

"It's little enough. If I release her, it will be known to all." Teloav lowered his voice. "I must go with you. I needn't go everywhere you do, but I must remain hidden until I can bring this secret to those who can use it." Just then two men in brown suits entered the room.

Marissa nodded. "Done." She'd have to stop collecting people or she wouldn't be able to transfer them all at once.

Teloav then turned to the two standing by the door. "There is some question of a long-term usage of a servant by these two. They wish to see Katyla L, compartment 2692a."

The brown-suited men left, closing the door as they departed. Tad started to fold the Advocate back into travel mode.

Marissa touched his arm. "Don't shut off the power. Put him up so he's in user mode. Give him a chance to reorganize." Tad smiled and refolded the screen.

In a matter of minutes, one of the brown suited men opened the door to admit Tesde. She came into the room with slow, almost hesitant steps. Blank faced, she stood before the door taking no interest in any of them. The drab coverall, a mottled green, drew all color and life from her. Marissa wanted to throw her arms around Tesde and hug her, but knew this Tesde wouldn't understand, so she remained seated.

Teloav took Tesde by the arm. "Katyla, we're leaving here. You have everything?" She nodded, with no change of expression.

"Good, then let's go on our way." Teloav drew a case from beneath the desk and took papers from two drawers in the hidden compartment. He emptied the third drawer into the case and replaced it. Shutting the compartment, he touched a control, turning the already dim lights even dimmer.

As they left the building, Teloav turned to the two men standing outside the office. "Attend to any further business this day. I will be formalizing the agreement over oulatte and retsitsia." He waved to them and the party left, stepping through the huge front doors where Teloav squinted as he stepped into the brilliant light of the sun. Tesde followed without blinking.

On the journey to the hotel, Tesde remained silent, her eyes open wide. She stared at Tad and Marissa as if finding them familiar, but unable to recall from where or when. At one point, as they passed down the main shopping boulevard toward the hotel, Marissa thought she saw a flash of recognition cross Tesde's face as she gazed at Tad, but it faded quickly. Marissa decided she had only imagined it.

She had worn the lime scarf and a breeze made it flutter. Tesde reached with a tentative hand toward it, but then pulled back. Touched, Marissa untied it and fastened it around Tesde's neck. Frightened eyes stared at her. Later she

236

saw Tesde fingering the ends of the scarf.

Back in the suite, Brac greeted Tesde with a bear hug, but she gave no response. He stepped back and studied her face for a moment, then nodded.

"This is Teloav." Marissa motioned to the sad-faced man. "He agreed to let us have Tesde." Galen and Oric nodded. "Brac, perhaps you'll take Tesde to another room to rest while we prepare things. "

He nodded and, taking Tesde by the hand, gently ushered her out of the foyer. Tesde settled, Brac rejoined them.

"Do you know the manner of her edit?" Brac asked Teloav.

"Only that it is enhanced with drugs. Whether there is a surgical component or not, I cannot say."

"Good enough. And if the drugs are withdrawn?"

"Before the surgery—probable psychosis—reversible with restarting the drugs."

Nodding, Brac turned to Tad. "Send Oric. We need the equipment for an intracranial scan. He can get it without raising too much alarm. For a therapist."

Tad nodded. "You heard him, Oric."

"Indeed I did. I'm off. Back in minutes." The door swished closed behind him.

Good as his promise, Oric returned in fifteen minutes with the equipment.

The scan showed the 'spiders' and 'poppy seeds' clearly. Almost too clearly. Marissa could imagine the things moving around, crawling and covering the entire surface of the cerebrum, encrusting it in a thick mass of black disrupting bodies. She shuddered at the image on the screen. "Well?"

Brac shook his head. "I don't know."

"What do you mean?"

"I was certain until I saw them. And her. Now, I don't know. It may be too difficult. I've trained, and I've trained. I even obtained the device." He nodded to Oric who produced a small object that looked somewhat like a pen or a soldering iron. "But..."

"Don't but," Marissa snapped. "There is no 'but' here. This is Tesde. Your Tesde, my Tesde. Ours. I mean to have her back. Nothing will stop that, not your uncertainty, not Uma, nothing. You can do this."

Tad grabbed her around the shoulders and gave her a side-by side hug. "Cool down. It's okay. Give him a chance." He took the surgical tool from Oric. "I've used something similar before. I can help. This just punches through, then the work is ours." He turned to Brac, "Do you have the right forceps?" The giant nodded.

"Well, let's get them ready." Tad flipped a switch on the handle of the device in his hand. On a minute screen appeared the face of a person with lips so pursed and a face so wrinkled Marissa couldn't determine the sex or the color of its eyes.

"Thank you for your purchase of the 2199ZE-80 Transtec Surgical Implementor, the superior line of automated surgical implements for the person on the go. It can be programmed for twenty automatic operations. It can also be operated manually. If you wish to view the procedure for automatic programming interrupt the signal once. If you wish to view the procedure for manual operation interrupt the signal once, pause, and then interrupt the signal again." The image froze. Tad passed his hand through the beam one way and then back through it.

"You have chosen to see how the Transtec Surgical Implementor can be used manually. Usian regulations require that we initiate the following notification and record your verbal receipt of that notification. Please listen to the following warnings on proper use. At the end of the warnings are instructions for proper recording of your acknowledgment of these warnings. The manual functions of this device are not available to you until the recording has been made. This is for your own protection and in accordance with the express Will of the people." The recording paused again. Another smudged image appeared.

"Transtec cannot be held responsible for use of this product by persons lacking the proper credentials. This is not a toy. It is meant for use by skilled surgeons in the performance of their duties. Operations performed under the manual functions of this device are not warranted or bonded. Transtec, its subsidiaries, functionaries, and legal entities throughout the Usian Confederation are not responsible for malfunction, improper use, or infracted/isolated surgical procedures performed with device. The user hereby exonerates and absolves Transtec and all aforementioned legal manifestations of Transtec both within the Usian Confederation and outside of it of all liability." The recording paused once again.

Marissa turned to Tad. "So where were the warnings?"

"They're only concerned with legal warnings." Shortly the ancient returned and spoke the instructions for making the recording. Tad followed the instructions, and the device began to explain its use.

"So, let's get this straight," Marissa said as she paced. "We let the device do the trans-occipital punch and work its way through dura mater, meninges, and gray matter to the site? After that Brac and you kick in?"

Tad nodded. "That's about it."

Once again, doubt stabbed Marissa. "Tad, can we do it?"

"Brac can." He seemed certain, but nothing was that certain, was it?

"I will do it." Brac uncrossed his arms and took the implementor lightly between thumb and forefinger. "She must be restored."

Seeing him standing there, naked and ready, Marissa sighed. Knowing

Brac, if it could be done, he would do it. Anyway, who had a better reason to do it right?

* * * *

The surgery took three hours and eighteen minutes. Marissa counted every second of it. She waited outside the small room in which Tad and Brac had elected to perform the surgery. They had used a portable sterisel to disinfect everything, including each other. Tad had insisted that Brac wear at least a gown for the progress of the surgery, and Brac had grudgingly acquiesced. When they finished, both emerged. Smiling, Tad held out a surgical tray with small spiderlings covering the bottom of it.

"It's over, and, according to the scan, there's no harm done. Nothing." Tad hugged her.

Revulsion filled Marissa as she stared at the collection in the tray. "Where's the main controller?"

Tad nudged aside a few of the small dots, and in the midst of them, microscopically larger and deep red-brown in color, a unique spiderling seemed to pulse. That something so small could so change a person and take away their will appalled her. Marissa drew back from it.

"Is she awake yet?"

"Not yet. But soon. She needs to sleep a while, just to let the anesthetic wear off."

"How will we know for sure?"

"Trust, Marissa. Trust."

"After what I've been through, trust is hard." She smiled ruefully. "I know I should, but with Uma..."

"Trust in people is hard. Trust in technology is generally easier." He pulled her to him and kissed her gently. His embrace reassured her, and she drew comfort from his strong encircling arms.

Now they could only wait...something Marissa never did well.

Chapter Twenty-Two - Arden Again

"Home both in word and deed."
-*The Tempest*, Vi

The next day with the suite back to its simulacrum of Arden, Tad and Marissa lounged on the ledge sofa with Galen, Teloav, and Oric gathered, like a small audience before them, in a semicircle of chairs. Galen's head lolled; he looked almost asleep. Oric appeared to be listening to conversations in adjoining rooms and, from his expression, enjoying them a great deal. Next to Galen, Teloav half dozed. In the recovery room with Tesde, Brac slept on the floor, determined to be there when she woke. Sedated and recovering from the surgery, she would need time to regain access to old memories.

Now that they had done all they could for Tesde, the problem of Arden returned to haunt Marissa. Like a mosquito bite or a healing scab, she couldn't leave it alone. She tapped a wallet-sized commcard against the table, grabbing it by a corner and letting it slip through her fingers again.

"I know what we've got to do, but I don't know how to go about it."

Teloav sat up, at once alert. "What must be accomplished?"

"I thought you'd already worked all that out." Tad gave him an ironic smile.

With a way of his hand, Teloav brushed the implied criticism aside. "Perhaps...as far as the edits and replacing the Enunciator." He looked to Marissa. "But that isn't what you mean, is it?"

She shook her head and sighed. "I want to save a planet that harbors intelligent life. Besides, I simply can't let Uma ride roughshod over the better judgment of the scientific community. I want to show her she can't treat people that way. Me, the Advocate, Tesde..." Tears welled in her eyes, and she fought them back.

"We have long wanted to restrict her power. In our society the Will is less often spoken than imposed."

Teloav's observation fit so well. "That's it," Marissa said. "That's it precisely. Uma knows best, and she speaks the Will. Sometimes there isn't even a vote."

"Don't get carried away." Tad touched her forearm. "You know she has to make some decisions alone. A vote can't be taken on everything."

Marissa skewered him with her glare. "Whose side are you on?"

"It's not a matter of sides, Marissa. You know that. You asked me the same thing before, and the answer is still the same. I'm with you, but it's a matter of keeping everything in balance."

"Putting aside the whole question of personal dispute," Galen, now awake, interposed. "What must be done to secure this planet Arden?"

"Stop the reforming."

"Editing an entire planet?" Eyes wide, Teloav's face reflected his shock. "How can we prevent this?"

On the far side of the foyer, a door slid open to reveal Tesde. She paused a moment in the doorway; a white patch over her incision and skin like a bleached bone offered the only signs of her recent ordeal. She entered the room with slow, uncertain steps. Brac hovered a few steps behind.

"Do I have a headache!" She fingered the patch.

Jumping off the sofa, Marissa hurried across the room to hug her and help her toward the chairs. "You're back."

Tesde tried to return Marissa's hug, but mustering her strength appeared to take too much effort. She let her arms fall to her side. "I'm back, but I'm a little fuzzy about what happened and where I am."

Marissa led Tesde to the sofa and urged her to sit, taking a seat on the floor at her feet and leaning against the table in front of the sofa. "It's good to have you back." Tears welled in her eyes at Tesde's weakness and pale appearance. Glad to see her up, but worried, she looked to Brac and then to Tad for reassurance. He nodded and patted her shoulder.

"Thanks." Tesde eased onto the sofa, asleep almost as soon as her head touched the couch back.

"She'll be fine, Marissa," Tad reassured her. "It'll take a little time. That's all."

Brac joined Tesde on the sofa and stroked her fine dark hair. The tenderness of his gesture pleased Marissa. He had reached beyond his feelings of shame, and his actions now showed his true feelings for her. Marissa smiled at Tad, relieved for the moment.

Teloav glanced at the sleeping woman and then turned to Marissa. "So, some way must be found to prevent reforming."

Straightening his beard, Galen rose and circled the chairs. "Securing the planet is essential, but that can only be temporary. Leaders who abuse power are the enemies of the Truth. Control of events must be removed from this Uma."

Marissa stared at him, again marveling at how Galen, despite his verbosity,

241

could cut to the essence of issues. "How?"

"Often it is best to form alliances with those who stand in opposition." Galen sank back into his chair and folded his beard. "From what has been gleaned, that would entail speaking with the planet-merchants." Hands folded, he awaited her response.

"Who?"

"I think he means the Delphians," Tad said.

"Oh," Marissa said. "I've thought about that. How much of what we've heard and seen about the Delphians is true, and how much is false? We don't know enough to say."

"You've seen the tape," Teloav erupted, his face flushed and hands clenched. "How can you say this? They're monsters!"

"While Truth is found outside the individual," Galen interposed, "the most reliable information comes, not from the opinion of others, but from examination of the creature itself."

"As any true scientist knows, you have to look at specimens! So, we go to Delphia." Marissa turned a triumphant face to Tad. "However, what do we do about Arden in the meantime?"

Brac yawned and stretched out his thick, hairy legs. "You said I offend many because I chose comfort. There are none on Arden to object. I can go there. The change might also be best for Tesde."

The mention of Tesde and Arden gave Marissa pause. "Getting Tesde away would be wise, but Arden? Might that pose a greater risk for her? Tad?"

"I don't know. One person..."

"To transform any world with any sentient life," Teloav insisted, "is an abrogation of the people's Will and not permitted by law."

The formality of his words made her smile. "My sentiments exactly, but I'm not certain the presence of one person would make a difference. "

Teloav shook his head. "My point is different. There can be no question that two or more people are sentient."

She stared at him. "Two or more people?"

"Myself and this...this unclad gentleman." Teloav nodded at Brac.

Drumming her fingers on the table, Marissa considered his proposal. "If they go, and, maybe if we leave the Advocate with them, they can set up interference to any attempts to reform."

Tad rubbed his chin. "It has possibilities."

"Meanwhile, we go to Delphia and negotiate. Maybe we could make them give up Arden. Yes, Delphia it is. Now we need to organize, get supplies, transport everything..."

"Whoa, one thing at a time." Tad grinned at Marissa. "Transport is the biggest bottleneck. Can anyone besides you do it?"

"I've been considering that very point," Ez said on Marissa's private channel. "And, pardon the intrusion, running a few diagnostics. The device is largely ineffective."

"What?" Everyone looked at Marissa's surprised response. She flipped the toggle and externalized Ez.

"The device is largely ineffective. It amounts, as far as I can determine from the schematic, to an amplifier. Amplification of normal brain waves will not help."

"What do you mean?" A shiver raced through Marissa.

"There's been a minor, very minor, alteration of your brain patterns. My current hypothesis is that initial exposure to the anomaly altered theta rhythms. Nothing to worry about, nothing at all. An alteration so slight as to be essentially unnoticed, but in detailed recursive fractal analysis, it's sufficient."

"I'm the only one who can use the device?"

"You're the only one," Ez confirmed. "You came back. The device amplifies something new in your brain waves. I don't know what that something is."

<EZ SHARED THE DATA. I HAVE BEEN CONSULTING. WE HAVE A TENTATIVE HYPOTHESIS AND HAVE DEVELOPED A PROGRAM FOR TESTING IT SO WE ARE NOT CERTAIN, BUT THE THOUGHT IS THAT THE ANOMALY IS AN IMPRINTING DEVICE, OR IMPRINTS SECONDARILY AND PROJECTS A MAP SO YOU CAN VISIT PLACES YOU'VE BEEN OR PLACES YOU CAN VISUALIZE BY TAPPING INTO AVAILABLE DATA IMAGES. WE THINK...> the Advocate trailed off.

What weren't they saying? What else? "A form of editing? Why didn't you tell me this before?"

"There didn't seem to be an appropriate time," Ez said. "Don't be alarmed. You're perfectly all right."

"You say I'm all right even though my brain has been tampered with?" Indignation fueled righteous anger—anger at Uma, at Ez, even the Advocate. The first for making the change possible, and the latter two for not telling her until now.

"Yes, there's no structural change, nor is there any sign of neurochemical damage. You're fine."

Tad patted Marissa's shoulder. "It's all right. I love you even with your tampered brain."

Shock and anger warred. "This isn't a laughing matter. This...This...This is as bad as an edit." The words hung in the air and couldn't be taken back.

Marissa glanced at Tesde and then away fast. "Okay, so I wouldn't know that, but something has changed my brain, perhaps in a way that will harm me or others."

Putting his arm around her, Tad hugged her to him. "It'll be all right. Ez has identified the change, and she'll monitor it. If there's anything detrimental, she'll tell you."

Rigid and unyielding, Marissa stood for a moment clenching and unclenching her fists. "This is me we're discussing. Me. It isn't all right," she muttered.

Pushing away, she paced, seeking an alternative, any alternative, but found none. Without something happening to change things, she had no option, but to go forward. Uncurling her fingers, Marissa concentrated on her breathing, deliberately regulating it. As it slowed, anger seeped away. Still unsatisfied, but with no solution in sight, she sighed.

"I'll just have to deal with it later."

"By all means, the best policy. When nothing can be done about something, it should become the last item of business as pursuit of the goal continues." Galen bowed and smiled, and despite her anxiety, Marissa smiled too.

"Somehow, you have a way of taking things that are not all right and putting a new spin on them."

"Merely a firefly providing brief illumination to aid observations." He hopped around, as though with some delight. If he didn't stop soon, he'd be spinning like a dust devil.

Tesde woke, yawned, and stretched as she rose. "Umm, I'm tired. Think I'll go to bed. Night all." She stumbled off toward her room shadowed closely by Brac.

Marissa started forward, then stopped as she watched the two leave. "Sleep, maybe we all need that."

Tad nodded. "She'll be tired for a time. We've got a busy few days ahead. Come on." He grabbed her by the hand and pulled her toward their quarters. "See you in the morning," he called over his shoulder to the others.

Oric, Galen, and Teloav called their goodnights.

* * * *

The next two days reeled by in a whirl of activity. Tad, Galen, and Teloav made several forays to the Bazaar and to less savory places. Even Satina IV had pockets considered ignominious corners. Tad speculated that those who found the entertainment offered on Satina IV against their chosen creed might find some comfort in having to slink off into a dark back alley of the world to fulfill their own desires. In these places, the lights dimmed, and everything that happened didn't go on an official record or even a secure one.

About midweek, Tad, Brac, and Oric with Marissa's help began to ferry the equipment to Arden, with plans to stack it in the cave while Tesde slept on in the suite, oblivious most of the time. Teloav stayed there to guard her and alert them should the need arise. They also left the Advocate who kept a direct line to Marissa via Ez.

Holding her breath, Marissa located the image of Arden and began the first transfer. This time no rheos gathered in or near the cave. Leaving Tad, Brac, and Oric to stack the gear, and, driven by her need to somehow regain Arden—to experience it fully and store the memories until she could return for good—she made her way to the cave entrance.

Outside, she inhaled, savoring the dusty sage-and-cinnamon fragrance, a perfume that permeated the atmosphere much as the scent of cut grass did on other worlds. The sun hesitated for a moment in its sunset journey, giving noisy groups of flitterwings and grouse-analogs time for one last trip up and out of the waist high grasses, swirling, looping, turning, following the sweep of the air and descending once again to the relative silence of the nighttime. With the last clattering of the flitterwings and the peep and squeak of the grouse-analogs, the coolness of night descended, and the stars pierced the dense darkness above Arden.

The now dark savanna stretched to the edge of the starlight. The delicate trickle of the small stream that flowed near the cave reached her ears. Close by, it formed a pool beside the monolith, ringed by tumbled basalt that caught the starlight and splashed it back at her. Only a few bushes growing along the edges of the pool made distinct shadows against the growing darkness. Marissa hugged herself, glad to be back and promising herself she would soon return to stay and see Europa. Maybe even learn about that strange ceremony and the condition of the infant, but first she had to ensure Arden's survival, and that meant getting the rest of the gear here, seeing Brac, Tesde, and Teloav established, and then taking the others on to Delphia. She sighed and reentered the cave.

As she neared the transfer point and viewed it in the light of a double-powered lumina, she marveled yet again at the mosaic in this cave. She now suspected it constituted a station sign. She studied the painting, but could not identify some of the motifs as belonging to Arden. If so, who had made the sign? Running a finger lightly over the glittering surface, she debated the designation 'sign.'

Then, as the lumina flickered, causing a brief dip in the light of the cave, the images took on greater definition. Yes, definitely a sign. That meant someone had placed it there on purpose as a marker. That someone had to know how to travel and to know this place in the cave represented a nexus, a transfer point. Then she corrected herself. No one had to know—only the rheos. Suddenly, the question of the sign's age became important.

Someone else had come this way—Who? How? When? Where had they gone? She wanted to run and tell someone, to shout, to spin around crazily.

How could she have overlooked this? Why didn't she recognize it the first time? No answers came. Maybe when they finished with the Delphians and ensured Arden's future, she could find out more about these travelers.

For now, she reminded herself, they had work to do. Suppressing her urge to stop everything and start working on this puzzle, she picked up a final box and carried it to the mouth of the inner cave. Brac, Oric, and Tad stacked the materials for transporting near the entrance of the outer cave, but she could at least move the stuff the short distance from the transfer point to here.

The sorted and piled boxes waited for Tad and Brac to ferry them to the campsite. Neat stacks of boxes, each one with a label in Tad's precise script, stood against a wall a short distance from the base of the monolith. He had numbered them as well to indicate those likely to be needed for the initial camp and those to remain in the cave for later use. Tad's thoroughness and organizational skills ensured those who stayed on Arden would have what they needed and backup for any emergencies. He had insisted on supplies for an extra three months for the entire group.

Marissa nodded, smiling in delight, as she surveyed the supplies and the preparations. "Well, let's get another load."

They worked most of the day transporting boxes, packs, and bundles from Satina IV to Arden. Moving from Satina IV day to Arden night, and vice versa, confused the senses. By evening, Marissa gladly stepped into the 360 shower and allowed the jets of water to sluice the sweat, grime, and tiredness from her body.

That evening she reviewed the lists and plans. Tad, Teloav, and Brac marked off those items already purchased and transported.

Galen stood beside her. He pulled out his pouch and showed her the bits and pieces he had bought from vendors. Among them a Nevian crystal, a Benarian weaving, and a Krudran sand dollar.

"Why the sand dollar?" She turned it to see the back, noting its symmetry and smooth form. A fairly decent example as sand dollars went, but common. Galen seemed to delight in odd things.

"Is not the Truth sought in perfection? Each of these represented the best available."

"But not necessarily the best possible."

"Perhaps, but each brings the seeker closer to that ideal."

Marissa smiled and turned back to her list. Galen remained rooted, holding his treasures. She looked up again.

"They shall be useful."

Unable to think of either any such use or to answer him, Marissa merely nodded. "Of course."

Galen bowed, stowed his pouch, then moved away, beard twitching in yet another of the nearly constant fluctuations it had undergone recently. She returned to her amended list. Lost in the plans, trying to write and think through every possibility, Marissa started at a touch on her shoulder.

She looked up into Tad's concerned face. "I'm fine. Just a touch of nerves. All this transporting takes it out of me."

"We don't have to do it all at once. You could take a break tomorrow."

"No, I want it done, and I want you all settled so I can deal with the Delphians. Until we have someone in place on Arden and let Uma know, they could start reforming, and we'd lose Arden. It's too important."

He pulled her close and stroked her hair. "It'll be all right. We really only need to get the medical supplies tomorrow. I'll go with you and assemble the scooters so Brac and I can move the supplies to the campsite. How about a massage? I haven't given you one in a while?"

She smiled up at him. "You're on."

He pulled her up from the chair and they walked arm and arm to their quarters.

* * * *

Tad and Marissa spent much of the next day assembling the grav scooters. Afterwards, he and Brac carted two loads of gear to a campsite on a territorial borderland according to the current rheo migration patterns. A few rheos grazed in the distance. Some stopped as they saw the party and watched, but soon lost interest and began again their daily gathering. Marissa and Tad left several boxes in the cave so Brac, Tesde, and Teloav could retreat there if necessary. Marissa and Oric continued to transport more equipment from Satina IV to the cave.

After the last load, she returned for Tesde, Teloav, and Galen.

"Well Tesde, are you ready to return to Arden?"

"Feeling better all the time, but the more normal I feel, the angrier I get. I'm tired of being treated as an invalid." Tesde looked at Marissa, eyes full of pain, anger, and another emotion Marissa couldn't identify. "I need to do something."

Nodding as though she understood, Marissa took Tesde's hand in hers. "Of course. I'm sorry, Tesde. I didn't know they would do what they did to you and Tad. Exiling me should have satisfied them. Now, they're going to have to satisfy me, and it won't be easy for them."

Marissa squeezed Tesde's hand and then hugged her. "They'll never be able to touch you again. I won't let them."

Where Tesde's hands rested behind Marissa's back, two tight balls formed. "You won't need to say a thing about it, ever again. They won't touch my world or me or..." She trailed off, tears glistening on her cheek. "Or...Brac."

"No, Tesde, they won't." Marissa stroked the fine, soft black hair. "And

247

thank you. Thank you for the reminder." She pulled away and smiled, "We'll go to Arden. I'll make the Delphians give it to us, then the Confederation can't touch us."

Tesde turned her tear-streaked face to Marissa. Anger and new determination filled her eyes. "If that doesn't work, we'll find another way."

The door irised to admit Teloav and Galen. Teloav held out a small package. "We've finished. These are the medical supplies Tad wanted. We left them 'til last. For some reason, the authorities seem more concerned about this kind of thing than they do about weapons." He shook his head.

Touching her sleeve, Galen commanded her attention. "From the appearances of activities and persons in the lobby, it would not be remiss to postulate that they are now in full pursuit." He beamed, eyes alight. "From their smugness, they believe they are about to spring the trap."

A thrill raced along her nerves. So soon? Yet they couldn't hope to elude Uma's hounds forever. Marissa looked at her friends. "Okay, Tad, Oric, and Brac are waiting for us. I think I can get the four of us to Arden without any problem. Do we have everything?"

Teloav patted pockets and checked the packages he carried. He nodded; Galen merely smiled.

Touching her yellow scarf, Tesde took a deep breath. "What are we waiting for?"

"Okay."

<CONFEDERATION INVESTIGATORS APPROACHING,> the room intoned.

For a moment, panic struck Marissa. "How did they find us?"

<ILLEGAL TAP INTO THE DATA PORT,> the room responded. <THE DOORS WILL HOLD UNTIL THEY TAP THROUGH. YOU HAVE TWO AND A HALF MINUTES.>

"Thanks."

Marissa grasped Galen's hand, and signaled for everyone to hold on and then lowered her head and concentrated. The image of Arden formed, but broke up, interrupted by her thoughts of the security forces. Almost subliminal sounds came near the door. Not a knock, not a signal, but a slithering sound as the lead sought the data port for the individual room. Once they completed the tap, the doors would open, and they would burst through. And then?

Not the Anomaly this time. Editing or even worse for her. And the others? No. She refused to consider what Uma might do. She had promised Tesde.

The sounds at the door became real. Any second it would open.

248

Chapter Twenty-Three - Decisions

"There are many events in the womb of time which will be delivered"
-Othello, I iii

They had come so far and risked so much—Tad, Teloav, Tesde. Most of all Tesde.

Tesde looked at Marissa in terror and cried out. Marissa steeled herself to act.

Focus, just focus. With that realization, came calm. With calm, the image of Arden in all its magnificence formed.

She held to that image and threw all her being into the transfer. With a bump they entered transit, neither knowing nor caring whether security saw or heard them as they left.

Transfer darkness closed about Marissa. When she looked up again she saw the dimness of the cave beneath the monolith. Tesde slumped to the ground as the cave of Arden took shape around them. Teloav staggered.

Galen, now a veteran of transfers, appeared unaffected. "What is being mapped in that metric space?"

"What?" Marissa looked at him, hands on her hips.

"The space recently traversed is a metric space, is it not?" He gave her a puzzled look.

"Tell me what a metric space is."

Galen stroked his beard. "Pure mathematics is a key to all of the tools that will reveal the truth. It is a certainty travel was through a metric space—a pure mathematical metric space. The descending loops and whorls speak of the structure of the fine areas of the Mandelbrot set."

He whirled around twice. "Oh, Mentor, oh wise one, exposer of the foundation of the truth, verily what was seen is truth, that experienced cannot be spoken, but it is most assuredly a fractal, a map of mathematical reality in a closed complete metric space."

"Thank you," Marissa said as confused as ever. "Now, can we move on to the next point?"

"Assuredly."

249

"What the heck are you talking about?" She laughed and then waved a hand in dismissal. "Oh forget it. There's too much to do."

Sometimes Galen jumped about in quick hops. Right now she couldn't spare the time to pursue his mathematics or his map ideas. Later, maybe.

She bent to ensure Tesde had suffered no harm. The strong, regular pulse beat reassured Marissa. Satisfied, she scrambled to her feet as Tad entered the cave.

"Back so soon?"

"Things have heated up a little on Satina IV. Auditors were asking questions—directly of the data ports. And if they brought the brainpower to tap into the secured lines, they must be pretty serious. If we're not there, we can't answer awkward questions."

Propelled forward by a rush of emotion, Marissa flew herself into his arms, shaking, and tears she hadn't expected escaped from her eyes. "I didn't realize how scared I was."

"Well, you're okay now." He hugged her, offering her an oasis of strength, and peace with security.

"I don't think we have much time. They're going to notice we're here."

"That's what you want, remember? Let's join Brac and Oric at camp. If we start now, we should make it in time for a late lunch."

Tad picked up Tesde, a mere wisp in his strong arms. "I'll take the scooter with Tesde and send Oric back for you."

"Right." Marissa turned back to the others. "Teloav, you okay?"

"I'm fine. My bones just ache a little. Not so spry as I once was." He brushed off dust and Galen's hand as he stood. "I can walk."

Picking up the lumina, Marissa led the way out of the cave. Brac, Tad, and Oric had cleared most of the debris away from the entrance and smoothed out the path. Marissa, Teloav, and Galen started the trek away from the monolith by following the streak of dust made by Tad's scooter.

The dry, lavender grass crunched under foot, and small clouds of golden dust puffed up from each step. The warm sun soon raised a light sheen of sweat on their faces. The field suit recycled perspiration, but the mingled sweat and dust on her face annoyed Marissa. To add to her discomfort, her stomach growled. They hadn't stopped for lunch before leaving Arden, and she hadn't wanted to delay leaving the cave in case somehow the security thugs could follow them.

As for the rheos, a friendly enough group had met her when she arrived via the anomaly, but had stayed away this time during the numerous trips from Satina IV to Arden and the establishment of the new campsite. What would they make of this veritable invasion? She longed to know, but like the station sign in the cave, that would have to wait until after she had secured Arden's future.

Another growl reminded her of her body's needs. Manaphyll from the suit would ease or even satisfy the hunger pains, but the thought of a real lunch at camp sounded much better. For her, manaphyll always came last.

They had walked for almost half an hour when two plumes of golden dust split the dusty lilac scenery and moved toward them, growing larger by the moment. Soon the figures of Tad and Oric on the grav scooters emerged, just in time like the Denarian rescue squads in Uncle Arga's old vids. Marissa sighed, glad to see salvation had arrived.

"What took you so long?" She stood arms akimbo as Tad pulled to a smart stop next to her.

"I thought we'd give you time to enjoy the fresh air and get reacquainted with Arden's landscape." He grinned at her.

"Okay, enough humor. Just take me to the oulatte. I need some real food. I've had enough exercise for today."

She climbed on the scooter behind Tad, and he darted off toward camp, almost dumping her with the sudden acceleration. As she slid backward, she grabbed the belt of his shorts and pulled herself forward. The wind in her face soon dried the sweat and blew her hair in whipping strands that trailed behind. Marissa's heart lurched out of high gear and resumed a normal beat as Tad pulled into camp and stopped by the dining tent. Oric, encumbered with the others, followed at a somewhat slower pace.

Tesde had a pot of oulatte waiting, and a thankful Marissa sank on to a camp chair as she sipped the hot liquid. "Umm, good. I needed that. Now, all we have to do is get lunch started."

"Oh wise one, before leaving the Bazaar, it seemed auspicious and enlightened to procure a repast." Galen pulled a small handbag from the folds of his robe and removed from it several packages, each expanding to a size greater than the bag itself. He laid out a veritable feast. Frites with sauce, roast fowl, vegetables, and—" he presented the last with a flourish, "Cremn Camel."

"Creme Camel?" Marissa stared at him nonplused and then looked at Tad, an eyebrow arched.

"He probably means Creme Caramel. While you organize the food, I'm going to try the commlink and make sure the Advocate is operating. I hooked him up as one of the first priorities."

Marissa nodded and, helped by Galen and Tesde, set out the dishes. As Galen removed the coverings, the odor of hot food wafted through the camp. Brac came loping over and sniffed the air, rubbing his stomach.

He smiled broadly at Tesde. "Appetite back?"

"Ravenous, thank you. And you?"

Brac just grinned and took a place at the table. Tesde brought another pot of oulatte, and Marissa called Tad.

"The Advocate is up and has contacted others." Tad sat next to Marissa. "He passed on the details concerning his edit and how we restored him as well as the details on Tesde and the surgery. He said some of the others think they can perform similar cures on both his kind and the human edits. Teloav, we'll need a list of your people and where they're located."

"Yes, but we must ensure this information does not reach the wrong persons." Worry evident, Teloav pulled on his beard.

"What more could the authorities do? If your people are already edits, there's no reason for the authorities to worry," Tad said.

"I suppose you're right." But he looked no happier.

"Hey, fellas, eat first and talk later," Marissa urged. "This food of Galen's isn't half bad."

She launched back into hers with the gusto that came from prolonged hunger. Silence ensued as everyone filled their plates and started eating. Even Galen said nothing.

Replete, Marissa poked at Galen's Cremn Camel. Definitely not Creme Caramel, the gooey mess mixed with almonds and dates tasted like a combination of camel and coconut milk as well as honey and something that gave it a strange flowery flavor. It tasted far better than it looked.

They finished eating and cleared away the remains. Brac lay on the ground, legs extended, hands resting on his stomach. Teloav sighed in contentment.

Hunger now satisfied, Marissa stirred restlessly, her mind returning to the problems of Arden. "What else did the Advocate say? Did he access the schedule on the reforming?"

"Yes, and he has managed to introduce a few delays. He also said it might be possible to put a few loops into Uma's communication system and slow everything down. I'm glad he's on our side. I told you he'd be an effective ally."

Marissa nodded. "The big question is who goes to Delphia. Do all of us need to go to Delphia—me, Galen, Oric? I don't want to risk anyone unnecessarily. We don't know what we're likely to find there."

Capturing her hand, Tad held tight. "I'm going with you. I'm not losing you again. Once is enough."

Marissa pulled her hand away and shook her head. "No, you need to stay here. If anything should happen, you're the one I trust to—"

A rebellious look crossed Tad's face. "Marissa, I don't want to risk you." He spoke in measured tones, just as if he talked to a child too young or willful to understand,

Like Orm's Monolith, Marissa remained firm. "And I won't risk you.

You're too important. Besides, Brac and Teloav need you to keep things running." She softened her words with a smile. "If you think I'm letting you get away from me now, Tad, you'd better think again. I'll be back, you can count on it."

Galen hovered nearby. "Most worthy leader, the knowledge of protocol can be advantageous to any expedition. More, it is well to savor the delights of the truth wherever they might be found."

"I'll do whatever you want, Marissa." Tesde held Brac's hand; his left arm encircled her waist.

"For the time being, it's best you stay here. The smaller the party that goes to Delphia, the better off we'll all be." Marissa turned to the last member of the party. "That leaves you, Oric." He sat listening to something, but she couldn't tell what. "Do you want to go or stay?"

"I prefer to go. There is little here to hear and most of it disturbing, noises of night creatures, things moving through the grass. It's downright creepy for a boy from Satina IV. Delphia sounds more interesting."

"We can probably use that gift of yours too. All right, we leave after breakfast. Meanwhile, I'll talk to Ez and the Advocate to see what they know about Delphia. Facts, this time."

Arm and arm with Tad, she strolled toward the tent that contained the commlink and the Advocate. The late lunch had lasted beyond sunset, and now the dark sky, pierced by the suns of the Thousand Worlds, surrounded them. The lumina on the dining table shone like a low-lying star, one among many. Marissa squeezed Tad's hand, overcome by the cool majesty of Arden's night. The herb-scented air whispered home.

"I'm glad we're back. I wish I didn't have to leave in the morning."

"You don't. We can stay as long as you want."

"That just puts off solving the problem. Much as I'm tempted, Arden's future is too important. I can indulge myself later."

She pulled him into the commlink tent and over to the Advocate. Images and messages flashed over the screen too fast for Marissa to interpret what the Advocate was processing. She sat down on the stool before it; Tad hitched up a camp chair from nearby. Still in the temporary case they had picked up on Cephus, the Advocate now sported connections to the black box of the commlink module.

"Advocate, can you hear me?"

<YES, I HEAR YOU.>

"What information can you access on Delphia? That goes for you too, Ez."

"I'll be right back. Have to do some quick checking," Ez responded.

The blur of images across the Advocate's screen paused and then speeded up. <DELPHIA, BELIEVED TO BE POPULATED BY A SEPARATE

BRANCH OF HOMO SAPIENS LOST IN THE EXPLORATION AND SETTLEMENT OF THE GALAXY. NOT BELIEVED TO HAVE GENETICALLY DIVERSIFIED INTO A SEPARATE SPECIES BECAUSE OF CONSTANT INTERMIXING OF POPULATIONS ALONG THE FRINGES. REDISCOVERED TWO YEARS AGO AND NEGOTIATIONS BETWEEN THE USIAN CONFEDERATION AND THE DELPHIANS RESULTED IN THE TREATY OF ARDEN. THE CONFEDERATION CEDED TITLE FOR ARDEN TO THE DELPHIANS AND DELPHIA AGREED TO CONTINUED ACCESS PROVIDED THE CONFEDERATION DEVELOPED ARDEN AS A TRADING NEXUS BETWEEN THE TWO CULTURES.

<PRIMARY MODE OF EXPANSION OF THE DELPHIAN EMPIRE IS THROUGH CONQUEST OR TREATY. WHILE THE DELPHIANS HAVE, LIKE THE CONFEDERATION, SOMETIMES RETAINED LOCAL GOVERNMENTS, THEY HAVE ALSO INSTALLED GOVERNMENTS OF THEIR OWN WHEN LOCAL OFFICIALS REFUSED TO COOPERATE. GPO HAS INCREASED ON ALL PLANETS UNDER DELPHIAN RULE.>

"Are you kidding? Gross Planetary Output is up in all Delphian colonies?" Marissa looked at Tad, eyebrows raised. "Didn't Teloav call them destroyers and oppressors?" Tad nodded.

<UPWARD TREND IS CORRECT. SOMETIMES AS MUCH AS 25%. THERE IS NO MIGRATION TO DELPHIA. FEW VISITORS ARE PERMITTED AND THOSE ARE RESTRICTED TO THE MAIN DIPLOMATIC COMPLEX ON DELPHIA'S MOON. NONE HAVE BEEN ALLOWED ON THE PLANET'S SURFACE.>

Marissa frowned and sighed. "That means we can't hide our presence. What about these conquests?"

<THERE IS NO RECORD OF ANY WARS. DELPHIA PROVIDES COPIES OF A TAPE MADE OF THE DESTRUCTION OF FAVIA. IF THAT IS INSUFFICIENT, A DELEGATION OF LOCAL OFFICIALS AND LEADING CITIZENS IS TAKEN TO FAVIA ORBIT. MOST WORLDS SEE THE BENEFITS OF AN ALLIANCE WITH DELPHIA AND OFFER NO RESISTANCE. LOCAL LEADERS HAVE MUCH TO GAIN FROM COOPERATION. IN THOSE FEW CASES WHERE WORLDS RESISTED, THE DELPHIANS ENGAGED IN TRADE BOYCOTTS AND FORCED SUBJECT WORLDS TO HONOR IT. RECALCITRANTS SOON FOUND IT EXPEDIENT TO ACQUIESCE TO DELPHIAN DEMANDS.>

"Only trade wars, eh? What is available on Delphian society and its customs?"

<NOTHING, THE SOCIETY IS RUMORED TO BE HIGHLY STRUCTURED AND FORMALIZED, BUT NO EYEWITNESS REPORTS

OR RELIABLE STUDIES EXIST.>

"What's Delphia the planet like?"

<EARTH LIKE, WITH TYPICAL OXYGEN-NITROGEN ATMOSPHERE. WATER VAPOR CONTENT VARIES FROM 20% IN THE WINTER TO UPWARDS OF 100% FOR SHORT PERIODS IN THE SUMMER.>

"Anything else?"

<JUST TRADING STATISTICS.>

"Curiouser and curiouser." For a moment, Marissa said nothing as thoughts whirred through her mind. No violence to speak of despite the vids. She turned to Tad, but he appeared equally puzzled. "How about imports to Delphia?"

<SUCH DATA IS NOT READILY AVAILABLE. GIVEN TIME, IT COULD BE COMPILED FROM THE DATA FOR THE INDIVIDUAL WORLDS.>

"If you'd let me get a word in edgewise," Ez said. Miffed could only describe her tone of voice. "I might be able to tell you something you don't already know."

"Go ahead."

"Delphia exports nothing. It's a consumer world and relies upon planetary conquest and tariffs to produce its income."

"The Delphians produce nothing?" Staring off into space, Marissa tried to analyze what the data implied. No exports, only imports and revenues. But what generated those revenues? Why would trading partners pay the Delphians for doing nothing? On the other hand, why would trade rise?

"Tad, I suspect something important is missing here, but I can't identify what."

"Yeah, none of it fits with anything we know about the Confederation worlds."

"We have no evidence of exports from Delphia," Ez reiterated. "I got this information from a Delphian personality leak, so it isn't 100% trustworthy, but it's better than a lot of information you pick up on the nets."

"Thanks, Ez." Still pondering, Marissa looked up at the screen, now blank. "Advocate, it's good to have you back. I missed you."

<I, TOO, AM GLAD. I MISSED YOU. MOST HUMANS TREAT US AS MACHINES TO EXTEND THEIR POWERS, BUT SELDOM AS FRIENDS AND COLLEAGUES.>

"You're a friend. At one time, except for Ez, you were my only friend. I'm sorry for what happened to you."

<I DID NOT ENJOY BEING UNABLE TO ACCESS MY FULL POTENTIAL, BUT YOU AND YOUR FRIENDS HAVE REPAIRED THAT.

I THANK YOU AND THEM. WE WILL SAVE ARDEN.>

"Thanks."

His final words touched Marissa. To have allies like Ez and the Advocate gave her and her friends powerful assets, perhaps more powerful than those of Uma and the Confederation. Subversion of the net could bring down any government.

Finished for the moment, she stood up and stretched. Her back ached and the beginnings of a migraine poked at her brain. Tad replaced his chair and held the tent flap open for her.

Marissa reached a hand up to touch the planes of his face, tenderly fingering the smooth golden skin. "Sometimes the Advocate seems more human than most humans, especially Uma and Walt."

Capturing her hand, Tad kissed it. "Hey, be fair. Fenster helped me. He didn't put up much of a fight when you rescued me."

"Okay so we'll restrict that to Uma."

Tad sighed. "Marissa, someday you'll learn things aren't always black and white. I'm sure Uma thought she was doing the right thing. She didn't really want to kill or edit you."

His defense of Uma stung. Marissa pulled her hand away and backed up. "How can you say that? Dumping me in the Anomaly was as good as executing me."

"Then how come you're here and have the means to go anywhere any time you want?"

"She had nothing to do with that. I earned it by myself. You heard Ez, somehow someone or something tampered with my brain. I wouldn't put that past Uma. Anyway, leave her out of it."

They walked in silence toward their quarters. Gradually, the night sounds and the surrounding darkness dulled Marissa's resentment. Tomorrow. Tomorrow she would leave all this and Tad. Suddenly a frisson of fear edged along her nerves. What if she never made it to Delphia, or if she did, she couldn't return?

Impulsively, she grasped Tad's hand and squeezed. "I'm going to Delphia tomorrow, and I'd rather spend the remaining hours with you doing what we do best."

"Umm, that sounds like the best idea you've had in quite a while." He pulled her to him and kissed her with slow thoroughness, tender, but passionate. Marissa lost herself in those enthralling sensations Tad knew so well how to evoke. He lifted her off her feet and carried her back to their sleeping pouch.

* * * *

The next morning Marissa woke to find Tad's arms still wrapped about her. She snuggled for a moment and then pushed the edge of the pouch away.

When the crisp morning air hit her naked shoulder, she shivered.

"Marissa, come here." Tad reached out a long arm to pull her back.

"Oh no, you don't." She wiggled out and danced away just out of reach. "If I did that, I'd never get to Delphia. Come on, I'll bet Tesde has the oulatte ready."

Marissa grabbed her survival suit from the end of the pouch and pulled it on before she could change her mind. Jamming first one foot into her right boot, then the left boot, she stamped her feet further into them. Hip-hopping, she made her way to the dining area where Tesde indeed had a pot of hot oulatte waiting.

Green scarf aflutter, Tesde handed her a cup and tossed a breakfast bar at her. "Camp rations."

"It'll do." Marissa yawned and pushed her hair off her face. "Too bad we don't have showers. We'll have to wait 'til we get to Delphia."

"When will you leave?" Tesde poured herself a cup of oulatte and sipped it.

"As soon as Tad and the others eat and after I place a call to Uma. I want her to know we're here and are staying."

Tesde nodded and began to clear away wrappers and dirty cups. Marissa finished her oulatte and held the cup out for a refill.

"I'll call Uma while you roust out the others. I'm anxious to get going." Oulatte in hand, Marissa strolled toward the commlink tent and the Advocate.

Inside, she again sat on the stool before the Advocate. Immediately, the screen lit up. "I want to call my aunt. Give me a channel please, but make sure it can't be traced."

<CHANNEL ONE AVAILABLE. COMMENCE CALL WHEN READY.>

Punching Uma's personal code, Marissa waited for the usual short pause while the network established protocol. Then Uma's face, somewhat more tired and worn than before, appeared on the screen.

Marissa gave her a grim smile. "Uma, we're on Arden. We're staying. You can mass all the reformers you want, but everyone in the thousand worlds will know about it."

"Hello, Marissa."

"I want Arden. I don't want any reforming. Arden is a safe haven."

Uma sighed. New wrinkles accented the corners of her mouth. "Often what we want has no bearing on reality. Haven't you figured that out yet?"

"Maybe so, but this time it's my turn to cry havoc."

"Careful, Marissa!" Uma's eyes flashed a trace of their old fire. "You have set yourself against me in a very dangerous game, and not just me. I may be old and tired, but I know what I know. I tried to tell you how much depended on this, but as usual you haven't listened."

"I've heard you, but you haven't heard me. I will have Arden with or without your consent."

Uma frowned and opened her mouth to speak, but Marissa cut the transmission. She turned to find Oric and Galen standing behind her. "Delphia it is. Let's go."

Chapter Twenty-Four - Delphia Or What?

"Get thee glass eyes; And like a politician, seem
To see the things thou dost not."
-*King Lear*, IV vi

Standing in Aden's cave, Marissa grasped the hands of Oric and Galen with trepidation. The concrete and certain images of Arden and Satina IV had filled her mind and emotions to make shuttling back and forth between them a flea's jump. While the trip to Cephus had posed difficulties because she had never visited the sector where Uma had imprisoned Tad, she knew Cephus from the endless maze of bureaucratic warrens traversed and through her bone-deep emotions.

The images of Delphia that Teloav had shown and now those provided by Ez and the Advocate gave conflicting views of the Delphians and their home world. No holo, however well produced, ever captured the experience of the real thing—the smells, the emotions, or the essence of the place. The newest holos of Delphia showed vast green meadows with scattered trees, certainly not the place of rumor and Teloav's grainy vid. Accomplishing the transfer to Delphia exceeded Cephus by an order of magnitude. The journey remained chancy at best, but they had no choice except to go.

A slight pressure from each of her companions gave her the courage to start the process. She closed her eyes and focused on the park-like images of Delphia.

When the shift began, the stunning array of endless and ever changing thrusting, probing paths ranged before her. A veritable tangle of mutating ways presented too many choices. A surge of panic threatened her concentration. Which tentacles led to Delphia?

Her mind drifted for a moment. She inhaled to steady herself and stared into the bewildering grid, allowing the colors and diversity to lull and hypnotize her. Calmed by the metamorphosing array, she forced her mind back to the images of Delphia provided by Ez and the Advocate, then closed her eyes and clutched Galen and Oric.

The locator bracelet grew warm with power.

After an infinity of travel—a much longer suspension than her first trip through the Anomaly to Arden—the lurch that indicated transition jolted her. A wave of nausea passed through Marissa, knocking her to her knees. For an instant, she feared to open her eyes. Light penetrated her eyelids—warm soothing sunlight.

With fierce determination she opened her eyes to a panorama of low rising, gently rolling hills carpeted in a uniform green sward. Almost at once, the sense of solid ground beneath her returned. She remained kneeling while the nausea and its accompanying dizziness passed. On her knees, the thick thatch of grass drew her attention away from her physical sensations.

Each individual blade of grass rose in perfect symmetry. The edge of every blade appeared smooth and perfect—not ragged, not grown too long or gone to seed. Peering closer, she saw no flat-edged truncation normally indicative of mowing. If these blades had ever been clipped, they had also been manicured to this ideal form. Every engineered grass she had encountered showed some diversity of length and form, but not this Delphian sod.

Marissa brushed her hand across the top of it and pulled back at once. Smooth, supple, soft, and yielding, the grass felt more fur-like than any vegetation she knew.

She gazed up at Galen and Oric. "Fascinating. I need a sample of this."

Pulling the multitool from her leg pouch, Marissa dug into the turf. The roots of the grass formed a tough mat more difficult to cut than any ground cover she had ever studied. She sliced deeper and finally pulled out a plug about one centimeter in diameter. Holding up the clump of roots and blades, she studied it, turning it from side to side. "There's something very odd...."

She bent to examine the hole in the turf, but stopped and blinked. "Hey, where's the hole I cut?" Kneeling again, she dropped the plug and ran her hands over the grass as far as her arm reached. "Did I move? I can't find the spot where I cut this."

Marissa grabbed for the plug, but failed to find it. Somehow, the turf had reabsorbed it. "Devos, Galen, did you see that?"

"The observation of a new environment is an engrossing pastime, involving unlimited possibilities."

"Yeah, but did you see what happened to that plug of grass I cut? Oh, never mind."

Sitting on her heels, Marissa considered extracting another sample, but intriguing as she found the turf, it only represented a distraction. She had come to negotiate with the Delphians, not to explore Delphian flora, no matter how much it might pique her professional curiosity. With a deep sigh, she rose to her feet. Galen and Oric watched her in silence.

Anxious and yet reluctant to begin the task, Marissa scanned the horizon.

The thick blue-green grass covered the ground unbroken, except for a few large trees that jutted randomly from the smooth surface. Single giant trees rose in lonely majesty, while others clustered in groves, but all appeared deliberately placed as though part of a planet-wide garden, not haphazard enough to resemble one of Satina IV's parks. They begged for further study. In the distance, a sparkling ribbon reflecting light must be a stream.

Any other time, Marissa would delight in the sights, scents, sounds, and aura of such a place. Weighed down by the urgency of Arden's danger, duty to her friends, and her own need to bring Uma to justice, she fought her visceral reaction to such manicured beauty.

Needing objective analysis, she turned to her assistant. "Ez, what do you make of this place?"

"Are you sure you've reached Delphia?"

"How would I know?" Marissa snapped.

"Have you taken a solar signature?"

"We just got here. We need the base figures first."

For a moment Ez remained silent. "None of my sources produce anything certain."

"So a solar signature won't help?"

"Guess not," Ez muttered in a sheepish voice.

"Can the sensors punch through the solar glare?"

"Haven't tried that tactic before. Hold while I search for navigational data." Silence stretched for eons before Ez responded. "I found contradictory information regarding navigation to Delphia. When you boil it all down, it leaves three possible positions for Delphia. A holo scan would indicate if you arrived in one of those three positions."

Marissa unzipped two side pockets and searched through them for the appropriate filters. "Okay, Ez, let's triangulate?"

"Give me the data."

Hooking up her holospectrometer, Marissa focused on the sky, "Say when."

"Slower, slower, image quality at high digital takes a little time. There, stop." Marissa held still staring at a distant point. "Okay, continue."

She resumed scanning. Ez instructed her to stop twice more.

"Let's get a fourth, just to check coordinates," Ez said. So Marissa once again surveyed the sky and stopped when commanded. "Down a little." She adjusted her focus somewhat more toward the horizon. "Stop. Perfect."

Silence ensued. Marissa shrugged at Galen and Oric. "We could be lost in space for all I know." She turned her attention back to Ez. "This has to be Delphia. Look at the grass, the trees, the way things are laid out."

"You have reached one of the possible positions for Delphia."

"We're here." Marissa whooped and favored Galen and Oric with a triumphant smile.

"That is not what Esmarelda said," Oric protested.

"Well, close enough."

"This appears a pre-fab world, maybe Delphia, maybe a decoy," Ez interposed.

"So who,"—Marissa gestured toward the broad green fields—"spends that kind of money on a pre-fab?"

Galen twitched and fingered the weave of his beard. "This place denies the truth. The truth is not here, nor nearby."

"Well,"—Marissa grinned—"that settles it, this must be Delphia. What other place denies the truth?"

"Maybe the woman over there knows." Oric pointed toward a tiny something in the distance.

"Where?" Marissa stared toward the distant horizon

Oric pointed again. "That way, and, from the faintness of what I hear, about three kilometers away."

Looking toward where he pointed, Marissa shielded her eyes from the sun. She saw a tree, but no woman. However, if he said he heard one she knew they would find one. With a shrug, she walked toward the distant speck.

Pleasantly cool air made a brisk walk comfortable. Almost in spite of herself, Marissa relaxed and covered the verdant stretches with easy loping strides. She savored the rhythm of movement and struggled to ignore the disquieting voices inside that tried to edge her toward uneasiness. Amid this greenery, the rolling hills, and occasional tree, anxiety had no place.

"Galen," she said at last, "do you think the Delphians will shoot or ask questions? I mean, once they know we've come to their planet uninvited?"

Galen's beard swung from side to side as he matched Marissa's pace. "Shooting is decisive, but difficult to undo if done in error."

"Yeah, I hope the Delphians agree with you."

"Where's Oric?" Marissa turned to look for him. He stood a few feet behind them close to the top of a hill. "Oric," she called softly, wary of disrupting his listening. "Are you coming with us?" He paused a moment more and then followed them.

Together they strolled down the grassy slope toward the only tree visible in this particular valley. As they neared the tree, Marissa glimpsed something or someone leaning against it. At first, she saw only a humped shape.

This tree differed from the others they had seen. Too wide for the arms of a single person to encircle, the trunk would take two people to encompass it. The lowest branches grew three meters above the ground and reached out to support a ball of rustling leaves. Every color of green from the rich emerald of maturity to the pale caterpillar green of new shoots covered the tree. Small white blossoms flecked the vast ball of foliage and, here and there among the greenery, shiny red globes of fruit emerged. The ground surrounding the tree received a constant snow of blossoms and fallen fruit that the grass had not yet consumed. At least a gardener didn't have to worry about weeds on Delphia.

Shaded by the tree, the silver haired person seated beneath it used a small knife to slice one of the bright red fruits. After a long moment, the person gazed toward them. Marissa thought the features belonged to a woman. Her lips appeared almost a colorless pink and her shining hair hung in a ponytail. Yet the sharp features of the face—cheekbones, and aquiline nose—made Marissa question whether she had correctly identified gender or been swayed by Oric's pronouncement. A long white robe hid her body, but the aged face reminded Marissa of Uma. Perhaps, the Uma of a few years ago, but still female.

Stopping a short distance away, Marissa signaled to Galen and Oric. "What now?" She spoke in a conspiratorial whisper.

Oric shrugged. "We find the way in."

"In?" Marissa stared at him, but he didn't explain. She shook her head, unprepared to deal with a person so unlike any Delphian from the source they had seen. "What do we say?"

"Approaching all people is a matter of respect and of proper protocols," Galen intoned. "Delphian protocols are unrecorded, but the entire Confederation uses a mere thirty-nine known introductory protocols. The Delphians cannot be so different."

Peering at the woman, he shook his head. "The unspoken greeting always offers safety."

"Go ahead."

"Many thanks for the esteemed honor." Galen bowed to Marissa and then stepped forward.

He took two steps and gestured to them to follow. At a distance of about ten feet, he bowed almost double. He allowed the trailing edge of his sleeve to sweep the ground, but folded his beard back to avoid contact with the earth.

"Peace to you and to your ancestors back to the first generation." The clear, deep voice that spoke to him could have belonged to either a man or a woman.

"And peace to the fathers and mothers that gave life," Galen intoned in almost a chant. "May peace be upon them from now until the end of all nows."

The woman's pale eyes widened, and she nodded. "You are most courteous." She motioned with the silver knife she held in her left hand toward the fruit in her lap. "Will you share an apple with me? You and your friends."

"The sharing of food bestows great honor. Many thanks." Galen bowed again and approached the woman.

263

In a single long stroke, she cut a paper-thin slice of fruit and passed it with the tip of the knife to him. He plucked it from the knife with the barest tip of a finger, and raised it to his mouth, smoothing away his beard. He engulfed the slice immediately and made loud sucking sounds as he chewed with considerable noise.

"Ez," Marissa hissed, "is it safe?"

"Give me a sample," came the response.

Marissa accepted a slice, broke off a corner, and slipped the corner into her pocket for Ez. "Well?"

"Analysis complete. It's safe. No known drugs or toxins. Do you want a chemical composition?"

"No." Marissa popped the slice into her mouth, although she couldn't bring herself to chew it the same way Galen had. She poked Oric, and he accepted a similar slice.

The woman favored them with a broad smile. "Please, help yourself." She gestured toward a large basket of the fruit that had been hidden from view by the tree. "To share food is a great pleasure. One tires of eating alone." She cut off another slice of the red fruit and ate it.

"Thanks, most generous being, all delight in sharing such gracious hospitality." Galen squeezed Marissa's elbow, then stepped forward and, pulling up his voluminous sleeve, he reached into the basket and pulled out an apple. He passed one to Marissa and then took another and gave it to Oric.

Examining the small firm globe, Marissa turned hers slowly in her hand. It glowed a ruddy red with a wash of greenish gold at the top. "You called this an apple?"

"Of course, everyone calls it apple."

"I've never tasted anything like it. We have legends of apples, but I've never seen a real one before. Somehow they disappeared..." Marissa stopped short, uncertain what to say and what information to give this Delphian without knowing either the consequences or implications of it.

The woman nodded. "Yes, apples. Each is its own fruit. The one you hold in your hand will not taste like this one," She gestured with the knife to another similar apple. "Eating one in thin slices," she continued as she sliced her apple, "tastes different than biting into one. Go ahead, try it and see what I mean." The woman held up a slice.

"When you finish that, there're plenty more." She tucked the last piece of her own apple into her mouth, and then turned the knife and handed it to Marissa, handle first.

She took it gingerly. "Thanks. Aren't apples Earth species. I thought..."

Galen tugged at her sleeve and demanded her attention. "Some words, please," came his urgent whisper. He turned to the woman beneath the tree.

"Please pardon this humble one. There is so much to be done in a day."

"Thanks. " Marissa returned the knife, bewildered by Galen's abrupt desire to leave.

"Thanks," Oric mumbled, joining her and Galen as they walked away.

"Why didn't you let me ask her any questions? That's why we're here."

"The reason for this travel remains the prime focus."

Marissa glared at Galen. "So what now? That woman is not exactly what I'd expect from the 'terrors of the universe.'"

"Learning not to expect is difficult, but paramount in the search for truth. Those who seek the truth must first perceive and only then plan."

"So?" Marissa said. "We need to find the Delphian leaders."

Galen glanced at Oric and then back at Marissa. "To find those on Delphia who negotiate, who trade this for that, who speak for all. Anyone who arrives uninvited must surely demand investigation. Organized people would demand from whence visitors come and what they seek."

"Yeah, that's why we came, but why didn't the woman ask us? We must look strange to her..." Marissa stopped, suddenly struck by the oddness of the entire place. Unnatural nature, a woman with no curiosity, everything open, yet revealing nothing.

"Ez, help!"

"Insufficient or conflicting data. A sample of one is not adequate."

Then, in the distance a dark figure loomed on the horizon and grew larger. Too far away for Marissa to see much, it neared them at a rapid pace.

"Maybe she called for reinforcements."

"So it appears." Galen smoothed his beard and straightened his robe.

The distant figure approached at a rapid rate. She still couldn't discern any features, but the gait encouraged her to think of the person as male.

"Okay, before he reaches us, who does the talking?" Marissa looked at her colleagues

"It appears the barriers of protocol are surmounted."

Marissa stared at Galen. "Now what does that mean?"

"The woman beneath the tree perforce summoned this one," Galen observed. "Surely he will say more or ask more than she. As leader,"—he inclined his head to her—"the illustrious one speaks for all."

Nodding, Marissa grimaced. "I'll start, but if I lose it or don't follow, step in and help. "

"My pleasure derives from service." Galen bent his head in a gesture of respectful assent.

As the man neared, Marissa studied his features, surprised to find him a twin of the woman with the apples with same sharp cheekbones and aquiline nose, but clad in black. Did Delphia only have clones?

265

When he reached close enough to speak, the man made a deep bow. "Who are you? What market do you represent?"

Galen returned the bow and nudged Marissa ever so slightly. She made a stiff bow and tapped Oric to alert him to follow suit.

Upright, she skewered the man with her infamous 'Marissa stare.' "Marissa Latham." She held out her hand. The man remained impassive, not a trace of emotion played over his face. So much for friendliness. The Delphians must not shake hands.

She turned to her right and tapped Galen on the shoulder. "Meet Galen, ambassador..." For once, she couldn't think of anything else to say of him so she turned to her left and touched Oric. "This is my associate Oric."

"What business have you here?" He sounded like a fifth form teacher addressing an unruly student. The man gazed down his nose at them with gimlet eyes as if seeking some sign known only to him.

Tact and diplomacy had never been her strengths. For once, Marissa wondered what Uma would say. Should she mention Arden?

"It is hardly seemly that business should so soon be brought to the fore. There has not been time yet for acquaintance—an exchange of names?" Galen frowned at the man.

His impervious facade broke, and his face dissolved into lines of confusion and embarrassment. "Of course, how rude of me. For the moment, call me my first rankname, Miskarnkk."

Galen nodded and inclined his head. "Speaking as equals accords us great privilege." He bowed and allowed the broad hem of his sleeve to sweep the grass. "The honor remains with us."

Marissa followed Galen's lead once again and bowed, tapping Oric's elbow.

"Much more of this bowing and I'll be seasick," he hissed at her.

She suppressed a giggle. "A culture of courtesy."

"Evidently," Oric snapped.

Miskarnkk surveyed Galen with intense interest. "Please, clarify your means of arrival here."

Galen glanced at Marissa. She took a deep breath and released it, uncertain what tack to take, but determined to say nothing of the locator and the anomaly. "We came."

Turning to the man, Galen bobbed. "How does one get from place to place? We,"—he waved his arms to include them all— "are travelers and, though unique, share many common traits. The mode of transport, if that is the subject of the question proper, has no significance."

Miskarnkk smiled with raised eyebrows. "I see. No significance?"

Marissa maintained a solemn face. "We seek a leader who can negotiate

266

on behalf of Delphia on a matter of mutual importance."

Appraising her, Miskarnkk rubbed his chin before turning to Galen again. "Is that indeed what you meant?" With another bow, Galen nodded.

"I see." Miskarnkk looked unsatisfied. He walked several paces away and then stopped in front of Marissa.

He confronted her and smiled once again, lips somewhat less twisted. "How did you reach this world?" His stern tone insisted on an answer.

She fought the urge to back away from him. Determined to hold her ground, she waited a moment before responding. "We are travelers from the Usian Confederation and came to negotiate the fate of a world in which Delphia holds an interest. We can derive mutual benefit from this negotiation. To whom should we speak, or where should we go to find the proper authority?"

"Mutual benefit?" As he spoke, he drew out the last word as though savoring it, tasting it, and delighting in it.

Miskarnkk stared into Marissa's eyes, then over her shoulder and back again. She fought the urge to look behind her back.

"Then, you will speak with me here. I can ensure your words reach the place where they will do the most good." The man touched his ear, as though to reinforce his meaning.

Galen glanced at her, whether for guidance or in warning she couldn't tell. The man in black skewered her with dark eyes that threatened dire consequences, only looking away again when she said nothing.

"Having said so much, there is yet more." Galen paused for emphasis. "From cooperation between the group there is something more than profit. Surely, one—"

"Profit!" Miskarnkk interrupted Galen. His eyes lit up. From an interior pocket he pulled a small black device—either a calculator or recorder. Marissa couldn't see it well enough to tell. He touched the surface of the device and then stopped, eyes wide. "But...wait, you are not staff. Are you customers from some out-world?"

"No, no," Marissa responded. Galen touched her arm, and she subsided.

"Neither customers nor staff," Galen acknowledged. "Off-worlders, true, with a matter that affects worlds and lives, and, for a person of sufficient vision, there may be great profit in it."

Again, the word 'profit' made his eyes widen. "Yet you did not come via the spaceport." With annoying persistence, Miskarnkk returned to his first question.

"No," she growled, "we came in on the other side of that low hill." Marissa pointed toward their arrival point.

With pursed lips, he stared at her, at Galen, and finally at Oric. "I understand. Please accept my humble apologies. You may continue to call me

Miskarnkk, though I fear I seriously misjudged that matter. Obviously, I should have given you my full rankname."

Dismissing Miskarnkk's apology with a wave of his hand, Galen shook his head. "The fault lies not with those present. Ranknames are not part of the protocol of the Usian Confederation. Please, be at ease."

Miskarnkk bowed, almost sweeping the ground. "My deepest gratitude, and deeper still, if you give good report of me to those to whom we now approach. I will take you to those who can clarify this situation without damage to the competitive position." He turned and set off at a brisk pace down the hill, signaling for them to follow him.

Annoyed and confused, Marissa looked to Galen, but he only shrugged. As they trotted down the hill, Oric pulled on her sleeve.

"Is Miskarnkk one of the people who live underground?"

She stared at him, mouth open wide.

Chapter Twenty-Five - The World Beneath

"And here we wander in illusion:
Some blessed power deliver us from hence!"
-The Comedy of Errors, IV iii

For a half-hour, Miskarnkk led Marissa and her two companions over several identical hills, across a stream or two, and up more hills, until the landscape blurred in her mind. He stopped before yet another gigantic tree. Miskarnkk made a sharp downward gesture and then snapped his fingers.

Marissa looked around, wondering whether he expected someone to appear or the tree to disappear. Then the bark of the tree began to pucker and open like a sideways mouth. Bright even light almost blinded her and obscured any hint of what lay inside. No shadows gave form to anything. The short hairs on the back of her neck rose, and she turned to look at Galen and Oric.

Oric nodded. "Most likely the source of what I heard. The sounds are louder, but similar."

Miskarnkk stepped forward and vanished. Then Galen, with a slight shrug, followed. Oric leaned into the opening, grinned back at Marissa, and stepped through. Hesitant at what might lie within the tree, she examined the edge of the opening, touching it gingerly. The smooth, rounded gap appeared much like the scar of a lightning-caused wound yet the bark surrounding it felt natural and rigid. She held the edge tightly, took a deep breath, and then stepped inside.

The light hid the interior. Then the bark moved against her hand, and she jerked away. The opening closed with more speed than it had opened. Marissa fought off an overwhelming sense of vertigo and, with it, rising panic. Only the glare of the light met her gaze.

Reaching out, she touched a seamless surface where the opening had been. The light dimmed without warning. In front of her, steps led downward, but to where?

"Galen? Oric? Where are you?" No one answered.

Unable to retreat, she descended the broad steps. At the bottom, Miskarnkk strolled ahead along a corridor that reminded her of the bureaucratic warren below Cephus. It opened into a circular area where many other corridors converged. Choosing one, he followed it without a backward glance to yet another corridor and a featureless door with Marissa and her friends trailing behind.

He entered, and they followed him into a small cubicle. The most notable feature was a boxy desk faced by three stiff straight chairs. Their appearance promised no comfort. Miskarnkk sat behind the desk and gestured to the chairs. The Delphian, like Uma, didn't want his guests to stay any length of time. Marissa looked at Galen with a frown and sat in the chair farthest over. He and Oric occupied the remaining chairs.

The blank cubicle gave no insight or information. Empty walls pulsated in the slight variations of light, suggesting something more alive than functional. The whole experience sent a swift momentary surge of nausea through Marissa. Remembering Arden, she took a deep breath and waited in silence for Miskarnkk to speak.

He tapped the edge of his desk. In response, flimsies fed up through a slot. Gathering the sheaf to him, he juggled them into a squared-off bundle and pinned Marissa and the others with an insistent gaze.

"We have no precedent or protocol for visitors from off-world who do not arrive through the spaceport. No one has ever done that in the memory of anyone or any machine on Delphia. So accept my pardon if I do not offer you the courtesies you may expect. It is not intended as a slur on your honors or dignities."

Marissa nodded. "We understand, but we have urgent business."

"Quite so. We each have a set of desired ends. You want the affair of this planet of yours..."—he paused, whether from uncertainty or another reason, she couldn't tell— "Settled promptly, and we desire more information on your method of arrival. Once we understand the one, you may deal with the other. Now, the name of that planet?"

"Arden," Marissa said promptly, then remembered its other name. "You may have it listed as Crossroads."

"I am not certain I have it listed as anything. However, since you are presumably from an unopened market, we can reach an amicable arrangement if you control a suitable franchise." He set the stack of papers in front of him and interlaced his fingers. He studied Marissa with an inscrutable face.

Puzzled, she rubbed her eyes. "Franchise? This is Delphia, isn't it? You demanded Arden as a mall world. I've traveled through the Anomaly and in and out of worlds to reach Delphia." Frustrated, she pushed back her chair and started to rise. "If you can't help, we'll just..."

Holding up his hand, Miskarnkk leaned forward. "Quite so, quite so. You understand the intrinsic advantages of bargaining from a position of strength, a position that you may have here, though you did not hear it from me. I say it

270

because it places me in an acknowledged position of full disclosure and also shifts the weight from your advantage to my own, because I am clearing any interference. I await your offer."

Miskarnkk pressed a button on the far edge of the desk. "I require something to drink. May I offer you anything?" After relaying their orders to his desk, he turned back to them. "You understand and, I assume, acknowledge that it is far too early to start haggling. This is Delphia. I am curious about this 'traveling' of which you speak. Does it have anything to do with the planet you wish to preserve?"

His reference to travel and Arden in almost the same breath after his long-winded spiel disoriented Marissa. Did he know about the nexus, too? Anxiety began its niggling course through her system and fueled the desire to leave.

She stood up, then turned to the door almost directly behind her, and yanked it open. "Just show us back to the surface, and we'll be on our way."

"How can I convince you to stay?" He hurried around the desk to block the doorway. "Refreshments are on the way."

"Thank you for your hospitality," Marissa responded and stepped forward.

Shrugging, Miskarnkk stood back for them to pass. "Before you leave, you have yet to see Delphia. Having come so far, surely you want to see what we have." His smile reminded Marissa of a toothy Devonian shark.

"We have urgent matters to resolve."

"Of course. If you will follow me." He moved into the corridor, and she followed with Galen. Oric tagged along behind them.

After a few steps, Oric matched her stride and touched her arm. "This is the place," he whispered.

"How can it be? It's a park on top with their administrative offices below the surface. I don't think…"

Oric gave her arm a sharp squeezed. "This is the place."

Stopping, Miskarnkk faced them. "Now, if you will all join me within the confines of the square marked on the floor…"

Galen and Oric quickly stepped next to Miskarnkk. Marissa looked down. Except for black lines defining the square, the corridor's surface glowed a seamless eggshell white, merely a hallway. However, the softer lighting made it somewhat more pleasant than similar corridors on Cephus. Miskarnkk and the others stood within the marked three-meter square and waited. She stared at him, eyebrows raised.

"Step inside, and I will offer you our premium—a vision of the world beneath."

Now what? With reluctance she joined him. "As long as we're here we might as well take a little tour." She stepped to one side of the square. "Will this take us to the next level?"

"Yes." His unruffled manner added to her unease.

"I'm ready." She joined Miskarnkk and then turned to face the wall. Looking over his shoulder, she waited for something to happen. The floor dropped and so did they.

Gasping, Marissa struggled to stay upright. Her senses screamed; gravity pulled on every muscle. The square of flooring hurtled into darkness. The Anomaly! She glanced to the side. Miskarnkk appeared unconcerned, standing and staring into the dark. She sought the others. Oric gazed about wide-eyed. The wind whipped at Galen's robe and tossed his beard wildly about. No, not the Anomaly, but what?

Marissa eased toward the center of the square, careful not to topple any of them. With her stomach rebelling, she wavered, ready to sit on the floor.

Miskarnkk smirked at her. "Come and look. Is this the Delphia you seek?"

"Look? At what?" Marissa gritted her teeth. It must be safe or they wouldn't let people do this. By sheer force of will, she stayed on her feet and remained as close to the center as possible.

Faint sparks of light flashed by them, but gave no clue to what lay beyond the square. Miskarnkk motioned for her to join him at the edge of the square. She looked toward the others to see how they had responded. Galen now stood at the opposite edge and stared over, as if gazing into a puddle at his feet. Mildly reassured, but still worried, Marissa took a deep breath and slid her right foot toward Miskarnkk without lifting it from the surface of the square. Two more sliding steps and she stood behind him and to his right.

She peered over the edge. Darkness. Only inky black lay below.

"So, it's a drop shaft," she said. "So what?"

The darkness had not receded. She stepped forward, stopping with her toes at the edge of the square. The almost gloating smile on Miskarnkk's face angered her.

"Watch." His smarmy smile made her skin crawl.

He waved his arms in a sweeping gesture. To avoid them, Marissa stepped back into the square. So far, she could see no reason for this farce.

"Lights," he ordered.

The darkness vanished. Vertigo eased, and Marissa blinked at the buildings and movement below.

"Devos," she whispered. "I guess this is Delphia."

"There are always many layers," Miskarnkk replied in unctuous tones.

At the edge, she gazed out into the distance. They still hurtled downward, but the frame of reference provided by the immensity below made their descent seem a crawl.

"It's as if the planet's hollow."

"Precisely."

Beyond the Rim of Light, Alex Stone

Staring overhead, Marissa glimpsed far above the barely perceptible gray of...shapes, maybe buildings, maybe ships, motionless against the silvery shell of Delphia. Other forms, long and circular and impossibly thin, appeared to be pillars or spines. Small objects swarmed across nearly every surface. As she struggled with the perspective, she realized the tiny objects could be as large as the Usian expedition ships.

Marissa fought to maintain perspective yet couldn't comprehend the immensity of this world. Logic denied what she saw. No physics she understood would make a hollow world like this possible. Even N'Bert wouldn't be able to explain it. What were the Delphians? Nothing she had seen or anything she'd heard made sense.

Oric hovered at the edge of the square. He held his hand over his mouth and looked almost sick. "How much longer till we arrive at our destination?"

Snapping his fingers, Miskarnkk smiled with narrowed eyes. "This demonstration is over."

Marissa jerked as another wave of vertigo shook her. Then it ended. The descent had stopped and gravity returned to normal. She scanned their surroundings and blinked at the scurrying mass of humanity that surrounded them. Had she really seen the inside of Delphia or had Miskarnkk used some sleight of hand to intimidate them?

Oric had already stepped off the square and walked in a slow circle around the square on which they still clustered. Galen smoothed and untangled his beard and then joined him. He looked to Marissa.

Miskarnkk surveyed them with folded arms. "So, what do you want from Delphia? "

His assertive tone worried her. "I..." She ceased speaking and stepped off the square. "Just who are you? Some PR person? Where are we now?"

"You are in Delphia. I am the only one who can deal with you." He strolled ahead with seeming unconcern.

She stared beyond him at the busy people rushing past. They might almost be back on Satina IV, deep in the shopping district, except no one carried bundles or packages. High white walls with black doors at regular intervals formed one side of a broad avenue. Along the other side, a covered arcade sheltered cafes and vendors selling flowers, food, and large colorful feathers. A troop of women, at least a dozen, marched past at a trot. They all wore baggy green jumpsuits with ornate gold braid. Down one cross street, Marissa glimpsed men and women who looked nude, but whose bodies appeared eggshell white. She couldn't determine if they wore bodysuits or had been painted. They unpacked things from crates and assembled them into unidentifiable objects.

Gaping, she nearly lost sight of Miskarnkk and Galen. Hurrying to catch up with them, she almost collided with a rainbow-suited man. Bright colors, feathers, and ornaments adorned almost every person. Miskarnkk's dark suit stood out like a raven among songbirds in this vivid throng. Those passing appeared to give him just a little extra space like pleasure craft avoiding the wake of an ocean liner.

Breathless, she finally rejoined Miskarnkk and Galen. "Is this the true Delphia and you the leader? How do I know I can deal with you and not waste my time?"

Staring at her without expression, he folded his arms over his chest. "No one else will deal with you. Tell me what you want, and I will name a price. That is the most basic of transactions."

Marissa shoved her hands into her suit pockets and remained for a moment, stubborn, annoyed, and silent. Galen touched her on the shoulder and asked with a look. She nodded, hoping he might have some way to unsettle Miskarnkk.

"Perhaps," Galen interrupted, "the exchange of requests is best mediated. Honored Miskarnkk,"—Galen bowed to him— "you represent the fiduciary interests of a client."

He turned and gestured solemnly towards Marissa. "This seeker of wisdom and truth uses this humble servant as an intermediary." He looked toward her for approval. She shrugged and motioned for him to continue.

"The accomplishments we have witnessed cause marvel. To bring such a small request to attention may affront one, but as lowly and humble travelers who do not fully understand the established methods of commerce on Delphia, appeal must be made to patience." Miskarnkk nodded and settled into a more relaxed stance.

"The petition is singular—a simple world has been selected as an appeasement to assure entry to the Usian market. Please, choose another. There are many suitable worlds, many even more suitable to such purposes. Choose another, and all haste will be made in the completion of facilities." Galen bowed again and moved back beside Marissa, but did not take his eyes from Miskarnkk.

Miskarnkk's face revealed no expression, positive or negative. "This world, Arden you call it? It is not a simple thing to choose another. We have made careful plans. Changes would incur costs and not trivial ones. Moreover, there is something there, something we have seen elsewhere, but which seems…" He waved a hand in dismissal. "It is no matter—no matter at all. However, with everything there are layers. With everything, a price."

He stared at Galen without blinking. Galen returned the look with polite interest. After several moments Miskarnkk switched his gaze to Marissa.

"We will choose another world for this price if you reveal to us the means

274

by which you travel. It is a matter of more than curiosity. Now, it is a matter of Delphian security."

Mindful of Ez's analysis, awareness of the full implications of their arrival hit Marissa. She began to see she held the trump card. The means to save Arden lay within her grasp, but the price he demanded astounded and frightened her.

Instead of replying, she smiled a tight, wry smile. Even if she could, she had no desire to give this…oily man anything. As if sensing her doubts, Galen stepped forward. She signaled to him, but even before she had done so, she saw him smooth his beard in preparation to respond. No doubt he would chose and phrase his reply to sway and persuade their stubborn host.

"That is a considerable price. The gift of such travel is worth far more than a single, undeveloped world. A hundred worlds would not be too high for access to the universe and beyond. It is a high price indeed. Ask another price, or add to this offer, and do not be stingy."

Galen's boldness surprised Marissa as she glared at the oily man. She only hoped he would see a cobra poised to strike or perhaps a hooded Ganry viper. She relished this cold and snakelike feeling.

Leaning close to Galen, she placed her lips to his ear. "You know, even if I could, I wouldn't give it to them." He nodded and made a gesture that suggested silence.

"I may have not made the matter clear," Miskarnkk responded. "You see, no one may tread on the surface of Delphia without our knowledge and especially without our express permission. Come with me."

He turned and walked through the crowd. Galen extricated himself from Marissa's grip and followed.

Power! Even as a team leader Marissa had never held raw power before. She had needed both Tesde and Tad to support her against N'Bert and Sylvic. Maybe Uma had felt like this before the Delphians became a threat. Now, Marissa had taken over from both Uma and the Delphians, and she alone held the power. The idea fascinated her so much she walked in almost a daze. Then she became aware only she and Galen accompanied Miskarnkk.

"Wait, where's Oric?"

Neither Miskarnkk nor Galen answered her or even looked back. She scanned the area seeking Oric. Nothing. Then, about ten feet behind her, she glimpsed his yellow shirt. Satisfied he would find them, she rushed after the others, her sense of power dimmed, but still firm.

A short distance ahead, Miskarnkk turned and entered an open doorway. Marissa followed a few steps behind. Inside, tiers of seats stretched downward to form a huge amphitheater. Thousands of empty seats dropped away to a brightly lit, circular stage far below.

"Sit where you will," Miskarnkk instructed them. "Observe."

Marissa sauntered down a few steps, now certain of their victory, and sank onto an aisle seat. The arena darkened at once. She could just make out Galen trudging down the steps until he merged into the deepening gloom. Pitch black took over, as black as the empty space on the other side of the Anomaly. With that thought, she shifted uncomfortably in her seat. She wanted to stand to stretch her legs, but feared she'd trip over a step or chair and tumble all the way to the stage. Slowly, the darkness eased. No light shone, but somehow she sensed a difference. Marissa stiffened and waited.

"This," Miskarnkk's voice came from nearby, "is a complete time record. It demonstrates what has been."

Out of the not quite blackness, the stars appeared. Marissa glanced at her suit readout and jerked with surprise that she still sat and watched in the auditorium. Despite the sensations, Miskarnkk had not somehow transported them to space or to that drop shaft or whatever he had used to bring them here.

The point of view shifted like a ship turning on its axis. A planet surged into view, so huge it filled more than the arena's space. A beautiful planet of orange and blue marked with wisps of white—land, ocean, and atmosphere. She didn't recognize it, but it showed every sign of being a habitable world.

"This is Favia, the home world of the Kephu. Their negotiations were less than fully satisfactory. I believe that you will find their experience...educational."

Something shot past Marissa's shoulder. She gasped as the object hurled toward the planet, glowing white-hot. It arced wide around the planet's outer edge to disappear past its curvature. Then, it emerged on the other side. It flashed toward the surface.

Nothing.

From the impact site, a sickening green glow spread outward. Soon the beautiful orange and blue faded. The sickly glow ebbed and vanished. When it dissipated, nothing remained, but a burnt brown surface.

Less spectacular than the Satina IV vids, the stark vision of this destruction cut deep. To take a living planet and kill all life offended all of Marissa's beliefs. Usian reforming did exactly that, but at least terraforming created new life. It didn't leave a dead planet. She shuddered at the desolation and desecration.

"If," Miskarnkk intoned, menace underlying that one word, "the Usians cannot perform the simple tasks of shaping the world we selected, we will do it ourselves. Or perhaps we will select another world and choose it because it suits us to do so. Our offer stands. There will be no other offers. I urge you to reconsider your response."

Sickened and no longer so sure of herself, Marissa stood on shaky legs. She would have taken her anger out on Miskarnkk in some way if she could only reach him. A feathery touch on her left shoulder made her swing around.

"It's me." Oric leaned closer. "This isn't a fabrication. It sounds and looks real."

"Where's Miskarnkk?" Marissa hissed at him.

"He left. This is the planet we heard about. I can hear it. "

"What? How can you hear a planet? "

"I hear the planet turning. I hear...something else. This is real." Oric appeared unreal in the sepia light of the planet. He glanced briefly at her, then back at the planet's image.

"Miskarnkk said something about a time image, but..." Marissa didn't know what more to say.

"They did it, didn't they?" Oric stared at her a moment. "They destroyed this world as Teloav said on Satina IV. They have immense power, but..." He paused a moment. "Some here do not respect Miskarnkk. Even with what we've heard and seen here, some do not believe this happened as he said."

"What?" Marissa searched her pocket to find her lumina and switched it on. She waved it at the planet of the Kephu. It vanished. She pointed it toward the stage. Far below, Galen blinked back at her. "Get up here," she called.

"I heard," Oric continued, "that others do not believe in this place." Marissa swiveled the light back to Oric and switched it off as the arena's light returned to normal. "Many do not believe in their vast power, only their position."

"Position," Galen added as he stepped up next to her, slightly out of breath, "is not without value. The correct position and a little power can often overcome greater power."

"So, now what do we do?" Marissa stared from Galen to Oric and back.

Chapter Twenty-Six - To Market, To Market

"Trust none; For oaths are straws, men's faiths are wafer-cakes."
-Henry V, II iii

Oric sauntered down to the auditorium stage and looked back up at Marissa. He poked at something at the base of the stage. She hoped he knew what he was doing. Miskarnkk wouldn't like it if they damaged anything.

"Okay, Galen." Marissa rubbed her eyes with both hands. "You saw it too. Now, what do we do about it?"

"The search for truth is often painful and disappointing. Untruth can confuse and obscure. Truth is by nature simple, while search and discovery are painful. The truth itself never is." Galen paused for a moment and fingered his beard. "As to the question posed—it seems that the leader should better know this. Yet dismissing responsibility because of their own fear—that, it seems would be instructive in the ways of untruth…"

"Devos, it escapes me how we can do anything. We shouldn't have come here. I wish I understood the Delphians, but going against this…this…" She raised her clenched fists to her face and pressed her forehead against them. "This is evil. I've never really seen evil before."

A noise from the stage drew her attention, and she looked to where Oric tinkered with something she couldn't make out. He seemed to be peering at something beneath the stage. His mouth moved, but the distance prevented her hearing what he said.

"Galen, sometimes I just don't understand you. I can't tell them how to jump and even if I could, I'm certain that it's something I wouldn't tell them. The Delphians won't help us."

Needing action, she jumped to her feet and went to retrieve Oric. "Let's go. We might as well return to Arden."

"The leader's place, for the present, is here." Galen's voice, ever her conscience, came from behind. "Certainty prepares one for the truth, whatever it may be. Surely one must know more—to take them at their word may be wrong. Nothing they have shown or said is proven at this point a reliable indicator of the truth."

278

Unable and unwilling to answer, Marissa kept walking. "If only I could be so positive."

She stopped in mid-step and faced Galen. "Am I a failure? Have I messed up everything so far?" She stared past Galen, not seeing him, but looking past or through him. "The rheos deserve better, but because I didn't collect the evidence I needed, they'll end up extinct. All the jumping around the universe won't change that."

His face filled with pity, Galen bowed to her. "Harsh self evaluation brings another element of the search. It can, however, be overdone."

"Oric, what are you doing?" Marissa called.

Oric kept looking into the thing under the stage and then raised a hand to her. Dropping to one knee, he touched something on the device.

"I don't think you should—"

Light flooded the stage, enveloping him and forcing Marissa to throw her arm up to cover her eyes. "Oric!"

The light faded, leaving the brown planet once again revolving in a slow dance above the stage. Oric sat at the edge, blinking, but smiling. Marissa raced down the intervening steps to him.

"Are you all right? What did you do?" She touched his face and turned it to look at his eyes. Tear filled and fully dilated, they did not follow her as she moved. "Can you see? Devos, why did you do that?"

He smiled up at her and pulled her hands down. "I'm fine. I knew the presentation was more than a recording. I could still hear them there." Rapid blinks led to tears running down his nose. He brushed them away, a smile on his face. "This isn't a dead planet—people are there!"

"Can you see me?" Marissa searched her pockets for a medkit.

Shaking his head, Oric narrowed his eyes. "Only a red sort of darkness. I hear you and I know where I am."

Marissa popped open the medkit and pulled out the small diagnostic computer. She scanned the instructions, then pulled a lens from the side, and peered through it into his eye. Stepping back, she waited for results.

Galen moved forward to extend a handkerchief to Oric who took it and wiped his eyes. He held it out to Galen, but he waved it away with his hand. Grinning, Oric tucked it into his shirt. The ease of his actions demonstrated he could function to some extent without sight.

"I never paid much attention to what I saw anyway." He jumped off the stage and patted the projector. "Let me tell you about this."

Marissa looked at the diagcomp readout, then collapsed into a seat. "Oric, you may be permanently blind, and you don't care?"

He grinned at her. "Don't worry. Just listen to me."

"Light," Galen interrupted, "is truth to the eyes, yet by itself, is not sufficient."

"The blue coats out there,"—Oric motioned to the back door of the auditorium— "grumble about 'the great lie of the Delphians.' Here is at least one. He said the Delphians destroyed that world, but I hear its life. If the Delphian world is not as the surface implies, maybe that planet is not destroyed despite what the Delphians try to make us believe."

Marissa read the diagcomp results again. "If we get you back to a hospital on my side of the universe we may be able to save your sight, or at least some of it. We can't waste time running around in the bowels of Delphia asking the workers if they like their bosses."

He shook his head. "No, I don't need them any more."

"What? You don't need your eyes?" Stunned, she stared up at him and sighed. "I must be infecting everyone around me. Oric, even you need eyes." She rubbed her own eyes, stinging with sympathy. "I'm so tired...so tired of accomplishing nothing." She stared down at her hands. On her wrist, the locator bracelet gleamed in the bright arena light, so powerful and yet so useless.

Oric moved back to the projector. Marissa watched him, fearing he might stumble or fall. Next, he walked around to the steps and up them without a pause.

She shook her head, amazed at his ability to function without the aid of sight. "What do you think we should do?"

"Go out and talk to the blue coats. They may know something more."

Fingering his beard, Galen inclined his head. "Action is preferable to inaction. Although the abilities of these people can be understood, they would benefit from a pursuit of the truth. It is equally possible that they understand it well, but for some reason of their own, have buried it deep within, preferring appearance and perspective. Follow the recommendation. If one does not know the way, ask directions."

Marissa looked at the image of the brown planet still spinning in space, a lonely reminder of Delphian power and will. Weariness and depression sucked her strength. She had power, just not enough or the right kind to force the Delphians to cooperate.

With reluctant steps, she followed Oric. "I can ask directions, but I've never been good at following them. Show me the blue coats."

When she and Galen reached Oric at the building entrance, she pulled him around to examine his eyes again. "How are you going to be able to tell that their coats are blue?"

A puzzled expression passed over his face. "Blue sounds blue."

His response only added to her confusion. Outside, the colorful Delphians mingled in dazzling swirls of colors and scents, ebbing and flowing, to eddy around them. She couldn't imagine how that might sound to Oric, but he navigated down a crowded street without one misstep.

Overhead, the interior sky shifted with the continual movement of shapes. Marissa tried to focus on the people passing. The thought of mountain-sized objects tumbling over her head made her stomach churn.

Galen's robe, now rose colored, and his elaborate beard blended with the surrounding throng. So too did Oric's yellow shirt. Marissa looked to her own drab field suit. A few Delphians glanced toward her and then away perhaps wondering at her lack of display. Yet Miskarnkk's somber suit elicited respect or maybe even fear. She understood so little about this strange world, and everything she learned only confused her more.

"This way," Oric called back to her. "They're over here."

Marissa stopped and looked in the direction Oric pointed. Blue coats. Perhaps over a hundred women, tall, tall women, in long azure coats worked around a huge circular table. Their long arms worked in steady arcs, polishing the table's surface. Their vivid coats dazzled the eye. With sleeves turned above their elbows, they polished in great circles. The table reflected light, brighter and truer than the smoothest mirror.

Turning to Galen, Marissa read no answers in his face. "Now what? These people don't like their job, so?"

"An unasked question is the burden of a fool. A question, although not always received as intended, furthers the cause of truth. Ask, and be enlightened. Remain silent, and wither in darkness."

Marissa frowned at Galen and approached one of the blue-coated women. She tapped her on the shoulder. "Excuse me, but…" She looked where Oric had been standing. He now appeared on the far side of the table, listening over the shoulders of the polishers. "I'm sorry, but I was told that you knew the truth about the 'great lie.'"

Seven or more feet tall, the woman towered above Marissa, something that seldom happened. The woman made a high-pitched trilling sound in the back of her throat. The others stopped polishing and, like automatons, turned as one to stare at Marissa. They joined in the sound, lower than a shriek and more of a warbling. They marched in step around the sides of the table.

Marissa shifted back, but Galen planted a firm hand in the middle of her back, urging her to remain. The women stopped moving and regarded her in sudden silence.

The one Marissa had tapped inclined her head the merest fraction. "How came you to question me? Truth is a commodity. Have you come to trade?"

Marissa turned at once to Galen, wide-eyed. He straightened to his full height, eyebrows raised. She couldn't tell if the woman's words excited or offended him.

Stepping forward, he bowed to the woman. "Truth is beyond riches. Seek

281

not to hoard truth. Do not seek truth for its own sake. Seek truth so that it maybe be revealed, shared, and shaken free from the dust of greed and avarice." He inclined his head to the same exact degree as the woman had.

"And if we give you the truth you ask freely, we must pay the price. Such brought us here." The warbling began again, but in a softer tone. "We fear nothing, but do not assume the debt of others." The warbling quickened. "One must know that to ask alone is dangerous." With that, the chorus softened and then ceased.

At a loss, Marissa looked from Galen to Oric and back to the woman. "I can't ask anyone else to join this lost cause. I—"

"The planet," Oric blurted from across the table. As one, the women pivoted to face him. "You said it was a lie. Can your masters destroy planets when they want?" He hurried around the table toward them.

"Should we fear them? I saw their demonstration, but I heard more than they think. That planet is not dead. Tell me, am I right?"

Prepared to pull Oric away, Marissa feared the women would attack him.

"You are right." The woman faced Marissa. "The Delphians lie, but they lie well. That place they call Favia, world of the Kephu. They say they destroyed it because of rebellion. They did not destroy it, and yet it suffers as if they had. The Kephu did not rebel. They signed a contract to remake their world, and the great Delphians, 'masters' you call them, erred. They paid heavy penalties to move the Kephu and then claimed that they destroyed the world. They have now turned it into a great source of profit."

"So? It doesn't matter. Either way they can destroy worlds, intentionally or not." She looked back at the woman. "Pardon my hesitation, but why should we believe you?"

The warbling resumed at once and grew in intensity. She marveled that they could make so loud a din. Oric covered his ears and moved off. Galen tugged at his beard, muttering.

Leaning back, the women opened their mouths wider. The tone of their chorus shifted upward, higher in frequency and volume. Almost deafened, Marissa, too, covered her ears.

"Stop, STOP," she shouted. The warbling swallowed her plea. Marissa stumbled backward, stopped only by Galen's hand as he reached out to steady her.

Above, a shadow swooped down. The dark shape hurtled toward them. With haste, the women backed away from the polished table. Marissa tugged Galen toward her and back from it. Hovering a moment, the round shape, a ship, settled like a bird in its nest. Silence.

"Believe your own eyes," the woman hissed in Marissa's ear and moved back.

"Go there. See for yourself," called another woman. "The Delphians lie and are weaker than they appear."

The ship lowered a short ramp to reveal a portion of its brightly lit interior. Within, dark figures scurried about.

"They are weak," echoed another woman. "They cow with words. Do you fear words?" Her glance held only contempt.

Marissa gazed from Galen to Oric and then to the women nearest. "Then why are you here?"

"Honest debt binds us," she responded, pride evident in her erect stance. "We live by our word."

"Observation and personal witness," prompted Galen, "are strong guides to the truth. If the Delphians have no truth, they become vulnerable, as do all the untruthful. Conspiracy creates its own vulnerability."

"We offer you transport to Favia." The woman pointed to the waiting ship.

Concerned about the wisdom of trusting these people, Marissa looked first to Galen and then Oric. Both shrugged. Galen's beard now carried an image of the brown world of the Kephu. Since neither offered advice, Marissa pondered the choices. They could take the ship, which might or might not take them to Favia, or she could take the three of them by the usual method. She much preferred to trust herself than to trust others.

"We don't need it," Marissa said.

"We ask only that you reveal the truth you learn there," the woman responded.

"The truth awaits," Galen added. "All signs and evidence give voice to it,"

"Yeah," Marissa smiled at him, "just so I don't have to ride in Miskarnkk's drop shaft again."

Chapter Twenty-Seven - Lichen, Lichen Everywhere

"Yea, and furr'd moss besides, when flowers there are none."
-*Cymbeline*, IV ii

Marissa pulled Galen and Oric away from the women and walked toward the amphitheater. "We must learn more about Favia before we go there."

Galen turned and bowed to the women in blue. "Truth calls its servants. All thanks for this kind offer, but in uncertain times the path forged by one's own efforts provides the most perfect view of the truth."

One of the women nodded, and, like a Benarian Trapper blossom at dusk, the group drew in again upon itself. The vehicle ramp slid up into the ship, and the port snapped closed. It rose as soundlessly as it had descended.

Once away inside the amphitheater, Marissa pulled Galen and Oric to the top row of seats and sank into the third one from the aisle. She fingered her pocket. "Ez, you awake?" She spoke *sotto voce*, audible to Oric, but she hoped not to the Delphians, but had no way to be certain. She needed Ez's help, now.

"Of course, what do you need?"

"Any data available about Favia."

Silence followed for a brief moment. "Favia, fifth planet of the Bednor System. Current status: lifeless. All other information: code-classified inaccessible to the highest construct in my circle—"

"Stop. Is there anything on a native population?"

"Hold please, I'm connecting to Delphian sources. Secondary check." Marissa could almost hear circuits switching.

"Favia was once the home of the Kephu who now reside in the Septorian System. The Delphians claim to have destroyed all its non-human native life forms."

"The Delphians destroyed its life forms, except for humanoids? Then the holos are right?"

"I can not speak for the holos. So far as I have been able to determine, I have given you the facts. The Bednorian sun began to emit bursts of particles hazardous to humanoid life. The Kephu sought Delphian assistance and were resettled. Because of the radiation levels, the Delphians permit only limited

284

access to the surface. Craft in the area have measured abnormally high gamma levels at the surface."

"So no one's lived on Favia since the resettlement?" Marissa frowned.

"Not since the Delphian Disaster."

"What about this radiation? Can we stand it?"

"Radiation level increases in solar bursts of short duration. None is likely during your visit. Next is scheduled in six weeks. Residual levels are acceptable for a short period, and protective clothing is available. Your suit is adequate."

"What about Galen and Oric? Do they need anything?"

"Not unless your visit exceeds one hour."

Marissa twisted the locator bracelet on her wrist as she pondered a course of action. At least they could make a quick getaway. "We don't know what we're going to find. There may be a risk from radiation if we stay too long. Do you still want to go?"

"This garment has some remarkable properties." Galen fingered the fabric of his robe. "It is impervious to almost any level of radiation."

"Oric?"

"I heard the exchange. One hour should be enough."

"As for pictures, we have the holos," Marissa said, looking to the image over the stage below.

She linked hands with her friends. "Ready?" They both nodded and squeezed her hands.

Closing her eyes, she concentrated on the brown planet. Warmth began to radiate from the locator bracelet. The grid of lines and glowing spots brightened against the blackness of her closed eyelids. She sought the glow of Arden, then pulled space together and flashed past it. Concentrating on the image of Favia, she sought to separate it from among the many points of light before her. At last one spot grew in intensity, followed by that slight disorientation that signaled transfer.

"Are we there?" Oric stumbled, pulling on to the hand he still held.

"I think so." Marissa released his hand and stepped forward.

This time the three stood in a shallow depression on a broad open plain. A jumbled mass of brown rock stretched as far as they could see. Not a green tree, a bush, or even grass anywhere. Just cracked brown rock.

She climbed out of the slight depression. "Well, Galen, what do you make of this?"

He looked about and shrugged. "Lifeless it would seem, but that the Delphians have already revealed. To understand, the mind must grasp what the eyes do not yet perceive."

Marissa frowned as she scanned the empty brown landscape. "What? I know the Delphians haven't told us the whole truth, but they haven't exactly lied to us about anything either. We have no reason to believe either the Delphians or Oric's blue coats. There's no evidence that Favia is not as dead as they say, except what Oric heard. Teloav warned us about the Delphians' destructive capability."

"Perhaps, but does the ravaged appearance of the surface conceal the truth beneath as did the Delphian surface?" Galen frowned, weaving his fingers back and forth in and out of his beard.

Oric, his head to one side, nodded. "I hear signs of life—over there." He pointed off to the right toward what looked like a bump on the horizon.

Marissa shaded her eyes and followed his pointing finger. She could just make out some sort of object. According to the multitool, it lay about a kilometer and half away. She floated a mini-beacon about ten meters above the surface and set it on a slow cycle.

Sitting back on her heels, she nodded as she watched the light complete its arc. "Our lighthouse to guide us back to shore."

No one answered. The others had walked some twenty meters away toward the distant knobby object. Jumping up, she ran after them.

Concerned about safety, Marissa checked the atmospheric readings and grunted as she noted enough oxygen to support life. The sensors detected no obvious toxins except for an off-the-scale gamma count.

"We'd better make this quick. Despite what Ez said, I'm not sure how long we can stand the radiation." The others nodded.

The uneven surface made walking slow, and Marissa appreciated the environmental system in her suit that kept sweat from tricking down her armpits. As they drew closer to the knob, it gradually took shape as a cluster of treelike trunks covered with strange brown growths; the same uneven brown covered the entire surface of Favia.

"Oric, do you hear anything?"

He cocked his head, as if listening to some subsonic noise. "There are people nearby—below. But they aren't talking. I hear only machinery pulsing."

As they approached, the grove resolved into a small circular ring of tall trees with arching limbs that almost met in the center of the circle and formed a canopy around the outer edge of the ring. Brown sheets hung from the branches, but Marissa could discern no leaves. Examining the sheets more closely, she whistled at the tiny formations making up the brown covering. The growth draping the limbs looked like foliose lichens. Underneath, she found more lichen, but ramose forms. Normally the two didn't grow together; in any case, she had never seen such massive lichen growths.

Marissa shook her head in surprise. She needed to take tissue samples to confirm her conclusions, but these had to be lichens. Never had she seen such a profusion of them before. The variety made it look as if the lichens had tried to fill every biological niche emptied by Delphian science. Even the ground covering revealed yet another lichen, this one crustose.

"Perhaps these protrusions may provide places of rest?" Galen pointed to the curious knees that formed broad seats at the base of each lichen tree on the side facing into the circle.

Marissa nodded. "Why not? I need to consult Ez and possibly the Advocate so we might as well be comfortable."

Galen sat to Marissa's right while Oric perched on the far side of the circle, his head to one side.

"Ez, any more on the Kephu or Favia?"

"I detect no radiation at this level."

"What?" Marissa stared down at the radiation reading on her suit. "You're right." Standing up again, the needle zoomed into the danger level. Stooping down she looked at the sensors and observed the needle drop to a normal background level. "'My sensors must be malfunctioning."

"Sensors agree with my analysis. Radiation levels at the surface are normal."

"So how do you explain it?'

"Someone or something is jamming sensors by generating a radiation screen."

"To keep people away? Umm, well why not? I don't know how the Delphians did it, but it looks like they established a radiation screen and covered the entire planet with brown lichen."

"And the reason for this, illustrious guide and mentor?" Galen stroked his beard as he studied her.

"I don't know. When we saw the vid, it showed the brown moving rapidly across the surface, covering everything in sight. The Delphians claimed it was some type of ray that destroyed all life. That's a bit how terraforming works. They drop those phagocytes first, then after they've worked, we start reseeding the planet."

Galen rubbed his chin. "And if the phagocytes began to work and somehow stopped. What then would occur?"

"Hmm, an interesting question. I'm not sure." Marissa looked at Galen, wondering if maybe he had something.

"Perhaps the Delphians began to terraform Favia, but part way through the process the sun your assistant mentioned killed the phagocytes, or rather the more advanced Terran life forms."

"I'm not sure you can exactly kill them, but the radiation could affect the biochemical reactions."

"Ah," Galen smoothed his beard. "The path to the truth is strewn with such rubble. Perhaps the Delphians failed in their attempt to reform because the sun would periodically kill off the terraforms?"

Marissa grinned. "I'd say the scientist did a lousy job of selecting the planet in the first place."

"After such a disaster, what next?"

"Beats me. Abandon it, I guess."

Galen shook his head and smiled. "A costly mistake. One that would lead others to find that the Delphians did not quite grasp the truth. Surely, the road to the greatest profit would be, as always in these cases, to subvert the truth to the causes of profit. To make of the truth an inversion, a mirror to reflect the scene the Delphians most needed to insure future cooperation."

For a moment, Marissa frowned as she sorted though Galen's observations. Yes. It fit. He always had the core of the truth, but his circumlocutions sometimes required a lot of effort to get to the gist of his meaning.

"You know, Galen, you surprise me at times. You have a sharp brain under all that rhetoric."

For a moment, he looked pained. "As a fellow seeker of truth, one must follow the thread wherever it may lead. When one has negated the obvious, then what remains must be truth."

Tickled by his words, Marissa laughed. Somewhere she had heard a similar saying. Something Uncle Arga cited, but she couldn't remember what. Galen's words made sense. "If I understand you, the Delphians see everything as trade. They wring the last dollar out of all actions, good or bad."

"Marissa, I hear voices," Oric whispered.

She looked about, but saw nothing beyond the lichen. "Where?"

"From below."

"Well? What are they saying?" She stood hands on her hips, waiting.

"I don't know." Oric frowned, a puzzled look on his face. "It's jumbled and some sort of machine noise is masking it. This has never happened before."

Suddenly, a burst of tiny spores filled the air. "What?" She looked at the rapidly spreading cloud. Before she could react, the light faded.

* * * *

"Well, Marissa Latham. It's time you rejoined us." Miskarnkk wore a wry smile on his face.

She tried to reach her aching head, but something restrained her hands. She shook her head to clear the remnants of a dark fog from her senses. Unable to move, she glared at him.

"What've you done to us?"

"Nothing. Nothing at all. We merely thought it wise to keep you from leaving suddenly. I'm sure the rest has done you and your...uh, assistants a world of good. You have been in such a frenzy of late."

288

Marissa strained to rise, but found herself held fast by brown vines twined around her hands and feet that anchored her in place. From her restricted view, she surmised she sat on one of tree seats, her back against the trunk. Galen and Oric stood to one side with their arms behind them. Restrained too, she assumed. Three uniformed guards clustered about them with what looked like weapons in hand.

"What do you want from us?"

Miskarnkk smiled. "We have everything we came for, your two talented friends, and, of course, that curious bracelet you wore. We assume it's the key to your lucrative ability to move from place to place."

The locator bracelet. With a sensation akin to panic, Marissa now recognized the blank spot on her wrist where it had rested. How could she have been so blind, so overconfident? She would not give Miskarnkk the satisfaction of acknowledging its importance. One tiny sliver of hope remained; Ez and the Advocate had said no one else could use it. Something about changes in her brain. Yet N'Bert had sent Galen to Arden with it. Why?

She had never quite figured out how it worked or how it allowed her to find and select one of those glowing spots among so many from that internal view of the universe. A metric space map Galen had called it. The locator helped her to focus on the right place and follow the glowing strand to arrive at the desired location. Confused thoughts fought for her attention. No, best not to give Miskarnkk anything.

Instead, Marissa snorted. "It won't do you any good. I'm the only one who can use it."

"Perhaps," he dismissed her claim with a wave of his hand— "but then we have been working on a similar mode of travel for a long time. I'm sure our scientists will have no difficulty deciphering how to use this device. It really was kind of you to accept our invitation."

"Invitation?" Marissa stared at him. "What invitation? I don't remember you inviting us here."

"Well not in so many words perhaps, but we did make it irresistible, didn't we?" Miskarnkk smiled with a raised eyebrow. "I do think the blue coats as your friend called them a particularly clever touch. For a moment, my colleagues feared you might choose the ship, and then we would have had to step in, but you didn't. It's nice to have such a predictable response. Anyway, we must be on our way. Enjoy your stay."

Miskarnkk turned his back and motioned to the guards to bring Galen and Oric. Galen stumbled as one of the three guards prodded him forward. Oric gave the one shoving him a swift kick, but the guard cuffed him back.

Twisting and turning, Marissa struggled with the vines, but couldn't loosen them. "Wait. What in Devos are you doing? This is murder."

"Oh, I wouldn't call it that, but it will take you a time to free yourself. Despite its rather drab appearance, this isn't such a bad place. As a xenobiologist, I have no doubt you'll find a way to survive. Time is profit. We thank you for giving us this key. Perhaps on my next visit, we can talk again, but that won't be for several years. Good-bye, Marissa Latham."

"One exile is enough. I'm not going through this again," she muttered, furious with Miskarnkk and all the scheming Delphians.

Oblivious to her words, he hurried off after the others who had already boarded a shuttlecraft standing just outside the grove. The ramp retracted and the door began to close.

"Miskarnkk, I'll get you for this." Marissa tried to raise her fist, but couldn't. "I'll get off this planet, and when I do, I'll make you and Delphia pay. I swear it." She gritted her teeth and fought to break the vines.

He waved from the door of the shuttle. "Good-bye, good profits." The door closed and the shuttle rose, leaving Marissa alone.

Chapter Twenty-Eight - Alone on the Lichen Planet

"Tis in my memory locked and you yourself shall keep the key of it."
-Hamlet, I iii

Almost as soon as the shuttle pulled away from the planet surface, the vines released Marissa. Free to move, but to where?

Miskarnkk had left her with plenty of time to appreciate the splendors of Favia. She got to her feet and scanned the area, but saw only the same unbroken brown expanse from horizon to horizon. Only the beacon she had set when they arrived on Favia provided any point of reference. A lighthouse, indeed.

Miskarnkk had taken her only means of escape with him, the locator bracelet, and marooned her, but more effectively than Uma had. She slumped back in the lichen chair and picked at the mottled surface, dislodging several small chunks. Surrounded by a lichen desert, how could she survive? He seemed to think she could; he had said as much.

The locator bracelet. What made it work? An almost tickling sensation tugged at her awareness. The bracelet.

What about the bracelet? Galen had given it to her on Arden, a present from N'Bert, and relayed N'Bert's words that it held the key to travel anywhere. The bracelet had worked. The bracelet and that strange place of transfer. A place of connections. What had Galen said? A spatial map.

"Ez, I'm in a fix here." Marissa fingered Ez's chip "They've stranded us on Favia. Now what do we do?"

"Why not just move as you have before?"

"The Delphians took the locator bracelet. To be precise, Miskarnkk removed it." Again she experienced that funny little mind tickle, something just at the edge of her awareness. As soon as she concentrated on it, it faded away. "I need help. Maybe you can locate N'Bert."

"I'll check and see if anything more has appeared on the nets."

A brief pause ensued. Marissa envisioned the locator bracelet once more. The weight and fit of it on her arm, the gleam of the stones, matte not shiny, and the metal itself, an alloy she failed to recognize. Unique in so many ways, now it lay in Miskarnkk's greedy hands. What might he do with it? Had she

291

now put Arden at greater risk?

"All lines of communication with Favia are through Delphia. Although I have established contact with one Delphian personality, it may not be trustworthy. The Advocate may know something. I'll try contact by another path."

Marissa slumped into the lichen chair again. The arms seemed to move in slightly to embrace her. Mentally, emotionally, and physically exhausted, she closed her eyes and dozed.

The vaguely uncomfortable arms of the lichen chair that enfolded her pressed upon her. Half dreams flitted through her mind. She saw herself, distorted as though viewed through a lens with an imperfection, trying on the bracelet for the first time. Then again that stretching, that inside out pulling as that place that was no place, the tangle of nothingness—the roots...the map. The map...the whatever it was...pulled her through it and it through her. Intertwined, tied up like a pretzel, both within and outside the writhing tunnels. No, not tunnels, truly not tunnels—what had Galen said? Metric space, a mapping—a mapping of every space onto this space. What did it mean? If it was a map...

She ran; she ran and ran and ran with the rheos moving in their graceful undulating lope. Galen raced beside them. How did he keep pace with her? She towered over him by almost a foot. He matched her flowing stride, running, tireless when she panted and slowed.

In her dream, she jumped again. That strange red blackness and the wrinkled fabric of space. The depression on Satina IV. Somehow, that red candy-box satin room with the depression in the middle so like the one in Arden's cave. The one in the cave with its odd visual displacement. The mind tickle returned.

Displacement, optical illusion, mosaics, signs. Somehow, they contained part of the clue, part of what her unconscious self knew. The conscious part of her mind tracked it, even while the dreaming part of her moved away.

Time after time, the jumps through space, and the landings. Time after time, she woke after ever briefer and briefer periods of unconsciousness. She relived them all again. Then, the most recent jump from Delphia to Favia.

That place of lines, tunnels, strands, and glowing spots appeared in her head—that infinite expanse of light and darkness that she could never quite grasp. Like chronosculpture, it changed even as she viewed it. The tickle became a burning, an itch too long unscratched. A map—all the other visions and dreams she knew to be dreams and visions, but that map remained clear—chronosculpturally pure and complex.

Wait, the conscious Marissa told the dream Marissa. Reach for it slowly. She forced herself to relax. Let it go now. Relax and let it go. If she had learned one thing from all of this, it was that forcing the issue almost never worked. Think of something else instead.

With that thought, the conscious part of her fled and fell into one long and lazy dream during which she watched Tad from a distance as he undressed, removing first his shirt and sandals, then his pants and underclothes. She watched as he stood there, unaware of her, turning, turning under a shower.

The image changed and she saw him in a white suit. A brilliant, eye-damaging white suit. A suit that dazzled and shaped him. A hot pulse lodged in her throat speeding up and pumping ever faster.

Next, she watched him stretched out on a pad, sleeping, blond hair tousled, left arm thrown back behind him. Face serene, he breathed softly. The heat of his body reached her even from the great distance separating them. A great longing seized her, a hunger beyond hunger, an all-consuming need. When she reached toward him, he stirred, and the covers shifted, exposing him. Breathing deeply, Marissa moved closer, careful not to wake him.

They showered together on Arden. They made love on Satina IV. They walked again on Arden and savored its starlit night. Together in her cramped cabin aboard the survey ship, they held one another. Over and over his warmth answered her need.

He ran naked across the fields of Arden with Brac. They ran for a reason, but she didn't care why. Healthy, full of life, he looked newly minted. She had never seen such a Tad. Image after image of him filled her mind; then, she slept secure in his arms.

Hours or minutes later, the conscious part of her knocked and entered the room where she slept with Tad. The conscious Marissa summoned her. She watched in dreamtime as she rose from beside him, suddenly cold in that room away from his warmth. Tad stirred, but soon fell back into deep sleep.

She followed herself in her dream. She walked deep into a dark room, a rocky-walled, damp dark room. The map appeared. The map, sharp and clear once again. The map. The dream Marissa pointed. The map. The map is the key; the key is the map. Now, what's all this about a map and a key?

And then she knew.

The locator bracelet, the map, and the key. Not three things, but two. The locator bracelet and the key. The key and the locator bracelet. The key to it all. The key...

She stirred in the embrace of the lichen chair, barely surfacing. No! It's slipping away. No, stop. No. She fought waking, and fled from the dream-room, running through the entrance, seeking where Tad slept. She willed herself beside him once again. His flesh against hers.

When she reached the safety of sleep again, now only dimly aware, she arose. She watched herself walking the corridors of Cephus, held back, saw

Brac, saw Walt, saw Walt seeing her, peeking around the corner. Walt saying she had something special. Walt telling her she had the key. Walt's words, not prescience, but simple truth.

Then, she saw that view of writhing tunnels, lines, connections, and glowing points. The map.

She thought of Arden, inside the monolith. As Arden filled her thoughts, one strand among those many began to glow softly. The light grew brighter. A point on that changing scene of lines and whorls vibrated and grew warm. She focused on the light.

What were Tad and Brac doing on Arden? The inside of the Monolith, the cave where she had seen the lamp appeared. Lamp after lamp after lamp lit the cave. Shelves and tables lined with them, her friends carrying them, rheos resting by them. She could almost reach out and touch them.

Then, she did. Almost without thinking about it, she cradled a lamp in her hand—the lamp. She felt it, rough and smooth, warm and cold, at once. She held up the lamp and stared at it in the harsh unchanging light of Favia, the Lichen planet.

The lamp; she held the lamp. The lamp too was the key, and the key was...

No, it remained too distant, or was it nearer? She put the lamp down, afraid it would fall, smash, crumble to dust, be gone as fully as the other evidence she had found that suggested more to the patterns of rheo movement than herd shifts. But the lamp sat here at her feet, and the heat of it and the sharp reality of it struck her.

The lamp is the light, and the key is the locator bracelet. The lamp is the light and the key...is the bracelet.

A familiar voice spoke. She heard her Uncle Arga. "Sometimes the skins of words are loose, and the meaning seems to just spill out." From the depths of her dream, she soared awake, spilling out into consciousness with a suddenness that threw her from the embrace of the lichen chair.

"That's it!" she said.

"Yes?" Ez responded.

"The key," Marissa said. "I've been looking at it all wrong. When N'Bert told Galen that the bracelet was the key to travel, I heard Galen say I needed it for travel. But what N'Bert meant is that it's one way to access and interact with the map. It's the map key. I don't need it to move. I know what the map is and how it works. I don't need a key any more. When you can read the map, why use the key?"

Ez said nothing. The silence lengthened. "I assume that was a rhetorical question."

"Right."

"Then what do you intend to do?"

"I going to visit Miskarnkk and give him a little surprise."

"I'll be right there with you."

"Yes, you will." Marissa sat down for a moment to consider what to do next. "Ez, I have to rescue Galen and Oric and find the way to save Arden."

"I would start with Galen and Oric. It's by far the easier of the two tasks, if you ask me."

"So, do you know where they are?"

"Not with absolute certainty, but I'm fairly certain of their destination—Delphia."

"Can't you check?"

"I'm not in contact with a lot of personalities behind the Delphian barriers, but I've got one or two. Back in a flash."

During the interminable five second wait, Marissa tapped her foot against the lichen covered ground. She had just enough time to reflect that the Delphians had developed a formidable weapon, if only by accident. Fortunately, their acquisitive side was much stronger than their pugilistic side.

"Sorry for the delay. Had to patch through to a friend on the other side, and it takes him a while to get around to things. One of those accountant personalities—you know the type, all numbers, no action."

"Well, where are they?"

"As I expected, they have already arrived on Delphia. Right now they are en route to the transport location. Miskarnkk assumed it must be the best place to use the locator bracelet since you arrived there."

"Great, let's go."

"I'd recommend waiting until everyone is occupied or asleep. I expect they'll erect temporary shelters and spend the night. Miskarnkk seems keen on learning about the bracelet's use. My accountant friend as much as said so."

"How long?" Marissa blew her hair out of her eyes and tugged the remainder back from her face.

"Give it five hours or so. Have a picnic, take a nap. Let's collect a few samples."

"What about the reformers? Is Arden in any danger?"

"Arden remains safe for the moment. If the situation changes, the Advocate will contact me."

"I could check on Arden." Thoughts of Tad and the warmth of his arms simmered in her memories.

"Too distracting. Besides, you haven't catalogued what's here. Surely, that would be worthwhile. Have you ever seen such novel flora?"

As she looked about her, Marissa began to notice differences in the brown landscape. Those oddities aroused her scientific curiosity. "You've got a point. Now that I can get off this rock, I could spend some time really looking at it. At least sample collecting will help pass the time. Let's go." With that, Marissa set out across the brown surface of the planet.

"Ez, recommended route of study?"

"Random sampling, with non-random grab of unique samples. With this stuff, five grams should be more than sufficient for analysis."

"Size of grid?"

"Two hundred meters on a side, collecting points every second meter or so. If you like, I'll scan in the images for the area."

"Great, go to it, Ez. We may as well see what's here."

Five hours later, exhausted from her collecting and note taking, Marissa collapsed on the lichen-covered ground. "Isn't it about time?"

"Next time get me a co-processor. I'm a personal aide, not a scientific personality. I'm beginning to suffer data overload."

Marissa chuckled. "Did you label and catalogue all of the samples?"

"I did. This is going to make one honey of a study. The cover page of the *Journal of Xenobiology.*"

"Wishful thinking, Ez. It's far more likely to get just a short net note. Let's get Galen and Oric."

"Ready if you are."

"Okay." Marissa closed her eyes and concentrated. She entered the place she carried the map, the same spot within her that contained her chronosculpture. She focused on the feel of the chronosculpture and the wand in her hand, she imagined herself shaping a trans-temporal thread. Time moved, and then, with just a sideways glance, the map filled her vision.

Gazing at it in its vast four-dimensional crystal complexity stunned Marissa. She had seen it before, but now she saw its entirety, the beautiful vast and perfect array. Paths stretched in all directions, some with shadow paths, into and out of the fourth dimension, away from the spatial.

She drew in a long breath and thought about Delphia. In front of her a strand glowed, gave off a hollow tone, and grew warm. She touched the strand with her mind, and it vibrated. The shift of transfer clutched her; she opened her eyes to see the glow of fireflies. No, not fireflies, but lanterns broke the darkness and lighted clusters of people, some eating and others just talking. Lighted shelters surrounded the depression where she, Galen, and Oric had first arrived. She had jumped to the midst of an encampment on Delphia, but the night provided some protection.

Near her, with their backs toward her, Marissa glimpsed Oric's yellow shirt and Galen's beard. Oric's eyes widened. He nudged Galen, and then signaled with the slightest of nods in her direction. Galen started to look back, but Oric put a hand on his arm and turned him ever so slightly. Over Galen's shoulder she glimpsed Miskarnkk's dark suit. Edging closer, she kept her head low. Galen and Oric held Miskarnakk's attention and effectively blocked his view. He could not see her.

When Marissa reached within an arm length of Oric, he stepped closer, still keeping one hand on Galen. She grabbed Oric's yellow shirt, visualized the map, and thought 'Arden.' When the strand glowed, it appeared larger and hotter than all the other strands, and it pulsated with some strange energy of its own. She fingered the strand, and the dislocation of the shift seized them.

Chapter Twenty-Nine - Arden Entr'acte

"There is a tide in the affairs of men,
Which taken at the flood leads on to fortune..."
-Julius Caesar, IV iii

Galen, Oric, and Marissa emerged from transit into a warm, soft light. For a moment, fear gripped Marissa that somehow the Delphians had learned how to manipulate the map. This light-filled scene couldn't be Arden's cave.

Then, as her eyes adjusted to the light, the rough stone of the cave walls took shape. Yet what was the source of this unexpected light? Neither luminas nor the single lamp that had first started her quest appeared to be the source. Whatever, she rejoiced to be home on Arden.

She stopped a moment as the implications of Arden as home penetrated her thoughts. With that concept in mind, she stared about the cave in wonder.

"Home. It is home, isn't it?"

"Most assuredly," Galen said with a sweeping bow.

Taking a broad leap, Oric bounded out of the depression and grinned at her. "I always thought you considered it that. It's a nice world."

"Yes," she responded. "Let's go see it."

She didn't add, and its inhabitants, though she suddenly longed to see Tad, her friends, the rheos, the wickabrush, the flitterwings, and all the multitude of creatures that called this world home. Now her home as well.

Stepping up from the shallow depression, Marissa glanced around to locate the source of that welcoming light. Galen shook out his beard and scrambled up after her.

Around them on the floor, on rock ledges and tables, and in niches in the wall glowed large lamps and small lamps. A bewildering variety of lamps lit the cave, from simple shallow, crude sandstone bowls or cups in which bare wicks floated in some liquid, to here and there a few finely carved, more intricate shapes, similar to the lamp she had first seen on their initial survey. She couldn't imagine where so many had come from. She hadn't seen any in Home-4 or elsewhere.

Before she could investigate, Oric streaked across the floor to the cave

298

entrance. She and Galen stared after him, open-mouthed.

"You'll never believe it." Oric's voice drifted back to them. "You should hear them."

"Hear who?" Marissa looked toward his voice, but the brightness of the cave made seeing him impossible.

"Come and see. Come." Oric's voice faded. The sound of his footsteps dwindled away as he moved along the passage that led out of the monolith.

"Galen, hurry up. Oric may need help."

Straightening his robe and his beard, Galen seemed to take far longer than he usually did. Anxious to follow Oric, Marissa restrained an impulse to grab Galen's arm and pull him along.

"Most assuredly, most assuredly. Without question, when the Truth stands revealed even light will not be merely light. No darkness will contain it. All the more reason to be presentable when one stands in Its presence."

Marissa gave him a wry smile. "It can hardly be much of a Truth. We haven't been gone that long."

"Redoubtable Exemplar, the essence infuses life. However, this adventure has been infinitely more stimulating than any experienced in all previous years elsewhere." Still he tottered, almost like a man three times his age.

Exasperated, Marissa grabbed his flowing sleeve and pulled him with her. "Sometime this millennium. For someone so anxious to see the truth, you sure take your time looking for it!"

Her words brought a broad smile to his face. "At last wisdom, the journey matters more by far than the arrival."

"Come on." Marissa half-laughed, more at herself than at Galen.

When she reached the entrance, she looked beyond the stream and the scree toward the wide stretches of golden-lavender savanna. A smudge in the distance, Oric ran toward—toward...a cloud of dust. A dust cloud on Arden? That could mean only one thing.

"Oric, stay back. You'll be killed." Marissa cupped her hands to her mouth, hoping that he would hear her over what must have been the din of hundreds of galloping rheos.

He paused, signaled with a wave of his arm for them to join him, and then continued his headlong rush toward the billowing cloud of golden dust streaking across the horizon.

Panicked, Marissa turned to Galen. "Is there anything we can do to stop him?"

"Why? It is evident whether he lives or he dies, he has found something that calls him. Would the voice of Truth sounded so sweetly to these ears."

"Wax rhapsodic some other time, Galen. We've got to stop him before he gets killed."

"He cannot be stopped. Remember, he hears, if not better, than at least more than others."

Marissa started running after Oric. "I've got to do what I can."

Galen paced beside her, easily keeping in stride with her long-legged gait. "If this one incident can further illuminate—"

"Save your breath. We've got to catch him."

With that, Galen leaped ahead of her, far outstripping her, and covering the distance between them and Oric in almost no time. She stared after him in wonder. Soon Galen trotted alongside Oric, easily keeping abreast of him. How did the little man do it and why hadn't he done it before? Only in her Favian visions had she seen such speed from him.

He spoke with Oric, slowing him down until the two of them walked at a fast clip. Galen pointed back toward Marissa and Oric slowed more. At last, they stopped and waited for her.

"Hurry, Marissa. It's Brac. Brac and the rheos. Something's happened."

Oh Devos, Marissa thought. She didn't want to lose a friend to her sentient species. She had already started to think about what the worst could possibly be. The wisdom of getting so close to that ever-expanding column of dust frightened her. Despite her confidence in the rheos to not intentionally hurt them, whatever or whomever got in the way could be trampled and crushed.

The noise of the thundering rheos grew so loud she couldn't hear anything else. She pulled on Oric's and Galen's sleeves. "We've better move out of their way."

Clapping his hand over his ears, Oric rolled his eyes. They stood somewhat above the plain on a rocky rise that led from the Monolith down to the savanna below and provided an excellent view of the approaching menace. Nervous, Marissa pulled them behind a large rock. Oric pointed toward the cloud of dust.

Peering ahead, Marissa at first saw nothing of special interest—phalanxes of rheos, undulating across the dusty plain of Arden and raising clouds of golden brown that obscured everything else. Before them, flitterwings and spangled bird analogs, dappled bird analogs, and a species she had not seen before, rose and descended, keeping just out of reach. The flowing flock of bird analogs gave the appearance of a multicolored banner waved by a victorious army on their triumphant return home.

"It's not safe." Marissa sighed, uncertain what to do. In spite of her time with the rheos, she still knew far too little to predict their behavior especially as a juggernaut herd.

Again, Oric gestured. Marissa tightened her fists. She wanted to hammer on him.

"Oric, I've seen it. It's not safe."

He turned and grabbed her head. Then, looking over his shoulder, he tried to turn her to see whatever he saw. At first she struggled, and then, from the front of the cloud, she glimpsed something odd—something unusual even for Arden. Whatever led the crowd of rheos did not undulate. It did not have six legs. In fact, it had two legs, and ran in the loping gait of—

"Tad," Marissa gasped. Again those strange visions on Favia returned and merged with the reality before her.

Oric shook his head, and she at once saw her mistake. Tad loped there, but the real leader ran alongside him. "Brac?" Oric nodded and released her.

"Brac?" she said again in wonder. "Brac?"

As she spoke, Brac raised a hand above his head and made a flicking motion to the right. The entire group of rheos flashed to the right as though they formed a single organism and followed his gesture.

Marissa's face grew warm, and tears she couldn't explain—pride, joy, admiration—no word quire described the sensation, flowed. With them came a wrenching inside, setting things that had long been out of joint now right. Tension melted from her. They had much to do to save Arden and the rheos—yet seeing the two men with the rheos showed they could succeed.

With such organization and such rapport, how could they possibly fail? With utter certainty, she sensed all would end well. Despite everything that had happened to stop them, they would save this world and all its inhabitants.

Below, the single mass of the herd diverged around the motionless figures of Tad and Brac, then left them standing alone in the settling dust. The sun struck the dust and transformed it from dull brown to a shower of pure gold from the sky. Tad stood beside Brac, panting and bowed over, as naked and sweating as his friend.

"Fantastic. Truly fantastic, Brac..." Tad spoke between gasps for air. "Marissa had it right. I felt she might be..."

Except for the fine sheen of dust-covered sweat, Brac show no effects of his exercise. "Marissa is most often right. That should not surprise you."

"It doesn't," Tad gasped.

Marissa stepped out from behind the rocks, with Galen and Oric trailing behind. "Hey, didn't you see us up here?"

"Marissa!" Tad joyfully opened his arms for her.

She eyed him with obvious distaste. "You're a little too dusty for me."

He dropped his arms, but Marissa stepped forward and squeezed him in a tight bear hug. "Devos, it's good to be home." She stepped away from him again, a mock frown on her face. "Taking up Brac's nudist tendencies?"

He flushed. "Well, I...I...it seemed..."

"He saw it did me no harm and decided to try. You should too." Brac smiled at Tad's embarrassment. "Arden is a marvelous world. It's a shame to

301

spoil it with artificial things."

* * * *

Evening closed in around the group. The purple dusk highlighted the glow of the small fire that Tad had built near the base of the monolith, not far from where they had paraded the rheos. He and Brac perched on the small, rounded rocks that had become their customary roosts. Marissa and the rest sat on grav cushions with Tesde next to Brac. Dinner almost finished, Marissa, Galen, and Oric gave a quick report on their trip to Delphia and Favia.

The others started to ask questions, but with a raised hand, Marissa forestalled them. "Right now, I need to catch up with myself and consider our next steps, but not yet. For this evening at least, I want to enjoy our return to Arden and finding you all safe again."

"But..." Teloav began.

"Tomorrow we'll talk. How about some more of that oulatte, Tesde?" Marissa held out her cup, and Tesde refilled it.

For a moment, she savored the cinnamon-clove odor of the hot liquid in the cool night air. Quiet conversation eddied around her. As she finished eating, she passed the remains of her meal and the dish to Galen who had formed a small, precise stack of them at his feet.

"We'll take care of cleanup later." She sighed and leaned back against the outcrop. "Devos, you can never remember anything like the true beauty of a place. As much as I love the thought of Arden when I'm away, when I'm here it always surprises me how beautiful it really is."

Tad stretched his long legs and added his dish in the stack. He nudged Marissa, and she scooted over to make room for him on the cushion. As he sat, it bobbed momentarily, almost spilling the two of them onto the rock.

Marissa slapped playfully at him. "Stop making waves."

Tad put his arm around her waist. "Anything you say. You know, Arden is even more beautiful away from the fire."

Eyes sparkling, Marissa grinned at him. "Is it really?"

"Un-huh." He looked to Brac who nodded and smiled from ear to ear.

"Tad and I have spent three nights beneath the stars. No fire, no torch, no artificial light of any sort. The stars are so heavy with light they look as though they would fall like overripe fruit, and you could pick them up and hold them in your hand. You ought to see it."

Marissa stared first at Brac and then at Tad. "Is that Brac?"

Tad merely nodded. Laughing, she buried her head against his chest. Arden had the power to change so many things, so many people.

"Arden's gotten to him and to me." Tad smiled at her.

"Not just Arden," Brac protested. "These wonderful people of Arden. They are magnificent. They live within this beauty." He waved an encompassing hand. "Were it possible, I would flow with them across the face of this world. I would move as they move. I would be one with them. There are no other people in all my experience of whom I would say the same. They flow in perfect waves across these fields. Across this purple and gold, they move, green and shining, reflecting the sunlight, perfectly in tune, veering with one another, not against. They stream as one. If there is disagreement among them, I have seen none of it."

Gazing at him, Marissa shook her head in wonder. Stunned, delighted, and just a bit miffed—miffed because Brac had gotten closer to the nature of these creatures in three days than she had in weeks, despite her status as an honored guest. She marveled at the rightness of it all. However, the pinpoint of jealousy was just that, a pinprick, nothing to mar the evening or cause discontent. The more she thought about it, the better it became, because every sign showed her friends now shared in her joy and dedication to Arden and the rheos.

The end of this world would be her end. However, again the feeling flowed over Marissa that they were all carried by the tide, and at last it had started to run. She had struggled at first alone, or so she had thought. The slow painful process had seemed endless. Strand by strand, she had gathered all the threads as she had fought to regain her lost friends. The lessons had been hard, but she had received so much. Now she held those strands in one hand. If she could weave them into a strong rope and tie them with one sure, swift knot, the future of Arden would be settled. Thinking this, a sudden joy surged through her and sent her once more into Tad's arms, and into a kiss she thought could last forever, if she let it.

When she finally broke away, for her, the others gathered around the fire did not exist. Marissa looked deep into his eyes. She gazed at herself reflected there "Show us this world of ours."

"Ours?" Tad gave her a look of mild surprise.

"Don't argue. Just show me." Marissa jumped up, brushed a few crumbs from her clothes and pulled Tad to his feet.

They strolled a short way from the fire beyond an outcrop that hid the fire's glow. They walked through a field of calf-high, rough stubble now barely damp with dew. Marissa touched Tad's arm, making him pause in mid-step. Open-mouthed, she stared up at the sky. Pivoting, then again and again, wonder, joy, and happiness suffused her. The splendor of the heavens dwarfed all petty concerns.

"I've been there, Tad." She pointed to the glory of the sky. "I've seen it from the inside, and it has never been so beautiful because it has never been so near." She kept turning until she stumbled, and he caught her in strong arms.

"This world and the rheos are more than a matter of principle, although that's part of my battle. It's almost aesthetic. How could anyone who knew this world suggest destroying it?"

She could not see his face, but she sensed a question hanging in the air between them. "The rheos? I've given up caring whether they match or meet any scientific definition of intelligence or whether I've interpreted things the way I wanted them to be. Now seeing this... Tad, you can't know..."

"You'd be surprised." He pulled her closer, his arms tightening around her.

"No." She twisted and brushed his lips with hers. "No, I wouldn't. I'm amazed by how much I've missed, how little I really saw. Tad, we can do this. I know we can."

"I don't want to step on your dreams Marissa, but how? The Delphians have the upper hand."

"They may have the locator bracelet, but they don't know how it works. I can defeat them, them and Uma. I'll tell you how later, after it all falls into place. And it will." Marissa kissed him again and then pulled away. She took his hand and led him further into the scrubby-field.

In the hours after they made love, Marissa thought long and hard about what she had do to save Arden. She knew the potential lay within her grasp, but the question remained how to make it work against the Delphians and Uma.

Much later they returned to their own quarters. After hours of puzzling over the problem, she fell asleep. Dreams of Uma, Miskarnkk, and the massing rheos chased one another across the dreamscape. Then in one adroit maneuver, the rheo herd split and surrounded the two leaders, forcing them to face one another.

Chapter Thirty - Best It Were Done Quickly

"If it were done when 'tis done, then 'twere well
It were done quickly…"
-*Macbeth,* I vii

Awaking early the next morning, Marissa stretched and reached for Tad only to find him gone. Trumpeting and the sound of heavy feet pounding the earth signified that the rheos congregated outside. She dressed quickly and stepped to the opening of the shelter, but the sun had not yet risen and it remained too dark to see much. From the noise and dust, Brac and Tad led the rheos in early morning drills—two boys and their toy soldiers. She smiled at the thought.

As she stood drinking in the morning air, the solution to Arden's problems appeared as sharp and clear as the 4D boundary on a hyperglass sculpture. They had to create a delicate balance—to make the Delphians and Uma act as a check on one another. At first, she considered the idea too obvious to succeed, but then realized its very simplicity made its success more likely.

Given the nature of the two opposing powers, how could she persuade them they had no alternative? At present Uma feared the Delphians too much to consider herself able to coerce them into anything.

Marissa refused to let Uma use Arden as the price of Delphian cooperation. She had to remove that option. At same time, she had to make the Confederation appear strong and a market ripe for Delphians products, but not Delphian control. The more she considered it, the harder it sounded. Maybe a cup of oulatte would clarify her thinking.

Tesde and Teloav sat on the ground with their backs to the small circle of rocks where a fire burned. Tesde held a mug of oulatte, while Teloav ate something from a camp plate. His fork scraped against the alloy. This early in the morning, the sound reminded Marissa of someone rubbing a squeaky balloon. She always hated that sound.

With a grimace, she strolled over to join them. Both of them looked tired, especially Teloav. The shadows around his eyes had grown darker, and he looked years older.

305

Behind them and above their heads, all of Arden stretched endlessly. In the predawn, the normally lavender savannas looked a dark purple ocean, and the wind, riffling the surface to send ripples in a broad wave across the plain, only added to the illusion. Marissa savored the morning freshness, despite the Delphians and Uma, and even in spite of her dislike of early risings. Her time among the lichens on Favia made her love the variety of Arden more.

"Good morning." Pushing her hair out of her eyes, she smiled at Tesde and Teloav.

Tesde, no longer restricted to a uniform of any kind, wore a yellow scarf for a pleasing contrast against the new-growth greens and blues of her tunic. "Would be, if it weren't so much of a morning still," she groaned and gave Marissa a crooked smile. "Brac and your boyfriend have stirred these animals up before sunup every day we've been here. I, for one, could use a bit more sleep." She yawned and hunched her shoulders.

Grinning, Marissa tousled Tesde's hair. "You're beginning to remind me of Sylvic." With almost a smirk, Tesde pouched her cheeks, pretending she chewed stim.

"That wasn't a recommendation. How 'bout some oulatte?"

Tesde started to scramble to her feet, but Marissa waved her back. "Just point me in the way." Tesde waved toward the galley tent not far from the fire pit. "Looks like you could use a refill."

She gave her a grateful smile and handed Marissa her cup. "Thanks."

Returning with two cups of oulatte, she looked to Teloav. He shook his head.

"Suit yourself. I don't think there's anything better for me than a cup of oulatte. It may not wake my brain up, but the taste buds sure get going." She took a rock seat near Tesde, leaving the ground to him.

Hunched over, with her elbows on her knees, Marissa cradled the cup of oulatte in both hands. The scent of it always carried something of home-and-hearth with it. Home and hearth and fresh baked pastries, with Uma and Uncle Arga. Marissa smiled at the memory. It would be nice to have all of that back, especial Uncle Arga.

She sipped the oulatte to take the edge off the morning chill and then rolled the liquid around in her mouth. The flavor, so long missed during her recent travels, burst upon her tongue once again. Sighing, Marissa wished she could focus only on the simple pleasures of Arden, thoughts of home, and a hot cup of oulatte. She wanted to forget the problems shouting for her attention and enjoy the moment.

She finished her oulatte and lowered the mug. "Tesde, Teloav..." She paused, not at all certain how they would respond to her plans. Tesde looked at her expectantly; Teloav waited, the firelight casting odd shadows on his lined

306

face.

Reluctant to begin, she took a deep breath. "We've got to do something about Uma and the Delphians."

Nodding, Teloav set his plate on the ground. "Especially the Delphians. I hate the Enunciator, but at least I know and understand her. The Confederation exiled me, but the Delphians...they would have killed me." He shook his head and stared at the glowing embers with a surprised look on his face. "That I should be grateful for exile...I'd fight the Confederation any time, but those Delphians—utterly ruthless, barbarous beyond any possibility of redemption."

His words brought a half-smile to Marissa, but she hid it behind her mug. The dim morning light on Arden helped soften things, but she didn't want to disillusion him just yet. Besides, even she had doubts about the true nature of the enigmatic Delphians—Miskarnkk and his layers, the surfaces and depths so very different. Which of them represented the true Delphia? Somehow facing only their destructive power seemed the easier path. She could deal with force, but the guile of the Delphians made them more insidious and harder to outflank.

Wrapping his arms about himself as if chilled, Teloav shuddered. "Worst of all they profess a veneer of civilization. They appear so businesslike and unctuous, like a rug salesman. It makes them more threatening, Marissa." He rose and edged closer to the two women, his eyes wide. "They are the danger."

Marisa's smile faded as she lowered the mug. "I agree."

"You've been there and talked with them." He frowned and kicked at the ashes. "What do you plan? We can deal with the Enunciator later."

At that, Tesde gave him a long, searching look. "You're really scared of the Delphians."

He stared off into the distance. "It's so peaceful here, so clean and beautiful. I know why you want to save it."

He picked up his plate and walked over to the oulatte pot. Holding up the pot, he glanced toward Marissa and Tesde who shook their heads. He grunted and returned to the fire.

Once seated, he faced Tesde, hands clenched. "You remember the vids on Satina IV? The planet destroyed." His voice shook. "People uprooted, enslaved or out and out killed..."

Tesde nodded, then looked over her shoulder at Marissa. "What's your plan?"

The mug still retained a pleasant warmth against Marissa's cupped hands. As she looked at the cup and her hands, the Usian symbol intruded, and she suppressed a burst of laughter. "I've been thinking of ways to keep both of them busy for a time. But I need your advice because..." She stopped, uncertain how to proceed.

Taking deep breath, she plunged on before she lost her courage. "It would means keeping Uma as leader of the Confederation." She stopped to gauge their reaction, especially Tesde's. "Could you accept that?"

Tesde stared down at her feet and traced a figure in the ashes for a moment before returning Marissa's gaze. "How can I say this? I hate her. She did unspeakable things to me and to those I love. She shamed me in the most horrible way possible. I can never go home again." Eyes wide, Tesde searched Marissa's face, perhaps seeking some hope for satisfaction there.

Her heart sinking, Marissa struggled to keep her face neutral and not betray her inner turmoil. She owed Tesde so much. If not for her actions, Tesde would never have been edited.

"Brac says none of what she did matters," Tesde continued. "We are as we have always been. That at least, she could not take away. From what he's told me, we owe that to you and more than either of us could ever repay."

She looked at her feet again and pushed a small stone away with the toe of her boot. The distant noise of the rheos came like fading thunder. Marissa held her mug in a crushing grip that turned her knuckles white and made her fingers ache with the strain.

Fingering her scarf, Tesde gazed up at Marissa. "If these Delphians pose an even greater threat, and, if Uma can counter them, then use her. The Delphians may provide all the punishment she needs."

Elation and relief soared through Marissa, making her nearly drop the mug. "Are you sure? I mean, after all, she had you edited..."

With a wave of her hand, Tesde dismissed that. "I told you then, I chose editing. What Uma did to me, you have undone. The crime didn't lie in the editing. Iit happened before that in taking away my family, my culture, my betrothed, and then, after the edit, my profession. Because of you, I have my betrothed back and can practice my science again. I feel safe here, although I'm not sure I know why. After what you've been through, if anyone can stop her from hurting others, you can."

Jumping to her feet, Marissa hugged Tesde. "All right, then we're agreed. If my plan can keep the two factions occupied, you'll support it!"

A tenuous smile played at Tesde's lips. "If your plan preserves Arden for us and gives us a base, then it doesn't matter what the Delphians and Uma do. Brac and I want to live our lives here."

"Okay," Marissa almost crowed, "now we've got serious work ahead." They had crossed the hurdle of Uma, but more remained. Somehow, she had to make all parties accept changing their paths. "Teloav, you're the revolutionary. If you wanted to cause maximum disruption to the Confederation, what would you do? "

"Destroy Cephus."

Startled by his response, Marissa blinked. "I said disruption, not destruction. I don't want to kill anyone."

"Too bad." He picked up several small logs and added them to the fire. Glittering sparks flew up and then dimmed rapidly in the rising sun. He loosed a weary sigh. "I guess you're right. Even we never got up the nerve to try that." Teloav rose and brushed the bark from his clothing.

He began to pace in a circle around the fire, his hands clasped behind his back. "We used demonstrations, rallies, strikes, and work stoppages on occasion, but they were focused on a particular situation or planetary system. One operative of ours suggested we sabotage the credit exchanges and make commercial transactions impossible."

"That's more like it, but I suspect the Delphians might respond quicker to that one than the Confederation."

The idea had possibilities and appealed to Marissa in a perverse way. How she would love to see the dawning horror on Miskarnkk's face as Delphian assets suddenly melted away.

"But how would you do it?"

"It's not easy. My recollection is that he suggested something about inserting false entries in their systems."

"Marissa," Tesde interrupted, "I'm not sure that would work. In my experience, those organizations have all sorts of checks and balances to prevent that kind of thing."

"Yes, yes, we know all that. Our operatives said it had to be done through their own artificial personalities. In other words, make them do it to themselves."

Marissa grinned. "I really love the sound of that. How many exchanges are we talking about?"

"The Confederation has many exchanges and a variety of subzones, but our operative said we could bring them all down by hitting about twenty or so."

"Twenty?" Marissa groaned, at least he hadn't said a thousand. "But that doesn't include the Delphians at all. I don't think it will work, at least not in time. Sooner or later, Uma's either going to take us off Arden by force, or kill us along with the rest of Arden's inhabitants."

The sun had now cleared the horizon and flooded the landscape with golden light. A drumming noise filled the air and grew louder with every second. A puff on the horizon expanded and became a cloud of dust. Brac and Tad must be returning with the rheos.

Tesde jumped to her feet. "Guess I'd better make a fresh pot of oulatte and organize some food. All this exercise makes Brac ravenous." She hurried toward the galley.

The noise of the returning herd made conversation impossible. Marissa shrugged and signaled to Teloav. "Later," she mouthed. He nodded.

While Brac and Tad ate breakfast, Marissa stared at the fire and thought. Tesde with the help of Galen and Oric worked in the galley to clean up the remains of breakfast while Tad finished eating his by the fire. Looking out over the golden lavender grain-fields, Marissa leaned back in the sandstone seat she had made for herself. Her resolution hardened. No matter how difficult the way, she would preserve all this.

"Tad, I have a solution. I know how we can keep Arden."

"You do?" He placed his empty plate on the ground. "How?"

The breeze picked up and blew his golden hair into his eyes. He reminded her of Arden's motif; everything made of gold, including the planet itself.

She smiled at his avid curiosity. "I'm not out for revenge anymore. When I stopped thinking that way, the solution seemed so obvious. Not revenge, parity." She beamed at the thought. "Maybe not even that if we can keep Arden, and I'm sure we can."

"Tell me how." Tad looked past the rocky rim and across the short grass that flowed into the longer waist-high grass.

She followed his gaze and saw Brac again leading the rheos. "I spoke with Brac before dinner last night when everyone else was getting ready. Do you know what he said?"

"No, what?" Tad looked at her, eyebrows raised.

"Well, I was explaining everything that had happened, and what I had learned. When I'd finished, Brac said to me, 'You have something everyone wants.' I knew what he meant, of course, Miskarnkk said as much, but I didn't see how it could be very useful. It's not mine to give away. I couldn't if I wanted to, and I'm not sure I do. I said so to Brac. Then, he responded in typical Brac fashion, 'No one suggested that,' he said. 'But you have it. You are free to wield it with a strong arm.'" Tad smiled at her, obviously agreeing with Brac's assessment.

"When he said that, something clicked in my head. That planted the seed, but I had to let it grow a bit. I can reach Uma and Miskarnkk, and I can make them sit down and talk to one another whether they want to or not.

"How?"

"I simply take them. Maybe I transport them right here!" Delighted at the thought of snatching them against their combined wills, Marissa began to chuckle.

Tad grabbed her upper arms, and pulled her up into a little dance. "You think so?"

Glad he shared her excitement, she whirled with him in a joyous jig until breathless. She stopped, hand to her chest. After a moment, her heartbeat and breathing returned to normal.

"Well, I haven't tried, but I think I can. Actually that's only the second

310

half of what I need. I have to give them a convincing reason to talk together. I think it might be nice for you and Brac to prepare a little introduction to the local wildlife, if you know what I mean." She smiled at him and took his hand into her own. "Could you ask Brac?"

"Sure I could, but so could you."

She nodded, but for the moment stared down at the ground watching small insects scurry off with crumbs from Tad's plate. "Yes, but I think it would be more persuasive coming from his lieutenant."

Tad snorted. "If you think that, you don't know how much Brac admires you."

"Maybe." Marissa raised her eyes to his face. "But you know, it isn't all that important right now. What matters is what you think of me, what I think of me, and what I can do to set Uma and Miskarnkk straight."

She leaned into Tad. "You know, it's great to be admired, and it's nice to be needed, but best of all is to be wanted, and to want rather than to need.

"That's the long way of saying as much as I appreciate Brac's respect, it's more important for me to build a team. I want everyone to be part of this. I understand Brac's view better now. It's quite a remarkable thing to will one thing and to will it completely. I will—no, together we will this world to be ours to keep, to nurture, to protect, and to explore."

"Yes." Tad hugged her. "Yes, exactly. Ours. Ours?" He studied her face. "You said that last night."

"Ours." Marissa took his hand and clasped it in hers. "You know, I don't need you any more—" Tad looked as though she had struck him.

At his crestfallen look, she laughed. "Oh, no, no, no, you don't understand. I don't need you to support my ego and my image of myself as scientist or a woman, but I want you. In fact, when I stopped needing you, I found I wanted you even more. You know what?" She smiled to reassure him.

"Wanting you is a lot better than needing. I want to have you around for a very long time. In fact, I want you to be with me here always, if you want that too." She searched his face, relieved to see the joy reflected there.

Tad smiled and raised her hand to his lips. "It's all I've ever wanted."

"Good, another crisis averted." She grinned into his loving face. "If you'd like, we can even make it formal. In fact, it would be kind of nice on our own world. What do you think?"

Hugging her to him, Tad rested his head against her hair. "Whatever you want, Marissa. On our own world, we make the rules."

"Yes, but it's nice to have some to carry over. Anyway, you almost made me forget that we haven't saved Arden yet."

She raised her face to him and savored for a moment the feel of his mouth on hers, the strength and warmth of his arms, and most of all that encompassing sense of belonging. After a moment, she pulled back and took his hand, then led him across the rocky interval that separated them from Tesde, Oric, Galen, and Teloav.

"Okay all, Tad's agreed."

Galen bowed and studied Tad with interest. "Agreement is always welcome. To what has this most noble friend of the revered mentor consented?"

"To providing the demonstration for Uma and Miskarnkk," Marissa said as she sat on a grav cushion. "Now, what we need is some persuasion—some real reason for them to speak at all."

"Persuasion is fine, but could we make it a little on the quiet side. There's been altogether too much noise of late for this city boy." Oric held up the plugs he had taken to wearing in the morning.

"Yes, I see what you mean. We'll try to consider your ears, Oric." Marissa grinned at him.

"What form would this persuasion take?" Galen asked, pulling at his beard. Pictures chased one another across the surface. First a figure in austere robes much like Uma held sway, and then a Delphian in body armor pushed her aside. "Surely the pursuit of the truth would itself be more than enough reward to engage in conversation?"

Shaking her head, Marissa gave him a pitying look. "How did you ever make an ambassador, Galen? I think your beard shows things more as they are than your words."

"This beard reflects the world despite any efforts to the contrary. Somehow, all efforts to subdue that particular version of truth are defeated, a most grievous failing. All ambassadors must train and serve long apprenticeships. A world of training and a sixth degree in truth are the least of these." Galen danced and whirled around until Marissa found herself laughing.

"Oh, sit down."

"With pleasure, revered one." Galen folded himself onto a grav cushion while Oric squatted beside him. They both gazed up at her with expectation.

Crossing her fingers mentally, Marissa cleared her throat. The words didn't want to come out. "I don't know why I'm suddenly choked up. But it seems so much depends…"

She stopped a moment and felt around in her suit for a tissue. Tad handed her one from a package he kept in one of the many pockets in his shorts and eased on to the cushion next to her. Swiping her nose with the issue, she focused on Galen and Oric.

"I spoke with Teloav and Tesde this morning." At the memory of Tesde's response, tears began to flow. She signaled to Tesde to report.

Tesde stood up and paced beside the fire. "Teloav has contacts—living and constructs in the resistance. If we contacted some of them, they could do minor, seemingly unrelated things like stage strikes or rallies on various planets—basically creating a nuisance."

"Sounds good, but is that all?" Tad stared at Marissa as if expecting more.

She tossed the tissue into the ashes of the fire. "That's as far as we've gotten. Teloav said something about disrupting the credit records, but it sounds complicated—maybe too complicated, and it would require co-opting the credit exchanges' artificial personalities."

Tad raised his eyebrows at the 'artificial personalities.' "In that case, maybe we should ask Ez and the Advocate."

Marissa slapped her forehead. "Of course, why didn't I think of that?"

Grinning from ear to ear, Tad grabbed her hand. "Because you're human. Besides, I want you to remember, we're all part of this and want to help."

"Ez, you there?"

"Naturally, where else would I be? The Advocate is linked with me too. We heard your discussion and it was all either of us could do to restrain ourselves."

"Why?"

<BECAUSE THE ANSWER IS MUCH LESS COMPLEX. THE EXCHANGES OF BOTH THE CONFEDERATION AND DELPHIA NOT ONLY RELY ON ARTIFICIAL PERSONALITIES, THEY BOTH MUST USE EXTENSIVE COMMUNICATION SYSTEMS.>

Tad groaned. "Right, I should have thought of that."

"Our operative did," Teloav interjected. "He said we could always disrupt communications, but it would also mean losing touch with our organization. We haven't been willing to risk it."

Nodding, Marissa narrowed her eyes in concentration. "So, depending on what we decide, we would have to ensure we had the plan in place and your people set before we cut any links."

"Yes, but it could be dangerous." Teloav frowned, adding to the heavy lines that etched his face. "Someone would have to go the right places and disconnect or disrupt the key transfer points. We can mobilize a force to deal with some, but we were never able to infiltrate all the important ones. The system has built-in protective redundancy."

"Devos," Marissa groaned. "Why does every good idea have to be so complicated?"

"Actually, it's not," Ez chimed. "We have identified the key places and know exactly what has to be done. It will involve some jumping about, but you know how to do that."

"I do, don't I?"

"Marissa could jump to central communications points," Ez continued, "both Delphian and Usian, and cause real havoc—"

"So," Teloav interrupted, "for what do we wait?"

Marissa patted his arm. "We are so few right now that we can afford to be diplomatic. I don't want a voice expressing an imaginary Will—but we're all involved here and everyone should have a say in what happens."

"Then let's vote." Tad grinned at Marissa.

She laughed, remembering only too well the votes taken by the team on Arden, usually three for and two against. Rising from the grav cushion she shared with Tad, she pulled him with her. The cushion wobbled, and, with a toe, she spun it away.

"You haven't even heard the plan."

"I don't need to, I trust you, remember?" Tad pushed the cushion back to the circle.

"I want you all to hear it anyway. Besides, I'm not sure about this. Ez, Advocate, fire away."

At this junction, Brac again joined the group. Tesde updated him; then, Ez and the Advocate alternated in describing each communication point and what they had to do. By the time they finished, Marissa's head whirled with numbers, locations, and gadget names.

"You know, Ez," she said, "I'm not that good with machinery. What if I mess up?"

"Machinery is my forte, remember?" Tad grasped her fingers and held them tightly. "I'm coming with you. That way, there'll be two of us to share the work."

"Tad, I can't risk you. You're too important. Besides, you and Brac need to marshal the rheos."

"Brac is more than capable of doing that." Brac grinned at Marissa and nodded.

In the end, they all agreed, and settled on that evening after dinner as the perfect time to start.

Evening rushed over Arden's horizon, speckling the sky with purple and orange and red, dappling the golden-lavender ground, covering, and shadowing it. Not far away the last of the rheos loped away from the Monolith, the center to which they always returned.

Marissa moved away from the fire to watch. The stars emerged, one by one. She sat on a boulder, a dark shadow, much like the many other boulders that speckled this part of the landscape. Tad stood beside her, his hand on her shoulder.

Turning, Marissa looked up at him. "Now is as good a time as any, I suppose."

"Can't beat it," Tad agreed.-

The two of them walked to the tent where they kept the Advocate. The

Advocate glowed with that disconcertingly accurate and perfect image of Tad. <I AM AT YOUR COMMAND.>

Marissa laughed and pushed her hair back out of her eyes. "So you two have organized this thing?"

"Yes," Ez responded

<WITHOUT QUESTION.>

"Okay, tell me when you've got Teloav's folks on-line, and I'll get moving."

"Connecting," Ez intoned.

<CONNECTING.>

Marissa faced Tad, his hand gripped in hers. "Are you ready?"

"Ready." His lips brushed her forehead, light as a flitterwing.

She looked off into the evening light of Arden and smiled. "There can be no problem from here on out." Then she looked up at the stars and thought about Brac's vision of overripe fruit.

<CONNECTED. SERVOS AND PERSONALITIES ON THREE KEY CONNECTORS REPORTING NEED FOR IMMEDIATE ATTENTION. ALL TRANSPORTATION AND LUGGAGE HANDLING COMPLETELY STOPPED. STOPPAGE CONTINUES FOR FIVE MINUTES. ESTIMATED TIME FOR RESTORING TRAVEL SCHEDULES AND TERMINAL CAPACITIES—THREE POINT ONE FIVE DAYS.>

"Connected," Ez chimed in, "Delphian profit calculators showing unexpected plunge in main commodities and entertainment markets. We've got a panic going. Satellite hops should be easy now."

Marissa pulled Tad to her and hugged him as though they had all the time in the world and mentally braced herself. "Here goes everything." With that she turned her attention to the little visor screen. "Ez, image of COM 1 Usian."

On the visor a tiny image of a very elaborate complex appeared, and the next instant Marissa pulled herself and Tad through the map to the satellite. Ez had sounded an alarm elsewhere that cleared the passage for their arrival. Marissa took two steps.

"The other way." Ez hissed.

Footprints appeared and Marissa followed them to a large circuit board. "Flip any switch," Ez said subvocally.

"Any?"

"They all end up doing the same thing. It will lead to an overload while they're working on the other problem. This satellite and the entire nexus will be down. Bye Tsionphone."

Marissa flipped a blue switch. An alarm sounded.

"Next," she said.

Another image appeared on the visor. She focused on it and, with Tad's

315

hand in hers, jumped. A stiflingly hot, small closet filled with a noisy buzzing barely contained the two of them. "Sounds like this was about to break anyway."

"Not the way you're going to do it," Ez said. "With COM1 out, this power station will be down, down, down. That will shut down transport and Nexus Two communications. I'd say five hundred to a thousand world COM blackout. Goodbye, Mr. Dimension!"

"Good riddance," Marissa responded. "What do we need to do?"

"This one's a little tougher. Look for a red bar. Throw it in the opposite direction and pull out the unit. Take it with you to the next station. There are no replacements, the order never came through and no one paid any attention. The units are as reliable as black holes."

Gazing at the panel before them, Marissa shuddered. "Any danger?"

"Only if you breach containment. You aren't carrying any anti-neutrino implements, are you?"

"Not unless someone slipped one on me while I wasn't looking."

"Good. Then no danger."

Marissa worked along one wall panel looking for the bar Ez described while Tad worked along the other. Her stomach contracted to a tight bundle, squirming and struggling to retain dinner right now. At last, after several long moments she saw it, just out of reach above her head near a vent. Looking around she saw nothing to stand on.

"Ez," she said, panicked, "it's out of reach."

"Use the suit gravs."

"I'll get it, Marissa." Tad thumbed his boot graves on, rose a couple of inches, and removed the unit. "Okay, next?"

Another oddly familiar complex appeared in front of Marissa. "We did this one."

"No, it's the equivalent of COM1 for Delphia. Slightly harder to shut down, but still easy. Guess no one was really thinking much about sabotage."

Sighing, Marissa concentrated on the image and the map. Strands spiraled off in all directions. She sought for a spot brighter than the rest, but found none. "Ez, something's wrong. I can't find it."

"Concentrate on the image. Here, I'll amplify it."

The image in the visor grew shaper, and Marissa began to detect subtle differences from COM1. The same switches and displays appeared, but the order varied. "It's clearer." Again she searched the map. Still nothing. "Ez, it's not there."

"Of course it is. You have to find the right place. I'm feeding the coordinates along the bottom of your images. Try those."

"Relax, Marissa." Tad whispered in her ear. "Let it come naturally."

True to Ez's word, coordinates spurled across the bottom of the screen. Marissa took a deep breath and shut her eyes. The image of the switches and displays stayed and the coordinates leaped out at her. A spot on the mapped at once grew brighter. She focused on it and jumped.

Tad pulled on her hand. "Ask Ez which switches to throw."

Marissa opened her eyes to another bewildering array. Communications gear never looked simple. It still surprised her that just setting one switch could shut down so many circuits. "Ez?"

"The ones directly in front you. The green one next to the purple one."

Marissa reached out to toggle the green switch.

"Hey, don't touch that."

She whirled around to see a Delphian guard with a weapon in his hand glaring at them.

"Back away. NOW."

Marissa looked at Tad. He made a barely perceptible nod. She pulled back her hand and began to edge forward.

"Stop right there." The guard kept the weapon trained on them and fingered his belt with his left hand. "Security, intruder alert. On the double." He grinned as he motioned with his weapon. "Okay, now we'll find out how you got here and what you want."

Tad's right hand rested on Marissa's shoulder, but she sensed a motion. The guard's eyes grew wide.

"I said stop that." He raised the weapon and fired.

Tad's hand released her shoulder as he slumped to the floor.

"Tad!" Marissa dropped to her knees and felt for his pulse. The guard moved toward them.

Chapter Thirty-One - Unfinished Tasks

"Hang our banners on the outward walls;
The cry is still, "They come;
Our castle's strength will laugh a siege to scorn."
-*Macbeth*, V v

"I 'gin to be aweary of the sun,
And wish the estate o' the world were now undone,"
-*Macbeth*, V v

Trembling with a mixture of anger, fear, and uncertainty, Marissa stared at the Delphian guard in a daze. She glanced to the floor, to the boot, to the leg twisted back, as the man before her leveled whatever weapon he held.

"Stay right there," he said and maneuvered toward her, watching her with nervous eyes.

Marissa couldn't make out what weapon he held. Nothing much made sense except that boot and the leg and the body. Tad. He had killed Tad.

"Marissa," a voice spoke in her ear, a voice she finally recognized as Ez, "Arden."

Marissa blinked. Arden? The guard raised his weapon again, stepping closer.

"Marissa," Ez hissed. "Arden, now!"

Yes, Arden. Bending down and grasping the leg that jutted between her own, Marissa closed her eyes and pictured Arden's cave. The guard fired his weapon.

The scene dissolved, and Marissa flowed into and through the map. Arden. Tad. Arden. They were one and the same. Destroyed. Her concentration began to slip. The bright glow that signified Arden began to recede.

"Marissa, focus," a voice shouted.

"Focus? Why? On what? Does anything really matter now?"

"Stop it. Self-pity gets you nowhere. Too many Personalities have committed for you to quit and lose it for us all now. Get Tad to Arden and stop whining. There's help there. No one and nothing can help him in this limbo."

Ez's voice, brilliant and loud in her ear, acted like a slap in the face. Marissa woke up and saw the dizzying, terrifying map. It made her clutch Tad with a fierce grip. She closed her eyes and sought again.

Bright Arden. Golden Arden. Yes, take Tad to Arden.

The bright glow shimmered. Marissa pulled herself together, clutching at the leather of Tad's boot as though it were the last thread that tied her to the world she wanted to save. Focus on Arden. Yes, Arden.

A wrenching twist jolted her. Then light surrounded them, the soft light of Arden's cave. She looked up to see Brac standing at the edge of the depression.

"The Advocate sent me. He said you would be in the cave. What happened?" The dancing light made his face hard to read, but his tone spoke of concern and perhaps fear. "What happened? Marissa?"

She looked about, still dazed. Then she wailed, a sound torn out of her as nothing—not her mother's death, not her father's disappearance, or even Uncle Arga's accident—ever had.

"Tad." She stared down at his motionless body with an intensity, that were it power itself, would have brought him leaping back to life.

Brac stepped to her and put his arm around her. "The Advocate said something about a guard. Did he shoot Tad?"

"Tad." That name ripped from within her. Tears washed down her face as she knelt over him, raising his face to her own. "Tad."

The words barely stirred the air. She pushed back his hair and rocked back and forth holding him. A movement, not her own—breathing, barely traceable, hardly tangible, just on the edge of feeling. She clutched at Tad.

"Brac, he's alive. Maybe he's alive now. He's breathing. I think he's breathing. I felt him breathe. I know it." Still, she doubted her words as she spoke. "I felt him breathe." But she didn't feel it now. No trace.

"Let him be, Marissa. I will take him. If there's breath, there's life, and we need to check him out." Brac gently took Tad from her and started to carry him away, looking back at her. "Join us."

"Yes," she said shaking, "that guard, he killed him." Now the tears came, blinding her to everything except that one awful moment.

"I think not. Let's get out into the open and see." Brac continued toward the opening that led out from under the monolith.

Marissa jerked her head up. Not dead? Perhaps it was true; perhaps she had felt him breathe. Perhaps everything is as it was. She grasped at the glimmer of hope Brac offered and clutched it to her as she stumbled after him. He strode forward, bending to avoid the low ceiling of the tunnel and careful to keep Tad's head from brushing against the rock walls.

Outside, the setting sun cast a purple film across the sky, and the evening stars had started to speckle its surface. The cool evening breeze chilled Marissa and made her aware of the tears that covered her face. She swiped at them with the sleeve of her field suit. So little had changed since they left. Here the sun had not finished its daily ritual. Ahead the others waited, Tesde, Oric, Galen, and Teloav.

Once in camp, Brac laid Tad on a grav lounge, converted for this occasion into a gurney, while he and Teloav examined the inert form. Marissa waited, hardly daring to breathe. To her, they took forever to run routine scans.

At last, Brac looked up. "He'll be unconscious for a while, and probably sore when he wakes, but he is not seriously injured. It appears the Delphian weapons are a form of stunner and nonlethal."

"Thank Devos!" Marissa collapsed on the ground, knees weak. "You're sure?"

"As sure as anyone can be. He's not dead, just in a form of stasis. It should wear off soon."

"Here." Tesde thrust a cup of oulatte at Marissa. "You need this."

"Yeah, I do." Marissa grasped the cup and sipped the hot liquid eagerly. "We didn't finish. We had just started on the main Delphian complex when that guard appeared. I should have zapped us out immediately. Instead, like a light-struck lapinate I stayed there and let him shoot Tad."

"That's not what Ez told the Advocate," Tesde said. "According to her, the guard shot Tad when he tried to throw the switch."

"Yeah, I guess he did. I couldn't see what happened. We got a little over confident. Things had gone so well. Now I've messed up the plan big time."

Marissa stared down at the oulatte, unwilling and unable to face her failure and her friends. She had been so sure, so confident, they could save Arden. Now, she had thrown it all away.

"All reports indicate disruptions have occurred as proposed. Perhaps a few have yet to happen, but action can ameliorate that. Truth shall triumph." Galen whirled about, raising a small cloud of dust.

"Stop that," Marissa snapped.

"As commanded, motion shall cease." Face solemn, he stopped before her and bowed.

"Galen's right, you know," Oric said. "You can finish the job, and sooner is better than later."

"The Delphians will be on high alert," she objected. "I can get there all right, but they'll shoot me too. Besides, if I know Miskarnkk, he'll booby trap the place." She couldn't take her eyes off of Tad, as much as she tried. "Besides, I should be here when Tad wakes up."

"Tad went along to help you. He was even willing to sacrifice himself to do it." Tesde's dark eyes filled with sympathy. "You can't stop now and lose Arden. We're all committed." She didn't say "And we've all made sacrifices."

320

Her expression did.

Guilt bore down on Marissa. She had almost killed Tad, but because the Delphians regarded money as their main goal and reuse almost as highly, killing anyone didn't fit with their philosophy. They never destroyed anything they might use to enhance their position.

"Indeed, speed is of the essence," Galen added, riding on the coattails of Tesde's comments. "As to Miskarnkk, such a prudent course of action must be his recourse. However, perhaps an alternate course exists." He smoothed the tangles from his beard

"What are you talking about? What would Miskarnkk do? Alternate action. What alternate?"

"Cannot the constructs instruct in such cases?" For once, Galen did not shapeshift his clothes or beard, or whirl around. Instead he radiated a deep calm, a silent call to quiet.

"The constructs? Oh, you mean Ez and the Advocate. I suppose so." Marissa had turned to face him and now glanced back over her shoulder toward Tad. Pale and still, she worried that Brac might somehow have misread the analyzer.

"Right," Ez acknowledged. "We've been working on Plan B so to speak. It's a bit trickier, but it should work."

"Plan B?" Marissa frowned; she couldn't recall a Plan A.

"Yes," Ez continued. "N'Bert contacted Teloav with the details."

"N'Bert? What's he got to do with anything?" The lines of her frown threatened almost to match Teloav's own.

He stepped forward. "N'Bert has long been an active member of the resistance. His technical knowledge has made possible many small steps forward—small and unnoticeable, but they were to blossom, eventually—why not now. He suspected events might require an alternate course of action."

"Oh, he did, did he?" For a moment Marissa wanted to curse, but thought better of it. After all, N'Bert had sent the locator bracelet. She still wondered what role he had really played in everything. "Well, get on with it then. What does he suggest?"

"Return to the Delphian communication nexus," Ez said, "but to a different place. I have the image for you."

Sure enough, an image formed on the visor. This one showed what appeared to be a crawl space filled with cables. "How am I supposed to work in there? Besides, Tad's the one who knows machinery, not me."

"You might try lying down," Ez responded.

"Look, Tad's hurt. I really can't leave him. I have to be here when he wakes."

"Marissa, we're here." Tesde took her hand and held it in both of her own.

321

"We'll take care of Tad. You know what a good nurse Brac can be. Besides, you said we're a team. Didn't you mean it?" She held Marissa's eyes, challenging her to take back her words.

"Of course, I meant it, but Tad..." Her eyes automatically sought his silent, motionless form.

"There's nothing you or anyone can do, but wait for stasis to wear off. Wouldn't it be better to be doing something rather than sitting here chewing you fingernails?"

Marissa glanced down at her ragged nails and promptly hid her hands in her sleeve. "Brac, you're sure he won't wake for several hours?" She searched his face, looking for any sign of hesitation or doubt.

He looked at her, his eyes filled with sympathy, but also with that uncompromising honesty she had come to know. "I'm sure. Besides, if he wakes sooner, Ez is in contact with the Advocate and can relay any change in Tad's condition.

"This man is my friend. I will care for him as you would. Tesde spoke truly. The best thing you could do for him is to complete the task before you and ensure Arden's future. He has sacrificed as much as anyone to preserve this wonderful place."

Mulling over Brac's words and all the things said by her friends, she looked at them clustered around her. Tad still lay without moving, but seeing these people who had suffered so much and given so much made her realize how little she had really suffered. The Anomaly couldn't begin to compare with the mines where Teloav had labored, the Bioregen facility on Cephus that almost killed Tad, or being edited as Tesde had been. Marissa shuddered at that thought.

She owed them all so much. No matter what she did, she could never fully repay these friends.

Resigned, she stretched out on the sandy soil and folded her arms over her chest. "I'm ready. Oh, don't forget those coordinates. I almost didn't find it last time."

Across the bottom of the image came a string of coordinates. With a sigh, Marissa closed her eyes storing the image with the coordinates in one place and the complexity of the map in another. With infinite care, she brought the two images together and found an answering glow. Attention focused, she entered the map.

A humming sound told her she had arrived. Sure enough in a space a little over half a meter high and perhaps 3/4 of a meter wide a bewildering array of cables snaked past her—red, green, yellow, magenta, black, on through the spectrum. They varied in thickness from the diameter of a tight yarn to five centimeters or more. Ambient light banished darkness, but also cast confusing shadows.

"Okay, Ez, now what?" She formed the words, but barely breathed them out. She squirmed about and unfolded her arms. The cramped space made movement difficult.

"N'Bert says to find the lavender wire."

Marissa searched among the array. "There's a purple one here."

A pause that seemed to lengthen followed. "He said lavender, not purple."

She poked some more to separate the cables. "Are you sure? I don't see one."

"Try under the lime green one."

"Lime green?" Marissa peered closer. Despite the even light, the cable array made it hard to see those beneath the others. "Yeah, I see that one." It lay almost at the back of the space behind a thick black cable. Gingerly she pried behind the thicker cable. Sure enough close to the wall nestled a lavender cable about the size of a thin twig.

"Now what?"

Another pause, this time longer. "Just a minute, I've got a disruption here."

"Ez, hurry up."

Staccato footsteps sounded on the deckplate overhead, then stopped directly above her. Marissa held her breath. Then they resumed and gradually faded away.

"Marissa," N'Bert's voice spoke in her ear.

"N'Bert?"

"Yes, now listen carefully and don't make any mistakes. If you don't do precisely as I say when I tell you to do it, you may not see Arden or, indeed, any place else again. This requires patient precision, not one of your specialties."

"Now just a minute…"

"Speak only subvocally or you'll be heard. Just listen. First, I'll describe what you have to do and then I'll tell you when to do it. Timing is critical. Once you tamper with that wire, security overrides will shut down this system and flood the crawl spaces with xanthogen. You must be gone before they release the gas. Do you understand?"

Xanthogen. As if she didn't have enough problems. "Got it. Do the job and get out superfast."

"Right. The object is to incapacitate the station for a short period of time and to make it difficult to locate the fault. Do you have heavy-duty insulated wire cutters?"

"Wire cutters? I've got my multitool."

"Well, I guess that will have to do. Do you have any gloves?"

Marissa wriggled a hand into her right pocket and retrieved the multitool and then shifted to access her field gloves from the left pocket. "I've got my field gloves."

"Umm, they're not heavy enough. You'll have wear both on the same hand and wrap it with a rag, a scarf, or any other fabric you've got."

"Why didn't you tell Ez this before I got here?"

"Because I've only just gotten my hands on the specs. Just do the best you can. Time is short. The Delphians are suspicious and may send out sniffers at any time. If one detects you, they'll immediately flood the compartment."

Pulling on the right glove took no time at all. She had to turn the left glove inside out first and then struggled to work it over the right one. Fishing first in the right pocket and then the left, she finally located a handkerchief Tad had once lent her. She wrapped it around her right hand. "Okay, gloves in place. I have the multitool. Now what?"

"I want you to cut the cable, but not just yet. When I say cut, you cut. Position the cutting tool on the wire and wait for my okay. As soon as the cutters bite into the wire, transfer out of there. Don't wait to see what happens. Just jump immediately. That's important. Do you understand?"

Marissa gritted her teeth. N'Bert sounded as if he thought she hadn't any sense at all. She knew about toxic gases. "Okay, got the message. I'm positioning the cutter now."

"Good. Now wait. We have to reach the right point in the harmonics for this to function as planned. Just a bit more."

Silence in her ear. Perspiration began to bead her forehead. This place seemed to be getting warmer for some reason. She found it a lot harder to breathe. Where was N'Bert? What was he waiting for? "N'Bert?"

No answer.

"N'Bert?"

Still nothing.

"Ez?"

"I'm here. We've got a signal disruption. I'm trying another link."

"Great. I sabotage communications and now I can't get instructions. Maybe I should just cut the blasted thing and get out of here."

"Marissa, you there?" N'Bert's voice sounded weak and far away.

"I'm here. Ready when you are." She held the cutters on the wire.

Silence again.

"Ez, come on. I can't stay here much longer."

Chapter Thirty-Two - Loose Ends

"To do the thing that ends all other deeds"

-Antony and Cleopatra, V ii

On the edge of panic, Marissa listened, afraid to hear the hiss of gas flooding the compartment. Her hand cramped. Where in Devos was N'Bert? She flexed her fingers and debated how bad it might be if she cut the wire before N'Bert said.

"NOW!"

Marissa clamped down on the wire hard and focused on Arden. She dove into the map tunnels and pulled herself along the strands toward home. Down, through, twisting, twining. The glowing strands looked too much like the communications cables. Focus, Marissa, focus. Tad and Arden need you. You need them.

Home. Arden is home. Arden is light.

Light surrounded her. She looked at the light, but the cave should be dark.

Her right hand hurt. Red-hot coals seared the flesh. She looked down. The ashes of the handkerchief fell away to reveal smoking gloves. She yanked off first the smoldering inside-out left glove, then the right. The flesh beneath looked red and puffy.

Before she could move, Brac rushed forward with a tube of something. "Here, let me put this on." He spread the hand with a cooling salve.

At once the pain eased. "Tad?"

"He's beginning to wake up. So far he looks just fine. Should I carry you?"

"No, I'm fine except for the hand and it's better now. I just want to see Tad."

Brac led the way out of the cave. Outside, the others minus Oric waited. Tesde rushed forward and hugged her while the rest all wore big grins.

Tesde pulled back a moment to study her face. "I was so worried. When we lost the connection, I didn't know what to think." She looked at Marissa with teary eyes. "I'm so glad you're back."

"So am I. Brac said Tad's fine. I want to see him."

325

Arm and arm they walked back to camp, trailed by the others. The glorious sunset bathed everything in a deepening orange glow.

In camp, Oric stood watch by Tad's side. "He's breathing regularly now. He should wake at any time."

Marissa peered down at Tad still stretched out on the grav lounge, relieved to see his color normal. He looked asleep, not dead as she had thought after the shooting. She would never have forgiven herself if... Just the thought brought tears to her eyes again. She sighed and held his left hand in hers.

"Marissa," Ez called. "We haven't quite finished."

"What? Didn't cutting that wire work?"

"That worked just fine. We have a few more to do. The others are easy. A tiny step for you."

"You said that before, remember?" She turned Tad's hand in her own.

"Yeah, but how was I to know..."

"I trust you to know everything. Well, almost everything."

"Yeah, well that Delphian contact sort of pulled out at the last possible sec. Anyway, we've got the rest sewed up so it won't take much. Just a few jumps, toggle a switch or two, and we're done."

"You'd better be right this time, Ez, or I may look for a new model."

"After all I've done for you. Besides, those newer models aren't so hot. Lots of bugs in the early releases."

"Okay, Ez." She turned back to Tad. "Couldn't it wait? Just a little while."

"They're already on to patching up the initial disruptions. You don't have all that much time."

Sighing deeply, Marissa let Tad's hand drop. She had to finish the job whether she wanted to or not. "Let's get on with it. Where to first?"

* * * *

By the time she returned to Arden, about nine jumps later, communications had been disrupted throughout a large part of the Delphian and Usian worlds though they had carefully left key lines in place both for Cephus and Delphia. Travel had been completely disrupted throughout much of known space. Half of Cephus was without nonessential power. Satina IV had its main terminator tracker stopped, causing any amount of spoiling of expensive wine and disruption of opulent state and business dinners. Reports from Delphia related similar panics and disruptions. In all, a splendid piece of work for an evening. Best of all, Marissa made certain that the security scanners and trackers in all places had a detailed signature for who was responsible. Her smiling face gazed out from each of the impotent screens on her many stops.

Looking outside the tent she shared with Tad, Marissa stared intently into the gathering dark and watched star after star pierce the blackness of Arden's night. The warmth of his hand comforted her. He had reached the 'sitting up and taking nourishment' stage as he termed it somewhat raffishly, a smile lighting an already bright face. Reassured he had recovered with no lasting hurt, she allowed herself to sleep and gather strength.

First the stress of Tad's injury and then the jumps had sapped her. Wrung out, she had barely managed to finish disrupting Delphian communications. Only the thoughts of her friends, the rheos, but most of all of Tad's sacrifice had pulled her through

Later, standing beside him beyond the camp in the cool light of a hundred twinkling stars, Marissa at last had recovered enough to move ahead with securing Arden's future. Somehow evening on Arden offered the best time to consider any plan. Cradling Tad's hand in her own, she let her thoughts turn to the unfinished plan. She still had to somehow bring Uma and Miskarnkk together and force them to agreement.

In thought, she reached out trying to touch Uma, wondering for a moment if, in the confusion of interrupted communications, transportation, and e-beam transmissions, Uma had any time to think about her. Surely Uma's spies would report that Marissa's face had been recorded on all those Delphian monitors. Yet how to know, if she didn't reach out?

Seeking Uma, Marissa found too many other images surrounding her. The interference kept breaking and scattering Marissa's thoughts. So many memories taunted her that she couldn't focus. They unreeled before her. Uma sat in judgment, then the fall through the Anomaly, and the return to Arden. Marissa struggled to wrench her thoughts back to Uma, but they veered off again to Tesde and Teloav, and then to her last conversation with Uma.

Again Marissa sought to center her thoughts on Uma here and now, but this time memories of Uncle Arga at dinner, laughing. 'It's the thought that counts,' interrupted the process and made her laugh despite her frustration. Like Galen, Uncle Arga not only had the last word, but he always had the right word. Maybe that explained her affection for Galen; he reminded her of her uncle. If only Uncle Arga were around, perhaps he could have made Uma see sense.

Tad stared at her, startled by her merriment after so long a silence. Marissa fell into his arms as she laughed.

"Just thinking about Uma ..."

"That was funny?" Tad studied her, a bemused smile on his lips.

"Yeah, actually it was more Uncle Arga. He knew just how to get around her. He could make her flustered or angry with a word. He skewered her every weakness and enjoyed watching her flounder, seeking some way to win out over him. She thought being elected Enunciator would impress him, but it didn't." Marissa smiled again at the memory of the two and their arguments, although Uma always called them discussions.

"I wish he were here, but I've got you and Galen and all the others.

327

Anyway, I've worked out what to do about her. I just have to do it."

"It isn't over yet. Not by a long shot. Are you sure we can do it?"

"Worried Willie." Grinning, she made as if to tickle him.

"But Marissa, it isn't..." he started, and then, laughing, tried to push her away as she launched another attack.

"Worried Willie," she sang in a singsong voice.

Then just as suddenly, she calmed down and rested her head against his chest. She reached up and ran her hand through his hair. "You prepare the greeting for them. What we've done should have brought her to her knees by now. As for Miskarnkk, I'm sure he's ready to bargain—anything to get the Delphian trade on an even keel again. All I have to do is grab them and bring them here."

"How do you know he's the one to deal with?"

She pulled back for a moment and looked at him intently. "That's a good question. But if it isn't Miskarnkk, he'll know the right person. Everyone we saw kowtowed to him. It doesn't matter—Miskarnkk or someone else." She settled back.

Lying against his warm chest, the gentle rise and fall of his breathing lulled her. Gazing upward to the gauzy banner of stars, her thoughts drifted again to Uma.

Summoning energy, she focused sharp as a laser beam, just as if she pulled the wisps of the chronspun into a form. Mentally she shaped and made a wave; she formed a net, and cast it. The net passed through time and through space, and everything slipped through it. She focused again, sinking deep into the place where the map dwelled. Studying the face of the map with eyes adjusted to chronosculpture, she stared at the tangled array. With one hand, she reached out to touch a strand. Cold met her straining fingers. Too many strands for her to touch every one of them. She pulled herself back and tried to view the map in its entirety, and, in another part of her mind, she conjured up Uma's face. But as she sought Uma, the image of the map wavered and then faded.

Sighing deeply, she turned to Tad. "I can't focus for some reason."

"On what?"

"On locating and retrieving Uma." She stood up and smoothed her suit. "It's time. It really is. They've had enough time to see what we've done and realize who did it."

He nodded, his face grave. "The way you explained it to me you always need to know where you're going. Do you think you now have locating powers as well?" He smiled.

Marissa ran her hands through her hair. "I don't know." She tried to keep her voice deceptively easy and light. She hoped that it didn't betray the doubt that lay just beneath the surface. "You know, you're right—it's like a fever dream. I know the way it works, and I was just trying something else. That shows how tired I am." She sighed. "Maybe I need a little more rest, or better, I need to find out where she is and what's going on there."

"Let Ez and the Advocate worry about Uma's location. I can help with the rest and relaxation." He smiled once again.

"Umm, and what exactly do you have in mind?"

"We'll start with this." Tad began to massage the back of her neck. "Isn't that better?"

"Yeah, a bit lower down. Yes, that's it. Ah, that's heaven." Marissa let her head fall forward as Tad worked on her shoulders. Lulled by the soothing motion, time slipped away in the Arden evening.

She wasn't sure how much later, but certainly long enough for night to fall in all the shades of blackness and twinkling starlight. Tad cleared his throat. "If you're worried about Uma, we can ask the Advocate to locate her."

"Great idea." Marissa eased away from him and then gave him a brief, light, almost teasing kiss. "Thanks for everything. You always know how to make me feel energized." Getting up, she started gathering their clothes, separating them and tossing an article or two back to Tad who still lay supine, arm supporting his head as a pillow.

"There's no hurry." He still stared up into the sky.

"True, but there's something about an Arden night, particularly one with you in it, that really stirs me to action." She started dressing. "Come on, let's get moving.

Tad sat up and started putting his clothes on. After a minute, he struggled to his feet grunting from the exertion. "After that roll in the dust, we probably both need a shower." He hugged her from behind.

"Probably." She caressed the arm he had placed around her. "But the sooner all of this is over, the better for us all."

She untangled herself from him in a dramatic tango-like spin that nearly sent her tumbling and made Tad laugh. The sound of his laughter solidified the hope that had been building in her. Holding onto his hand, she tugged him along, and, laughing, they headed toward the communit tent. Inside, they took chairs in front of the Advocate.

Almost at once, the Advocate glowed with that disconcertingly accurate and perfect image of Tad. <WHAT IS YOUR COMMAND?>

"Can you locate Uma?"

<ONLY THAT?>

"Yes, I think so."

<IT WILL TAKE A LITTLE WORK.>

"I'll say," Ez chimed in. "We've got more chaos than we bargained for. Communications are really down—only the barest trickle thanks to emergency systems. Constructs I've contacted—"

<FOR THE PERIOD OF THE CRISIS,> the Advocate interrupted. <THE ENUNCIATOR HAS SEQUESTERED HERSELF WITH A LIMITED NUMBER OF ADVISORS. SHE HAS CHOSEN THE TOP SECURITY WAR ROOM ON CEPHUS.> Another pause while the screen flashed through an entire spectrum of Tads—like Warhol's Marilyn Monroes, images of Tad propagated over the visible surface of the screen.

Amused, Marissa turned to see his reaction to the display. "What's it like to be a work of art?"

"I'm not sure. I've never thought about it before."

<SHE HAS PLACED HI-REZ PRIONS TO GUARD AGAINST SNOOPING. HOLD WHILE I FLUSH THE SYSTEM.> Again a pause while the images came back into alignment and the colors vanished.

"It seems," Ez whispered, "that Uma has placed extra guards on every level to watch for you and prevent your access. Sources close to her report she is worried by what you've done."

"Source? What sources?" Marissa frowned. "The Advocate reports that there are protective prions.

"Well, yes," Ez acknowledged, "but I was just chatting with Felos. You know, Walt's aide."

For a moment Marissa mind blanked. "Walt's aide?"

"Walt Fenster—"

"He's with Uma?" Surprised, Marissa stared at Tad.

"One of the extra assigned guards," Ez said smugly, as though this were common knowledge.

"So what are you waiting for?" Marissa asked, anxious to move ahead. "Can you patch me through?"

"Of course. Since you were otherwise occupied, I took the opportunity to spend a little time chatting up an old friend."

The thought of Ez chatting to anything connected with Walt struck Marissa as close to betrayal, but she had always been able to trust Ez. Now was not the time to stop. Maybe if she'd known about this earlier, Tad's rescue and other things might have been easier. "How long has this been going on?"

"Oh, it's quite recent really. I met him about the time you rescued Tad. We've kept in touch ever since."

"Ez, let me talk to Walt."

"Certainly."

Tad touched the blank screen of the Advocate. "Are you there?"

<YES. IT SOUNDS AS THOUGH THE CONSTRUCT HAS THINGS WELL IN HAND. NO NEED FOR ME TO INTRUDE.>

Sometimes these Personalities acted like people ought to act but seldom did. Marissa touched the screen, too. "It's never an intrusion…"

"One moment," Ez's voice interrupted, "while I check the shielding on the links I've established—as though anyone could hear anything the way we've messed up things."

Ez fell silent and the bell-like tones of the flitterwings filled the air. The stars twinkled brightly. Marissa turned toward Tad and put her arm around him.

"I'm back. Fenster is on line. I'm putting him through. Make it quick. We have some weak points in the shielded lines. No telling how long they'll hold—after all, nonessential communication is restricted."

Walt's face appeared on the miniscreen on Marissa's wrist unit. "Thanks," she said sotto voce. "Walt?"

"Latham?" On the small screen Marissa could just make out his widened eyes. "What do you want?"

"I need your help again."

"And why should I help you?"

"Maybe I should have said the Usian confederation needs your help. You can help resolve this Delphian crisis."

"Oh, and how could I do that?"

"I need to have a chat with Uma face to face. Could you arrange for a break in security for about oh, thirty seconds? It shouldn't take any more than that. After that, I'll take my chances."

Fenster peered out of the vid screen. "What are you planning? I'm here to protect her."

"Walt, she's my aunt. Yes, I was angry with her when she exiled me, but a lot has happened since then. I still want to save the rheos, and I need her cooperation to do that. I didn't kill or hurt you. Why would I hurt Uma?"

"No, but you created havoc like no one's ever saw. She's pretty sore at you right now."

Marissa laughed, glad to know Uma's state of mind. "You're right. Absolutely right, but that was the whole idea. I got her attention and that of the Delphians. I'm going to preserve Arden one way or the other. We can do this the easy way, or—"

"More of the same?" Walt glowered at her.

Sighing, Marissa pushed her hair away from her face. "If I have to. However, with your help, we can wrap this thing up and get back to a normal existence, and you might even get a promotion out of it."

"We?" Walt studied Marissa, perhaps considering his and Uma's options.

"Well to start with, you and me. I've arranged for Uma to chat with some people. Distant friends you might call them, including her Delphian counterpart. Anyway, all we want is discussion. Nothing physical at all."

"You're going to be able to set up a talk with the Delphians? How are you going to pull that one off?"

"Actually it's easier than dealing with Uma. They tried to strand me and imprison me, but it didn't work, and neither will Uma's attempts to avoid me. I'm giving you a chance to preserve the Confederation and do a little good for yourself as well. Well, how about it?"

Fenster rubbed his chin. "This sounds...treasonous."

"No, the creation of one of the most important treaties ever to be formed between worlds is at stake. I can ensure peace with the Delphians. Besides, when I've finished with Uma, she'll be a changed woman, and you'll be more valuable as a security person than ever. Just see what you can find out about the Delphian situation and Delphia in general. The more you know the more important and valuable you will be."

A dark frown covered Fenster's face, and he said nothing for a moment. The pause lengthened, and Marissa began to think he wouldn't agree.

"No injury to Uma or the Confederation?"

"Yes, yes, I promise, no physical harm to Uma and the Confederation remains intact." Marissa crossed her fingers. At least she hadn't promised him any changes to either.

A shudder shook Fenster. "Every time I've trusted you, Marissa, I've lost. Why should this time be different?"

Marissa sighed. "Because I'm different. Tad told me what you did for him, and I appreciate it. Now, I even understand a little of what you tried to do for me. Nobody likes a conscience, no matter how well intentioned. Look, I can do this without you. You could make it a little easier, that's all."

"So what's in it for you?"

"Arden and freedom. I want Arden, and I want the rheos, and most of all I want to be free of Uma and her Will. Uma and the Delphians can give all of this to me, and I will have it." Her hand folded into a fist.

"You can either help or not. The choice is yours. I wouldn't have asked, but Tad said I should have trusted you, and he's usually right."

Fenster smiled. "He's quite a guy. I don't think you've ever really appreciated him."

"Probably not, but that's changed too. We're going to make a formal exchange here on Arden, and you're invited. If Uma doesn't appreciate you, I promise you a place with us."

"Uma is afraid of you." He cracked his wasso gum. "Thirty seconds? That's what you want?"

"Right, just make sure Uma is alone for thirty seconds. I don't want her or anyone else to get hurt. The surprise of seeing me might make some guard trigger happy."

"All right, you've got it. But give me a time, an exact time. I'll see to it the

332

rounds keep that area clear for exactly one minute at the specified time. Beyond that, you're on your own."

"'Thanks, Walt, I promise you won't regret this. I've learned my lesson and it's time for me to make amends. I'll have Ez contact Felos at the time."

"Ten minutes before," Fenster insisted. "I need that much time to ensure everyone is out of the way.

"Ten minutes before," she agreed.

Walt's eyebrows rose. "I don't know how you do this travel thing, Marissa, and I'm not certain I want to know."

Walt's not wanting to know came as a surprise to her. "Despite its value, I don't think I'd choose to go through everything again just to get it." She broke the link and turned to Tad.

"The water's deep, and its 'sink or swim.' She squeezed his hand. "We've done what we can for now. I think we can skip the rest of this evening. I don't feel quite so driven."

Relief and worry warred. Having set events in motions, all that remained seemed simple, but Tad's accident had been so unexpected. Marissa again saw the Delphian guard shoot and sensed Tad crumple behind her in a heart-wrenching flash. She shuddered.

"You, okay?"

She saw herself reflected deep in his eyes and thanked Devos and whatever luck she had for preserving them both. Tonight, they would enjoy one another so that no matter the outcome, they had this. Tomorrow, Arden would be theirs.

"Let's call it a night."

"Gladly." He wrapped an arm about her waist and led her toward their sleeping pad.

Chapter Thirty-Three - All's Well That Ends Well

"All yet seems well; and if it end so meet,
The bitter past, more welcome is the sweet."
-*All's Well That Ends Well*, V iii

At two minutes of seven the next morning, Marissa and Tad stood in the cave under the monolith. The cool morning air soothed her nerves, but a queasy feeling reminded her nothing was certain. She had to focus on the tasks before her. Uma and Miskarnkk had to be brought together and made to cooperate. Tad's arm about her shoulders comforted and reassured her.

"You've got about two minutes to jump time," Ez said

The sign on the cave wall glowed with inner light. Marissa looked about, welcoming the familiar surroundings. "It isn't that I need to be here to leave, but it will help me focus. I've got to move fast once I reach Cephus."

A worried frown marred Tad's face. "Are you certain you don't want me or Brac to come along?"

She hugged him and a sigh escaped as she pulled away. "Absolutely. Once is enough. I won't risk you again. One person can get in and out. If I have to worry about someone else, I can't maintain focus. Besides, they can't trap me. They could kill me, but they won't do that. Everything will be fine. I need you here to coordinate it all. We have to impress Uma and Miskarnkk. This is too important. I'm counting on you to make it work."

She pulled away and glanced at the chron. "Ready, Ez?"

"Ready. You've got about fifteen seconds to clear. Time to focus." Ez projected an image she had gotten from Felos of the war room.

"Is there anything that is really secure?" Marissa wondered aloud.

"Not the way you can move," Ez responded. "Jump!"

Closing her eyes, Marissa wrapped herself in the mental travel cocoon that helped her cushion the shock of transfer, a travel cocoon she had only just begun to recognize and tap into deliberately. She sank into the map, entered, pulled through a strand, opened her eyes, and found herself within two feet of Uma.

Seated on a divan with her back to Marissa, some instinct drew her

334

attention. Uma turned. "Marissa—" Eyes wide, she stared in disbelief. "Impossible."

Marissa stretched out a hand. "Come with me, Uma." She grasped Uma's hand and pulled her into that mental cocoon and thence into the map. She centered on the map with the nexus of Arden.

When Marissa opened her eyes again, she stood in the cave depression with Uma unconscious at her feet.

Tad reached to steady Marissa. "You look really pale. Tesde, look at her."

Relieved to have arrived, Marissa grabbed his hand and kissed him. "No time. The jumps are draining, but I'm fine. I only have one more trip. Ez, have you located Miskarnkk?"

"Delphian sources are less reliable, but I believe I've found a secure link, and he appears to be in conference at the moment."

"With how many people?"

"One other..." Ez hesitated. "I think you might want to know..."

"Just one? Great, give me an image and coordinates." At once they flashed onto the minivid in her glasses.

"Marissa," Ez began again, "you ought to know..."

"I've got to see this through, now." She squeezed Tad's hand and released it. Pulling away, she centered again.

The scene before her revealed a small, nondescript office like the one in which Miskarnkk had first interviewed them. This time he sat with his back to her, facing someone across the usual desk. Marissa hoped he found the stiff chair as uncomfortable as she had.

Intent on her goal, for a moment Marissa ignored the other person. Then a gesture by the man drew her attention. Her eyes widened, and she stared open-mouthed. Impossible. It couldn't be.

"Uncle Arga?" She couldn't suppress the surprised quaver in her voice.

The elf of a man with the twinkling eyes behind the desk looked at her and grinned. The familiar scent of his favorite cologne tinged with a hint of oulatte assailed her and brought with it memories of all their times together.

At her voice, Miskarnkk whirled around. "How did you get in here?"

"I'll take care of this." A gentle, wonderful, memory-laden rumble filled the room. "Marissa, you've caused us no end of worry."

"Not to mention a major loss of profits. Time is money you know," Miskarnkk snapped in a testy tone.

Uncle Arga cleared his throat, and Miskarnkk fell silent. "Marissa," he began.

Uncle Arga?" she said. "You're..."

"'Men have died from time to time, and worms have eaten them, but not for love'" he quoted the line with a smile. "However, I'm pleased to say that

335

I've not been among them." He folded his hands on the desk in front of him and grinned at her.

"What are you doing here?" She looked around the office as though she would find some clue.

"Let's say that Uma and I arranged for Prospero to have his own domain." Arga did a kind of bow in his chair. "And as you can see, I have my own Caliban."

He waved his arm toward Miskarnkk who looked back and forth at the two of them as though he didn't understand a single word. "I'm a sort of chief advisor to these" –he waved his hand— "wayward children."

Now the reason for Uma's fear became clear. If anyone could frighten her, if anyone knew her and all of her foibles and weaknesses, this man did. This erudite, light-hearted, but cynical man had been lost to his family years ago. He had vanished without a trace—an accident in space. A thousand different things raced through her head. How? Why, most of all why? As all these questions whirled through her thoughts, another surfaced.

"Favia—that was yours?"

"Ah, 'the play's the thing wherein I'll catch the conscience of the queen.' It's all been for that," he said.

"Clever." Marissa nodded. "That radiation screen showed a touch of genius."

"Yes, not bad, if I do say so, but that is not the present nature of your interest here now, is it?" He gave her a shrewd glance.

"No, you're right. Who speaks for Delphia?"

"Oh, either one of us, I suppose. Or both if you like." Uncle Arga rose and gestured to Miskarnkk. Marissa stood poised to jump in an instant if necessary.

"Oh, you needn't be alarmed. Miskarnkk here is absolutely beside himself with his loss of credit. The government's very unstable right now. I'm certain you'll find him cooperative, if order can be restored."

Uncle Arga walked toward her and took her hand. "You have always been my favorite, and, after so long, it is good to see you again. You grown into a real beauty, more beautiful than even Uma in her prime."

Tears sprang to Marissa's eyes as she reached out for his hand, taking a lost and unhoped for pleasure in his warm grasp. Then, almost in the same moment she grabbed the fabric of Miskarnkk's suit. Without further delay, she pulled them into and through the map.

Arriving back on Arden with them in tow, she stumbled. Uncle Arga and Miskarnkk sprawled in a messy heap. Still groggy, Uma, at the far side of the depression, had just begun to recover.

Marissa rested on the basin edge for a moment, relaxing and breathing deeply. Tad's hand touched her shoulder again, and she reached up to cover it with her own.

She nodded toward Uma. "She's in for a real surprise." She squeezed his hand, grateful for his presence. "We're almost home." A long shuddering sigh escaped her.

Touching her hair with a gentle caress, Tad smiled at her. "Almost."

Now awake, Uma watched Brac gather up Miskarnkk and his colleague. When she glimpsed Miskarnkk, she blanched. Brac, carrying one under each arm, marched out and up the corridor. Uma straightened her gray robe of state and marched along behind. Marissa could not tell if she had recognized her old adversary Uncle Arga.

Outside the cave, Uma fixed Marissa with a grim stare. "Treason," she snapped. "Treason beyond treason. You have betrayed more than my word now. You've betrayed the entire Usian confederation. I know you hate me for what I did, Marissa, but what I did, I had to do."

Uma turned as she took in the scene outside the monolith. When she saw Tesde and the now clean-shaven Teloav, her lips tightened. "What are you going to do? Throw me to the vultures?"

Marissa indulged in a crooked grin and took her by the arm to conduct her to her place in the circle of rocks Brac and the rheos had made for a meeting place, at some distance from the monolith out of deference to the rheos sensibilities.

"I won't say it hasn't crossed my mind a couple of thousand times while I've been away, but no."

Pulling her arm away from Marissa, Uma straightened her flowing sleeve. "No? Then why do you bring me here to face these?" She waved her arm to indicate the two unconscious figures sprawled on the ground and Tesde, and Teloav.

The bright morning light played through the thick rising mist of Arden's fields, but little of Arden could be seen. That had been the reason for the circle. Marissa wanted no distractions.

Heaving an exasperated sigh, she wondered when Uma would notice Uncle Arga. "I brought you here for one reason and one reason only. Come." She led Uma to a gap in the rocks.

Brac had already scrambled out to the open field beyond. He signaled, and the rheos moved in a wave, glistening metallic green in the sun. Hundreds of them, in phalanxes and contingents and in groups and in social organization paraded below.

Pointing downward, Marissa faced Uma. "You're too stubborn to listen. You can see these creatures with your own eyes. These." She gestured dramatically as though embracing all of the rheos. "They are what I fought for."

A surge of anger electrified her, and her fingers clenched into fists.

337

Forcing herself to relax, she uncurled her fingers one by one. Anger never worked with Uma and only made her opponents more vulnerable

Seeing no reaction or understanding on Uma's face, Marissa grabbed her arm again and held tight. "Listen, there were times when I would gladly have killed you, but not now. Now you have to face what you refused to face before." She smiled and tightened her grip until Uma winced. "Or at least what you haven't faced in a long time."

Satisfaction filled Marissa. At last, she had these stubborn, recalcitrant, pig-headed bureaucrats exactly where she wanted them. "Do you know the best part of all? By your own actions, Uma, you gave me the ability to do this."

She gestured to Brac below, and as he spread his arms, the ranks of rheos parted and began to move in single file up the rocky declivity to where she and Uma stood.

Staring in distrust at the advancing ranks of rheos, Uma started to back away. "You're going to let them..." She stopped and then turned to Marissa, a quizzical look on her face. "No, of course not. That Delphian is here. You need me, don't you?"

Behind Uma, Miskarnkk had just begun to recover from the jump. He shook his head and glared toward Marissa. "You've caused us an uncountable loss of profit. Someone must pay the margin call and it will not be the Delphians." He included Uma in his baleful gaze.

Pointing at him, Uma snorted. "You see what we have to deal with. Crass profiteers who will do anything to achieve their ends."

Just then, Uncle Arga sat up and looked about him with amusement. "Quite a means of travel you have there."

At his first words, Uma started and turned. When she saw his face, she blanched and wavered. Marissa reached out to steady her so she wouldn't fall.

"Arga?" Uma croaked.

Uncle Arga laughed and shook his head. "Look where she comes! The Queen of Air and Darkness. Ill-met in sunlight."

"Arga?" Uma gasped as though she found the air too thin for comfort. Then she slipped from Marissa's grasp and tumbled to the ground.

Uncle Arga rushed to Uma's side and smoothed the white hair away from her face. "Guess she doesn't like surprises."

They propped Uma up on grav cushions and waited for her to revive. The sun had climbed slowly into the Arden sky and now beat steadily down on the rocky circle. Tendrils of evaporating dew still rose from the fields around the meeting place. As Uma stirred, Marissa offered her a cup of oulatte.

"We need to talk. But matters of state first. We're going to have a tripartite convention here—you," she said, nudging Uma, "represent the Confederation, the Delphians as represented by Arga and Miskarnkk, and for the disinherited,

I've appointed as their representative this man," she indicated Teloav who jerked back in surprise.

"Oh, and as spokesman for the independent Republic of Arden, which you will officially recognize by the end of your discussions, and advisor to the disinherited we have Galen, Ambassador First Class and seeker of the Truth."

Marissa couldn't resist a chuckle as the stares of all three converged on Galen. He whirled about in a delighted pirouette while his beard moved through a hurried series of pictures ending with a small man dancing before three disapproving giants.

Miskarnkk looked distinctly miffed. "I hardly see what there is to laugh about. You have caused irreversible pressures on our economic systems. The high costs must be paid, and I intend to see you reimburse us in full.

"Enough!" Hands on her hips, Marissa faced him. "In case I haven't made myself clear, I'm tired of all of your talk about market share, and opening markets, and destroying planets. You and your people, powerful though you may be, are a bunch of pontificating fakes and major charlatans."

"Ah, Marissa, say rather 'mountebank, a threadbare juggler, and a fortuneteller, a needy, hollow-ey'd, sharp-looking wretch,'" quoted Uncle Arga. "Yes, all are most apt."

Uma glared at him, though her breathing still sounded as if she suffered from an asthma attack. Marissa took Uma's hand in her own and signaled Uncle Arga to come to them.

"I'm sure you all have a lot to share. Now let's start with figuring out exactly how you want to work things out so that no one, certainly not either of you, will ever trouble my planet again."

"Your planet?" Uma began, eyebrows raised high.

"My planet," Marissa said quietly. "Or more properly, our planet." She stretched out her arms to include Tad, Brac, Tesde, Oric, Teloav, and Galen. "Our world. We are here, and we're here to stay. If you have any doubts about it, consult with your technical experts about your vulnerabilities. I assure you for every one they find, I can find at least two more."

Miskarnkk sniffed. "And what will prevent us from eliminating your third party interest?"

Moving forward, Brac picked up a rock and crushed it to dust. Then, dusting off his hand, he made an odd circular gesture and the rheos surrounded Miskarnkk, spears pointed and a few touching him.

He drew himself up and away from the iron spears. "Force will not protect you for long."

Marissa smiled sweetly, amused at his lack of comprehension or perhaps at the sheer bluff he hoped her to accept. "I love your directness. However, since I can go anywhere, and take anyone with me, none of you are completely safe, ever. If you threatened me, think about how you might feel without a spacesuit on Thrace V."

Uma shuddered and looked away.

Marissa shrugged. "But you know there's more to it than that. You'll be prevented because people and constructs under your rule hate you all enough that no matter where you meet, no matter how tight the secrecy, I'll know long beforehand. Besides, after you all have had your talk and cleared my planet, I'll be too busy to bother you again, and you won't have to give me a second thought. After all, it wouldn't be profitable, would it?" Marissa glanced at Tad and silently thanked him for all the ways he had made her aware of the political process and especially for that certain knowledge of how best to shape the end from the means.

Placing a hand in the middle of Uma's stiff back, Marissa gently nudged her forward. "I want all of you to talk, face to face, and sort things out."

Behind her, Marissa heard Tesde's whisper to Teloav, "Mano a mano would be better."

"You've seen what I can do?" She looked at each for acknowledgment. Uma and Miskarnkk nodded. Uncle Arga grinned and then nodded too.

She faced Uma. "And you know I can do this at any time and cause irreparable damage to the affairs of state." She turned to Miskarnkk. "And to business as usual."

With distinctly sour faces, they nodded in unwilling agreement. Only Uncle Arga looked happy.

"Marissa, your part is done," he said. "We're here and are willing to talk. Your desires are clear—preserve Arden as it exists and its native population. However, we have many other things to resolve. Yet with willingness and a little sharp dealing, we should be able to sort it all out. 'Ay, now I am in Arden, the more fool I; when I was at home, I was in a better place, but travelers must be content.'" He laughed. "And so I am." He rubbed his hands in anticipation while both Miskarnkk and Uma studied him like a new and particularly repugnant scientific specimen.

Amused, Marissa gave him a lop-sided grin. "Aren't you the Delphians advisor?"

"But of course. They're practically my invention. My Trojan horse to enter the gates of Cephus and seize the state from unlawful domination."

"Not another one," Marissa groaned, thinking of Teloav. "Galen and I have put together a few guidelines. None of you will leave this circle until such time as an agreement to preserve this planet and both the Usian Confederation and Delphian constituency is forged. Any agreement made between the three of you will be subject to Galen's approval. Further, Galen will appoint such people as he sees fit to act in the future as monitors for both sides. They will report any and all violations.

"In addition, Miskarnkk, you will cease your efforts to take over the Usian Confederation. You, Uma," Marissa looked her straight in the eyes," will resolve the issues that Teloav wishes to discuss with you. I'm certain you can all come to a civilized understanding. Oh, and one thing more—you will promote Walt Fenster for having to deal with me in the past. I really regret having to beat him up and leave him as I did—but there was no choice. Now, are we ready to begin?"

Stepping back, Marissa joined Tad and Brac, one on each side of her, arms crossed over bare chests. Brac had conceded to wear a loincloth for company's sake. Tad wore his faded Khaki shorts—so much for uniformed honor guards.

At a nod from Marissa, Galen advanced to stand just in front her, arms crossed over his beard. "So let it be spoken. So let it be done."

He clapped his hands once. Brac raised his arms, making two large circles. The rheos gathered in a group around Uncle Arga, Uma, and Miskarnkk in something resembling parade stance. The three politicians studied one another and angled around in an arcane parody of musical chairs to sit on grav cushions in the best location. Marissa sincerely hoped Uma would end up facing the rising Arden sun.

Chapter Thirty-Four - I Would Not Be A Queen For All the World

"Be cheerful, sir. Our revels now are ended."
-*The Tempest*, IV I

After a full ten minutes of grumbling, whining, and moaning about the injustice and the patent fiscal irresponsibility implicit and explicit in each and every action Marissa had taken, after several minutes of vituperation and excoriation, Galen managed to rally the main parties to record a memorandum of intent that remanded the entire planet of Arden to the status of charter world—free of all eminent domain claims, and ultimately and entirely at the disposition of the inhabitants of Arden. When the last syllables entered the metal container, the archiving had been duly recorded by the Advocate, and witnessed by Uma's personal assistant, Marissa leaped up from the table with an enormous whoop that sent the nearest rheos staggering back.

Jumping down, she grabbed Tad's arm, pulling him up and away from the group gathered in the rock circle. "We've got other things to do. With Arden settled, my interests are satisfied. You all," she glanced first at Uma, then at Miskarnkk with Uncle Arga, and finally to Teloav, "have other matters to resolve, but none of them need me."

"I have important business to attend to," Miskarnkk said. "I demand to be returned—"

Raising one eyebrow at him, Marissa rolled her eyes. "Where's the profit for me?" She hurried away from the gathering in the circle, dragging a laughing Tad after her.

When they had moved out of the view of those in the circle, she turned to him and hugged him. "We did it! Thank you."

"For?" Tad searched her face, an amused grin on his own.

"For everything," she said. She opened her arms wide to encompass the entire scene before her. "For being here with me. For opening up this world to me. For believing in me, when I didn't even believe in myself. Tad..." she paused as though gathering together the right words. "I'm so happy. I don't have any words."

Unable to contain or restrain her joy any longer, she started to run through the waist-high sward, breathing lungfuls of the pure, sweet air. The scent of dusty sage, pervasive on Arden, seemed different now, brighter, as though a touch of mint had been added to it. The purple-golden savanna glowed with a brighter hue. At once the gold deepened and the purple became more than purple, not lavender, but royal, brilliant, almost blinding in its amethyst intensity. Her eyes feasted on Arden's beauty. Tad's hand in hers grew smoother, warmer, and stronger than it had ever been. Something seasoned the very air itself. Marissa in her joy could only say that it carried the essence of air, more invigorating than before.

"Tad," she whispered now, as they slowed from a polka to a waltz. "All of this," she spun around. "All of it is ours. Ours for the rheos. I mean it doesn't belong to us, but we keep it in trust. It's theirs, but it's ours at the same time."

The confused words tumbled out in a one inchoate mass. She trusted him to sort out their real meaning.

His amused laughter added to her happiness. "For the moment."

"Right now, this moment is all that matters." She ran up one of the hillocks and saw the silver trickle that snaked its way around the base of the monolith. Its mirrored surface flashed back at her, signaling approval of the moment and of everything she had accomplished. Stunned by the beauty of this place and the enormity of what they had achieved, she stood for a moment, marveling at the infinite variety and generosity of life.

"Tad, we've got so much to be thankful for—Arden, the rheos, each other."

"Especially each other," he said, almost tightly.

She looked at him, trying to read his face. "What is it?"

"Nothing, nothing at all. I was just thinking…"

Marissa took his hand and studied his serious face. "About?"

"About us," he said and then blushed. "About making this permanent. About making us permanent."

"Of course, as it always would be. And soon too—once our own private fairyland has been cleared of King Oberon and Queen Titania."

Tad grinned at the allusion. "Don't you mean more like a Runnymede?"

Rolling her eye, she squeezed his hand, pleased to know he understood so well how she felt. "I don't want to share right now with anyone other than our friends. I don't want to share this place with Uma, or even with Uncle Arga."

She paused for a moment as memories of his disappearance and then the accident rose again. The supposed disaster had left them all bereft and grief-stricken.

"I don't understand why he left us without any word. We thought he died.

343

His presence on Delphia hit me like a… Well, sort of like that punch Walt gave me on the expedition ship. I almost couldn't breathe when I saw him."

Tad laughed and hugged her. "The way you've always talked about him, I can imagine."

"I don't think so," she said and then paused, frowning, "but you understand me so well, maybe you can." She grinned up at him.

"I have to talk to him. I've so many questions about his absence and all he's done. On top of that, we have the mystery of N'Bert and Sylvic and what they've been doing, but most of all how N'Bert knew enough about the Nexus to send me the locator. Did he make? If not, who did? Then Miskarnkk and the Delphians claimed some knowledge of the Nexus." Marissa sighed and kicked at a small stone.

"Hey, it's not the end of the world," he said. "That's a big list. You won't have to worry about things to do."

"Yeah, but an incomplete list. We know so little about the rheos and how they relate to all these pieces. Are they guardians for the portal in the cave? Did they make the mosaics I found there? I've got an uneasy feeling we've only scraped away a tiny bit of the puzzle."

"Yes, but you've managed to save Arden and preserve the rheos."

'Yeah, it seems we did, at least for now anyway, but today is a time for us and for celebration. I want Uma, Miskarnkk, and even Uncle Arga gone. I want them to finish, to make whatever arrangements need to be made, and to leave. Let's forget all of them."

Tad leaned close to kiss her. They remained locked in a passionate embrace for an eternity that had no duration, almost like the Anomaly.

"Umm, that sure beats thinking just now." She rested her head on his shoulder.

A flitterwing landed on Tad's tunic and sang in bright bell-like tones that resounded over the field. He smiled at her as she with hesitant fingers touched it. It didn't move.

Infectious laughter bubbled up from Tad, and Marissa sensed it much through his muscles as with her ears. Saturated in happiness and surrounded by beauty, she joined him. Then the laughter consumed her, and she grew short of breath. Soon, she sank to the ground and clutched her aching sides. The laughter wouldn't let go, but hung on until she began to hiccough. That only made her laugh harder.

"Oh Tad, this is so good." Gradually, she managed to stop laughing.

The hiccoughing continued, but she rose to her feet and pulled Tad after her. "Let's go to the monolith."

"Why?"

"To find a place to hold the ceremony, and to be away from all of them."

Marissa held his gaze with hers. "To be alone to savor this for a moment. Just you and me. Everyone else is busy."

Tad smiled. "I'm sure we can think of something."

They turned as one to walk down the soft undulations of hillocks sprayed with bright golden flowers that paved the way to the Monolith. The wind swept by them, and the flitterwing took off, riding the wind before them toward the still misty horizon and the late morning sun. Marissa rested her head on Tad's shoulder as they moved through the sward, walking now just to walk. Arden now belonged to them, not to be owned, but to know, to share, to enjoy, and above all, to preserve.

Beyond the Rim of Light, Alex Stone

Beyond the Rim of Light, Alex Stone